BELFAST CONFIDENTIAL

Colin Bateman

headline

First published in 2005 by
HEADLINE BOOK PUBLISHING

2

British Library Cataloguing in Publication Data

ISBN 0 7553 0925 1 (hardback)
ISBN 0 7553 0926 X (trade paperback)

Typeset in Meridien by Palimpsest Book Production Limited, Polmont, Stirlingshire
Printed and bound in Great Britain by
Mackays of Chatham plc, Chatham, Kent

Headline's policy is to use papers that are natural, renewable and recyclable products and made from wood grown in sustainable forests. The logging and manufacturing processes are expected to conform to the environmental regulations of the country of origin.

HEADLINE BOOK PUBLISHING
A division of Hodder Headline
338 Euston Road
London NW1 3BH

www.headline.co.uk
www.hodderheadline.com

For Andrea and Matthew

1

Mouse never liked cats.

Nothing to do with the name, just he never liked cats. He valued loyalty, and friendship, and long walks. Cats aren't loyal, they're not your friends, and you can't take them for a walk, unless they're in a bag, weighed down with stones. So when he came round to help me move house, and he saw the Siamese playing with a dead sparrow in the middle of our newly sown lawn, it was natural for him to lift the rock. It was natural for him to throw the rock. He was a big man, with a strong arm, and he hefted it with all the grace, power and directional acumen of a major league pitcher.

For Mouse, if it's worth doing, it's worth doing well.

If I had thrown a rock at all, it would have been to merely frighten the poor creature. Not to half cleave its head off, the way Mouse did.

If I'd thrown it, it would have fallen short, or smashed into next door's greenhouse, and the cat would have given me a haughty look, picked up the bird, juggled with it for a while, then tossed it to one side before nonchalantly wandering off. That way, neither of us would have lost face. Mouse's way, the cat lost face. And ear. And top of skull. Before rolling over dead. Stone dead.

We stood and looked at it. We could hear my wife, singing to herself inside. Something by Abba.

Mouse said, 'Oh.'

I said, 'Oh.'

From the other side of the high wooden fence, our new neighbour said, 'Psssss-wsssssss, psssss-wsssssss, Toodles.'

They say that moving house is one of the most stressful things you can experience: it's in there with giving birth, burying your parents, taking the driving test. I think people ought to get out more. You get pursued by religious maniacs, shot at by rampaging terrorists, threatened by drug-crazed movie stars and pummelled by heavyweight champions, you soon realise moving house isn't stressful at all. It's a walk in the park. Till someone kills the neighbour's cat, and you have to scoop up the body, brains an' all, and stuff it in a box in the garage until you can decide what to do, all the time cursing Mouse under your breath and him grinning stupidly at you. And then you wander back out, blood still on your hands, and the neighbour suddenly appears head and shoulders above the fence, balancing on a stool, 'Nice to meet you! I'm George, this is my wife Georgie, and you didn't happen to see Toodles anywhere, did you?' And Patricia, *my* wife – she would say 'longsuffering', but then don't they all? – comes down the garden innocently shaking her head while I shrug and Mouse stands there grinning like an idiot. *That's* when moving house gets stressful.

Instead of thumping Mouse I introduced him because I could tell they weren't sure which of us was the husband, and then they took a proper look at him and said, genuinely surprised and impressed: 'You're *that* Mouse?'

Mouse grinned.

'Right enough,' said Georgie, 'I've seen you on the telly. And I never miss a single issue.'

They were talking about a weekly magazine called *Belfast Confidential* and looking at Patricia and me curiously, wanting to know what the Editor, owner and all-round celeb magnet and virtual-brandname Mouse was doing in our back garden. We were clearly not celebs, so that surely meant we were the other sort that *BC* delights in exposing – frauds, or thugs or sexual deviants or born-again Christians or terrorists. Except Mouse had a can of beer in his hand and he looked quite at home. Maybe we were relatives. Dim country cousins moving to the big city.

It used to be that I was the well-known one – I had a column in the local paper, I stirred up all kinds of shit – but just as terrorists eventually hang up their guns and enter politics, I had long since resigned myself to the security and boredom of the post-Troubles newsroom. Belfast is like any city that has suffered war or pestilence or disaster – hugely relieved to no longer be the focus of world attention, but also slightly aggrieved that it isn't. In the old days you could say, 'I'm from Belfast,' anywhere in the world and it was like shorthand: a thousand images of explosions and soldiers and barbed wire and rioting and foam-mouthed politicians were thrown up by that simple statement. You were automatically *hard*, even if you were a freckle-armed accountant in National Health specs; you earned the sympathy of slack-jawed women for surviving so long, and you habitually buffed up your life story like you'd just crawled out of the Warsaw ghetto. You joked about the Troubles, but in such a way that you made it seem like you were covering something up. Perhaps you said you were once in a lift with that Gerry Adams and you thought he bore a remarkable resemblance to Rolf Harris, and you pointed out that you never saw the two of them in the same place at the same time, and your audience laughed and said, 'Right enough,' but at the same time you knew what they were thinking, that you were making light of it because actually you'd suffered horribly at the hands of masked terrorists or your mother had been blown through a window at Omagh or your father was shot down on the Bogside for demanding basic human rights. To say you were from Belfast was to say you were a Jew in Berlin, or a soldier of the Somme. But no longer. And as the Troubles had waned, so had the world's interest, and so had my star. Like a minor player in a soap opera who has been killed off, I no longer had access to (or, to tell the truth), much interest in the limelight. My job was boring, my wage was average, my family life was quiet, uneventful. But I was happy. I had seen and done too much; now was my quiet time. Mouse, on the other hand, had reinvented himself, and not just as a cat-killer.

'Could we have your autograph? Would it be too much trouble?'

Mouse didn't even bother to blush. The wife raced in and got her latest copy of *Belfast Confidential* and Mouse signed and dated it. He then obliged them with some TV gossip: Eamon Holmes was being wooed by Channel 4, and some local actor who used to be in *CSI: Miami* had checked into rehab again. Then we left Patricia to bask in the residual glow of his celebrity, saying we had to get on with the unpacking, but instead Mouse guided me to his new toy and I, who know nothing about cars, blinked at it kind of impressed. 'Is that a . . . ?'

Mouse nodded 'You betcha.'

The RA Jet is the kind of sports car you have to be young and beautiful or suffer the illusion of such to drive. I'd a fair idea of where Mouse fitted into the equation, but he was obviously deeply in love with it. He ran his hand down the sleek bodywork. 'This is one of only three working models in the entire world. They won't roll off the production line for another eighteen months.'

'So how come you . . . ?'

'Because if the Editor of *Belfast Confidential* has one, then it's *the* car to have, isn't it?'

I nodded. 'Good to see you haven't got an over-inflated sense of your own importance.'

Mouse shrugged. 'Doesn't matter what I have. It's what *they* think. So jump in,' he said. 'I'll show you what it can do.'

I wasn't the slightest bit interested in what it could do. I was never a car boy. Strictly A to B. Mechanically illiterate. But Mouse was keen to show off, so I sat there with a can of beer from the coolbox he kept in the back, while he put it through its paces. I said, 'Very nice,' a couple of times, and asked about cylinders and horsepower and satellite navigational systems and he went into considerable detail.

'I've to give it back next week. Liam Neeson is next on the list, and they're making *him* come here from New York to drive it.'

'Wow,' I said.

We'd been gone about twenty minutes when Patricia called my mobile. She said, 'Where the fuck are you?'

I looked at Mouse. 'Where the fuck are we?'

He pointed at the electronic map on the dashboard. 'Here,' he said.

'Where's here?' I asked, squinting down. The writing was too small.

'I'm not sure,' said Mouse. 'I haven't got my glasses.'

'Neither have I.' Sad, really. 'Trish, it's official, we have no idea.'

'Well, that's a big help.'

'I know.'

'If it's any consolation,' Mouse said, 'I'm going in for laser eye-surgery next week. Then I'll be twenty-twenty.'

'Patricia, he says he's going in for laser eye-surgery. Then he'll have twenty-twenty vision and be able to read the maps in his own fucking car. Unless of course the surgeon sneezes or something and they blow the top of his head off.'

Patricia sighed. 'Well, tell him good luck, and would you ever think of looking out the window and just telling me where you are?'

I glanced about me. We were moving up Great Victoria Street. Lavery's Bar was only a few hundred yards away. 'Nope. Don't recognise it. He's got us lost, love.'

Mouse's brow furrowed.

'On second thoughts,' Patricia snapped, 'I don't care where you are. Just get back here and help me do this, will you? It's not fair, leaving it all to me.'

'I know, I know, love, I'll be back as soon as I can. And we don't have to do it all in one day anyway, do we? We've got the rest of our lives.'

'Yes, Dan, very romantic. Now stop trying to slink out of the fucking unpacking and get back here.'

'Yes, Boss,' I said. I cut the line and pointed Lavery's out to Mouse. 'Some nights in there, eh?' Mouse nodded. 'Fancy one?'

He snorted lightly. 'In there?'

'Aye.'

'I think we're a bit past Lavery's, Dan.'

'Meaning what?'

'Well, it's all . . . you know, drunks and students.'

'So?'

'We've moved on a bit from that.'

'Speak for yourself.'

Then he had a brainwave. He clicked his fingers. 'Tell you what – you hungry? I have a table at Cayenne.'

'You what?'

'I have a table at Cayenne.'

'Yes, I heard what you said, I just don't know what the fuck you mean.'

'Dan, for god sake. Cayenne. The restaurant.'

I shrugged.

'They used to run Roscoffs. Remember Roscoffs?'

My knowledge of restaurants is largely confined to eating establishments that only get busy after the pubs close, but I remembered Roscoffs because before peace broke out it was the kind of establishment that politicians and PR people took foreign visitors to, in order to prove that every meal in Belfast didn't have to include chips. Anyone who was anyone ate there, and the owners were awarded stars, and their own TV show, and they joined the celebrity chef circuit. So I nodded and he said, 'They've redecorated and changed the name and it's a whole new concept in cooking and they've put the prices up. It's fantastic, and it's only around the corner.'

'And you have a table.'

'Well, it's not my own personal table, but they'll look after us.'

I sighed. 'Has it really come to this?'

'Come to what?'

'That you have a table. Or at least access to one. "I have a table." That's what you said.'

'Well, they're difficult to get.'

'So who gives a fuck?'

Mouse shook his head. 'They're friends of mine.'

'Good for you.'

'And besides, they want to make sure they're on the List, so it won't be a problem.'

'The List?'

'The List.'

'What List?'

7

'*The* List.'

'Lost me, Mouse.'

'The *Belfast Confidential* Power List.'

'Ah. Right.'

'Dan – you know about the List. I've told you about the List.'

'Well, I'm getting on, I don't always remember everything you say.'

He shook his head, because of course I knew the List. Everyone in town knew the List. On it were Belfast's top fifty movers and shakers. A canny mix of multi-millionaire industrialists, TV chat-show hosts, pop stars, gangsters and politicians – the people who shaped our booming little city. It was parochial to the extreme, and didn't mean a thing ten miles out in any direction, but in the three years since Mouse had launched the *Belfast Confidential* Power List, it had assumed an importance, a cultural relevance which was hard to quantify and difficult to pin down. It was just – *big*, and Mouse loved it.

'Okay,' I said, '*that* List.'

'You don't have to say it like that.'

'Like what?'

'Like that. It's important, Dan.'

'Uhuh.'

'I don't mean to be on it, *per se*. It just – gives us . . . a sense of identity, do you know what I mean?'

'Mmmmm,' I said. 'And by the way, do you think there's any danger of you disappearing up your own arse?'

Mouse gave me a sad look. 'A bit of support, once in a while, might be nice.'

He was my best friend. Thick and thin, mostly thin. 'I know. Sorry,' I said.

'We just don't throw it together, you know.'

'I know.'

'Every entry is scrupulously researched, expert opinion is sought, we discuss every single detail . . .'

'I know, Mouse.'

'We don't just pull names out of thin air.'

'I believe you, all right? Go to fucking Cheyenne then.'

'Cayenne. Anyway, I thought you had to get home?'

'I do.'

Mouse turned the car back towards Shaftesbury Square. We didn't say anything for a couple of minutes. I thought I'd better break the ice. 'So,' I said, 'these Cayenne people. Are they on the Power List?'

'Well, it depends what table they give me.'

2

Good table. Just where everyone could see you. Mouse loved it – being the centre of attention. Not just here. Everywhere. Being someone. Anyone. He had been my Editor for a lot of years, back when I had some kind of profile, largely based upon what was billed as a satirical column but which was really just me taking the piss out of the great and the good, and sometimes the bad and the bold. Usually it was the great and the good who came after you with a big stick; the bad and the bold just shrugged it off because they didn't care, or couldn't read.

Through all the threats and bollocks, Mouse was my rock – solid, dependable, supportive. He could blow and bluster and roar and scream with the best of them, but like most big, loud men, he was shy and lacked confidence and avoided the spotlight wherever possible. Not that it ever sought him out. He was a desk jockey, brilliant at his job, but perceived as not being dynamic enough to progress up the editorial ladder. He stayed anchored to the news desk, frustrated at his lack of progress at work, and living a quiet, repressed kind of life at home in the shadow of his abrasive wife. In my less modest moments I had sometimes thought that he lived vicariously through me. He pulled me out of holes and guided and advised but he did not put himself in the way of danger. That was my foolish lot. And since I had ostensibly retired from dangerous missions – or getting myself into trouble – Mouse was denied even that outlet. His nickname was sarcastic, but few people realised how deadly accurate it actually was.

The first time I noticed something different about him was on holiday in Cyprus. On the beach, me hungover, Patricia pissed on frozen Pina Coladas, Wendy, his wife, red raw and defiantly refusing suncream and complaining about the sunbeds, the pool, stones on the beach, jellyfish in the water, the price of heating oil at home, tribal strife in Rwanda and saying she didn't find Terry Wogan funny at all – and Mouse staring blankly out to sea. It was a look that I'd become familiar with up and down the beach: the grown man's fear of the Jet Ski. Mouse wasn't a doer. He desperately wanted to be, but he always held back. Never paraglided, never scuba dived, never went on roller coasters, lived in fear of speed cameras and never drank more than one pint if he was driving.

I was looking for headache pills in my wife's handbag, Wendy was yittering on about aviation fuel, and suddenly Mouse was standing jabbing a finger at her: 'You know nothing about aviation fuel! Shut the fuck up!'

Then he turned, strode down the beach, and a few moments later he was racing across the waves on this bright yellow Jet Ski, yelling and hollering.

We looked at him, agog.

Agog. Not a word you use every day.

Wendy blamed it on dehydration and made him lie down in a dark room for the next few days. And Mouse agreed. Docile and pliable, like it was a glitch, a sunspot. Or as it turned out, more like a virus. Soon his whole system was infected. Or affected.

He said later that it was the death of my own son that prompted it all. As a newsman he had dealt with violence day in day out for twenty years, but the murder of my boy just as peace was descending on us had brought home to him the fragility and shortness of life and a sudden, crushing awareness that it was passing him by, that it *had* passed him by. The Jet Ski was almost an unconscious decision to do something about it. The changes that followed were more calculated. Much to the consternation of his wife, he jacked his job in and took over an internet horse-racing gossip site called *The Horse Whisperer*. 'A midlife crisis,' said his wife. 'Away and fuck yourself,' said Mouse. Much to everyone's surprise, *The Horse Whisperer* was a huge success. Inspired, Mouse then came up with the idea for *Belfast Confidential* – initially another internet site specialising in localised celebrity gossip, insider business news and hard-hitting tabloid-style exposés. It was like a hybrid of *Hello*, *Private Eye* and the *News of the World*, the kind of magazine that could be astonishingly fawning towards you one week, and stick the knife in the next, without feeling awkward about it at all.

Again it was an instant hit – but whereas *The Horse Whisperer* relied on copious amounts of free gossip, *Belfast Confidential* needed journalists to ferret out its stories, and journalists need feeding – or at the very least, watering – which meant that Mouse needed advertising. Belfast businessmen are a cautious lot, however, and they weren't convinced of the effectiveness of internet advertising, so Mouse launched a print version of *BC*. And it was massive from issue one. It just struck a chord. A weekly magazine which lampooned and celebrated the rich and famous and successful in equal amounts. At least part of the secret was that it was a regional production, that the celebs were locals made good, that the business shenanigans were happening just down the road and round the corner. Advertisers, until now restricted to old-world titles like the *Ulster Tatler*, flocked to it.

It was a big, bright, glossy hit, and pretty soon Mouse started to become big and bright and glossy himself. He got a new hairstyle. He shaved his beard. He started a diet. He went to a gym. Muscles. Definition. A month after he had had a nose job, photos of himself began to appear in his own magazine. He appeared at launches, parties, on local television quiz shows. He became the voice of *Belfast Confidential*, and to some extent, the voice of Belfast; a cultural and topical news commentator. A master of the soundbite. And then he came up with the Power List.

We were eating Dublin Bay prawns with chilli and garlic in Cayenne. He chose. He seemed to know what he was doing. I would have settled for a ham bap. He asked for the wine list and discussed grapes with the maitre d' for a while. I've grown up a lot, and don't let people down in public so much any more, so I just took it as it came. I didn't even say anything when Mouse sent the first bottle of wine back, saying it was too dry for his palate.

At other tables, ash trays were whisked away from smokers and replaced virtually between puffs. It was very impressive. But Mouse tutted, because he didn't smoke any more and didn't see why anyone else should. *Belfast Confidential* had thrown its weight behind a campaign to have smoking in bars and restaurants banned, just as it was across the border in the Republic. The Government was taking it seriously, and had indicated that Northern Ireland might be used as a dry run for introducing the ban across the UK. Mouse was pleased with this. I wasn't so sure. The Government had a tradition of trying out unpopular policies at a safe distance from its voters. Like proportional representation and internment.

'So,' I rasped, chilli sauce burning my throat, 'how's wife number two, or are you already onto number three?'

'Very funny, Dan.'

'You know, Patricia's not forgiven you yet.'

'She seemed all right today.'

'Well, she's two-faced. You should hear what she says behind your back.'

Mouse gave me a look. 'Yeah. Right.'

'Swear to God, mate. I mean, you can't blame her, Wendy's her best friend.' I concentrated on my prawns for several moments. I sipped my wine.

Mouse said, 'What does she say?'

'She says you're a bastard for throwing Wendy over for some mail-order bride.'

'She's not a mail-order bride.'

'I know that. But she's from that part of the world – it's an easy mistake to make.'

'What're you talking about?'

'Mouse. Come on, she's from the Philippines.'

'She's from Thailand.'

'Same neck of the woods. And you know, she suddenly appeared and now you're married and . . . well, I mean, I don't want to tar them all with the same brush . . .'

'You don't, or Patricia doesn't?'

'Patricia, obviously. She thinks if your new woman's from the Philippines or wherever, she's more'n likely a mail-order bride. You know, because with all your money, you've gone a bit that way lately – you see it in a catalogue, you buy it. New car, new nose, new wife.'

Mouse shook his head in disbelief. 'You really think that?'

'Me? No, mate, you don't have to convince me. It's Patricia you have to bring round.'

Mouse blew hot chilli air out of his cheeks. 'She's not a mail-order bride. I didn't order her out of a catalogue.'

'I know that. I saw the wedding snaps in *Belfast Confidential*. Lovely beach. She's beautiful. She must be about eighteen. No reason why an eighteen-year-old beauty wouldn't find a forty-two-year-old man with a face like a bag of Comber spuds attractive.'

'She is beautiful, and she's thirty-two.'

'Seriously?'

'Yes, Dan. And she does happen to find me attractive.'

'Well, there you go. Still, she must be enjoying her new life. Nice big house. Flashy car. The holidays.'

'Dan, she married me. Not a house or a car or a holiday.'

'If you say so.'

'Dan, we're in love.'

'Not me you have to convince.'

'I don't have to convince anyone.'

'Fair point. But Patricia thinks you flew out there looking for a teenage sex bomb, and she saw an easy one-way ticket out of a straw hut in a swamp. Or maybe it was one of those go-go bars where they shoot ping-pong balls out of their holes. Either way she thinks you got suckered into it, being a horny middle-aged man suffering an identity crisis.'

Mouse took a very deep breath. His nostrils were flared, his brow furrowed, his eyes cool.

'And this is really what Patricia thinks?'

'Yes, it is.'

'And you – what do you think?'

'None of my business. Long as you're getting a ride, mate, I'm happy for you.'

He was gripping the side of the table now. His knuckles were showing white against skin. Colour was rising up his cheeks like a petrol gauge. 'You just can't stand it, can you?'

'Stand what, mate?'

'Seeing how well I've done. Seeing me happy.'

'Mouse, wise up.'

'You can't. You're jealous. I'm rich, Dan. I've a beautiful young wife who loves me. You're jealous.'

'I don't think so.'

'Well, what is it then?'

'What is what?'

'All this attitude. This fucking backstabbing.'

'What attitude? What backstabbing?'

'All this mail-order shite. All this cold shoulder.'

'Cold shoulder? Mouse, we're sitting here having lunch.'

'Have you invited us round, once?'

'We were moving house.'

'Not for the last six months you weren't.'

'Yes, we were. She's been packing and organising the whole time.'

'Right. Did you call to see us? Did you welcome us home? Did you make the fucking effort, Dan?'

He had a point. 'No,' I said. 'You're right. We should have made the effort. But it's nothing against your wife. We're just lazy. Didn't I call you to help me to move house?'

'No, Dan, I called you.'

'You did?'

'Yes, Dan, I called you and before I could say anything you asked me to come and help you move fucking house.'

'So I did. Well, what's the difference? Aren't we here now, having fun?' He put his knife and fork down and gave me another hard look. He dabbed at his mouth with a cloth napkin. I decided to defuse the situation. 'Are you going to finish your chips?' I asked.

He glowered at me for a further moment, then snapped, 'They're not chips. If you'd read your menu you'd know that they were sautéed Irish potatoes with a glazing of garlic and tarragon paste and then rolled in an egg and sunflower batter.'

Our eyes locked.

The restaurant was packed, but there still seemed to be as many staff as customers. The talk was hushed, the music subdued. It was harder *not* to listen to us.

'So have you finished with your chips or not?'

'When did you turn into such an arse, Dan?'

'Might it not be the other way round?'

'What, that you've always been an arse and I've just never noticed before?'

I smiled. 'Maybe you should lighten up, Mouse.'

He looked at me for a long time. Then he said, 'Yeah.'

I was happy enough to get a taxi. There was no point in rushing home. It would be like hurrying to your own execution. I should have phoned and let her know I'd been waylaid by Mouse. She would have said, 'You're old enough to make your own decisions.' But it was too late now. I could phone and say, 'Are you not finished the unpacking yet?' I suggested this to Mouse, and he advised against it. He was good with advice, especially now that he'd cooled down. We were like that, quick to explode, just as quick to make up. Like lovers really, without the sex or soppy cards or whining about the toilet seat being left up. So when I huffily suggested getting a taxi Mouse said, 'Wise up,' and led me to the car. There was a crowd round it, staring. Mouse said, 'Back off.'

We went into Lavery's for a pint. It was on the way.

'Jesus,' I said, looking around. 'You're not the only one's changed.'

It was much brighter and the thugs were better dressed than we remembered. I asked if I could peruse the beer list, then ordered Harp. I tried to send it back because it tasted like piss that had been passed through a soda stream. Then I remembered that that was why everyone liked it. So we sat down, and after a while Mouse said, 'You're right to be a bit strange with us. It must have come as a shock.'

'You bet. We'd Wendy round our place every night for weeks, crying her lamps out. We thought you had the perfect marriage.'

Mouse blinked at me. 'You're joking.'

'No, seriously, mate. You know Trish and me, always fighting the fucking bit out, but there was never a cross word between the two of youse.'

'Oh bollocks, Dan. Don't you know those are the ones you have to watch?'

I hadn't quite thought of it like that. 'I suppose,' I said.

He took a long drink. 'Dan, I married Wendy because . . . well, I didn't think I could do any better.'

'Mouse—'

'No, wait, let me say this.'

I glanced around the bar in case the locals were listening. The music was loud and the chatter was incessant, but it didn't mean they weren't listening with as much attention as in Cayenne. I was happy to let Mouse prattle away, but if he broke down and asked for a hug, I'd deck him.

'Okay. Just, you know, keep it down.'

He had a big, booming voice. He notched it down a couple. 'I just want—'

'Do you know sign language?'

He smiled and lowered it further. 'I just want you to understand, Dan. I've never had much luck with girls. You know that. So when Wendy came along, I knew she wasn't the prettiest or even the nicest, or to tell you the truth, the most faithful, but she liked me and I made do with that, Dan. I settled for what I thought my level was. But things have changed. I feel like I've seen the light, Dan – and I saw Wendy for what she is: a fucking moaning fat old cow.'

'Don't beat around the bush there, Mouse.'

'She made my life miserable, Dan, so I did what I've been dreaming about for years. I told her to fuck off. And she did. And I've never been happier.'

I raised my glass to him. 'Fair enough then.'

He nodded, happy to have gotten whatever it was off his chest.

I took a long sip. 'So where did the mail-order Philippino bride come into it?'

'Thai,' he said.

'Thai. The postage must have been horrendous.'

'Do you want to know where we met?'

'You were on a busload of sexed-up Western saddoes, and she was sitting behind glass waiting for her number to be called.'

'We met at Oxford.'

'Oxford?'

'We were both attending a symposium of magazine publishers.'

'What, like porn magazines?'

'No, Dan,' Mouse explained patiently. 'She is the daughter of one of Bangkok's leading publishers. She was Chief Executive of her father's company, responsible for twenty-six different titles with a net worth of over a billion dollars. She also managed her family interests in satellite television and computers.'

'God, it must be difficult to fit in the hooking on the side.'

He continued to smile. It seemed that now nothing I could say would stop him.

'You're serious?' I asked.

'Completely. She fell in love with *me*, Dan. She gave up her job and her family to come all the way across the world to become my wife, because she loves me absolutely and I love her absolutely. It's fantastic.'

I gave him a slow, searching look. How long could he keep giving me all this bullshit without cracking?

3

The cat was in a black binliner and we were tiptoeing through the grass seeds. Mouse had the torch, I had the shovel. We had a can of beer each, and I also had a small paper funnel of seeds to cover the area of soil we were about to displace. We found a spot down near the hedge at the bottom, then checked the eye-line up to the neighbours' house. The fence blocked out the kitchen, but the two upstairs bedrooms had a nice view of our nocturnal burial site. However, the lights in both rooms were out.

It had been a long walk down from the back door, so we popped our cans and each took a drink. I glanced back up the garden to our new bedroom. The light was on, but the curtains were closed. When we finally arrived home Patricia had shouted down, 'I'm having a doze.' I knew by her tone that only polite-ness towards Mouse was saving me. It was the lull before the storm. And, inevitably, the longer the lull, the bigger the storm.

'How deep?' Mouse asked.

'How would I know?' I pushed the shovel blade into the ground. It sank in easily. We'd had a delivery of topsoil the week before. Patricia got the idea that our own soil wasn't good enough, so we got rid of it and brought fresh soil in. She had read about this in a book entitled *Your Little Garden of Eden* by a local crackpot called Liam Miller; she claimed to have found a copy on a park bench. After the soil, she'd spent ages deciding on the type of grass we needed. I had thought there was only one, the green variety, but Liam Miller's manual went into considerable detail on about twenty-seven. Their consistency. Their hardiness. The fucking *shades* of green that might best match the colour of our house.

Well, at least the fresh soil was easy to work with. In five minutes I'd dug down about two feet. There was sweat on my brow and my shirt was stuck to my back. It was like being on a chain gang. A very lazy one. And they probably didn't get to wear Lynx 24-7 to cover up the smell.

'Come on, hurry up,' said Mouse. His eyes were darting anxiously about.

'Doesn't this make you feel at one with Nature?'

'No,' he said.

I gave it another couple of digs, then I stepped out of the hole. Mouse picked up the bin bag and threw it in. It hit the bottom with a dull clump.

I said, 'Please, show some respect for the dead.'

'Let's just get it over with.'

I said, 'How much would a photo of this be worth?'

Mouse looked about him, suddenly panicked. 'You're not . . . ?'

'Mouse, get a life, would you?'

'Just hurry up then, please. Here, let me.' He reached for the shovel. That was the agreement. But I held onto it.

'We should say a few words.'

'It's a dead cat, Dan.'

'I know, but we can't just . . .'

Mouse sighed. 'Okay, say something then, anything.'

I stood over the hole. 'Here lies Toodles,' I said, 'killed by a Mouse.' I looked up at the stars. 'I didn't know Toodles well, but by all accounts . . .'

'Oh, for fuck sake!' Mouse grabbed for the shovel again, and this time I let it go. He quickly began to throw in the topsoil. I drank my beer. When he'd finished he patted it down flat so that it looked like the rest of the garden. Then I sprinkled some of the leftover seeds on top.

'There,' Mouse said, shining the torch across the uniform earth. 'You'd never know.'

'No, Mouse,' I said, shaking my head grimly. 'We'll *always* know.'

'Oh, fuck off.'

We laughed. We returned the shovel to the garage, then went back into the house. We sat at the kitchen table and opened another couple of beers. There was still no sign of Patricia. I was working on the assumption that as long as Mouse remained, she would stay upstairs. I was also working on the assumption that Mouse wanted to talk. We were the best of friends, but we hadn't been in touch in months, then he'd called me out of the blue. He'd hung around all day waiting for the right moment. He was clearly pissed off that neither Patricia nor I had made any effort to welcome his new wife to Belfast, but we'd been through that earlier in the day and here he still was, so it must be something else.

I took a sip of my beer. He took a sip of his. I took a sip of mine. He took a sip of his. A pattern was emerging. I took a sip of mine. He took a sip of his. I looked at him, he looked away. He looked at me, I looked back. He looked away. When he looked back I was still looking. He said, 'What?'

'Awkward silence.'

'What?'

'Awkward silence. We never have awkward silences, Mouse. If you've something to say, just say it.'

'I don't have something to say. Do you have something to say?'

I shook my head. I took another sip. He took another sip. We sat for another three minutes. Then there was a clump-clump-clump from the stairs, and Patricia appeared in the doorway. Her cheeks were red and her eyes were wide and she was just about to launch into me when she saw Mouse. 'Oh!' she said. 'Mouse – it was so quiet, I thought you were away.'

Mouse just looked at her.

'We're just having a chat,' I said. 'But if there's anything you want to say to me, you can say it in front of—'

'Shut up, Dan.'

'Trish, come on . . .'

'Don't Trish me, you arse!'

'Trish, not in front of—'

'He's heard it all before!'

I glanced at Mouse. He had heard it all before. It didn't mean he wanted to hear it again.

'Maybe I should—' he started to say, and began to rise from his chair.

'Just stay where you fucking are!' Trish yelled.

He sat back down and she gave me her full attention. Patricia has never been one of those women who look more attractive when they're angry. Her eyes were wide and her nostrils flared, and when she began to shout, flecks of spit appeared in the corners of her mouth.

'I am *so* fucking tired of this!' she began. 'Every time it's the fucking same! Every time I ask you to do something it's "Yes, yes, yes, in a minute" and for a brief moment I have this little hope that you're actually going to do it, but oh no, I turn my eye for one moment, and away you go! Moving house, Dan, it's a big fucking operation and it needs both of us to do it. I can't do everything by myself. I need you here, not waltzing all over the place getting pissed.'

'I'm not pi—'

'Shut the fuck up! I went to see the houses. I did all the negotiating. I transferred all the money and did all the paperwork. I
packed up our house. I organised the removal. I changed the post.
I switched the phone. All I asked you to promise was that you'd
be here on moving day, that you'd help me through it, that you'd
stand up to those fucking removal men if they smashed anything,
and I should have known! As soon as you came through the door
you opened your first beer and you said "This is for the house,
this is for our lovely new home," and I should have known you
just wanted another excuse to get pissed. And then Mouse turns
up and I think, Great, he's going to help us out—'

'Patricia, I was—' Mouse ventured.

'Shut the fuck up, Mouse! Then I get stuck speaking to the
fucking neighbours and youse two sneak off and get pissed. It's
not fair, Dan, it's not fucking fair. I can't do everything.'

She pulled a chair out and sat down heavily. She put her
head in her hands. A tear rolled down her cheek and splashed
onto the table. Her hair was all over the place, her face was
covered in black smudges, her hands were red and raw and
her fingernails encrusted with dirt. I reached across and gently
moved her hands back from her face.

'Love?' I said.

She blinked tearfully at me. 'What?' she murmured.

'Is there any chance of some pizza?'

Mouse's chair scraped back across the linoleum, his face pale
at the expectation of sudden violence.

But Patricia just stared at me, and then the corners of her
mouth softened and the furrows of her brow smoothed out
and she let out a great guffaw of a laugh. 'Christ,' she said,
'what a day. I'm sorry, love.' She took my hand and kissed it.
'I always get fucking stressed out, moving house. Christ, I wish

I could take a leaf out of your book.' She stood up and kissed the top of my head. 'I'm going to have a shower, then I'll order some pizza, yeah? Mouse, you'll stay, won't you?'

Mouse just looked blankly at her. She took this for a yes and turned for the door. She ruffled my hair on the way past.

'Trish?' She stopped. 'Pepperoni. Extra onions.'

'Pepperoni, extra onions.'

The shower was running upstairs. Mouse said, 'She's some woman.'

I shrugged. 'She'll do.'

'How long have you been together now?'

'No idea.'

'But you work, you two, you work.'

'Suppose we do.'

'Though you wind each other up something dreadful.'

'Just the way we are.'

'It's nice, though, isn't it. You know each other inside out. You have a back story. You both know what Opal Fruits are and who Joe Strummer was and how good the Liverpool team of the eighties really was. You've so much in common.' He was turning his can in his hands, staring at the table. 'You know what May Li and I have in common?' he asked sadly.

I shook my head slowly.

'Four orgasms a night.' He said it so quietly that for a moment I didn't pick up on it. And then I looked at him and saw that the down-at-heel glumness had vanished. Now he had a big, stupid grin.

'You *bastard*,' I said.

'Four. Every night. Whether I want it or not. I'm fucking near dead, but it's fan*tastic*. Every position known to man, and a few others besides. She's incredible.'

I cleared my throat. 'I'm very happy for you, Mouse. But why are you telling me this?'

'I have to tell someone!'

'Okay, all right. You can stop smiling now.'

'Okay, okay . . . but sometimes she just gets hold—'

'Mouse! Too much information. Just . . . shut the fuck up.'

'You don't want me to talk about all the sex?'

'No, Mouse.'

'And all the things she can do?'

'No, Mouse, for fuck sake!'

He laughed quietly to himself.

I got up and fetched him another beer from the fridge. We popped together. I let him take his first drink. 'So, what else is this about, besides the sex?'

'Does it have to be about anything?'

'No. Doesn't have to be.'

'Can't I call up an old mate without there being an ulterior motive?'

'Course you can.'

We drank our beers for another couple of minutes. Then he shook his head and said, 'All right. Fair enough. You always could read me like a book. I just wanted – well, a bit of advice. It's . . . well, it's nothing really.'

'It's not nothing, Mouse, otherwise you wouldn't be sitting here.'

'What's that supposed to mean?'

'Mouse. We're mates. We always will be. But you're moving in different circles now. I don't mind that, fair play to you, I'm sure I'd do exactly the same if I suddenly came into some money. It happens, you know, people go in different directions, different social circles, some people get left behind . . .'

'We're not leaving you . . .'

'You know what I mean. Come on, mate, you've been hanging around like a third nut all day. If you've something to say, say it. Don't beat around the bush any more, because it's as flat as a fucking pancake.'

He looked a little bit relieved. 'We are mates,' he said, 'and we always will be. And what I said about youse not keeping in touch – well, that was as much us as you. May Li has . . . well, expensive tastes, and I didn't want you to feel . . .'

'Like third-class citizens.'

'No, I mean—'

'Like boring working-class poorhouse rejects.'

'No, Dan!'

'Then get to the point!'

'Okay! All right!' He clasped his hands together. Stared at the table. Took a deep breath. 'The thing is, Dan – I think someone is trying to kill me.'

It sat in the air for several long moments. I could hear the hair-dryer going upstairs, and Patricia singing 'I Heard It Through the Grapevine' over it. Mouse glanced up at me, and for the first time I noticed the bags hanging heavy beneath his eyes.

'You're serious?' I asked. He nodded slowly. 'Why the fuck would anyone want to kill *you*?'

'I'm an important man.'

He was Mouse, and I thought of him as Mouse, but I had to concede that in recent months he had indeed, in at least some respects, become an important man.

'So why are you telling me?'

'Well – one, the police would laugh me out of the station if I told them, and two, because people are always trying to kill you, I thought you'd know what to do. Help me out. You know. Maybe you could get to the bottom of it.'

The hair-dryer had stopped, and now I could hear Patricia coming down the stairs. I jabbed a finger at Mouse. 'Don't say a word,' I warned him, then smiled up as my wife came through the kitchen door.

'Right!' she exclaimed happily. 'Pizza Hut or Domino's?'

4

I couldn't sleep. I tossed and turned and Patricia barked at me to stay still. After a while I slipped a hand around her waist and snuggled up behind and nibbled at her ear and she purred for a few moments. Then she gave me a backwards headbutt.

She swore it was an accident. She was only trying to stop me from pawing her and could I please not bleed on the sheets. She handed me two cotton buds, and I pressed one up each nostril.

'Fucking great,' I moaned. 'Fucking *great.*'

'Sorry,' she said. 'You took me by surprise.'

'Next time I'll make a fucking appointment.'

'I'm exhausted, Dan. I need to sleep.'

'Right,' I said. 'Go ahead.'

Instead she turned and squeezed my arm. 'It's your first night in a new house, you're bound to be a bit unsettled.'

'Yeah.'

Of course I was unsettled. But it had nothing to do with the new house. It had to do with seeing a dead cat every time I closed my eyes. And the fact that someone was trying to kill my best friend. I couldn't mention either problem to my wife. She simply *would not* understand at all about our behaviour towards the late Siamese, and while she would certainly be sympathetic towards Mouse, she would totally and absolutely ban me from getting involved, no matter how superficial that involvement was. We'd been down that road once too often.

'Well, seeing as you can't sleep,' she suggested, 'why don't you do some more unpacking?'

She'd worked tirelessly all day, but the house was still chock-full of taped-up cardboard boxes, over-stuffed bin bags and rolled-up carpets. You accumulate a lot of crap in life, and you're always reluctant to part with it. Because one day that beige lampshade with the bent connection might come in really useful.

'Yeah, right, that's what I feel like doing in the middle of the night with blood pishing out of me.'

'Oh, poor soul. I'll put Emergency Ward Ten on standby. Make me a cup of tea then.'

It being the lesser of two evils, I tramped downstairs. The kettle was already unpacked. It took me a while to track down a cup. Most of our cutlery was still in a box somewhere, so I stirred in the sugar with one of the cotton buds. The clean end, obviously. When I took it up she was sitting with the lamp on, looking serious. 'What did Mouse really want?'

I laughed. 'Where did that come from?'

'I was just thinking about it. How we haven't seen him in ages.'

'That's why he turned up.'

'Balls. Youse were talking about something. Is he having trouble with the mail-order bride?'

'He's having four orgasms a night.'

Patricia raised an eyebrow. 'Seriously?'

'According to Mouse.'

She stared into the distance for a few moments, then half-focused back on me. 'I remember when we . . .' she began wistfully, then stopped herself. 'Oh, wait a minute – we've never had four orgasms a night. Nor three. Nor . . .'

'Very funny.' She smiled back, but then she went kind of quiet, and that got me thinking, and thinking led to worrying, so I felt it was important to remind her that we too had had our moments. 'Not that I'm keeping a record or anything, but remember FA Cup Day? You had two that day. Orgasms. The big O.'

'FA Cup Day?' she asked vaguely. 'Who was playing?'

'Liverpool and Man U.'

'No, I don't.'

'Yes, remember? One at half time, and one after extra time. You were wearing . . .' And then I stopped, because there was something not quite right about my memory of it. 'You were wearing . . .'

Patricia raised an eyebrow. 'What was I wearing?'

I sighed. 'A referee's outfit.'

She smiled sympathetically, but when she spoke it was clearly and precisely, as if she were addressing a child. 'That's what we call a *fantasy.*'

I folded my arms. She set her tea down, then crawled across the bed towards me. She put her arms around me from behind. 'Don't worry, love, one orgasm is plenty.'

'Do you mean that?'

'Of course I do.'

She kissed me, and we fell back in each other's arms. She kissed me again, and I responded. I was just removing her nightie when a cat meowed outside. I jumped up and raced across to the window.

'Dan!'

'Just a—' I ducked in behind one side of the curtain and peered out. Down below, turning circles on our freshly seeded lawn, its fine and shiny coat caked with soil and grass seeds, was a Siamese cat.

'Dan, what is it?'

'Nothing, nothing. Just a . . . cat.'

It stopped rotating. It looked towards the house. It looked towards *me*. A shiver ran down my spine. I banged suddenly on the window, trying to break the connection. But it just kept on staring.

I opened the window. 'Fuck away off!' I shouted.

'Dan!' Trish came jumping off the bed. 'What is it?'

'Yes, you! Fuck off!'

She was beside me, looking down. 'Dan – Dan. It's only a bloody cat!'

'I know.'

Mouse had killed the cat, its brains were all over the fucking place. We'd buried it in a bin bag, two feet down. And yet there it was, large as life. I shuddered. Patricia put her arms around me from behind and gave me a squeeze. Maybe cats did have nine lives. Or perhaps it was *Ghost Cat*. The concept was as horrifying as it was hilarious. Christ, maybe I was just tired and a little bit drunk. How could it possibly be 'our' cat? It was just some neighbourhood moggy out for a dander; maybe it had smelled the body down there. Or maybe it was just taking a dump. Yes, that was it. As we watched, it seemed to tilt its head towards us, and in that movement, as ridiculous as it sounds, I could almost have sworn that it winked at me. Then it darted quickly across the topsoil and leaped onto the wooden fence. It balanced for just a moment on top, then dropped gracefully down and out of sight into the neighbours' garden.

'Bastard,' I whispered.

Patricia laughed. 'Never known you to get so protective about a garden before.' She turned back to the bed and lay down. 'There's hope for you yet.'

I turned. 'Well, isn't it a good thing?' I asked.

'Not when you're about to screw me.'

'Am I about to screw you?'

'I certainly hope so.'

I smiled and crawled back up the bed beside her. We started to kiss. I finally removed her nightie and she dragged off my Liverpool top.

'I love you,' she murmured in my ear.

'Same here,' I murmured back.

'And I want you to know,' she whispered, nibbling at my earlobe, 'that I'm not keeping count.'

'Count?'

'Of the orgasms.'

'Trish . . .'

'Two would be good. I don't want you to feel any pressure to go for three. Although I'm sure four's completely beyond you.'

I jumped up. 'For fuck sake. Talk about putting someone off their stroke.'

She laughed, then rolled over away from me and pulled the quilt up. When she spoke, it was with a triumphant smugness. 'Well, perhaps you'll learn from this, Dan my love. If you want to lay me, first you have to lay the carpet. And that means not pissing off to the bar with your mates. Nighty noodle.'

She reached across and turned her bedside light off.

I remained on the side of the bed, fuming. She was an evil, evil, *evil* woman. And 50 per cent of me was waiting for her to roll back and say she was only raking and please screw me now, big boy.

Five minutes later I was still sitting in the darkness.

'Right,' I snapped, 'I'm going downstairs for a wank.'

Just as I reached the door Patricia said, 'Enjoy.'

5

Next morning, on the way to work, with the upstairs curtains still closed, I checked the ground where we'd buried the cat. There were faint paw prints, but the soil and the light coating of grass seeds was otherwise largely undisturbed. Satisfied, I turned towards our garage. Then I heard George, over the garden fence, going: 'Pssss-wsssss-wsssss. Pssss-wsssss-wsssss-wsssss . . .'

A few moments later, where the fence dipped as it reached the top of the garden, his head popped up. 'I'm looking for Toodles,' he said.

I nodded. 'Cats,' I said.

He gave me a perplexed look. 'What about them?'

'Never bloody home, are they?'

'Toodles is. He's Siamese. Like they used to have on *Blue Peter*. He's a home bird.'

'If I see him, I'll let you know.'

'Thank you. You're very kind.'

Sort of guy I am.

When I got into the office I called Mouse and told him I'd booked a table for us in my favourite Italian restaurant. The previous evening Patricia had hung around for so long that he hadn't had the chance to tell me any more about his fears, but now that I was offering him another opportunity he seemed suddenly reluctant to address them again.

'Look,' he said, 'maybe I'm just being paranoid. I've been under a lot of pressure lately. Maybe I'm just, you know, imagining things.'

'Maybe you are. But come for lunch anyway.'

We agreed on 1 p.m.

It was another busy morning in the news business, and in keeping with my low standing in work, I didn't get to cover the story I was interested in. One of my alltime heroes, the legendary Terry Breene, Liverpool's greatest ever star, had put together enough cash to buy Belfast's leading football club, Linfield, and its ground, Windsor Park. This was remarkable enough, a star buying a tiny provincial club, but what was causing most interest locally was the fact that Terry was born and raised a Catholic, and Linfield had always been Protestant-owned and run. Although Catholics had played for it, they were still few and far between. But when news of Terry Breene's purchase leaked out it had been widely welcomed, which was seen as symptomatic of the sea-change that had taken place in Northern Ireland since the end of the Troubles. In short, we all loved each other. I wasn't so sure. I wanted to be at Terry Breene's first press conference since taking over. I wanted to meet my hero, and gauge the lie of the land for myself.

It wasn't to be.

The thugs, who'd had difficulties with channelling their energies since the temporary suspension of paramilitary strife, had now decided to turn their attentions to the local Chinese community. It was the same old story, just with a different slant. Houses were burned out and businesses targeted for protection money. Kids were mugged and graffiti adorned dozens of gable walls. In one respect it was good to see that the hard men of Loyalism and the Republican freedom-fighters were at last sharing a common goal; wasn't great news for the

Chinese, though. So I spent the morning getting reaction to the latest savage beating. There's a standard formula for reporting this kind of a story: you interview the victim, if possible, and if not, his family, then you get reaction from the local community and its representatives. The neighbours say what a lovely family they are. The councillors condemn the attack and say we all have to work together to resolve this problem. The police say they are pursuing a line of enquiry.

This particular beating had happened just off the Falls Road, and the worthy councillor I got to interview came over all pious and meek and distraught at the thought of the kind of message the attack would send out to the wider world, and I'm sure he meant it, but I couldn't get out of my head the fact that ten years previously he'd been one of the IRA's top bomb-makers and had killed dozens of people, which hadn't done much for the tourist trade either. I try to forgive and forget, but it's diffi-cult. I'm glad there are people who can do it quite easily, because if it was left to me there'd never be any progress at all. What annoyed me even more was the fact that he insisted on being addressed by his full Irish name throughout. This was their peace dividend: we got to stay in the United Kingdom, but we had to address them by their Irish names. It wasn't a bad deal, over all, but every time I said his name I mispronounced it and he seemed to think I was doing it on purpose. His name was Padraig O'Mallaighourberhouchiecouchie or something equally stupid. It was a dead language, littered with modernisms, and anyone who insisted on using it was a pain in the hole.

On my way to meet Mouse, still pissed off at Padraig O'Mallaighourberhouchiecouchie, I was listening to Radio Ulster. David Dunseith was hosting his *Talkback* phone-in show. His was a rare voice of reason, dealing in a quietly exasperated fashion with that horde of lunatics otherwise known as the general public.

As I drove into the city centre, an ex-squaddie was explaining how he'd suffered nightmares for years about the time he'd served in Belfast, the horrors he had seen, and the treatment he'd suffered at the hands of the bigoted locals. He hated the Irish with a vengeance, but this hatred made his life so miserable he'd decided to confront his demons and return to Belfast for a short holiday. And to his amazement he'd found the city and its people totally transformed: everyone was lovely and friendly and helpful and he'd absolutely changed his opinion.

I phoned in. I did this from time to time. Deprived of my column, it was one of the few ways I could let off steam without getting sacked. I never gave my real name, and used a different one each time. I was in a queue of callers, but by the time I'd found a parking space outside the restaurant, I was on.

'. . . and now we have Frank from Bangor. Frank, what do you want to say?'

I affected a rather more cultured accent. 'Your last caller – the soldier – did he never hear of the expression "beauty is only skin deep"?'

'What do you mean by that?'

'That if he cared to look beneath the surface he'd find this place hasn't changed at all. It's just waiting to explode again. If he'd worn his uniform they would have torn him to shreds.'

'You're very cynical.'

'I've every reason to be.'

'Why's that now?'

'I lost a son.'

'Well, that's very sad. But do you not think that it might be time to move on? People have been lost on both sides. It's dreadful. But you know, we won't get anywhere unless we learn to talk to each other. Anyway, thank you for calling. We have another—'

'Oh, David?'

'Yes, caller?'

'I just wanted to say: piss, fuck, wank.'

I hung up. They had a delay button, but they never seemed to use it. I got them every time. I locked up the car and then took my usual table in Macari's front window. Mouse arrived five minutes later, parked across the road, and then spent ten minutes walking up and down trying to find the restaurant. Eventually I knocked on the window as he passed for the second time. He looked quizzically at me for a moment, then took a step back and looked up at the sign. He shook his head, gave a short laugh, then came in and sat opposite me.

'Very funny,' he said.

'What?'

'You said it was an Italian restaurant.'

'It is.'

'It's a fucking chip shop.'

'I know. It's run by Italians. They're the best.'

'I wanted pasta, not fucking pasties. I was running up and down there like a fucking lilty looking for Macari's Italian restaurant. How was I supposed to know it was this dump?'

'It's not a dump, Mouse. It's the best chip shop in Belfast.'

'But it doesn't *say* Macari's. It just says *Frank's Chips*.'

'Yeah. Frank Macari. Everyone knows it as Macari's.'

'I don't.'

'I thought you had your finger on the pulse, mate. And you don't even know Macari's?'

Mouse sat back on the wooden bench and sighed. A waitress with a huge lovebite on her neck and a thumping great boil in the middle of her forehead came across to take our order. I chose. It was my turn. Fish and chips, fresh from the freezer. Two cans of Lilt, with a thin coating of grease dew. The food arrived on two stained trays, on paper plates, with plastic knives and forks and three sachets of ketchup half-inched from McDonald's.

I tucked in.

Mouse managed several mouthfuls, then put his utensils down and dabbed his lips with a paper napkin. 'I get it now,' he said. 'You've switched sides, haven't you? The people out to get me – you're working for them.' He nodded down at the food. 'Another bite of this and my arteries will close for good and I'll keel over.'

I gave him a long, searching look, then nodded. 'Damn it,' I said. 'Got me in one.'

6

'Please, I need this,' said Mouse. 'I know you don't like to be seen in these places, but bear with me.'

He was sitting on an exercise bike in the Elysium gym, which was attached to the Culloden Hotel, about five miles out of Belfast. He was wearing Speedo shorts and a Gucci T-shirt and Nike trainers and he looked very much *the part*. If he'd gone for a hairband I would have ripped it off and set fire to it. I had my twenty-year-old *Fuck Art Lets Danse* T-shirt on, my battered bomber jacket and black jeans with knees which were about to go through old age rather than design. My trainers cost £13.99 in Dunne's and were white at the toes. I'd never worked out in a gym in my life, and the last time I'd been on a bike it had had stabilisers. Now Mouse was the one who needed stabilisers. Two before breakfast to start with. He was trying to work off both bites of his fish supper. That very same fish supper was in a plastic bag in the car. I was taking it home to Trish. Waste not want not. He'd signed me in as a guest, and I was sitting on the bike beside him, but I wasn't pedalling. Life is too short.

There was a bank of television screens on the wall above us. They were all showing the same thing: our First Minister Frank Galvin visiting a children's school. It was one of the main items on the news. He was announcing that Irish was to be introduced to the school curriculum of all schools in Northern

Ireland. It would help 'bind the communities to the island' and 'foster a fuller appreciation of our shared history'. I thought it would help foster some rioting in East Belfast. Most everyone else would take it lying down; perhaps people were getting lazy after so many years of Trouble. As ever it would fall to the dour working classes to make a stand.

Galvin was a natural on TV. He had to be really, as for years he'd been the public face of Sinn Fein, the political wing of the Provisional IRA. He'd had to explain away bombs and bullets and make it look as if this was a perfectly acceptable way of working towards a 'lasting and peaceful solution', and the thing was, he usually managed it, and as the PIRA campaign dropped the vowels and became a PR one he inevitably rose through the ranks until he was deputy leader of the party. It was widely acknowledged that Gerry Adams, the leader of Sinn Fein, would never be allowed to become the First Minister of Northern Ireland because of his controversial past; so eventually he stepped aside, retired to contemplate his pipe and the lucrative American After Irish Stew circuit, and Galvin, without a smudge on his CV, took over.

'How's your Irish?' I asked Mouse.

'Better than yours.'

He had a point.

'How much do you usually do?' I asked, nodding at the bike.

'Five hundred calories,' he said between breaths. 'Twenty-one kilometres . . . thirty-four minutes . . .'

'And you feel better for it?'

He nodded. His face was bright red and you could see the pulse vibrating on the side of his head. He'd only been going five minutes and there was already a puddle of sweat growing beneath the bike. I was no further along in finding out about what was bothering him.

It was a large gym, and as far as I could judge, state of the art. There were half a dozen fit-looking ladies on rowing machines towards the back, and off to our left three men with sculpted figures that would not have looked out of place on a billboard advertising underpants. Not that they would call them underpants. Boxers. Jockeys. Shorts. The old words were being phased out. Soon, if I walked into a department store and said, 'Take me to your underpant department,' they would look at me like I was some kind of half-wit. There were other words that I found myself still clinging onto – talc, gutties and products like Matey bubble bath and Pacers. I stopped myself from thinking about it, because once you start that train of thought you can go on for ever. There would soon be enough obsolete words and brands to create a dead language to rival Irish.

'Looking good,' I said. His body shape had certainly changed in recent months, but it didn't mean he wasn't setting himself up for a coronary. Sloth would do it, and over-exertion would do it. I preferred to tread the middle ground, which involved beer and crisps.

'My trainer says . . . another six months . . . and I'll be as fit as an Olympic athlete.'

I snorted. 'What, like the Paralympics?'

'He's serious . . . he means . . . for my age. I feel it. I feel . . . good.'

'Be a shame if someone kills you then.'

He kept his eyes on the electronic gauge on the handlebars which would warn him of approaching death. 'I told you, I . . . over-reacted.'

'Over-reacted to *what*?'

'To . . . Look, it was just something that was said. And a coincidence. The garage said the brakes could have gone at any time. I've been a bit lax with the—'

43

'What are you talking about, the brakes? Did someone mess with your car?'

'No, that's what I'm saying. It could have happened any time. I just put two and two together and got, like, seven. Relax.'

'Mouse, you were worried enough about it to come to me.'

'I was just stressed out. It's that time of the year – the Power List, it's always a bit frantic . . . but I'm fine. Honestly.' He upped the pedal rate for the final few minutes, then climbed awkwardly off the bike and winced as he straightened. 'They say they're state of the art,' he wheezed, 'but you've still got a numb arse when you're done.' He put one sweaty arm around me and squeezed. 'Now, Dan, I absolutely insist – come and have a sauna with me.'

I shrugged it off. 'Yeah. Right.'

'No, really, I insist.'

'You can insist all you want.'

'They have towels here. It won't be a problem.'

'No.'

'Come on. You'll feel great.'

'No.'

'Dan, come on.'

'No.'

'What are you scared of?'

'I'm not scared of anything. I just don't want one.'

'Have you ever had one?'

'No.'

'Well then.'

'Well then what? I've never stuck my hand in a fucking deep-fat fryer.'

'It's hardly the same, is it?'

'How do I know?'

'Then come and find out!'

The sculpted underpant men were looking at us now. I wanted to say, 'What the fuck are you looking at, underpant men?' but I was worried in case they blew me over.

'There's no need to be ashamed of your body,' Mouse said.

'I'm not ashamed of it!'

'Then come for a sauna. You'll feel great. It brings all the poison to the surface.'

'Great, I'll come out covered in boils. Mouse, I—'

'If you're worried about taking your clothes off in front of these guys, I'll make sure it's just the two of us.'

'Why the fuck would I be worried about that? You think I *want* to look like a muscle-bound cretin?'

They weren't just looking now, they were glaring. Mouse gave them the thumbs-up. 'He wasn't talking about you, lads,' he said. 'He was talking about different muscle-bound cretins.'

This didn't seem to placate them much, so Mouse quickly ushered me out of the main gym towards a small reception desk. 'Two sets of towels for the sauna,' he said. A T-shirted attendant smiled pleasantly and handed them over.

'Mouse . . .' I began.

'Tell you what, we'll treat it like a confessional. While we're in there you can ask me anything you want. About the thing.'

'The thing?'

'The thing with the death threats.'

'There were death threats?'

'I'll tell you in the sauna.' He lifted the towels and walked off.

'Okay,' he said. 'What do you want to know?'

'Apart from how long you can stay in here without dying? It's not what I want to know, Mouse, it's what you want to tell me. You called me.'

'Yes, I did.'

'And if you really and truly think it's nothing, we can forget about it and I can go back to a world of cool air and rain.'

There were several benches, at different levels, and you chose your position according to how close you wanted to be to the steam hissing out from the centre of the floor. I was on the top bench, Mouse was on the bottom. I did not feel better, or wonderful, and although we'd only been in there for forty seconds I'd already sweated out half a cod and nine chips.

'I have messed you around, Dan, but only because . . . well, because I'm still not sure.'

'Mouse, a death threat is a death threat.'

'I know, but things are said in the heat of the moment, you don't always mean them, or follow up on them.'

'Who threatened you?'

'I don't really know.'

'Mouse.'

'I mean, it was a phone call, and I didn't recognise the voice.'

'What did he say? I presume it was a he?'

Mouse nodded. 'He said, and I quote, "Stop your fucking interfering or you're a dead bunny".'

I nodded. Twenty-seven droplets of sweat rolled off my brow and hissed on the floor. 'What are you interfering in?'

'Well, *Belfast Confidential* interferes in rather a lot. But I imagine it's something to do with the Power List. That's our big issue. It's always a talking point.'

'Okay, is there something particularly controversial or revealing that you're working on?'

'It's impossible to say.'

'Well, try.'

'I'm not being reticent, I just mean, who can say what's important to any particular individual? It could be Daniel

O'Donnell thinking we're into his sexlife or the First Minister worried about his dodgy investments.'

'Daniel O'Donnell's on the Power List?'

'No, I'm just using him as an example. He *was* on the Power List, but then he got married and lost the blue-rinse brigade. His influence is on the wane.'

I shook my head. 'We're really at the cutting edge here, aren't we?'

'That's what's so great about the Power List, Dan – it's a real mix.'

'But as of this moment, you're not aware of any great revelation that might cause anyone to warn you off?'

'No.'

'So it could be something that you might discover if you *were* to investigate a particular individual.' Mouse nodded. 'I don't suppose you happened to record your call?'

'Nope.'

'Or notice caller ID or what is it, 1471?'

'No, it was all over so quickly. But it was from a callbox, because his money ran out.'

'If his money ran out, he must have said more than "Stop your fucking interfering or you're a dead bunny".'

'No, I think he just had to wait a while before he was put through.'

'So he must have spoken to your – what? Secretary, receptionist?'

'I suppose.'

'And she didn't ask for a name?'

'No, because a lot of the stories we run rely on caller confidentiality.'

I took a deep breath. I was starting to feel a little bit dizzy. 'How long are we supposed to stay in this hell-hole?' I asked.

'Give it another five,' said Mouse.

'There might not be any of me left in another five.'

'You'll feel better for it, I swear to God.'

'Yeah – famous last words.' I steadied myself on the bench. 'Okay. Look, Mouse, how many years did you work on the news desk?'

'As a reporter? Ten. I was twelve after that as a sub and news editor. You know this.'

'I'm just trying to make a point – which is, how often were you threatened? With violence or death or ex-communication?'

'About once a week.'

'And how many times were you actually beaten up, or killed, or chucked down the church steps?'

'Well, never.'

'So. What's different about this?'

'I told you. The brakes on the car.'

'You said they were about to go anyway.'

'And they followed me.'

'They?'

'Well, it felt like they. It could have been just one.'

'You actually saw someone?'

'Not exactly. I just . . . Look, I know this sounds crap, but it just felt like someone was following me. And when I came out of work, somebody had scratched my car.'

'The phallic-symbol car?'

'It's not a . . . it's a Jet. It's fantastic. I've my name down for one. It was May Li's idea. She says I deserve it for all my hard work.'

'And someone did what? Run a key along it? Chip the paintwork?' Mouse nodded. 'Mouse, for fuck sake, it's a natural reaction to want to damage a Jet. I could have done it. Everyone who will never be able to afford one would do it. It's jealousy.'

I shook my head. 'Mouse, someone gave you an earful on the phone. The brakes on your car gave up the ghost. You think you might have been followed. And somebody scratched your car.'

'Yes, I know, but put them all together . . .'

'Put them all together and you've got fuck all squared in a box.'

Mouse closed his eyes for a moment; he pushed his fingers into the corners and rubbed. He took the kind of deep, refreshing breath you'd expect to take at the top of a mountain, but in here it must have been like sucking on a volcano. He coughed a little, then opened his eyes again and looked across at me. 'You think I'm imagining it all?'

I thought about it for a few moments, forcing myself to concentrate because I was starting to feel a bit woozy. My stomach gurgled unhappily. 'Yes, maybe,' I said, rubbing at my tummy. 'If a psychiatrist was sitting here instead of me, I think he'd say you were having an MLC.' And when his eyes narrowed: 'A midlife crisis.'

'Crisis?' he laughed. 'No offence, Dan, but I'm rich, successful and I've a gorgeous young wife who can't get enough of me. Spot the crisis.'

'He might say that's exactly the point. You have all this but you're still not happy.'

'Happy? Are you joking?'

'Deep down, he might say.'

'Oh bollocks, Dan.'

'On the surface you might appear happy. You might *think* you're happy. But a psychiatrist might say that although you're now rich and successful, and have a beautiful young wife and you've got the flashest car in the country bar none, deep down you don't feel you deserve any of it, and that manifests itself in a kind of low-level paranoia. You're scared that someone's going to take it all away from you – your business, your wife, your car.'

'Christ,' said Mouse. 'That's a bit deep.'

'Yeah, I know. That's psychiatrists for you.'

'Forget the psychiatrists, Dan – what do *you* think?'

'Honestly?'

'Honestly.'

'Well, they say wanking makes you blind. If you're having four orgasms a night I think you're probably suffering from some kind of minor brain damage.' I reached down to squeeze his shoulder in a best-mate fashion, but his shoulder was damp with sweat and my hand slipped down and cupped his nipple instead. It was an awkward moment.

'Nice tits,' I said and laughed.

He looked at his chest and said, 'Enjoy them while you can, they're next.'

'Listen mate,' I continued hurriedly, 'if you're really that worried about it I'm the last person you should be coming to. You should know better – I'm a walking disaster area, so go out and hire someone to look after you, you can afford it. Some big doughnut with a gun or at the very least a black belt in looking mean. Get him to follow you around for a while, he'll soon . . . *shit*!'

The dizzies were back.

Then, very quickly, a bitter taste in the back of my throat.

And gurgling.

'Dan?'

'Sorry,' I gasped, my hand across my mouth.

I forced myself up and yanked at the door, stumbling out into the lemon-scented changing rooms. I'd had a sleepless night, a backwards headbutt, a hangover, an argument with a reformed terrorist, a fish supper, a can of rusting Lilt and then boiled myself for twenty-five minutes in a sauna. Now, as I clutched my towel for security and leaned against the wall for support, I could see the Adonai from the gym standing to my left comparing thongs. I threw up into a plant pot.

7

'You did what?' Patricia asked. Demanded.

'Is that a rhetorical question? Or is *this* a rhetorical question about a rhetorical question? Or is *this* a rhetorical question about a . . . oh, I could go on all night. The eternal—'

'Dan! Please! You're doing my head in. Why the fuck did you do it?'

It wasn't about throwing up. It was about something much worse.

'It just seemed like the right thing to do.'

'Without even consulting me?'

'Without even consulting you. Trish, I'm old enough to make decisions that will affect both of us without thinking them through thoroughly. I'm big enough to make decisions that will really piss you off without calling home first.'

'I really am going to swing for you.'

'Trish. Come on. It's long overdue. What was I supposed to say?'

'You were supposed to say, "Let me check with Trish and get back to you".'

'It would've looked like I was trying to squirm out of it. And if I had phoned to check, what would you have said?'

'I would have squirmed out of it.'

'Exactly. So I said yes on your behalf because unless we confront this now, we're never going to be able to confront it.'

'So what?'

'Trish – he's my best friend, and it's only dinner.'

'It's *only dinner*. Listen to you. That woman broke up *my* best friend's marriage, she stole my best friend's husband with her . . . with her Oriental ways.'

'Oriental ways. Listen to *you*! What're you talking about? You mean she put on a silk dress and made him a curry? You mean she did it *inscrutably*?'

'Yes! No! Jesus, Dan, I don't know. I just don't feel right about it. It's like betraying Wendy.'

'She doesn't have to know.'

'She'll know. She's bitter and twisted and she watches his every move like a hawk.'

We were sitting on the sofa watching *EastEnders*. I was drinking Harp and she'd opened her second bottle of Asti. She paused as she went to take another sip. I was laughing and she wanted to know what she'd said that was so funny. Clearly, it couldn't have been anything on *EastEnders*, which is like Largactyl for the masses.

'She's bitter and twisted and watches him like a hawk?'

'Yes, and why not. Can you blame her?'

'Would this watching him also mean following him? And vandalising his new car?'

'Following maybe. I don't know about vandalising his car, but I wouldn't put it beyond her.'

'The stupid bitch. He's got it into his head that someone's trying to kill him. That's what he came to see me about! Don't look at me like that, he made me swear not to tell you.'

'Why?'

'I don't know. I think he's scared of you.'

'Me?'

I cleared my throat. She gave me a wan smile. 'Anyway,' I

pointed out, 'if she's following him, and she's mad enough to run her keys along his Jet . . .'

'It's a Jet? Christ.'

'It's only a prototype. So maybe the brakes did just go of their own accord and it was just some pissed-off tosser who phoned in the death threat.'

'Mouse got a death threat?'

'Aye, that's why he's so jumpy. I mean, now that I think about it, I wouldn't even put it beyond her messing with his brakes or hiring someone to make the call. It doesn't *have* to be connected, but it makes sense. Christ, wait'll I tell him this.'

'You can't tell him this.'

'Why the hell not?'

'Because he'll go and have it out with Wendy, or have her arrested, or committed, and then she'll know it came from me.'

'How will she know that?'

'She will, she's bound to, and Mouse can't hold his own water, he'll tell her. Then I'll be in deep shit.' She finished her glass and poured another.

I said, 'I have to tell him.'

She sucked on one of her lips. She tutted. But eventually she said, 'All right. She's been a bit of a pain in the hole lately anyway.'

'And you'll come to dinner?'

She sighed. 'If I have to.'

'You never know, she might be lovely.'

'Yeah, right.'

We finished unpacking, quite drunk, at 3 a.m. We crawled into bed dirty and dusty but too tired to shower. Patricia lay back and said, 'Where's the carving-knife set in the decorative box?'

'Kitchen cupboard, top left.'

'What about the figures-in-glass dancers Mum bought us that you say is tasteless tack?'

'Third shelf, display cabinet, the lounge.'

'Where's the spare mobile phone charger?'

'Plugged into study, charging the spare mobile phone.'

'And the one hundred and twenty CDs that came free with the Sunday papers?'

'In the roofspace, where they belong.'

Patricia nodded. 'Well, everything seems to be in order. I think it's all right to have sex now.'

'Okay,' I said.

8

I hate press conferences at the best of times, but I reserve particular loathing for press conferences where the main focus of attention can't even be bothered to turn up, but instead make their appearance by satellite link.

The venue this time was Hillsborough Castle, the Government's playhouse just outside Belfast. Newspaper, TV and radio journalists crowded into an austere lounge and stared at an incongruous hi-tech plasma screen as First Minister Frank Galvin shook hands with Ryan Auto founder Jacintha Ryan in New York.

Jacintha Ryan was a real mover and shaker – a Northern Irish immigrant who was the living embodiment of the American Dream. Her parents had arrived penniless in New York, but had scrimped and saved to send her through college. Then she'd joined General Motors and begun a breathtaking rise through the ranks to the point where she'd been hotly tipped to become the first female CEO of that august American institution. Instead she'd shocked everyone by resigning in order to start her own motor company – Ryan Auto. She'd attracted hundreds of millions of dollars' worth of investment, despite the fact that she'd insisted that production would be based in Belfast. So fair play to her. There had been a lot of hype at the start, when it was first announced, but this was the latest in a lengthy series of press conferences and the number of new things you could say about a car factory were becoming increasingly few and far between. This particular one was to mark the handing over of the land, and Jacintha Ryan's pull was such that she could take possession without going to the trouble of leaving her New York office, but instead could insist that Northern Ireland's First Minister actually came to her to sign on the dotted line.

Eventually, after much posing and waffle, they got to the point where they asked if the reporters had any questions, and where once I would have been chomping at the bit to stir things up I quite happily stood at the back, eating their sandwiches and listening in. The fact was I didn't care. Cars. Fields. Build things. Sell them. It was the fourth such press conference I'd attended in recent months, as the whole Ryan's Jet project gained momentum, but I hadn't asked a question yet. The info was all there. They gave it to you in a nice press pack, with a Matchbox version of the Jet, so you could impress your friends and go *brmmm-brmmmm* with your kids. If you had any.

Jacintha Ryan was forty-seven, blonde, and as far as I could judge, expertly turned out. She spoke with a cultured American accent, which reminded me a little of JFK's. Mouse was at the press conference, of course. He asked the kind of arse-loosening *Belfast Confidential* questions that made the rest of us squirm.

'First of all I want to compliment you on the car. The prototype is fantastic – *Belfast Confidential* certainly approves.'

'Why, thank you.'

'What's your birth sign, Jacintha?'

'Gemini.'

'And are you a typical Gemini?'

'That's not for me to say.'

'You've never married?'

'No.'

'Are you in a relationship?'

'No comment.'

'I'm told you're planning a spectacular party when you come to Belfast.'

'Well, it's important to make an impact.'

'Do you want to tell us something about it?'

'Not yet – but if there are any ladies amongst you, think ballgown.'

Mouse sat again, then winked at me across the room. I shook my head disdainfully, and he laughed. Five or six other questions were asked, but they were the kind that everyone already knew the answers to. We were each clutching an exhaustive press pack which covered every possible angle. Back in the office I had three just like it. Then the questions dried up. Jacintha stared somewhat awkwardly at the camera, then glanced to the left, probably to some producer and asked if the satellite was down. She must have got a negative response. She looked a little surprised, then returned her attention to the camera. It was getting towards the embarrassing stage, and where once I would have revelled in it, I actually felt a bit sorry for her, sitting there with all her billions and nobody wanting to talk to her, so I shouted, 'You say you left Belfast when you were six. What do you remember of it?'

'Very little. Virtually nothing, in fact. Sorry. I can make something up if you like?'

Smiles through the press pack. She couldn't see them, of course. It was never going to be a real face-to-face conversation. It was strictly a one-way experience. 'So why do you want to set up here?'

'To give something back.'

'Something back to somewhere you don't remember.'

'Is that so strange? It's my heritage. It's what my father would have wanted.'

'Your father is – deceased now.'

'Yes. Fifteen years. Asbestosis. From working on building sites around Belfast.'

'Why did youse go to America in the first place?'

'For the same reason everyone else did. The Troubles.'

'You worked your way up from Sales to Management to the Board of General Motors. You were tipped for CEO.'

'By some obscure business paper.'

'But you were a high flyer, and you gave it all up to become your own boss.'

'I had a dream.'

'Is that Martin Luther King, or the Abba song?'

She smiled this time. 'It's the truth. That's the difference between America and Ireland, Britain, Europe – here, people believe in realising their dreams; over there it seems to be they quite often can't be bothered.'

'Those are strong words. You don't think people will be pissed off?'

'I would hope they'd be inspired.' She glanced at her watch. 'Okay, ladies and gentlemen – thank you.'

And the screen went blank. Just like that. We stood looking at it for several moments, then the cameramen began to pack up their equipment and the reporters turned off their tape recorders. I closed my notebook. (I still did things the old way.) But I hadn't made a single note. Nobody was dashing out of the door shouting. 'Hold the front page!'

Mouse sauntered across. 'Well, that was fun,' he said.

* * *

There's fashionably late, and then there's Patricia late.

We were due there at seven, it was a ten-minute drive, and it was already seven-fifteen.

'You're doing this on purpose!' I shouted up the stairs, and her lack of response suggested that I'd hit the nail squarely on the head. 'You know if we arrive late, they'll just add the time on at the end!'

I was pacing back and forth, jangling the car keys in my hand. I was itching for a drink, but I'd agreed to drive over, then get a taxi back and pick the car up the next day. I was enjoying one of those rare periods of actually being in possession of a driving licence. The next time I got caught I would probably be banned for life, and do some time, and keep pet budgies and get caught up in a riot in cell block number nine, and die.

'Trish! Would you come on?!'

'Dan!'

'What!'

'Do we have any ice?'

'What? They'll have ice there.'

'No – for my drink now.'

'Christ All Mighty!'

I charged up the stairs. Patricia was sitting in front of the mirror; she had the war-paint on, and a low-cut black top and knee-length skirt with black leather boots; there was a half-drunk half-bottle of Smirnoff vodka and a long, thin pint glass with an inch of Diet Coke in the bottom sitting on the dresser before her. Her eyes were slightly clouded and her cheeks, despite the make-up, had reddened up from the alcohol. She turned as I came through the door and her legs parted and her skirt rode up and clearly she wasn't wearing any pants. I stood for a moment and she smiled, and said, 'I know what you're thinking.'

'What am I thinking?'

'You don't know wever to fump me or fuck me.'

That's the way she said it: *wever* and *fump*. She would some-times lose the power of her 'th's when she was half-cut.

I sighed. I did not immediately melt into her arms, and in her state she took that as a rejection and quickly closed her legs and spun back to the mirror. 'Please yourself,' she said.

'We're supposed to be there,' I said. I folded my arms and leaned against the doorframe.

'I know. I'm just running a little late.'

'Trish.'

'I'm just nervous, okay?'

'What's to be nervous about?'

'*Everything.*'

'Christ, Trish, it's only dinner.'

'With the *enemy.*'

'She's not the enemy!'

I stormed off downstairs again. I opened the fridge and took out a can. One wouldn't do any harm. I lifted my mobile and phoned Mouse on his. That way, I was fairly certain of talking to him directly, rather than taking the chance of phoning his home number and May Li answering and me having to make crap excuses to her about why we were so late, and then having to repeat them because her English wasn't so good.

It was answered on the first ring.

'Mouse, it's me. We're running late, will you apologise to—'

'Who is this?'

'It's me.'

'Me who?'

I realised then that it wasn't Mouse at all. The voice was muffled, and slightly echoey, as if he was holding the phone away from his mouth. 'Dan,' I said. 'Is he there?'

'He's in a meeting right now. Can I take a message?'

'Well, I'm supposed to be having dinner at his house. Round about now. But if he's in a meeting . . . How long will he be?'

'Not long.'

'Well, will you tell him I'll see him there in about twenty minutes?'

'Will do. And who will I say you are again?'

'Dan.'

'Dan who?'

'He'll know.'

'Well, can I take your number in case he needs to call you back?'

'He has it.'

'Please yourself.'

He put the phone down. I shook my head. Mouse would say, 'You just can't get the staff these days,' but the real problem was he offered shit pay and you got what you paid for. The reporters that worked for him were probably straight out of college, anxious for their first break, all full of vim and vigour and attitude and not that worried about the money.

Vim – there's another one you don't get any more.

'Did you speak to him?' Patricia shouted from the top of the landing.

'Yes. He's really pissed off.'

'Really?'

'No, but we need to get going.'

'I'm coming, I'm coming!' she shouted as she hurried down the stairs, glass in hand.

As she passed me at the bottom I said, 'Just like last night.'

She stopped and cupped my chin with her hand. 'Although just the once.' She gave me a sarcastic smile, then stepped quickly along to the kitchen for more ice.

* * *

We sat in the car outside for five minutes, while Patricia fixed her make-up and finished a cigarette. She tutted as she examined her reflection in the driver's mirror, which, annoyingly, she had turned to face her.

'I look like an old hag.'

'No, you don't.'

'Look at the lines around my eyes.'

'I don't see them.'

'You're as blind as a bat.'

'Love is blind.'

'Oh fuck off.' She squinted and moved her head to one side. 'Have I too much make-up on?'

'No.'

'My hair's like straw.'

I sighed. 'Could we just go in?'

'Are you wearing aftershave?'

'No.'

'I like aftershave.'

'I know.'

'I bought you it for Christmas.'

'I know. I forgot. Can we go?'

She shook her head. 'All right, Grumpy Drawers.' She opened the door and climbed out. I gave a sigh of relief and followed her up to the front door. She smiled back at me. 'I'll be on my best behaviour. Promise.'

I nodded and rang the doorbell.

It opened almost immediately, and then she was standing there, May Li. It struck me for the first time that as she was Mouse's wife, we would be perfectly within our rights to refer to her as Minnie Mouse. The thing was, I had never seen anyone look less like a Minnie Mouse in my life. To say that she was stunning was to under . . . oh fuck it, in Belfast parlance, she was what you'd call a *ride*. It's coarse and it's demeaning, but it absolutely hits the nail on the head. Petite, black-haired, small angular face, white hesitant smile and green eyes – it's the eyes that almost always get me on a woman. You can just tell how much light and life and intelligence and humour there is in a woman by her eyes, even in that very first instant of seeing them.

Patricia, who I'd expected to be cold and aloof, surprised me by stepping forward immediately and holding her hand out and saying, 'Hi – May Li,' and then she gave her a hug. May Li hugged her back and said, 'It's so nice to meet you. I've heard so much about you. Please call me May.' There was hardly any accent at all; her English was perfect.

Patricia let her go, and May Li turned to me. She held her hand out, and I clasped it, and we both went, 'Oh!' There was literally a spark between us.

May giggled. 'I'm sorry, it's the static electricity – we have new carpets.' It was such an endearing giggle that I was prepared to believe her, but she'd shaken Patricia's hand and there was no spark between them.

'Come in, come in.' She ushered us into Mouse's palatial new home.

'That's a beautiful cocktail dress,' Patricia gushed. 'It's Dior. No, it's Gucci. It isn't Valentino, is it?'

May gave an embarrassed little shrug. 'It's a Valentino copy.'

'It's gorgeous! You'd never know.'

'Well, I bring the silk in from home, and Sadie from the Markets runs it up for me. No point in paying top dollar when you can't tell the difference.'

'Oh, I *know*.'

I sighed. It was going to be a long evening. Cocktail dresses? Christ, I was wearing my beer trousers and no one had said a thing.

May led us into a lounge that was dominated by a huge plasma screen. We sat on a white leather sofa. She got us drinks – red wine for Trish, Harp for me – and said, 'Do you want a glass with that?' My normal response would have been, 'Wise up, are you brain dead?' but she was beautiful so I said, 'Please.' Patricia was looking at me, so I quickly said, 'Is he not here yet?'

May shook her head apologetically. 'Mouse said he'd be home by now, but I'm sure he won't be long.'

Patricia giggled. 'I'm sorry, I just didn't think you'd call him Mouse.'

'What do you mean?' May asked.

'I mean – sorry, I just presumed you'd call him by his proper name.'

The endearing smile faded. 'He has a . . . *different* name?'

Patricia's mouth dropped open. 'I'm sorry, I—'

May exploded into laughter. 'Only rakin',' she said, like a native, and I think in that instant some kind of a bond was created between them. Patricia snorted wine up her nose and it dribbled back down onto the white leather sofa and threw her into a panic and May started going, 'It's okay, it's okay, we can get a new one,' and that made her laugh even more and they were getting on so well together that I would have felt left out of it if it hadn't been for the spark between us that still had me thinking, sitting there sipping foam from a half-pint glass and quietly dribbling it onto my beer trousers.

At eight-fifteen, with Mouse still not there and his mobile playing host to three voice messages from May, which would surely have been irate if we hadn't been there – I mean, they were married and no one is that patient in a marriage – I said maybe I should take a run down there, see if I could gee him along.

May said, 'He'll be fine, he is so committed to his work. Why don't we just start?'

Between us Trish and I had expected her to cook something Thai, to impress us, but instead she had made roast beef and roast potatoes and green beans, and she even put a plate of chips down beside me and gave me a little wink as she did it and I quickly took another slug of beer to cover up my embarrassment but Patricia hadn't noticed because she was going, 'Ooooh, it's so tender, how did you cook it?'

By ten, with no sign of him, May had grown a lot quieter, and every few minutes, as a car passed outside, she jumped up to see if it was him, but it wasn't, so she sat back down on the edge of her chair and clasped her hands in her lap. She chatted on, but she was distracted. I said, 'Listen, I'll take a run down and see what's keeping him.'

'Would you?' said May.

Patricia said, 'Haven't you had too many?'

I said, 'I'll be fine.'

It was important to drive normally. Drunk drivers either drive all over the place, or so cautiously that they draw attention to themselves. So, at a steady forty-two miles an hour, and sucking on four Polo mints from the glove compartment, I was confident that I could fool most of the cops most of the time. The *Belfast Confidential* offices were located directly behind the BBC, just off the Dublin Road, in a square that was fairly quiet by day but gridlocked at night because it served as hooker central. Belfast doesn't have many prostitutes, and most of them look like the back end of a bus, but for the farmers who flood in from the country it's a case of any port in a storm, and they do a roaring trade. I wasn't sure if the police just looked the other way, or took a slice of the action, but the hookers were always there.

I was just about to turn into the square when I saw there was a police motorbike parked side on, right in the middle of the road, blocking access, and a cop in a crash helmet directing traffic away. I wound my window down and asked what the problem was and he looked at me like I was an idiot, then glanced behind him. I followed his gaze. I'd been so busy paying attention to driving properly that I hadn't taken a proper look at my surroundings, but now I saw fire engines, and a lot of firemen running back and forth, and several ambulances, and crowds of onlookers, and hookers, staring up at the offices of *Belfast Confidential* and the flames leaping from its windows.

9

I jumped from the car, ducked under the flailing arms of the motorcycle cop and raced forward. There was a big, flash sign hanging outside the offices, but only the letters *BEL* and *CON* were still illuminated. Mouse's business occupied the top two floors of a four-storey building, and it was from these that smoke was pouring and flames were leaping. Most of the windows had already exploded in the heat, but even as I approached, others were giving way, showering the ground below with shards of glass.

'Keep back! Keep back!' a police officer was shouting; he and half a dozen colleagues were angrily shepherding onlookers away while firemen wearing breathing apparatus hurried into the building.

'Has anyone been brought out?' I shouted at them, but was ignored. Another policeman took me by the arm and tried to lead me away. I repeated my question. 'Just move back, sir!' he bellowed in my face. He was stressed out, and he had every right to be, but Mouse was my friend, and even though asking the question or getting an answer wasn't going to help him in any way, shape or form, it had to be asked and it had to be answered. I gave a sudden shrug of my arm, and it took the cop by enough surprise that I was able to wriggle free and dash back towards the burning building. I veered off to the right towards where two ambulances were sitting. One had its back doors open and two paramedics just inside it appeared to be busy making preparations for an imminent arrival.

'Lads!' I shouted. 'Has anyone been brought out? Is anyone hurt?'

One of them ducked under the doorframe. 'They're just bringing—'

I was grabbed roughly from behind by the cop whom I'd shrugged off, plus the motocycle cop from the entrance. 'You!' the biker shouted. 'This way!'

They each took an arm and bent it up behind my back, which wasn't a lot of fun.

'What the fuck are you doing?' I shouted. 'My friend's in there! My mate's in that fucking fire!'

'That may be,' said the biker, 'but you blocked the fucking road, arsehole, and you stink of fucking drink, and you're fucking done.'

They frogmarched me to the edge of the square and threw me into the back of a police car. They locked me in and went back to supervise the fire. I couldn't do a damn thing. Couldn't open a door or a window, couldn't call Trish for help because I'd left my mobile in my car, couldn't do anything but put my hands on the window and fight back the tears as I saw Mouse being brought out of the *Belfast Confidential* offices by a team of firemen straining to carry his new, muscular bulk on a stretcher. As he emerged, the paramedics quickly clamped an oxygen mask to his face, then secured him in the back of the ambulance. It roared away, siren wailing.

I slumped down, feeling sick to my stomach. Patricia and May were still at home, drinking wine and swapping stories and probably thinking that I'd picked Mouse up and lured him off for a drink somewhere. And now I couldn't even tell them what I'd seen, even though, really, it was very little. A fire, and Mouse being brought out on a stretcher. I'd seen his face for only a few seconds before the mask was applied, but it was enough to register that it was him, and that his skin was smoke-blackened. Such a big event, so little information. I sat fuming in the car, watching as the firemen battled to bring the blaze under control. They darted in and out of the lower floors for a little while, but at some point the decision was made that it was becoming too dangerous.

Eventually one of the cops who'd locked me in came back, chatting away to another of his colleagues. He opened the driver's door and I heard him say, 'Nah, it's half-price . . . Aye, in Woodsides . . . Sure, wait till I take this joker in and I'll give you a bell.'

They were talking about the mundane things in life, while my friend was lying injured in some hospital. It was just another night for them, but it was my mate.

'I need to go to the hospital,' I said.

'Why?' he snapped back. 'You better not have fucking pissed yourself, or you'll get your fucking head in your hands.'

This wasn't exactly the new face of the PSNI, or maybe it was, but I had to ignore it. 'Please,' I said, 'he's my friend, we were supposed to be having—'

'Shut it, arsehole.'

Another, different cop climbed in beside my driver. He glanced back at me. 'What's your story?' he asked.

'My friend—'

'Suspected DIC,' the driver interrupted. 'Here.'

He handed the new, younger guy a testing kit. I was kind of familiar with them. They read me my rights and gave me my instructions and asked me to blow into the bloody thing and of course I was over the limit.

The more I protested, the more annoyed they got, and the more annoyed they got, the more pissed-off I became; so it was a shouting match all the way to Donegal Pass police station, them threatening all kinds of retribution. They were to be applauded, of course, for not giving preferential treatment to members of the press – that would have been the kind of hypocrisy I might once have railed against in my own column – but that said, I half-hoped that I might have proved the exception to their rule. We all live by our own double-values. Not even Mouse's name seemed to register. Perhaps they didn't read *Belfast Confidential*, although that would have made them the only two in the city who didn't.

They hauled me into an interview room and left me there to stew. Eventually they came in to take a statement and I asked about my phone call and they said I couldn't make one. It wasn't a question of withholding my rights, but some other drunken arsehole had smashed up the phone they normally used and they were waiting for a technician to come down and replace it. They locked me in a cell then seemed to forget about me. I heard a lot of shouting and screaming and thumping. At about 4 a.m. an older cop brought me in a cup of tea and I asked him what all the noise was and he said, 'We had a riot of our own upstairs – lotta joyriders from up the Falls. We won. Five submissions and a knockout.' I asked about the phone and he said it was still being repaired. I asked him if he'd heard about the fire at *Belfast Confidential* and he said, 'Yeah, heard about that.'

'Did you hear what happened to the fella they brought out?'
'Sorry, no.'
'But if he was dead or anything, you'd have heard, right?'
He thought about that for a moment. 'Suppose. We don't get that many stiffs any more. Not like the good old days.' He

71

stood and looked wistful for a moment, then he smiled at me and said, 'Try and get some sleep.'

I nodded. I was tired. I slumped down on what passed for a bed. But sleep wouldn't come. Of course it wouldn't.

Turns out, they couldn't charge me. The cop who'd arrested me came in a little after eight the next morning, his eyes heavy, his uniform smelling of vomit. He was half-embarrassed, half-seething. With the phone being busted, I'd been denied my right to a phone call, and that meant that there was a possibility that I'd get off on a technicality, and they were only in the business of prosecuting certs. So he gave me a caution and reluctantly took me back upstairs. I was handed my car keys again. As far as he knew, my car was still parked by the scene of the fire. I asked again if he'd heard anything else about it and he said, 'Do I look like fucking Ceefax?' I asked him for his name and he said, 'Bartholemew,' and I said, 'Nice one.'

Outside I found the nearest phone box and phoned Trish at home, then her mobile. She answered on the second ring.

'Dan!' she exclaimed, then followed it with, 'Thank God!' and 'Where the fuck are you?' almost in the same breath.

I explained quickly. She said, 'I was worried sick. I'm at the hospital – Mouse is in the theatre now. May's in pieces. I thought you were in there! Do you hear me, Dan? I thought *you* were in there!'

'I know, I know, I'm fine. What about Mouse, did you see him?'

'No, no . . . they wouldn't . . . Christ, Dan, it's not looking good.'

They'd taken him to the Burns Unit at the Royal Victoria Hospital. I took a taxi across and stepped out into its chilling shadow. It was a cold morning with black clouds hanging low over the city. Perched as it was on the edge of the Falls, it wasn't very Royal but it was very Victorian. Or Dickensian. Everywhere in Belfast seemed to have gotten a face-lift in the past few years or been replaced with bright shiny newer versions, but for some reason the RVH had been left out; 'gothic' was too happy a word for it. Structural stitch-ons and subtractions in virtually every decade over the past century had given it an ailing, indecisive feel and an ambience of despair. As I raced along the corridors, the blue linoleum tiles seemed to suck up the dull light coming from the fluorescent tubes overhead.

But it wasn't the drab surroundings that made Patricia and May look so pale; it wasn't the stench of old folks and industrial-strength Dettol; it was the knowledge that a friend and husband was fighting for his life on the other side of a couple of sets of swing doors; the knowledge that even if he did pull through he might never be the same again. Broken bones are for Christmas, burns last for ever.

May Li sat on a plastic couch, her head down; Patricia was sitting with her arm around her, but she removed it as soon as I approached and came over and gave me a hug. Her eyes were heavy and her mascara had run. I kissed her dry lips and smelled stale wine. 'How is she?' I asked, which is one of those dumb questions you have to ask. Trish just shook her head. 'Have you heard anything about the fire? What happened?' She shook her head again, then motioned for me to follow her over to a drinks machine. She put some coins in and got us both a Diet Coke. We were just about out of earshot. 'They think it was arson,' Trish whispered urgently. 'There were cops here when we arrived, I heard them talking, said the place stank of petrol.'

I glanced back at May Li. She was still staring at the ground.

Arson.

It had now been nearly twelve hours since Mouse was carried out of his burning offices, and in all that time I hadn't thought about the causes of the fire. There had just been a crazy presumption that because it was Mouse, my old friend, there would be some kind of straightforwardly daft explanation; that perhaps while publicly campaigning against smoking, he had nipped into the office for a crafty fag and somehow managed to set the rubbish bin on fire; that he had skimped on the wiring in order to devote all his finances to the launch of the magazine and now it had come back and burned him on the arse. Something vaguely comical – but petrol?

If you didn't know him, it suggested two things.

One, that with a thriving business, a beautiful young wife and everything he had ever dreamed of, he had taken leave of his senses and decided to kill himself.

Two, that the death threats which I had patiently explained to him were a figment of his imagination, were in fact deadly serious.

I took a long drink of my Diet Coke, and then nearly choked as a scream erupted from behind and I turned to find May Li being grabbed by the hair and dragged backwards over her seat.

'You did this, you fucking slant-eyed cunt! You fucking did this!'

A large woman with nicotine teeth and wild rheumy eyes was now starting to rain blows down on her.

Enter the dragon.

10

'Wendy! Wendy, please!'

Patricia raced across and tried to drag the first Minnie Mouse off, but she had a firm grip, so that as she dragged Wendy backwards, Wendy dragged May.

I, knowing better than to come between two fighting women, held back and made tutting sounds. 'That's enough now, ladies!' I barked, just to show that I was taking a positive interest.

'She did it! She fucking did it!' Wendy was screaming. 'You did it, you fucking cow!'

May was coming out with high-pitched yelps as Wendy's nails dug into her head, but then she managed to twist around and began to tear with her own not insignificant nails into Wendy's hands. They were both screaming then. Between screams Wendy yelled, 'Get off me! Get off!' at Trish, while Trish shouted, 'You're just upset! You're just upset!' which is another of those bloody obvious comments, although I didn't have the heart to point it out to her there and then. Eventually a ward of nurses came scurrying across and managed to separate Wendy from May and Patricia from Wendy. They were each taken to separate corners, like it was some kind of lesbian wrestling match. 'I was only trying to stop them!' Patricia was shouting, but the nurse boxing her in clearly didn't believe her and wouldn't let her move.

Then Wendy slithered down the wall until she was sitting

on her bum. Her shoulders began to shake and her head drooped and she slipped into hysterical crying. The nurse guarding Trish relented and let her out and she hurried forward and knelt down beside Wendy and tried to soothe her with, 'It's all right, it's all right,' when it clearly wasn't.

The other nurses withdrew, but remained on standby for peacekeeping. May, who'd been pulled by her hair over the back of a sofa and then dragged across the floor, was on her knees, gingerly massaging her scalp and desperately trying to hold back her own tears. I went across to her and crouched down and offered her my Diet Coke. 'It adds life,' I said, hoping to raise a smile. It didn't, obviously. But she took it and drank, and half-choked on it. She coughed, wiped the back of her hand across her mouth. She looked half-scared, but defiant. She also looked quite astonishingly beautiful, which is nothing to do with anything, but worth noting.

From somewhere behind us, swing doors opened and a surgeon emerged; he was wearing a blue surgical gown and there was a mask pulled down off his face. He looked at the crying, clucking women with some confusion and said, 'Oh – did someone already tell you?'

The crying stopped instantly, and we all looked at him, and one of the remaining nurses shook her head vigorously.

'Oh,' he said. 'Mrs McBride?' And he looked first at Trish, and then at Wendy and then May. Wendy's mouth dropped open and she just stared for a moment and then began to try and get up, but Trish put a gentle hand on her shoulder and slowly shook her head. Wendy closed her eyes and began to shudder. Beside me, May slowly rose to her feet. The plastic bottle of Diet Coke fell from her hands and bounced once. The fizzy liquid began to spray out across the floor, the exact opposite of champagne at a famous victory.

'If you could come with me, Mrs McBride.'

May stepped softly towards the surgeon, who managed a sympathetic smile as he ushered her through the swing doors.

Not more than ten seconds later, May screamed.

I made a point of saying to myself, Zip it, shut your god-damn mouth. Because I'm self-aware enough to know that in times of stress I open my bake and say the first stupid thing that comes out, and that there and then, travelling back in the taxi with May crying softly behind me and Patricia feeding her tissues, my first instinct was to glance back from the passenger seat and say, 'Well, I guess that means you're available now.'

I didn't, of course; that's maturity for you – plus fear of Patricia. She was crying hard as well. She kept saying, 'Mouse,' and then, 'Mouse,' and then, 'Big Mouse,' and then back to 'Mouse.' I made some sympathetic noises. I couldn't think of words. The *right* words. It just seemed so – *daft*. I had caught a glimpse of him being carried out of the burning building, but that was all. I had not wanted – or indeed been invited – to go in and view his body. His burned-up corpse. I didn't want that particular vision anywhere in my head. But the very fact that I hadn't seen him meant that somehow it didn't really feel like he was dead at all. I had always despised people who described death in terms of *promoted to glory* or *he's just popped upstairs*, and God knows I had experienced enough death and disaster to know that it was so not a case of popping upstairs, but with Mouse, with not actually seeing him dead, it really seemed as if he had literally nipped out, or gone for a drink, or just gone to work and we'd see him later on.

At May's house the dinner-plates were still on the table. Mouse's place was set. May began to load the dish-washer.

Patricia said, 'Leave it.'

May continued on.

Patricia looked at me, then guided her away from it. I took the remaining plates and continued the loading.

May sat at the kitchen table and folded her arms.

Patricia made a cup of tea. May sipped it.

I've never been a tea drinker, and have never seen the therapeutic benefits of it. I opened the fridge and took out a can of beer.

'Why don't you go upstairs and lie down?' Patricia asked May Li.

'There's so much to do,' May Li said weakly.

'Later,' said Trish. 'Get some sleep.' Patricia led May Li upstairs.

I have never appreciated the therapeutic benefits of lying down either. I was wired. I needed to be *doing*. Not dwelling.

Patricia came down, looking dog tired herself. She stood in the doorway and said, 'He's dead. How can Mouse be dead?'

I shrugged.

'We should have had them over to dinner more often. We didn't call him. We froze him out after he married May. Why did we do that? Didn't he stand by us through everything? He was like a rock when Stevie died, wasn't he? And yet as soon as . . .' I was across to her by then, had her in my arms and she sobbed against me. 'He's dead, Dan, he's dead.'

'Shhhhhhh,' I said. 'It's going to be okay.'

As far as we were aware, May had no other friends in the city.

'Imagine if she woke up and there was no one in the house, and her husband dead,' Trish said.

So she elected to stay. She kissed me again and said, 'Are you going to be all right?' and I said of course. She gave me a funny look and kissed me again. 'You're not going to do anything silly, are you?'

'Like what?'

'Dan.'

I rolled my eyes. 'For god sake, I'm just going to pick the car up.'

'Promise?'

'Promise.'

It was a promise. She wanted to call me a cab but I said no, it was better to walk. It was raining, but not hard; it was cold, but not icy. I *needed* to walk. It was only about twenty minutes back down into the centre. That's the great thing about Belfast: it's a small city, you can walk most anywhere in a reasonable amount of time. And maybe the born again squaddie had a point. Every step of the way I saw smiley, happy faces, people going about their work with a jaunty enthusiasm, men and women standing outside their offices, smoking, bus drivers pumping their horns at each other as they passed, neon signs flashing high above Donegal Square promoting the latest gig at the Waterfront Hall, tourists with their cameras bundling into cabs to take tours of the huge stretches of garish Loyalist and Republican murals which were as irrelevant as they were freshly painted.

I reached my car. It was sitting in a space close to where I'd left it. There was a traffic warden just in the act of pushing a fixed penalty ticket under the windscreen wiper. I didn't say anything, and he looked relieved. I opened the car and climbed in. I sat behind the wheel and looked up at the burned-out offices of *Belfast Confidential*. All of the windows were empty of glass now, their frames either missing completely or blackened and warped. There was a tap on the window and I turned to find the traffic warden smiling in at me. I wound down the window.

'Your tax is up,' he said.

I nodded.

'Just to let you know.'

'Thanks,' I said.

He gestured towards the burned-out building. 'Terrible thing,' he said, and tutted. 'Suppose that's what happens,' he continued, 'when you stick your nose in someone else's business.' He nodded to himself, then turned away.

I sighed. I wound up the window and checked my mobile phone. There were six messages, all from work. I called Davie Mahood, the News Editor.

'Dan! Where the hell are you?!'

'I'm . . . here,' I said vaguely.

'You heard about Mouse?'

'I heard about him.'

'Well, it's our lead, so obviously we need you. Look, mate, I know he was your friend an' all, but we need you on this.'

'Davie . . .'

'Dan, you're a reporter, we need you on this.'

'I know.'

'Then get your arse in gear. Christ, we've already had the wife on the phone . . .'

'May Li?'

'No, the other one. Christ, what a battleaxe. She's already screaming about the Black Widow . . .'

'The what?'

'Calling her a mail-order bride and all sorts of shit.'

'Look, Davie, I'm kind of . . . upset, you know. He was—'

'I know. Look, let me put one of the boys on. You can give him some quotes – what about that? Keep us going till you get in. That okay?'

I sighed. They put someone on. I didn't know him and didn't catch or care about his name. He asked the kind of questions I would have asked. Ease in with biographical stuff, work your way up to 'Was his business in trouble?' or 'Did he have any enemies?' I gave sparse, mundane answers. More than once I caught myself talking about him in the present tense.

'They are treating it as murder, aren't they?' I asked at one point.

'Or suicide.'

'Mouse wouldn't have committed suicide in a million years.'

'Yeah, I sort of gathered that. Kind of makes the Philippino bride a very rich woman though.'

'She's not Philippino, she's Thai. And she's not a bride. I mean, she's not one of those—'

'Well, we can't confirm what she is as she's not answering her phone, and no one but the ex-wife will say anything about her. *She* says—'

'I don't give a fuck what she says.' I cut the line. I sat fuming. I punched the dashboard. I said, 'Fuck it, Mouse, what did you have to go and bloody die for.'

I had no intention of going into work. My head wasn't right. I drove home, took a beer from the fridge and some vodka and some Bailey's which had been sitting there going off since Christmas, and put The Clash on the CD player and cranked it up loud. 'Armageddon Time', a slow reggae about war. 'Death or Glory'. 'White Riot'. 'English Civil War'. I hadn't played any punk in a long time. A lot of it hadn't aged well, but great songs were still great songs, and there were enough to see a drunk man through an hour and a half of reminiscing about an old, dead, murdered friend. The sudden cataclysmic end to the Dead Kennedys' 'California Über Alles' had just sounded when I became aware of the door bell ringing. It was the final track on a compilation CD, so I had to get up anyway. I staggered to the door and opened it and the neighbour was standing there with a Siamese cat in his hand.

'Holy fucking shite,' I said, looking at it.

The neighbour looked a little taken aback. He said, 'Excuse me, I hope you don't mind, but I wonder if I could ask you to turn the music down a little. My wife has a migraine headache.'

I said, 'Where'd you get the fucking cat?'

He looked from me to the Siamese and back. 'Topper?'

'Excuse me?'

'This is Topper. Say hello, Topper.' He lifted Topper's paw and waved it at me.

'I thought he was fucking Tiddles.'

'You mean Toodles.'

'Tiddles, Toodles, who gives a fuck?'

'Toodles is Topper's brother. Topper's a home bird, Toodles is always out wandering about.'

'Good for Toodles,' I said. Toodles's wandering days were over. I was drunk, but not enough to confess that he was literally pushing up daisies.

'Would you mind then, turning it down? It's the chocolate that does it.'

'The what?'

'Chocolate – it gives her the headaches.'

'If she knows that, why does she eat it?'

'Well, alcohol gives one a headache, but one still imbibes it.'

'Are you making a fucking point?'

'No, I—'

'And what gives you the fucking right to use imbibe in a sentence? And call oneself one?'

He blinked at me and said, 'Well, if you could just keep it down.'

He smiled weakly, then turned away. Topper kept watching me over his shoulder. Then the neighbour stopped and turned. 'It was really nice to meet that Mouse the other day. He seemed a very nice chap. Next time you see him, say hello from me and Georgie. And Topper. And not forgetting Toodles.'

And he waved that fucking paw again.

I closed the door. The tears were tripping down my cheeks. I stumbled back into my chair. Then I pulled myself up again and started flicking through my CDs. It was time for The Rezillos. It was time for 'Flying Saucer Attack'. Cranked up to eleven.

11

May Li asked me to say a few words at the funeral, so I said a few. They were not bright and witty, neither were they deeply personal or overly emotional. I found it difficult to put what I felt into words. *Sorry you're dead* was about the grand sum of it. A lot of people got up and said things, it was that kind of a service. They called it a celebration of his life. It didn't feel that way to me. They told funny stories featuring Mouse. Anecdotes. I'd heard them a thousand times before, only about other people. I didn't notice anyone who had featured in *Belfast Confidential*. They might have been there, I just didn't notice. Wendy was there, sitting in the second row, directly behind May Li. They did not speak. There was a lot of coughing and blowing of noses as his coffin jolted and shuddered through the curtains and descended into the crematorium proper.

Outside I mingled with a lot of Mouse's old colleagues from the paper. I didn't know what to say to them. All journalists are cynics, and most of them think they're pretty funny. One said, 'Do you think they got a discount? Sure, wasn't he half-cremated already?' At someone else's funeral, I might have said the same thing, but I found myself making a grab for this guy and had to be pulled off. Patricia led me away, growling. 'Fucking typical,' she moaned. 'Only you could get into a fight at a funeral.' She put me in the car and left me there while she went back to talk to May Li. I watched as Wendy hurried away, head down, all alone. They'd had a lot of friends, but it seemed that with the divorce, nearly all of them had chosen to stay with Mouse. She was a bitter, lonely woman who considered herself a widow, but wasn't. That was May Li's job, and she hadn't been married more than six months.

There was a tap on my window, and I looked up to see someone nodding down at me. At first I didn't recognise him, but then he smiled and I saw that two of his front teeth were missing and I remembered: Bobby Malone. A cop. Lost the teeth in a riot and never got them replaced. Everyone called him Toothless. He loved it. He used to tip me off to stories.

'Bobby,' I said. 'Didn't recognise you without the uniform. You still . . . ?'

'Oh aye. Transferred to CID. Bad business, yer man, isn't it?'

'Aye,' I said. 'You knew him?'

'Oh yes. We had an arrangement.'

'Like our arrangement?'

'Similar, but with money instead of pints.'

'They were good pints.'

'They were, but I'm off all that now. Doctor warned me the old liver was gonna pack in. So I packed it in first.'

'So what do you hear?'

'About yer man?'

'Aye.'

He glanced up and across the crematorium car park. Mourners stood in small groups, chatting; others were climbing back into their vehicles. I could see Patricia standing with a comforting arm around May Li's waist. Toothless crouched down. 'I hear,' he began, his voice low, conspiratorial, 'that your guess is as good as mine.'

I gave him a thin smile. 'Thanks,' I said.

He made a little rubbing sign with his fingers. 'Are we on?'
I sighed and said, 'We're on.'
'Okay, give me a couple of days, I'll see what filters down.'
He winked and walked on.

I rolled the window back up and leaned my head against it.
What was I even thinking of? Mouse was dead and there was
nothing I could do about it. Let someone else find out who
was responsible. Let someone else put themselves in the line
of fire. I'd seen too much, I'd lost too much. I was too old for
it. I didn't care.

No, I did care. Just not sufficiently.

I should have called him back, I should have told him to
forget it, that it wasn't my job. But he kept walking and I kept
sitting there. I just didn't have the energy.

In the days that followed I found it increasingly difficult to
function. There was no reason for Mouse's death to hit me so
hard – we hadn't been close for quite a while. But every time
I thought of him my stomach got all twisted and sometimes I
had to sit down because my breathing felt all fucked-up.
Eventually Trish packed me off to the doctor, but he couldn't
find anything particularly wrong: high cholesterol was about
the height of it. 'But I can see you're stressed, and the breathing
– well, we call those panic attacks. I can give you anti-
depressants for your depression, and a paper bag for the panic
attacks. You breathe into it. It'll help calm you down.' I was
only there at Patricia's insistence, and didn't want or need any
of it, but I took the prescription and I got it filled and kept it
in the bathroom, and every night for the next five nights I took
out one anti-depressant and flushed it down the toilet. I got a
sick line out of it, which allowed me to sit around the house
and mope.

'Why don't you go out for a jog?' Patricia asked eventually.

'Why don't you go yourself, porky?' I said.

She slammed the lounge door on her way upstairs. I went out for a drive. I was gone about an hour, just driving, thinking, then I went home to apologise to her. I came through the door with a bunch of flowers and a bottle of wine, already saying, 'I'm really sorry—' but Trish was nodding across the room. May Li was sitting there. She was wearing a red silk shirt and black jeans and her long black hair was tied up in a pony tail. She smiled at me and said, 'Hello, Dan.'

Patricia said, 'I'll just make a cup of tea.' She moved into the kitchen and slid the divider closed after her. I didn't hear her filling the kettle or getting cups, just a slight scrape as she pulled a chair out from the kitchen table.

'So,' I asked, 'howse it hangin'?'

There are certain phrases that Linguaphone haven't gotten around to yet. May Li's brow furrowed slightly. 'I asked to speak to you alone. Patricia agrees as long as I don't ask you to do something stupid. I agree because I want to speak to you alone, and believe that stupidity is open to interpretation.'

'That's what I always say.'

We both smiled. I sat down opposite her.

She clasped her hands in her lap and said: 'You were Mouse's best friend, but you don't know me from a mad man.'

'Adam.'

'Adam?'

'Adam is the expression. You don't know me from Adam. Although I think it dates from a time when there were a lot more people called Adam.'

She nodded. 'I think this will be a lot quicker if you don't point out all of my linguistic shortcomings. I have only been in Belfast a few months – you can't expect me to talk like a nigger.'

'Native,' I said.

'I know,' said May Li. 'That was a joke.'

'Politically suspect,' I said, 'but otherwise right on the button.'

'Button?' asked May Li. We smiled at each other again. 'Mouse always said you were a smart cunt,' she observed.

'Alec,' I corrected, but she stood her ground.

'My husband has been murdered, and the police are investigating, but they do not inspire me with confidence. In my country, many police are corrupt, and if they are not corrupt, they are lazy and stupid. Is it the same here?'

'It's pretty much universal,' I said.

'I thought so. This is not my country, Dan, I do not have friends or relatives here, and my instinct is to go home, to sell off my husband's business interests here.'

'That's understandable.'

'But also – my husband loved this country. He loved the people and he loved the fact that he had become successful through his own efforts. Part of me feels that I would be betraying him if I allowed *Belfast Confidential* to be sold or to founder. Do you understand that?' I nodded. 'I don't know why he was killed. Perhaps to prevent publication of some fact or other, perhaps to gain revenge for some perceived slight, or perhaps it was some business disagreement. I don't know, Dan, but if I leave or sell without finding out, then I feel I will have dishonoured the memory of the man I loved.'

'You wouldn't be – but I know what you're saying.'

'And do you also know why I am here, and what I am going to ask?'

'Not exactly, but I'm starting to get palpitations.'

'Why?'

'Because I've had enough trouble and shite.'

'I want you to run *Belfast Confidential* for me.'

'I've been threatened and shot at and my life made a misery at every turn.'

'I want you to finish researching the Power List and I want you to publish it the way Mouse intended.'

'My son lost his life and I almost lost my wife.'

'I want you to find out who killed him and why, and I want that person brought to justice.'

'We've only just pulled ourselves out of that black hole, we have no desire to throw ourselves back into it.'

'In return I will give you a fifty per cent share of *Belfast Confidential*. My husband's accountants have valued the core business at more than six million pounds.'

'It's not about the fucking money.'

'I know that. But I am a woman, and we must address practical matters.'

'Yes, we must,' said Patricia. I had not heard the divide open. She was standing with her arms folded, looking at May Li.

'Trish,' I said, somewhat defensively, 'I haven't agreed to anything.'

'I know that.'

May Li produced a folded copy of *Belfast Confidential* from her handbag; she flattened it out on her lap, then smoothed the cover further with her hand. 'Mouse had finished this when he . . .' She took a deep breath. 'We got it to print and it'll be in the shops tomorrow. We're about halfway along with next week's issue, but we need someone to hold it together, to make the right decisions. I'm not a journalist, I'm not . . .'

The words trailed away. She smoothed the cover down again.

I started talking without really knowing where I was going. 'Look – May Li, I know how much you must be hurting. Believe you me, we've been there, and what happened to Mouse, it just makes us sick to our souls. But he's gone and he's not coming back and nothing we do will change that. And yes, the police are corrupt and stupid, but there are some good ones as well and I think that sooner or later, whether by design or accident, they will find out what happened and someone will be, as you put it, brought to justice. You should, you know, let them get on with it. You should go home, get on with your life, you should . . .'

She stood abruptly. Her eyes flamed angrily. 'Perhaps *you* should think about your great friend. He has been murdered and you are content to sit there and do nothing?'

'No, May Li, I'm—'

'You are content to let whoever killed him get their way?'

'No, I'm not saying th—'

'You are happy to have his memory insulted by doing *nothing*?'

'No, please, just sit—'

'And I offer to make you very rich indeed and you just throw it back in my face!'

'I didn't throw—'

'You are *not* his friend!'

I looked desperately to Trish. She remained in the doorway, her arms folded, an odd look on her face. 'Where's the fucking support?' I snapped.

'Well, I think May Li has a point.'

'She has a lot of fucking points!'

'Mouse was our mate, and we should do something about it.'

'When you say *we*, you mean me, don't you?'

'Well, obviously, yes, but you'll have my moral support.'

'Trish! This goes against everything you've ever—'

'Dan – it's for Mouse.'

I looked from one to the other. I slumped back in my chair. Shook my head. 'It's all right for you two, you can just hang back. What if they lock *me* in the office and set fire to me as well?'

'Well,' May Li began somewhat hesitatingly, 'at least we will have established a pattern.'

I couldn't resist that one. I smiled. She smiled.

And that, as they say, was that.

Later, when May Li had gone, all smiles and thanks and solidarity and support, I cornered Trish in the kitchen. She had a bottle of wine open and was making me a ham bap for dinner. I had a can in my hand and a befuddled, bemused, confused and perplexed expression on my face, which was enough expression for a whole family of faces. In short, I didn't know what the hell she was playing at.

So I asked. 'What the hell are you playing at?'

'I'm not playing.'

'Then what's going on? You *want* me to get involved?'

'Yes.'

'But it contradicts every—'

'Dan.'

'What?'

'We went through years of hell after Stevie. We split up, for Christ sake, and then we got back together and it still wasn't right. Because we let it fester.' She put her glass down; she wiped her hands on a drying cloth. She came towards me. Put her arms around me. 'We only got back on an even keel when you dealt with it. You went out to Florida and you dealt with it.'

'That wasn't me, it was—'

'It was *you*, and you came back a changed man. A better man. Still an arse from time to time, but a better man, and we're a better couple.'

'Then shouldn't we preserve that? If I get involved in this . . .'

'I know you're a shit-magnet, Dan. But that's just how it is. And I know you. You might tell yourself you don't want to get involved, but it'll eat away at you.' She lowered her arms and gave me a playful poke in the chest. 'You'll make yourself miserable, you'll make me miserable. You have to do this. For you, for me, for May, for Mouse.'

I half-laughed. 'For fuck sake, Trish. You just keep surprising me, do you know that?'

'Well, isn't that how it should be?'

'Up to a point.' She has me wound round her little finger. I am aware of it. 'Right,' I said wearily, 'okay. Whatever you say.'

'Good. And do you know what else I say?'

'Christ no.'

'I say come upstairs with me, right now.'

'Right now?'

'Right now.'

'For . . . ?' I asked. She raised a suggestive eyebrow. 'You're getting awful horny in your old age,' I tutted.

'It's that whiff of danger. It's a bit of a turn-on.'

'Are you serious?'

She rolled her eyes. 'Will you just hurry up?' She turned for the stairs.

'What about my bap?'

'Fuck the bap, Dan.'

I blew air out of my cheeks. 'I love a woman who talks dirty.'

She smiled, and began to take the stairs two at a time.

But still I hesitated. 'Trish?'

'What?'

'It's not about the money, is it? I mean, she's virtually giving us three million quid. Tell me you're not thinking I could just arse around with the mag and pretend to investigate and there's not a bloody thing she could do about it.'

She gave me a look. 'Do you think I could possibly be that cynical?'

I put my hands on my hips. 'Will my answer in any way affect the chances of me having sex in the next few minutes?'

She smiled.

I smiled back. 'There's not a cynical cell in your entire body,' I said, 'and just in case there is, I'm going to launch a search and destroy mission for it . . . right *now.*'

12

I recognised a few of their faces from the funeral, but for the most part they were complete strangers casting curious looks my way. May Li had called a staff meeting in a disused computer showroom we were going to use as a temporary office. It was more or less opposite the burned-out shell of *Belfast Confidential*. According to the books there were six journalists, a Deputy Editor, two photographers, three designers, two receptionist/secretaries and six advertising staff on the magazine. Only about half of them had turned up. May Li introduced herself first, because she'd only visited the magazine twice, and made all the right noises about being fully behind continued publication, about providing additional security and about not giving in to terror. I could have pointed out that half of our staff already had, but it didn't seem right to start on such a negative note. Then she introduced me, and I wasn't exactly overwhelmed by the warmth of their welcome.

I've never been one for standing up in public, unless it's to make a tit of myself, but I realised the importance of this first meeting. Trish had sat me down and settled my nerves and made me do the speech for her. She'd nodded positively throughout, then got up and gone to the front door and said, 'I'm not working for a pretentious wanker like you.' So we worked on the speech a little more, and a little more after that, and then I tried it again and she said, 'Not bad, but maybe you'd be better just being yourself.' We looked at each other then and laughed heartily, and went back to work on the speech.

So I delivered it, sitting on the edge of a desk, looking them in the eye, and I talked about Mouse and what a friend he'd been, and how he'd turned his life around, and how he loved Belfast and thought it was the equal of any place on earth, that there was as much talent here, as much creative energy as any city in Europe, and he wanted *Belfast Confidential* to reflect that. He believed that Northern Ireland had emerged as a better, stronger place for what it had been through, but it was important to always be aware that it could slip back into the abyss, and that was what *Belfast Confidential* was about as well, exposing the cheats and the charlatans and the recidivists, and that if Mouse was here today he would be urging us to get right back to work, not to give up, but to face the future with determination and bravery and also to crack a few jokes.

Or something like that.

When I finished there was a desultory round of applause. I hadn't expected to be carried on their shoulders down to the pub, but I'd hoped for a slightly better reaction. I heard someone say, 'Wow, just like *Braveheart*,' but it was heavy with sarcasm.

Virtually nothing had been saved from the fire, so May Li had splashed out on a new computer system, photographic equipment and all of the little things without which an office cannot work. Like coffee and staples. I let them choose their own desks. When that turned into a mad free-for-all I cancelled that plan and assigned them individually. Then I asked Mouse's Deputy Editor to meet me upstairs in my own office, which was, understandably, the best in the building. It was a perk. It looked directly across at the old offices, which was another one, a useful reminder of why I was there, and what could happen.

I walked May Li back downstairs to her car. She said, 'Good speech,' and I laughed. 'No, really, I mean it.' She put a hand on my arm. She was wearing a black shirt and a short black skirt. Patricia could have told me what designer labels they came from, I just knew that they looked good, but not as good as May Li did, with her black hair worn long and her warm fingers pressed into my freckled arm and her smile-with-a-hint-of-sadness which just made you want to pick her up and hug her.

I am a happily married man, and I have been known to be distracted in the past, but I wanted to do this *Belfast Confidential* thing, and I wanted to do it properly. I wanted to *prove* that I could do it properly. Prove it to everyone, prove it to Trish, prove it to myself.

'May Li,' I began.

She put a finger to her lips and said, 'Shhhh. I know what you're going to say. That you want to run *Belfast Confidential* your way, that you don't want me calling in every five minutes giving my opinion on how it should be done, or plaguing you every day to see how the investigation is going. I understand that. It was the same with Mouse. Strictly hands off.'

'Actually, I was just going to say, "have a nice day".'

She smiled. She was a good five inches shorter than me; she went up on her toes and kissed me on the cheek. She smelled of Imperial Leather and Colgate. At this time of the morning Patricia still smelled of last night's Lambrusco and quite often went to work with a Rice Krispie stuck to her cheek. It was easy to see how a man could be distracted by a woman like May Li. Not me, fortunately, as I had a world to put to rights.

Brian Kerr was waiting in my office. There wasn't much to him – a scrawny-looking soul, about forty years old, with thinning hair and wire-framed glasses. It's usually best not to judge a book by its cover, but sometimes you can, and I have found quite often that my first instinct about someone is the correct one. Brian looked like a whiner.

First thing he said was, 'She's gone and bought state-of-the-art computers. We were working on this cheap old crap, but at least we knew how they worked. It'll take us a good couple of weeks to get up to scratch on these'uns. How long are we delaying publication by?'

'We're not.'

He smiled. 'No, seriously.'

'Yes, seriously.'

'You're fucking joking.'

'I'm fucking not.'

'It's impossible.'

'They said Everest was impossible.'

'Hundreds of people died before someone conquered Everest.'

'Well, it's a good thing we don't have hundreds of people.'

I smiled. He didn't. He said, 'Well, we have more than this, but they're scared of coming in.'

'Scared of what?'

'Getting burned to death.'

'Can you call them and tell them it's okay?'

'Is it okay?'

'Well, I don't smell smoke. Will you call them?'

'Some of them are freelance, they'll have taken other work.'

'Well, try them.'

'And if I tell them you're sticking to the schedule they'll laugh in my face.'

'I think you should call them.'

'We can't do it. I mean, Jesus Christ man, this is Monday – we're due at the printers on Thursday.'

'Yup. That's the plan.'

He rubbed at his weak chin. 'Well, half our guys are working on the Power List issue – if we pull them off that and concentrate on just getting the usual magazine out, maybe we can do it. Scale down, cut back on the pagination, bump the Power List for six months.'

'The Power List appears as normal, three weeks from now.'

'That's impossible.'

'They said Everest was impossible.'

He looked at me. 'You obviously haven't edited a magazine before.'

'That's true.'

'It's not like a newspaper.'

'I'd noticed that.'

'It's not just about getting stories, you can't just phone it in.'

'I think I'm aware of that.'

'We've lost everything, we'll be starting from scratch.'

Behind his head, out of the window and across the road, firemen were hauling down the burned-out *Belfast Confidential* sign. He saw where I was looking. 'Are you not scared at all?' he asked. 'Of ending up like Mouse?'

I shrugged. 'Who do you think did it?'

'I've been through it all with the police.'

'I'm sure you have. Nevertheless.'

'I find it's best not to speculate.'

'Brian, you're a journalist, you're paid to speculate.'

'Well, to be strictly accurate, I'm a Deputy Editor. I pay other people to speculate.'

I smiled. I clasped my hands and put on my boss look. 'Well, to be strictly accurate, you're not anything. You were all on freelance contracts so I'm reinterviewing you all for your jobs. I'm pleased to say you've come through it with no colours at all.'

He said, 'What?'

I said, 'Your enthusiasm isn't exactly catching. Brian, I'm sure you're very good at what you do, but if you're going to be a real misery guts, then maybe we'd be better off without you.' He sat there. I stood by the window and looked across. Mouse, to all intents and purposes, had died in there. What was it, a firebomb? Or did someone tie him up and then torch the place? Was he overcome by fumes, or did he scream and scream and scream and scream and scream and scream . . .

'We could do a scaled-down version of the Power List,' said Brian.

'No, we do it properly.'

'We haven't the time. We need to use those resources to make sure—'

'I think we're in danger of going over familiar territory here, Brian.'

He stood up suddenly. When I turned at the scrape of his chair I saw that his sallow complexion had reddened somewhat. It wasn't exactly Custer's Last Stand, but he'd decided to make his point. 'I was next in line,' he said. '*I* should be in charge.'

'Ah,' I said.

'I know everything about *Belfast Confidential* and you know bugger all.'

'It's the truth,' I said.

'You know,' he continued, 'I heard you were an arsehole.'

'Yes, it's on my CV.'

'And you're fucking mental if you think you can turn this round.'

'If you say so.'

'You haven't the experience, you haven't the connections, from what I hear you're a fuckin' dipso anyway. What the fuck makes you think you can just walk in here and throw your weight around?'

'The fact that I own the place. Or half of it. Which is a half more than you.'

'Yeah, right. You *are* a fucking arsehole, Starkey, and if you think you're in charge you're a fucking bigger fool than I thought you were. You're the boss? You're the owner? You've got it all in writing, have you?'

'That's nothing to do with you, Brian.'

'I knew it. You fucking clown. The fucking Black Widow will suck you up and spit you out the way she did with Mouse. So fuck you.'

He walked out then, leaving the door open, and thundered down the stairs. I thought about getting down on my knees and begging him to stay, but something stopped me. I put my feet up on my desk and thought about what he'd said. He probably had a point about May Li. In the words of someone more famous than me, a verbal contract isn't worth the paper it's written on. But this wasn't Hollywood, and May Li was my mate's wife. She had a beautiful smile to go with all her other beautiful bits and she'd given me no reason at all to mistrust her. She'd made me rich, powerful, and had also kissed me on the cheek, any one of which was enough to earn my eternal gratitude and trust. Or at least a few hours for me to wallow in it.

13

Brian Kerr left, and took two of the four reporters who'd turned up, a designer and three of the advertising staff with him. They stopped short of standing across the road with a big banner saying *Wanker!* on it, but I was prepared to encounter the sentiment in the air as I walked through the office downstairs. But those few who remained didn't seem perturbed in the least. Most of them weren't long out of their teens, and *Belfast Confidential* was their first job. It was a cool, trendy, exciting, cutting-edge kind of a place to work, and in their eyes Mouse had been all of those things too, and Brian Kerr none. They were used to being underpaid and badly exploited and they weren't going to let a little fire put them off, or the fact that their new boss didn't know his arse from his elbow.

I said I appreciated them staying, and they said they'd nowhere else to go. I said we could be a great little team and they said, 'Like Man United, or Linfield?' I said Linfield for now, but I had high hopes. One of the reporters was called Patrick O'Hare, the other Stephen Fagin. I talked to them together for five minutes. They were keen in a way I hadn't been in decades. At the end of it I said, 'I'm making you joint Deputy Editors. You can split Brian's wages between you.'

'But we've never deputy-edited anything.'

'Well, I'll teach you everything I know. Put the magazine

together any way you can. You have complete artistic freedom, and try not to fight. There, that's everything I know.'

They looked at each other, a little bit shocked, a big bit excited.

'You're serious?' Pat asked.

I nodded.

'Seriously?' asked Stephen.

'Lads, with great power comes great irresponsibility. I'm throwing you in the deep end, but it's also your big chance to make your mark. We've got two days to put this baby together: are you up for it?'

They exchanged the briefest of looks, then gave each other and then me high fives. I've never been given a high five in my life, but I managed it with the suave sophistication of a gum-faced pensioner at an allnight rave. Party. Disco-thing. When they'd settled down again I asked them to explain how the Power List was put together.

'Well,' said Stephen, 'we sit down about six months before the publication date and go through last year's list and weed out anyone who's died or gone bust or been arrested for child abuse or generally fallen from favour . . .'

'And then we talk about any potential new entries,' said Pat. 'There's usually five or six – it's a pretty small country and not that much changes, so mostly it's a question of updating last year's entries.'

I nodded from one to the other. 'And were there any complaints about last year's list? I mean, serious complaints – threats, or legal action?'

'Well, you get the odd one complaining about their position in the Top Fifty, saying that we've exaggerated or underestimated their wealth or influence, but no, nothing serious. You didn't hear of anything, Pat?'

Pat shook his head.

'So as a starting point,' I suggested, 'we could guess that whoever torched the office might be someone who heard they were about to be included and didn't fancy it.'

They exchanged glances again, then nodded.

'Okay, so get me a list of the new guys and then meet me upstairs in ten minutes.'

'That's about all we'll have – names,' said Stephen. 'Mouse liked to deal with the new ones himself. It was his *thing*, you know? He liked to go and look them in the eye. He said he could always tell a good 'un from a bad 'un. His words.'

I left them to it. I spoke to the remaining advertising guys, and they seemed pretty upbeat. They never had much problem selling space; the interest in Mouse's murder alone would get us through the next few issues, with the Power List issue already shaping up to be the biggest ever. 'No disrespect intended,' said Alan Wells, the most senior of them, 'but there's nothing like a murder to push sales up.'

'If I murdered you, would it push sales up?' I asked.

'Well no, you'd really want someone with some kind of a life, or personality. And a job,' he added meekly.

Point made. When I went back upstairs Mary Brady, the receptionist who also doubled as Mouse's secretary, was waiting for me. She was considerably older than the remaining staff; she looked to be in her late fifties at least. Her hair was dyed a dirty blonde and she wore slacks and trainers and was using my can of Diet Coke as an ashtray.

I said, 'Mouse spoke highly of you,' as I took my seat. It was a lie, but I couldn't afford to lose any more staff.

'He did?'

'He did.'

'But he always shouted at me.'

'He just had a loud voice.'

'No, he shouted at me.'

'He shouted at everyone.'

'No, mostly just me.'

'Why was that, Mary?'

'He said I reminded him of his wife. His first wife. That's no reason to shout at anyone.'

'Well, you'd need to meet her.'

She smiled at that. 'I only came in to pick up my wages. I thought working here would be fun, and I suppose it was, but I lost my husband and my son to the Troubles, and I've had my fill of all that crap, so I don't need to be working somewhere it's going to happen again. Life's too short. Is it going to happen again?'

I took a deep breath. 'I wish I could guarantee it won't, Mary. But I can't.'

'He never spoke highly of me, did he?'

'No. To tell you the truth, he never mentioned you.'

'Everything I read in the paper since he died makes him out like some kind of saint, but he wasn't.'

'No, he wasn't.'

'He was arrogant and impatient and he thought he could call me any time of the day or night to fix him up with this or that. And to tell you the truth, when I heard he was gone my first thought was, Well, at least he's not going to shout at me any more. Isn't that terrible?'

'Well, yes and no.'

She put her cigarette out in my can. 'And he wouldn't let me smoke in the office. He made me go and stand outside, in the rain and snow.'

'I don't mind if you smoke.'

'Seriously? I'm forty a day, unfiltered.'

'Well, seeing as how the life expectancy of Editors around here isn't exactly fantastic, I don't see how some passive smoking is going to make much difference.'

'You're a bit of a sweet talker, aren't you?'

'You should get out more.'

She smiled and lit another one. When she'd taken a long drag she said, 'You don't remember me, do you?'

'I saw you downstairs.'

'I mean, from years ago.'

I gave her a long look. I shook my head slowly. 'I'm sorry, but if we have a love child somewhere, I can backdate the payments.'

'When my son died, you came around looking for an interview.'

'Oh.'

'You were very nice and you were very sweet, and I remembered that, because not all of them were. And the piece you wrote was sympathetic, and it was accurate, and I appreciated that. So I remembered your name and I used to read your columns and you were very funny and then you seemed to get into lots of trouble and I haven't seen your name in years, and now here we are. It's a funny old world, isn't it?'

I had to agree. Funny, or tragic. It's a fine line.

'You'll stay, won't you, Mary?'

'I'll stay, if you don't shout and you let me smoke.'

I put my hand out, and we shook on it.

'So what do you want me to do first?'

'I DON'T GIVE A FUCK!' I exploded, and it took her five minutes to understand that I was only joking; she was nearly away down the stairs to join the rest of the rats. But she calmed down and then she saw the funny side of it, kind of. I promised her a pay rise. When she asked again what she could really do, she kind of tensed before my response, but I'd learned my lesson. I asked her quietly if she still had access to Mouse's appointments book, and she said yes, she carried it with her everywhere because he really did call her at all hours of the day and night. So I asked her to get that, and then to track down Mouse's office and mobile phone records so we could put together a picture of his last few days to see if that would yield any clues. She said the police already had those, but that she could probably get copies.

Pat and Stephen appeared in the doorway, and Mary bustled away, all business. Pat took her seat, and Stephen stood behind him, leaning on the back of it.

'Well?' I said.

Pat handed over a single sheet of paper. There were six names written on it, with two or three lines of detail beside each one. I recognised four of them. I took a pen from my jacket and added a seventh. I turned the page round so that they could read it.

'May Li?' Pat said incredulously.

I nodded. '*Belfast Confidential* is the most influential publication in Belfast and it's worth millions. She's the new owner because her husband got burned to death by person or persons unknown. I think that makes her a perfect entry for the Power List. And add to that the fact that we know bugger all about her. Besides, I find it's always worthwhile knowing exactly who you're working for.'

'I understand your reasoning,' said Stephen, 'but do you think it's wise?'

I took a deep breath. 'Stephen, son, do you think that wisdom has ever played a significant part in my life?'

He looked at me for a long time, then he slowly shook his head.

14

A short while later Mary buzzed up that there were two police officers wanting to see me. I said, 'Is there a back way out?' jokingly, without realising she had me on the speakerphone, and judging by their faces when they came through the door they didn't seem to find it very funny. Or perhaps they didn't find anything very funny, given the nature of their work. Maybe with the cessation of the Troubles they'd expected to be able to put their feet up for a while, but it hadn't exactly turned out that way. There were a lot of bored ex-terrorists looking for kicks, and now that the war was over the thousands of ordinary decent criminals who'd kept their heads down for years felt it was safe to come back out and steal things.

I have no idea if they mismatch cops into partnerships the way they do on TV, but these two seemed to fit the bill. One was mid-forties, grey over the ears, wearing a smart sports jacket and slacks, thick across the shoulders and barrel-chested. He looked like he worked out. He introduced himself as Detective Sergeant Eric Mayne. The other, perhaps around thirty, was tall and thin; his face was dominated by a large hooked nose, the kind of nose that might bestow gravitas upon him in his later years, but which had probably made his teenage years a misery. He was Detective Inspector Brian Mooney. They sat down and nodded politely. They didn't show me their ID, but they didn't arrest me either, so we compromised on coolly appraising each other across my desk.

'We're investigating the murder of Mark McBride.' It was Mooney, he was younger but he was also senior. Fast-tracking. Probably went to college, whereas Mayne had come up the hard way. Mayne probably resented the fact that he was into middle age and Mooney was earning twice his wages and ordering him about, snotty-nosed kid. You could make up all kinds of shit just looking at people.

'Who?' I responded, and then it struck me. 'Sorry. Mouse. Mark McBride. It's so long since I called him that.'

'You knew him before?'

'Oh yes, we're old mates.'

'We've spoken to most of your staff over the past few days,' said Mayne.

'That's more than I can say.' I laughed.

'This isn't a laughing matter,' said Mayne.

'I appreciate that.' I clasped my hands together and tried to settle down. Cops made me nervous. It wasn't that long since I'd spent the night in one of their bed and breakfasts. 'How can I help you?'

Mooney pulled his chair forward slightly. 'This is more in the way of a courtesy visit, just to update you on the investigation and to ask you nicely not to . . . well, interfere.'

'Interfere?'

'Stick your nose in where it's not wanted.' It was Mayne. 'This is a murder enquiry, we don't want your pack of teenagers sticking their oars in and fucking things up. We spend half our lives clearing up the mess you lot create.'

I cleared my throat. 'Forgive me, gentlemen, I'm new to this, but it was my understanding that *Belfast Confidential* quite often unmasks the criminals and then you get to arrest them.'

'Bollocks,' Mayne snapped. 'You stir up shit and we have to deal with the fallout.'

'Well,' I said, trying my best to act like an Editor, 'perhaps we should agree to differ. Or agree to disagree. Or—'

Mayne cut in with, 'You think you're a real funny cunt, don't you?' He wasn't getting my statesman act at all.

'Well, a cunt's a useful thing.'

Mooney leaned forward. 'The point is, Mr Starkey, that we're aware of what you all do around here, and think it might well have been a contributing factor to the death of Mr McBride. As we don't want a repeat performance, we're asking that you, and this publication, desist from mounting any kind of an investigation into your late Editor's murder. We appreciate that you may still feel obliged to do it, but this is a small town, Mr Starkey, and we don't want to be trampling all over each other, perhaps scaring off potential witnesses or inadvertently contaminating evidence.'

'Well, perhaps we could work together.'

Mayne snorted.

Mooney said, 'I don't think so.'

'Well then,' I said.

'So you'll steer clear?'

I looked at him and said, 'Where are you now? In the investigation.'

'It's early days.'

'Do you have any leads?'

'We're following several lines of enquiry.'

'When I made my statement, I said someone else answered Mouse's mobile when I called him: has anyone followed that up?'

'It's beyond our remit to disclose that.'

'Did he have any other injuries besides the burns?'

'I'm not at liberty to discuss that either.'

'Has anyone claimed responsibility?'

'Those days are gone.'

'Did you lift CCTV footage from the cameras around the Square?'

'Most of them weren't functioning. But we've some.'

'And?'

'It's too early to say.'

'Did you talk to the hookers outside? Did they see anyone come or go?'

'I can't discuss that.'

I sat back. 'Well, thanks for updating me. When does the courtesy bit start?'

'It's the funny cunt again,' said Mayne.

'Do you talk like that in front of your mother?' I asked.

'No, I talk like that in front of yours, just before I fuck her.'

Even Mooney looked a bit taken aback by that one. 'Detective, please,' he said. 'Settle yourself. Here, for God's sake,' and he pushed my can of Diet Coke towards him.

Mayne gave me a hard look, then lifted the can and took a long drink. Then he gagged and spat and wheezed and doubled over and near-choked and hurled the can across the room.

'What the fuck, what the fuck . . .' he coughed.

'My secretary has been using that as an ash tray.'

'You fucker, you fucking fucker,' Mayne wheezed, his face pink and contorted, his finger angrily jabbing out towards me.

Mooney tried to soothe him – 'It was an accident – an accident.' – and patted his back.

'Do you want me to get you a fresh one?' I asked. 'There's cold ones down in the—'

'No, I fucking don't! Christ.' He flicked at the butts and ash sticking to his shirt and jacket. Then he rubbed his tongue over the back of his hand, and made a sick face.

Mooney smiled wryly across the desk at me. 'That's one way to put him off smoking.'

I blew air out of my cheeks. I glanced at my watch. I nodded from one to the other. 'You're very good,' I said, 'but I think you're overplaying it.'

'Overplaying what?' Mooney asked.

'The good cop, bad cop routine. You see, you're being okay, but you . . .' and I nodded at Mayne, 'you're a bit over the top. You're *too* bad. And I really haven't done anything to justify it. I mean, are you always like this, or is it just me specifically?'

'He's always like this,' said Mooney.

I laughed. 'See, there you go, you're being the nice guy again. I think you need to work on your material.'

Mayne pointed a finger. 'I'll fucking work on *you*.'

'There you go again – right over the top.'

Mooney stood up. Mayne followed, but not before giving me another long, hard look.

'Well, thank you for your cooperation,' said Mooney.

'No problem,' I said.

They'd only been gone a few moments when Pat and Stephen appeared in the doorway.

'What'd they want?' Stephen asked.

I crossed to the window in time to see the two police officers cross the road to an unmarked car. They appeared to be shouting at each other. 'We've just been warned off,' I said.

'But we haven't started yet.'

'I know.'

They joined me at the window. 'The big one,' Pat said, 'he's a right wanker. We ran a story about police corruption last year and he blew a gasket.'

'You named him?'

'No, that's the point. We'd never heard of him until he came in threatening everyone.'

'Curious,' I said.

15

I phoned Toothless Bobby Malone and asked him what he was up to, and he said now wasn't a good time and hung up on me. He phoned back five minutes later and said *now* was a good time, but that time was money and he was saving up for a Ryan Jet and did I care to contribute. I said okay. I told him about my visit from Good Cop and Bad Cop and he laughed and said they were just protecting the case. I told him I'd heard Mayne was open to backhanders and he said, 'You're telling *me* this?' 'That's a different sort of backhander,' I said, and he said, 'Is it?' We were in danger of getting into a deep moral and philosophical discussion, so I cut him off at the pass by asking if he'd been able to turn anything up since Mouse's funeral.

He said, 'Yes, but I didn't have a number for you. You move around a lot, and the *Telegraph* said you were off with mental problems.'

'They said mental problems?'

'Nah, but I kind of guessed. Losing a mate can do that, fuck you up for a while.'

'So what do you have?'

'That it's a professional hit.'

'Professional as in . . . ?'

'As in it wasn't some amateur who left like a receipt for where he bought the petrol, or fingerprints on a door or his mobile lying around. As in there's been thousands of murders here in the last thirty years, but I can hardly think of any that weren't straightforward shootings or bombings. Someone went to a bit of trouble with this one. Tying him up and gagging him. Spreading petrol in specific points to make sure the whole building went up. We're not just talking careless smokers. One might say someone was making a point.'

I took a deep breath. 'Okay, what else?'

'Nobody's talking. Not the hookers outside, or any of the usual movers and shakers.'

'Because they don't know, or because they're scared?'

'I would say the latter, because someone always knows.'

'You'll be able to find out more?'

'It's not my shout. But if you'll settle for hearsay and gossip, I'm your man.'

'Someone was with Mouse in the office just before he died – I spoke to him.'

'I saw your statement.'

'So he must be on CCTV.'

'You'd think that, but you know how it is, there's so many hookers around there that most of the offices switch them off at nights so they won't get pulled into any legal shit every time some poor hornball gets arrested.'

'What about the post mortem?'

'I have the shortform version, it's the three lines they released to the press; the long form's proving a bit harder to come by.'

'Any reason for that?'

'Nah, I don't think so. I think they're just playing silly buggers.'

'Can they do that?'

'Pretty much. Tell you the truth, I'd have gotten more by now, but I've been off myself, what with my teeth an' all.'

'Which teeth would they be?'

'My brand new pearly whites. They've been like this for ever, but the wife finally had enough of watching me trying to eat a Crunchie sideways. The rest were pretty rotten as well, so I have a whole new mouthful. Big fucking op. But I've a smile like Tom Cruise now. Cost a fucking fortune.'

'I thought you were saving up for a Jet.'

'I was, but I had a discussion with my wife and she made a valid point – that you can't fuck a Jet.'

'I see,' I said.

'But now I'm back on the case, and if you'll see me right, I'll see you right.'

'I think we see eye to eye,' I said.

I left that night at a little after nine. There is a lot to putting a magazine together, and even though I'd worked like a dog, it somehow felt as if I hadn't really done anything besides push pieces of paper around. I wanted a cool beer and the sympathy of my wife. I was parked just outside the new *Belfast Confidential* offices. I climbed into the car, started the engine, and just as I was about to reverse there was a tap on my window; a thin, blonde, tattooed hooker was smiling in at me. I shook my head. She tapped again. I rolled the window down and said, 'Not tonight, love.'

She said, 'Your tax is out of date.'

I said, 'I know.'

She shivered.

I said, 'Cold, is it?'

And she held out a warrant card. She told me she was a police officer and she was arresting me for kerb-crawling. I said, 'Get away to fuck.'

She said, 'Also using foul and abusive language to a police officer, and resisting arrest.'

I said, 'You're winding me up.'

Then there was someone standing behind her. She glanced back, nodded, then moved to one side and there was Mayne, smiling sarcastically. He crouched down beside me and said, 'See, Starkey, how easy it is?'

I just kept looking. There were a million things I wanted to say, but sometimes you have to hold it.

'So take this as a little reminder, eh?'

He laughed to himself, began to straighten, then appeared to have a bright idea. He leaned in through my window. I thought he was going to take my keys, but he reached down past me and I moved back and closed my legs, thinking instead that he was going to give me a dig in the balls; but his hand stretched further, until his head and shoulders were half-through the window. He yanked out the ash tray and turned it upside down in my lap. Except the ash tray was empty. He turned it up to examine it, and I kind of laughed because it was such a stupid situation. He was embarrassed then, and sometimes when big men are embarrassed, they strike out. So he struck out, and clipped my forehead with the top of the ash tray, and I started to bleed. Then he gave me a wink and walked away, and the hooker, who wasn't, watched him go for a moment, then shook her head. She opened her handbag, took out a tissue and handed it to me. Then she clack-clacked away on her heels.

It wasn't a bad cut, but it was annoying. I drove home with the tissue stuck to my forehead and told Trish about my day. She showed admirable restraint by not asking about the tissue on my head. She knew it wouldn't take long for me to get there. A woman can tell you a story and you'll never need to say to her, 'Give me that again, but with more detail,' because it will all have been covered, twice. 'Half the staff walked out,' I explained, 'then the police came in and threatened me, and then I nearly got arrested for kerb-crawling and then one of the original cops attacked me with an ash tray.'

She gave me a long look and said, 'Just another day at the office then.'

I nodded, and sat there, cradling my beer.

'Okay then,' she said. 'Let's just go over it once more.' And I knew that that was the rest of the night taken care of.

16

I was in a nightmare about my son, one of those ones where you know it's all in your head, but you can't get out of it. We were back on Wrathlin, and our son was dead and we were so devastated. Mouse was there, so I knew it wasn't real, and there was music in the background, from *The Omen*, which didn't help. Then miraculously my son was alive again, crying his little heart out in Mouse's arms, and we were so happy. Patricia and me and Mouse, we all hugged and kissed and bounced and the world was full of bright, vibrant colour and new, mystical Eastern sounds. Then as the images and sounds began to fade, the astonishing green of the island, the stiff, cool breeze, Patricia's laugh and Stevie's cry, I gradually became aware of our bedroom again, the vague furniture shapes in the dark and my wife's steady breathing, but there was still a vague memory of Little Stevie's crying. I didn't mind. It was comforting and familiar and I lay enveloped in its pleasant warmth, that lovely half-awake state that seems to last for ever.

Trish turned beside me, muttered something incomprehensible, then returned to sleep. I could still hear the crying. I listened, wondering if this was a dream within a dream. Then my wife of many years farted, and I realised it wasn't, but real, very real life; but the crying continued. Maybe it was a neighbour's baby and it was carrying in the silence of the night, the way a dog's bark will. Perhaps some anxious father was trying to distract a teething child by taking him out for an early morning walk. But it still seemed too close.

I rolled out of bed and padded across to the window. I slipped in behind the curtains and peered out.

And saw a Siamese cat in the middle of our soon-to-be-lawn. Moving in circles and crying like a baby. It pawed at the soil, hesitated, looked around, then pawed again.

Topper. Looking for little bro.

I turned from the window and slipped out of the room. I padded downstairs in my faded *Carpenter Joe* T-shirt and pair of black boxers. I opened the back door and hissed: 'Pssssss-wssssssss, fuck off!' and waved my arms. Topper just looked at me. It was early autumn and cold with it as I stepped out onto the damp concrete patio and repeated the warning. Topper crouched down, but still refused to move. I went back into the kitchen and spent five minutes trying to find where we'd put the pepper-grinder when we unpacked. When I finally located it I hurried back outside, only to find that Topper had vacated the scene. I crossed the lawn in my bare feet anyway – I am of that punk school which believes that wearing bedroom slippers is a clear indicator of approaching death – and began to grind the pepper over the soil. Maybe it was an old wives' tale about cats and pepper, but I had to do something. I laid it on good and thick around where I supposed we had buried Toodles, though since we'd had some heavy rain in the past few days, the first shoots of grass were now beginning to pop up, and the ground had taken on a more uniform appearance so it was difficult to tell exactly where that grave was. I emptied the container nevertheless, then turned back to the house. I glanced up in time to catch my neighbour staring out of his bedroom window. He quickly ducked back in behind his curtains. I continued up the garden, trying not to imagine the conversation he was probably having with his wife. According to the clock on the kitchen wall it was 4.35 a.m. A perfectly reasonable time to be out peppering your garden.

An hour later and I was dressed and armed with coffee and sitting at the kitchen table looking at the seven names on the list Patrick and Stephen had drawn up. The important thing to remember was that it wasn't a list of suspects. It was just some names for me to think about. Neither was it a Rich List. Even calling it a Power List was a bit of a misnomer, because although several of the names were undoubtedly powerful in the traditional sense, others were only there because they were cool and trendy or had somehow captured the public's imagination in the preceding twelve months. They might still be there next year, or have disappeared back into well-deserved obscurity.

The first of the seven potential newcomers to the *Belfast Confidential* Power List then was the singer Kieren Kitt. He had been one fifth of West Bell, a boy band who'd chalked up half a dozen chart hits, before being thrown out after confessing to a drug habit in . . . *Belfast Confidential*. But instead of disappearing off the radar, he'd cleaned up, signed a solo deal and was now a huge star all across Europe. He was coining it in, although he still hadn't cracked America, where the really big bucks were. According to the boys' brief notes, the only dirt we had on him was that he insisted on a songwriting credit on his hits, even though he'd never written a note or a word in his life. I knew enough about the history of pop music to know that this was pretty common practice – because it was the songwriters who made the big money, not the performers.

The second name was Patrick O'Brien, owner of *Past Masters*, just about Belfast's only private members' club. The boys had written: *Exclusive, snobby, expensive, but the place to be seen. Mouse was a member, and quite a few off the Power List as well. O'Brien likes to give the impression of being loaded, but Companies House shows he's just about breaking even.*

The third name was Christopher 'Concrete' Corcoran – and the first name so far at which I could have pointed the finger and shouted, 'He did it!' without having a shred of evidence to connect him. Concrete was a West Belfast hard man, equally at home with bomb or bullet who, when things got too hot for him in the city, moved to the country where, instead of retiring to tend cows, he set about putting the 'Bandit' into 'Bandit Country'. The end of the fighting had proved a windfall for him. Buying a farm which literally straddled the border, he'd found a hundred ways to use its position to smuggle goods back and forth – petrol, DVDs, computers, guns – whatever was cheaper on one side or the other.

With the Army mostly gone, and police checkpoints politically contentious, Concrete had had virtually free rein for a few years to build up his many and nefarious businesses. The cops were at last making some kind of an effort to put him away, but he was difficult to pin down. He claimed he was just a farmer trying to make an honest living. I knew all of this not just from working as a journalist, but because it was common knowledge. The boys' note merely said he was thought to be responsible for one in every three CDs and DVDs sold in the Province, and almost half of all the designer-label clothes available in the country were probably bootleg copies imported by him.

The fourth name was Jacintha Ryan. In brackets after it, the boys had merely written: *Cars!* Production of her high-spec sports car, the RA Jet, was due to begin once her state-of-the-art factory was built in West Belfast. She'd told me she was 'giving something back' to the land of her birth. She was rich and successful and Mouse, driving about the city in his proto-type Jet, was one of the best adverts she could have.

The fifth name was Liam Miller, and my first thought was that the boys were joking, because Miller was the kind of card-carrying charlatan that gave card-carrying charlatans a bad name. He had allegedly trained as a psychiatrist, but had developed into a kind of all-round lifestyle guru with his own UTV chat show – 'the empowerment hour' he called it – dispensing medical, social, DIY, gardening and horoscopic advice in a twee, ingratiating manner which had, inexplicably, become hugely popular. People really loved it, and many a slack-jawed woman lived her life according to Liam Miller's pronouncements. If you didn't get enough of the TV show, he was also constantly on sell-out tour, and if you couldn't make the gig there was always the book *Men Are From Mars, Women Are From Donaghadee*. He was a purely local phenomenon, and I suppose you had to admire him for what he had achieved with such obviously limited talents. Trish swore by him. 'There's that fucker on TV again,' she would say. Was he the sort to phone Mouse up and say: *'Stop your fucking interfering or you're a dead bunny'*? More likely: *'Stop your blessed interfering or I'll come round and pebble-dash your house.'*

Numero six was the ex-Liverpool striker Terry Breene. I'm a Liverpool fan, so Terry, the boy from the backstreets of Belfast who went on to wear the number ten shirt at Anfield, was always a bit of a hero. That was in the early 1980s, of course. His career was finished by injury prematurely, and he drifted for a few years, became a fixture of the tabloids for his sex 'n' drugs 'n' easy listening lifestyle before cleaning up and getting back into football, managing a succession of smaller English clubs with varying degrees of success, including one (losing)

FA Cup Final. After his last club fired him he'd lain low for a while before suddenly re-emerging in Belfast, using his not-inconsiderable fortune to purchase Linfield Football Club, that fiercely Protestant outfit which plays at our national stadium, Windsor Park. Like all new managers and owners he had predicted a bright new future for the club, but it was early days yet. Good material for the Power List? Well, potentially. Anything against Mouse? No idea.

The final name was the one I'd written. May Li. We would have to tread carefully. I'd already asked the boys to run a background check on her, but it wouldn't do any harm to check her out myself. Feed her a few glasses of wine, see if I could loosen her tongue at all. Maybe she'd let something slip, maybe . . .

'Dan?' I snapped around to find Trish standing in the doorway. 'What are you doing?' she asked.

'Nothing,' I said.

'You're staring into the void and you've got that kind of ecstatic look you get when you're lost in a sexual fantasy.'

I laughed. 'Bollocks. I'm thinking about murder.'

'Well, whatever turns you on.' She came across the kitchen, tying her dressing-gown, then filling the kettle again. She yawned. 'So, how's it going?'

I turned the sheet of paper round to show her. 'Well,' I said, 'I've narrowed it down to the seven names I started with.'

She secured the page with one hand, and ran a finger down the list. When she came to Liam Miller she looked up at me and said, 'If Liam Miller didn't do it, can we frame him anyway?'

'That seems fair.'

She smiled and started to move away, then stopped and came back. She lifted up the Bic pen I'd been doodling with and wrote another name at the end of the list. She turned it round for me to see.

'Wendy McBride?'

She nodded. 'The wronged wife. A woman scorned and all that. Aren't most murders domestics anyway?'

They were, but I still couldn't see it. 'Trish, come on. She's a bit of a dragon, but I don't think she's up to killing her husband.'

'Well, dragons breathe fire, don't they?' She returned to the sink, made her coffee and began to tramp back upstairs. 'Are you coming up?' she asked wearily, then stifled another yawn.

'No, I've a murder to solve.'

'All right, Sherlock,' she said.

17

When I left for work that morning, Topper was sitting in his front garden, sneezing hard. I gave him a *'Pssssss-wssssss, psssss-wsssss-wsssss'* as I passed just to show that there were no hard feelings and he coughed something up in response. As I drove away I caught a glimpse of Georgie, the wife, picking the Siamese up and stroking him, and her husband standing beside her, watching me go. It was kind of creepy. They were too nice, too well-defined. They were probably devotees of the cult of Liam Miller. Like a Satanic cult, but worse. If cleanliness is next to godliness, then fucking feng shui and designer breads are the work of a bigger, badder devil. This thought gave me a kind of sad, sick feeling, because I knew that sooner or later I was going to have to go and meet the annoying little guru himself. He was on the list, and I intended to talk to them all, face to face.

I reached the office at 8.30 with the intention of being the first one through the door, setting an example, but they were nearly all already there. Mary brought me the morning post which she'd already opened and organised in her version of its order of importance. On the top there was a gold embossed invitation on black card with a haunting-looking illustration of a puppet-like character in a mask. It read: *Jacintha Ryan and Ryan Auto invite the Editor of* Belfast Confidential *to a Masked Ball at Belfast City Hall to mark the start of Project Jet.* There was a date just over a week hence.

'Christ,' I said, 'a Masked Ball. There's two feet in the twenty-first century for you.'

'I think it would be fan*tastic.*'

I pushed the invitation across the desk to her. 'Be my guest.' She reached for it, and I pulled it back. 'If you can set up interviews for me with the following . . .' and I gave her the list, first taking a moment to stroke out, colour in and generally make indecipherable May Li's and Wendy's names. She examined it briefly, rolling her eyes at each name. 'You'll be lucky,' she said. Then her eyes fell on the photos I'd been examining for a swimsuit feature we were going to run in the next issue. They'd been shot up on the Strand in Portstewart. 'Jesus, where'd they take those?' she asked. 'Their goosebumps are bigger'n my nipples.'

I was still trying to get to grips with that image when Pat came in and said he had a copy of Mouse's post mortem.

'The press release? Yeah, I saw.'

'No, the Full Monty.'

'I'm impressed.'

Clearly he wasn't as toothless as Toothless. He didn't volunteer where he'd gotten it and I didn't ask. There were seven pages, and I hardly understood a word of them. 'Whoever got you this, I hope they explained it to you.'

Pat nodded. 'It's pretty gruesome stuff, but basically, yes, it confirms the earlier release which stated that the burns were what killed him. He was tied hand and foot. No evidence of other injuries.'

'Okay,' I said. 'Thanks.' He wasn't finished, but he looked awkward about continuing. 'What?'

'Page seven.'

I turned to the last page and perused it without anything striking me. Pat came and pointed it out. 'Cocaine in his system.'

'Mouse?' I thought about it for a moment. His drug of choice had always been Harp. But his circumstances had changed so dramatically over the past couple of years, there was no reason why his choice of relaxant shouldn't have changed as well. 'How much?' I asked.

'Heavy enough, according to my man, but not an overdose. Nothing lethal.'

'Did you know he partook?'

'Well, it kind of goes with the territory. You know, the whole media, showbiz set.'

'And do you use it?'

That surprised him.

'Me?' He cleared his throat. 'Well, I, ah, well, I mean . . .'

'I'll take that as a yes. What about Mouse, did he have a dealer?'

'Yeah, I suppose.'

'In here?'

'Here? Well, I, ah, wouldn't exactly . . .' He saw where I might be going with it, and panicked suddenly. 'It wasn't me!'

'Who then?'

'I don't know!'

I gave him a hard look, then lifted the phone and dialled Stephen's extension. He answered on the third ring. 'Stephen? Pat says you're the office coke-dealer.'

'The bastard!'

'Get up here now.'

As he thundered through the door Pat stared at him, wide-eyed, and shouted, 'I never said a thing! Swear to God!'

'Yeah! Right! You fucking—' Stephen seemed to remember me then. 'Well? You pay fuck-all wages, I have to do some-thing.' He took a deep breath. 'I'm fired then, am I?'

'No, Stephen. We're just trying to establish Mouse's drug intake.'

'I'm not fired?'

'Not yet. Was he really into it?'

Stephen shook his head. 'He thought he was, but he wasn't. I'm not either. It's just social use, and a couple of friends, you know?'

'What about May Li?'

'A little.'

'You ever see them take it together?'

'I don't really move in their circles. But once, yes – down at *Past Masters*.'

'The club?'

'Aye, in their VIP room. They took me down one night, more as a driver than anything. It was just innocent fun, you know.'

'I'm sure it was.'

'I've never taken it at work, Boss.'

'Okay.'

'I swear to God.'

'All right.'

'If you want me to enter some sort of a programme . . .'

'That won't be necessary.'

His brow furrowed in confusion. 'What sort of a boss are you?'

I shrugged.

'You're supposed to set an example.'

'Excuse me?'

'You should throw me out on my ear for dealing in the work-place. But you hardly bat an eyelid.'

'Well, I'm not your mum, you know?'

Stephen smiled across at Patrick. 'Well then – great. Ahm, do you want a spliff?'

I took a deep, invigorating breath. I clasped my hands and gave a gentle shake of my head. 'Don't get me wrong,' I said. 'What you do on your own time is your affair, but you keep it out of the office, and you turn up on time, and you do your work. All right?'

'All right,' said Stephen.

'Right, Boss,' said Pat.

As they went down the stairs, I heard them laughing. It wasn't a nasty kind of a laugh though, just buoyant with disbelief. I wasn't trying to be Mr Dead-on Trendy Boss. I had a magazine to produce and a murder to solve, and the simple fact of the matter was that I needed them.

18

Despite its name, I'd expected the *Past Masters* exclusive private members club to be a chic, post-modernist chrome and mirrors effort. In reality they'd taken three four-storey houses at the back of Great Victoria Street and knocked them into one. This would have been all right if the houses had been constructed to the same design, or they'd kept the façade and hollowed out the rest, but they'd gone the opposite way: new façade, and kept more or less to the original interiors, which were clearly from different pages of the architect's handbook. One side of the new, unified building was all narrow corridors and hidden alcoves, the central section boosted big, spacious rooms that were bathed in light from wide windows back and front, while the third was kind of a mix of both, which gave the whole complex an odd, higgledy-piggledy effect.

I pointed this out to Patrick O'Brien as he gave me a pre-lunch tour of the premises and he gave an exaggerated, 'Exactly! That's the point. Do you never have one of those days where you want to keep your head down in a dark room? And then an hour later you want space and light and air? We have all of that!'

'Or perhaps you just couldn't afford to have it all done to one design.'

'Oh, so cynical! It's a good job you've got free life member-ship, or I'd charge you double.'

'I have free life membership?'

'Well, more accurately, the Editor and owner of *Belfast Confidential* will always have free life membership – you're our recruitment officer, you are!'

He laughed, and continued the tour. He was in his mid-thirties, slicked-back hair, sunglasses glinting out of it, a black suit, white open-necked shirt. I complimented him on the black suit and its nice small lapels – a hatred of big lapels was another of my hangovers from punk days – and he opened the jacket and showed me that it was an Armani. 'You can never go wrong with Armani,' he said, and I thought, Well, you probably can if Concrete Corcoran is supplying it, and the chances were he probably was.

Another thing – I'd expected a lot of modern art on the walls, but he'd gone for bog standard landscapes. I pointed this out. Patrick stopped me beside one of the canvases on the stairs on our way to the restaurant. He waved his arm across it: 'This one's called *Hills, Trees and Bushes Outside Ballymena.*'

'So?' I said.

He smiled and said, 'Look a little closer.'

I studied the painting. I spotted hills, and trees and bushes, but I'd have to take the artist's word for it that it was outside Ballymena. I looked back to Patrick and shrugged. 'What?'

He pointed. Right in the middle, amongst the trees, I almost literally couldn't see the wood for the trees. But I could now see a giraffe.

'That's a fucking giraffe,' I said.

'I know.'

'In Ballymena?'

'Outside it. He's a very unusual artist. You should check him out for your Power List.'

Not unusual, I thought. A weirdo. But nevertheless I resolved never to think of him again.

O'Brien guided me into the restaurant, which was all dark wood and stained wooden floors. He handed me a menu and I was pleasantly relieved to see it was not only in English, but that most of the dishes were familiar. He saw me nodding appreciatively and said, 'Our chef's from up the road. Didn't see the point in bringing someone in from France or wherever. The clientèle we attract, you know they're always off at business meetings and they have to eat all this modern crap. When they come home here, they might just want pie and chips, you know what I mean?'

A waitress – blonde, tight black top, Eastern European accent, brought me a Harp poured into a pint glass they kept in the freezer. I ordered the aforementioned pie and chips and said, 'So business must be good?'

O'Brien nodded thoughtfully. He gave me a look, he raised an eyebrow. I raised one back and said, 'What?'

He said, 'You're enjoying this, aren't you?'

'Enjoying what?'

'Keeping me on tenterhooks.'

'Am I keeping you on tenterhooks?'

'You bet your bollocks you are. Come on, I'm not going to enjoy my lunch unless you tell me.'

I took a long drink of Harp and said, 'Tell you what?'

'Christ!' he exploded, although not in an angry way. 'You just love this, don't you? Come on, tell me! Are we in or not?'

And then the penny dropped. The Power List. I set the glass down. 'It's important to you, is it?'

'Of course it is! Look – look.' He opened his jacket and removed several folded pages. He opened them up. It was a photocopy of last year's list. He quickly flicked through the pages, pointing and saying, 'Look, there . . . there . . . here,' at entries he had previously circled in red. 'They're all members, this is *the* place to be seen, to have meetings; decisions are made here which shape this little city of ours. We really have to be on your list.'

The food arrived. We both sat back while a different waitress, but also blonde with a tight black jumper, laid it before us.

'What did Mouse say?' I asked.

'Mouse, God rest his soul, gave a clear indication that we were in.'

'He was a regular here?'

'Yes, he was. Two or three lunches a week, three, sometimes four nights.'

'With his wife?'

'At night? Sure. Not so much during the day.'

'I heard he liked a little snifter after dinner.'

'Snifter?' I touched the side of my nose. 'Oh – right. Well, I couldn't really say. We have a strict anti-drugs policy here, Dan.'

'So if I wanted a line right now, you'd throw me out.'

'I would ask you to retire to the privacy of our men's room.'

'Out of sight, out of mind.'

'Something like that.'

'Is there much of it goes on? I mean, London, New York, I can imagine, but I always thought of Belfast as, you know, a couple of Paracetamol being the limit.'

O'Brien laughed. 'Oh, you should get out more, Dan.' I shrugged. He said, 'Looking at you, I'd say you still think dope's a bit dangerous and Ecstasy's right up there with crack cocaine.'

'Well, isn't it?'

He smiled indulgently. The pie was good. Their chips were chips. He said, 'So?'

'So?'

'The Power List?'

'Well,' I said, 'it's obviously important to your business.'

'Yes, it is.'

'Which, according to our information, isn't going tremendously well.'

His sunny demeanour suddenly faded a little. 'Where did you hear that?'

'We research all of our entries thoroughly, you know that.'

'But you're not going to print that we're in difficulties?'

'Are you in difficulties?'

'No! But if you say that it isn't going well . . . As Liam says, "Negativity breeds negativity – banish it!"'

'That's what Liam says,' I agreed.

'So you can't print that.'

'Can't.'

'I mean, it would be worse than not appearing at all, appearing negatively. We're just a new business, it takes time to get to profit, you know that. Our membership's growing, our word of mouth is fantastic, but if *Belfast Confidential* includes us, we'd be eternally grateful, Dan.'

'In what sense?'

He put his knife and fork down and lifted his glass of white wine. 'In whatever sense you like,' he said without looking at me, but allowing his eyes to wander across the half-full restaurant. But he looked back to see what my reaction was. I keep a poker face in my bag for emergencies, so I slipped it on. 'Dan – it's how it works, isn't it? You scratch my back, I'll scratch yours.'

'Like the Masons,' I said.

'Exactly. But without the handshakes.' The waitress came to take my plate away. I said thanks. O'Brien said, 'Whatever you want, it's yours,' and his eyes flitted to her curvaceous rear end as it proceeded towards the kitchens.

I smiled.

He smiled.

I said, 'When's the last time Mouse was here?'

'Night he died. That's why I was so shocked to hear about it. One minute he's eating his dinner, and the next . . .' O'Brien blew air out of his cheeks. 'Well, you know.'

'Who did he dine with?'

'I'm not sure. Tell you the truth, I didn't actually see him, but he was signed in.'

'Can you check?'

'Of course.' He stood up and walked over to the maitre d'; they talked for a few moments, then they both disappeared into the kitchen. I counted waitresses for a while, then he came back and lifted his napkin as he sat down. 'He ate with Terry Breene.'

'The footballer.'

'The footballer. Mouse was booked in for five-thirty. Although when I say he ate, he only had a starter, a Caesar salad. Terry Breene had a prawn cocktail, a T-bone steak with a Béarnaise sauce and a Black Mamba Gâteau.'

'Black Mamba?' I asked.

'It's really Black Forest, but we try to sex things up a bit, you know?' He gave a gentle laugh. 'Anyway, Terry Breene.'

'Is he a regular?'

'Like clockwork. Hang around, I'll introduce you. They finish training at three, he's usually here not long after.' O'Brien took a deep breath. 'So, what's it to be for dessert? Something from the menu, or something, ahm, *off* menu.' And his eyes winked back to the waitresses.

I cleared my throat and said, 'I'm not hungry right now, but maybe later.'

'Later it is then.' He extended his hand, and I shook it. 'So make yourself at home, treat it like your own place.'

'Seriously?'

He nodded, although I was sure that he didn't get my meaning, but that was okay; few people did.

There was a bar upstairs. I took out my mobile and for the next hour conducted the mundane business of running *Belfast Confidential* from a corner table with a window which over-looked a set of traffic-lights. I sipped another Harp and thought about how relaxing it was working like this, and I wondered if this was how Mouse had done it as well, enjoying a cold pint and trading space in his magazine for the pimped waitresses at *Past Masters*.

19

I was reasonably intoxicated when Terry Breene came in a little after three-thirty. He went straight to the bar and ordered a Bush. O'Brien had promised to introduce me, but he was nowhere to be seen, so I walked up as steadily as I could manage and said who I was, and he said, 'You're the cunt trying to put me in your cunting Power List.'

'Yep,' I said.

'Well, you can go and fuck yourself.'

'Ah, if only,' I said.

He was in his early fifties, but looked about ten years older. Having a liver transplant can do that to you: make you sallow, and thin, with wispy hair like straw, but he'd once been voted Sexiest Man in the Universe, so even at his worst he still made handsome men look like they'd been beaten with the ugly stick. He knew it, women knew it, I knew it. He gave me a hard stare, then stepped around me and walked up to the table where I'd been sitting. He turned and shouted back at the blonde, tight-black-jumpered bargirl: 'Who's sitting at my fucking table?!'

'That would be me,' I said. I'd left half a pint, my mobile and a notebook sitting there. He gave me another tough look then sat down. He took a mouthful of his whiskey, then said, 'So what's this about?'

I managed to keep my smile in check. He was like any star who'd become a media fixture – on the one hand decrying his lack of privacy, and on the other desperately craving its attention. With the passing years the media's focus had shifted to the next generation, leaving the likes of Terry Breene out in the cold. So on the surface he was biting my head off, but really, he wanted to talk. I didn't mind. He was a Liverpool legend. I'd been a member of his fan club.

I said, 'I used to have your poster on my wall.'

'Used to?'

'Well, when I got married I had to take it down.'

'Aye, bloody women.'

'No – it's a gay marriage, but he still wouldn't allow me.'

His mouth dropped open a fraction, and for a moment he seemed genuinely lost. So I smiled and said, 'Only rakin'.'

He laughed then, but the laugh morphed into a long hacking cough, which he tried to stifle by inhaling a thick cigar. It wasn't entirely successful. When he was finished he rubbed at his chest, then ordered me another drink. I protested, although not very strongly, that I already had one. 'So what brings you back to Belfast?' I asked.

'I think you know that.'

'Yeah, but – I mean, London's where it's happening. Hardly anyone ever comes back here – and you've been gone thirty years.'

'Aye, well, it's still home though, know what I mean? And I was given this chance to take over Linfield.' He took a sip of his drink. I kept looking at him. 'And after the liver op, and all the publicity about my drinking, and cursing like fuck live on national TV, I'm pretty much in the Last Chance Saloon, so I thought, What the fuck, you only live twice, and you can't fucking take it with you, so let's take a chance on this.'

'And now that you're here?'

'Well, it's great. I mean, it's unrecognisable this place, ain't it? No soldiers, no roadblocks, no bombs, everything's dead modern, a bit flash, there's stacks of money around. You see the cars out there? Porsches, Ferraris, and once those new wee beauties get going . . .'

'The Jet.'

'The fucking Jet – name down for one of them, so I have. Brilliant. So yeah, it's pretty cool.'

'That may be, but Linfield?'

'Dream come true.'

'To manage an Irish League side?'

'Absolutely. See, I was – am – a Catholic, so my da never allowed me to go and see Linfield. I never got into hurley or anything, it was always a case of the grass is always greener. Or red white and blue, depending on your point of view.'

'Well. Fair enough. I just supposed you'd have bigger dreams.'

'It's all about potential, Dan.'

'The only potential they've previously shown is as a recruiting ground for the UDA. What's changed?'

'Europe, son, Europe.'

'They've never gotten beyond the first round.'

'Not yet. But that'll change. Look – I've built up a tidy wee nest egg, right, but not enough to go out and buy the likes of Liverpool or Newcastle or, heaven forbid, Coventry or Nottingham Forest. But at a stretch I've bought the home team in my home town. And you know what that gives me?'

'Depression?'

'The gateway to Europe. Look, take England. If you're a Premier League club, you've got to finish in the top four to get into the Champions League, right, which is where all the money is. That could cost you hundreds of millions and take you what, three, four years to buy in the right team and get them working together. But, no offence to the Irish League, it's dead easy to win, and all you have to do is invest a couple of million in the ground and a few thousand on a handful of ex-Premier League stars who're past their best, but still good enough to run circles around the locals. So you win that and you're in the qualifying rounds of the Champions League. All you have to do then is win a couple of *those* matches and you're into the League proper, and then you start to rake the millions in, depending on the draw. So you make money, you buy better players, and each year you qualify for Europe again and each year you do a little better, and you earn more money. It's like what that Liam Miller says, "success begets success; you just have to wrap your thighs around it."'

'He does,' I said. 'It sounds easy.'

He laughed. 'Well, that's the theory.'

'And if it doesn't pan out that way?'

'It will. I've worked it out. I've got a good team together.'

'And if it doesn't, you can still sell Windsor Park for houses.'

'You said that, I didn't.'

I signalled the bar, and they brought us some more drinks. 'Do you really object to being on the Power List?' I asked.

'Couldn't give a fuck one way or the other.'

'So what were you meeting Mouse about? The night he died.'

The waitress set the drinks down. Terry looked at her admiringly, and she smiled back extravagantly. I smiled at her and she ignored me. Terry took a sip from his new drink, then swirled the rest in his glass. 'Because he asked me to.'

'What do you mean?'

'I was in the bar when he came in and I recognised him from the press conference to launch our project. We got talking and he asked me to join him for dinner.'

'Simple as that.'

'Simple as that. Look, I've been gone from Belfast for the best part of three decades. I don't actually know anyone here any more.'

'You were lonely?'

'Not lonely, no. Just . . . sometimes it's good to talk to someone who isn't, you know, wanking all over you.'

'What about your players?'

'Well, it's not good to mix with them socially – fucks with the discipline. You need to keep them at arm's length. They can't afford it in here anyway!' He laughed. Swirled his drink some more.

'Who can?'

'*They* can.' I followed his gaze across the bar. Two men in grey pin-striped suits had just walked in. They carried brief-cases and the authority of bean counters on an expense account. 'Accountants,' said Terry, '*my* fucking accountants.' They began to scan the bar, obviously looking for him. 'Better be off,' he said, quickly finishing his drink and standing. 'See you around, mate.'

He hurried across to the suits, and extended his hand. They disappeared back out of the bar, and with the swinging of the doors I was able to see them head upstairs towards one of the private rooms O'Brien had shown me earlier. I sat for a while longer. I was enveloped in a warm glow, and it wasn't just the alcohol. My football hero had just called me 'mate', and it felt good, and I began to appreciate a little bit how Mouse must have felt, mixing with the celebs. But then I remembered that that mixing might well have led to his death, and that for all of his undoubted talent as a footballer, Terry Breene, thanks to a road-crash victim's liver, wasn't much more than a born again alcoholic with his eye on the main chance. He'd also just lied to me about his dinner with Mouse being an accident. It was in the appointments book that Mary carried everywhere. Next to it was a note that said: *Remind not to eat too much! Friends later!*

Friends indeed.

Outside, waiting for a taxi, I phoned Patricia and told her how much I loved her, and she said, 'Great, you're pissed again.'

I said it was all in the line of work and she gave a sarcastic laugh. 'So if you're getting a taxi home, why are you calling me?'

'Just to let you know I'm safe and sound and I'll be home soon.'

'More like to make sure your dinner's on the table.'

'The thought hadn't crossed my mind. Although if by chance . . .'

'Your boss called.'

'May Li?'

'No, the Belly Telly. It seems you gave them a sick line for a few days, and you haven't been back.'

'Oh that. Aye.'

'It seems that you never told them that you were taking on *Belfast Confidential*.'

'I was keeping my options open.'

'They say you're an arse, and I'm inclined to agree.'

'I'm on a freelance contract! What're they getting their knickers in a twist about?'

'"Common courtesy" and "loyalty" were some of the words being bandied about.'

'Shit, Trish, c'mon. I just didn't know how long I'd last with this thing. If it wasn't going to be any more than a couple of days there was no point in letting on, was there?'

'And you didn't think they'd find out? It being the best-selling magazine in the history of best-selling magazines?'

I shrugged. She couldn't see the shrug, but she probably guessed. I said, 'Sorry. But if it's any consolation I just got drunk with Terry Breene and he's my new best mate.'

'No, Dan, that's no consolation at all.' She fell quiet. I said sorry again. She sighed. 'You can't just treat people in such a cavalier fashion.'

'I know that.'

'You'd better call them and apologise.'

'I will.'

'Promise?'

'Promise.'

'Okay. So when will you be home?'

'Ten minutes, tops.'

'Okay.' She cut the line.

A taxi finally pulled up and I climbed in. The woman behind the wheel ducked down a little to look up at the *Past Masters* entry. 'So *that's* the fucking place. Top ho, what!'

There was something vaguely familiar about her. Her hair was short and spiky, and she was wearing a cap-sleeve T-shirt with tattoos clearly visible on each arm, although what they depicted was impossible to decipher due to their crapness. Despite the vehicle being plastered in No Smoking signs, she had an unfiltered fag in her mouth, with an inch of ash hanging off the end.

'Where to?' she asked, and I gave her the address. As she drove, she kept looking at me in the mirror. I tried to ignore it. I'd had a lot to drink and my eyes were heavy, and the gentle movement of the vehicle was making me feel sick. I was just moving towards the Land of Nod, but before I could claim citizenship she let out a whoop and said, 'It is you! Fucking Starkey, right?'

I nodded warily.

'Fuck sake, I gave you a ride about ten years ago. Not that sort of a ride, this sort of a ride. You were in my cab before all that stuff blew up. Remember?'

I hated to admit it, but I did. She was the Belle of Belfast City.

'So you're hanging out with all the fuckin' nobs now, are you?'

'Not exactly.'

'I never see your fuckin' name in the fuckin' paper any more.'

'No, I—'

'I mean, I never used to fuckin' read it, like, but my ould fella, he used to love it.'

'That's nice.'

'Aye, and so was he, then he fuckin' two-timed me, so I turfed him out.'

'Oh.'

'Fuckin' dead loss he was. So what're you doing now?'

'I'm a . . . well, *Belfast Confidential*.'

'Seriously? Fuckin' class. I love that. All the fuckin' movers and shakers, eh? All the fuckin' tit jobs and them wankers tryin' to pull a fuckin' fast one. Wouldn't miss it. And you work for them? Fuckin' brilliant.'

I nodded wearily. Her eyes met mine in the mirror. 'You married still?'

'Last time I checked.'

'*Last time I checked.* I like that. I'm fuckin' playin' the field, you know what I mean?' I nodded again. 'No use fuckin' tyin' yourself down – different fella every week.'

'No,' I said.

'Keep them on their toes, you know? I said to this fuckin' guy last night – I'd just given him a blow job like and he was all, "I love you, I love you, I love you" – I said, "One swallow doesn't make a summer, mate, know what I mean?"'

I cleared my throat, and this time closed my eyes and nodded vaguely, and she seemed to get the hint and concentrated on the driving for a while.

Next thing, I felt a hand clamp onto my leg, and a nicotine-tinged voice purring, 'Wakey, wakey,' as I jolted upright.

'Sorry, I . . .'

She removed her hand from my leg, and I tried to massage some life back into it. 'Four seventy-five,' she said.

I rummaged in my pocket, and gave her a fiver. As I climbed out I said, 'Keep the change.' I closed the door, and then stood there in some confusion. I knelt down to her open window. 'This isn't—'

'It's what you fuckin' asked for,' she snapped.

'But I don't live here. If you could just take me—' I went to open the door again, but she flicked on the lock. Her head appeared through the window; the ash was by now almost down to her lips. She looked up at the overcast sky. 'Is it raining, or did a bird shit on my face?'

I said, 'What?'

'Thanks for the big tip! Once a wanker, always a fucking wanker!' Then she rolled up the window again and sped off.

I stood in the middle of the road, watching her go.

I had my mobile, and I could easily have called another taxi.

Or I could have walked. However, I didn't have the brains, or gumption, to do either. You see, the subconscious is an occasionally wonderful thing. It had clearly brought me to this address for a reason, and now that I was here, I had to find out what that was. Clearly it had nothing to do with my advanced state of inebriation. Something deeper. So I marched right up to May Li's front door and rang the bell.

20

'Howdy pardner,' I said, just as the first true wave of nausea hit me.

May Li was in a flowered silk bathrobe, with her hair tied up. I was in a black, zip-up bomber jacket and black jeans and trainers. She had a surprised, then quizzical look on her face, and I must have just looked a bit gormless, and green.

'Dan?'

'I was just passing,' I said, my head now beginning to spin, 'and I thought you needed dated. Updated.' I lurched forward suddenly, cupping my hand over my mouth and gasping through it, 'Can I use your bog?'

'My . . .'

I charged past her up the stairs and threw up in her bathroom sink.

It would have been an idea to remove the bra soaking in bleach first, or indeed to use the toilet, but it was any port in a storm. It was the taxi ride, and maybe the *Past Masters* pie was past its sell-by date. That, or the unthinkable. That I was becoming allergic to alcohol. Or to be more strictly accurate, allergic to huge great amounts of it.

I was getting older, I couldn't cope with it any more.

May Li stood on the landing and said, 'Are you okay?'

I made a groaning sound and reached back with my foot,

gently pushing the bathroom door closed. A man has to have some dignity.

'Do you want me to call Patricia?' May Li asked through the wood.

'No,' I managed. 'That would not . . . be a good idea.'

She left me alone for ten minutes. Then she came back and knocked gently. 'Are you feeling any better?'

'Yeah . . . yeah. Thanks. I'll be . . . down in a minute.'

It was no word of a lie. I was feeling slightly better. I was reclaiming a toe-hold on an eternally spinning planet. As she padded quietly away I just managed to lift my head off the sink. I examined my reflection. Bleary-eyed and pale, but otherwise as stunning as ever. I looked back down at the sink. I pulled the plug and the water drained away, leaving a thick coating of vomit around the rim and all over May Li's lacy white bra.

I had kind of imagined encountering May Li's bra, unlikely fantasies being the justifiable preserve of the married man, but not boking on it. Boking was one thing, but explaining, justifying and worst of all, cleaning the offending lingerie presented a whole different range of problems. Avoiding the issue though, is a bit of a male art form, so I carefully lifted the offending article by its strap, briefly admiring the cup size, while allowing some of the vomit to drip off so that it wouldn't get on the carpet. Then I rushed across to the bathroom window, opened it up, then hurled the bra out as far as I could.

I returned to the sink and rinsed around the basin. I splashed water on my own face; I gargled with her mouthwash and then sprayed some of her deodorant around. Satisfied, I made my way downstairs. May was sitting on her leather sofa with her legs folded under her, looking concerned.

I sat opposite her. There was a glass table between us.

'Sorry,' I said. 'Something I ate.'

'I made you some coffee,' she said, and leaned forward to pick up a cup. Her bathrobe fell open a little, and after five minutes I averted my eyes. She moved her hand across to secure it, but she caught me looking, and I knew that she had caught me, and she knew that I knew that she knew.

'Thank you,' I said, for the coffee as opposed to the view, although it was pretty marvellous as well. 'Thai?' I asked after my first sip.

'Nescafé.'

I nodded. 'Good stuff.'

She looked at me, I looked back. She said, 'I was just opening a bottle of wine, but you probably don't need any more.'

I put my coffee down and said, 'Hair of the dog.'

Her brow furrowed, and I explained about hair of the dog. It was a long rambling explanation which involved going off on many tangents and entering a bewildering number of cul-de-sacs, but she listened attentively until I'd exhausted myself, and then she asked, 'Do you want a glass?' and I said yes.

We sipped our wine. A better man might have reflected that this young woman had recently been tragically widowed, and that her dead husband was my lifelong friend, but then a better man wouldn't have come here in the first place, and even if he had, he would have come armed with a better excuse for being there, and he wouldn't have thrown up on her bra.

I told her what had been happening at the magazine, and how I thought it was going quite well, considering. She asked about the Power List and I explained about the names we'd come up with as possible suspects. I asked her if any of them meant anything to her, and she said she'd been there when Mouse went to pick up his Jet from the airport, and that Jacintha Ryan had spoken to Mouse over a speakerphone from her office in America.

147

'What was she like?' I asked.

'Distant,' said May Li, with a smile. 'Professional.'

'In what sense?'

'That American have-a-nice day thing, you know? She had her man here take us out for dinner. He treated us well.'

'Where was this?'

'*Past Masters*. It's convenient and it's private, and they don't let civilians in.'

'Civilians as in ordinary plonkers like me.'

'You're not a civilian any more, Dan. You're a – what do they say? – mover and shaker.'

'Thanks to you. You go there much?'

'Not since . . .'

'But before, you were regulars?'

'I suppose, yes.'

'And I hear the coke's good.'

She hesitated, and a half-smile appeared. 'It's not a sin, Dan.'

'Well, technically, it *is* a sin.'

'You don't partake?'

'I'm not allowed.'

'Patricia?'

I shrugged. She smiled. Her legs were folded under her to the left, and now she shifted them to the right. The movement allowed the bottom half of her bathrobe to slip open. For just a second. It was the kind of moment you might freeze if it was a DVD, but it was too quick, and I was too drunk, and the lights were too subdued for it to be anything other than an accidental slip in the course of preventing her legs from cramping. I think. But then her eyes flitted to one side and she said kind of dreamily, 'The best sex you can have is cocaine sex, you can go all night.' Her eyes came back onto me.

'Ah,' I said. 'That would account for the orgasms then.' I

said it without thinking. My cheeks were reddening, and my T-shirt was stuck to my back. There's something terrible about being alone with a beautiful woman who mentions sex. Funny, crushing, mortifying, enticing. 'Mouse . . . ahm, was very happy. He didn't, ahm – mention the cocaine. I'm sure it's wonderful. You should – ah, try, ahm, Harp sex. You can go for entire minutes and you get a free migraine into the bargain.'

'Would you like some?' she asked.

'Sex?' I began, but then cleverly covered it with, 'What?'

'Coke. I have a little. Just to relax. After Mouse . . . it just helps. Will you join me?'

I gave a little shrug. 'Just to, you know, keep you company.'

She disappeared into the kitchen and came back with a small plastic bag, a steak-knife, a straw and a breadboard. She poured out the white powder and chopped it down and then took a long sniff. She squeezed her nostrils together and closed her eyes, then opened them again and smiled at me and offered me the straw. I have a strict rule about not putting things up my nose which have already been up other people's noses, but I compromised as I compromise with most things when confronted with no alternative or the opportunity. I sniffed up and she was just asking, 'How does that . . . ?' when everything went black.

21

It was getting on for dawn, and I was lying on the sofa with a tartan rug over me. My shoes were on and so were my trousers and T-shirt, and there was an empty basin and kitchen roll on the carpet beside me. I struggled up into a sitting position, and then bent down to pick up my head, which was made of concrete and needles, off the floor. I screwed it firmly back into place.

Christ.

Normally, at the newspaper, I would just phone in sick. But this was different. I was the boss, and in a few hours' time I had to send my first issue of *Belfast Confidential* to the printers. I still had to do what I'd been putting off for days: write an appreciation of Mouse. It was the lead article. There was a big white space waiting for it. There were twenty-six candid shots of his funeral already in place. It was kind of gross, but it was what I'd signed up for, and what the readers would expect.

I hauled myself up and staggered to the front door. It was raining steadily outside. I looked around for an umbrella, but couldn't see one. I pulled the door softly closed behind me and started walking. I could have made coffee and taken it up to her, but I didn't want to put her in the way of temptation. I could have sat downstairs and waited for a taxi, but really I just wanted out of there. I was not only consumed by guilt and embarrassment, I was chewed up and spat out by it. Also, I had the mother of all hangovers. I stopped twice to be sick.

I was having difficulty coping with alcohol, so I'd taken some cocaine to sort me out. There was some kind of epic madness to it which I might have appreciated if I'd been someone else. I had resolved, on setting out on this damp march, to never ever, ever drink again The cocaine went without saying. But, as ever, ever, ever, after walking for a while the rain and the cold and the exercise began to work on me. I decided I was being a little hasty in forever swearing off the drink. A few days to sort myself out, that was all I would need.

I took out my mobile. At some point I had foolishly switched it off. I checked my messages and saw that there were three, all from Patricia.

The first said, *'Where are you? Dinner's getting cold.'*

The second, an hour later, said, *'Dan, give me a buzz, will you?'*

The third, somewhere around 3 a.m. said, *'You wanker, don't even bother coming home.'*

I have spent many useful hours of my life desperately concocting believable excuses for things I have or have not done, but walking towards the city centre, damp, sick and feeling very, very stupid, I couldn't think of a bloody thing. It crossed my mind that it might be better just to tell Patricia the truth, and then I couldn't help but laugh out loud, because telling the truth has never, ever been a realistic option. Since when did the truth ever make things better? Lying and lying well was the answer. Another answer was the avoidance of confrontation, and a third was the total and complete denial of responsibility. In my favour I had the fact that Patricia should be well used to it by now. Apart from the time when we were separated, I have only once really and properly strayed, and that almost destroyed us. She knows that I am inclined to get myself into situations that usually end with me falling asleep. She has forgiven me countless times. This was no different. I was guilty only of drinking and falling over. That it was in a beautiful half-naked widow-on-coke's house was neither here nor there.

I got to the office at 7.30 a.m. Patrick and Stephen were already at their desks. I said, 'Don't you guys ever go home?'

And they said, together, 'Don't *you*?' and then explained that Patricia had been on the phone already.

I said, 'Oh. How did she sound?'

'Well, we've never spoken to her before,' said Patrick. 'But is she always that angry?'

'Not always,' I said, and then to change the subject quickly, followed it with, 'Are we nearly finished?'

'Just waiting on your article.'

I rolled my eyes.

Stephen held up a photo. I'd been looking at a lot of photos of blonde would-be models in the past few days, and at first this one didn't seem much different. *Belfast Confidential* employed a lot of non-agency girls for their photo shoots because they were cheaper and people seemed to prefer the girl-next-door look to the plastic production-line version. Although we didn't go in for nudity, we were still in the grip of that fashion look which favoured the exposure of the belly button, which meant we had a large stockpile of photos of blonde girls who'd eaten too many chips. But on closer inspection, this one looked a little classier. She had proper clothes on and her hair was in a neat pony tail and she had a nice smile; she wasn't looking directly at the camera, but concentrating on a Salman Rushdie novel. And there was something vaguely familiar about her.

'Ah,' I said. 'A bit of class at last.'

They exchanged glances. 'That's Jacintha Ryan,' said Patrick.

'Ryan's Jet Ryan?' They nodded. 'You're joking,' I said.

They laughed. I laughed.

'No, seriously,' I said. 'I saw her at a press conference the other day . . .'

'Seriously,' said Stephen, 'that's yer woman. Although it was taken about twenty years ago. She's what . . . forty-five now?'

Patrick nodded.

'Jesus,' I said, admiring the photo again, 'I really have fallen in with the beautiful people. She was gorgeous. And she's not bad now.'

'Well,' said Patrick, 'according to the people we've talked to, that beauty is only skin deep. They say she's as hard as nails. Doesn't suffer fools gladly. Will bite your head off and suck out your blood.'

'All qualities,' Stephen pointed out helpfully, 'that would be perfectly acceptable in a business*man*.'

I gave him a steady look and asked him if he was gay. He denied it, but then didn't help his case much by saying he'd just *die* for an invite to her masked ball. I said, 'Well, you're welcome to it, if you take Mary on your arm.' He didn't seem as distressed by this prospect as I would be. He kind of glowed at the thought of it. I took another look at Jacintha's photo. 'She's done well.'

Patrick passed me a second photograph which showed a more familiar version of Jacintha Ryan, taken in New York at the press conference with Frank Galvin that I'd witnessed from Hillsborough Castle. Frozen in a black and white photo, the First Minister looked rather smug. I suppose you can afford to look that way if you have the power to okay tens of millions of pounds of loans and tax incentives to attract something like the RA auto factory to West Belfast.

I said, 'Look at him – like butter wouldn't melt in his mouth. Didn't he pull some strings for her to get the land?'

'Oh yes,' said Stephen. ''Twas green, now 'tis brown i.e. there was this big whack of wasteland doing no one any good, but it was zoned green. Frankie boy Galvin thought it was better to have some nice American pump billions of dollars into our little economy than pay for the upkeep of three trees and a duckpond full of disused Tesco trolleys.'

'To be strictly accurate,' said Patrick, 'three trees, a duckpond and the yellow diamond daisy.'

'The what?' I asked.

'The yellow diamond daisy.'

'I heard you – just *no comprendez*.'

'This particular area is one of the only places in Ireland – nay the UK – where the yellow diamond daisy grows *au naturel*. That's why it got green status about twenty years ago.'

'I've never heard of the yellow diamond daisy.'

'That's because it's rare, and they try to keep it secret. But it's common knowledge among yellow diamond daisy aficionados.'

'Are you a yellow diamond daisy aficionado?'

'No, but I surf the internet a lot.'

'So what changed?'

'Well, someone picked the yellow diamond daisy.'

'Picked it? There was only one?'

'No, there were about a hundred and fifty, but someone picked them, and overnight the need to keep it green disappeared. Which was remarkably good timing, seeing as how there was a rich, hard-as-nails American just looking at exactly that plot of land.'

'You're not suggesting . . .'

Stephen held up his hands. 'Perish the thought. Although

there are yellow diamond daisy aficionados who will tell you otherwise.' I gave him a look. He said, 'No, really. There's a group of them tried to cause a stink about it, but one thousand jobs for beleaguered West Belfast seemed somehow more appealing.'

'I see,' I said. 'Was Mouse particularly attached to the yellow diamond daisy?'

'I think he was more attached to his Jet,' said Stephen.

'But you never know,' added Patrick. 'He was a bit of a dark horse.'

I had to agree.

In fact, not only was he a bit of a dark horse, he was almost entirely unrecognisable from the man who had been my best friend. He had changed his lifestyle so completely that I was investigating the murder of a man I no longer knew, at the behest of a woman I had never known, but who had recently knocked me out with a quick view of her breasts and some top-of-the-range cocaine.

22

I copped out of the Mouse appreciation. I found an old photo of him from our punk days, looking wild and spiky, and ran it alongside one taken at the launch of the first issue of *Belfast Confidential* with his designer suit and surrounded by celebs. I just wrote: MOUSE, WE'LL MISS YOU and put it in big, bold type. It wasn't just the lingering hangover. It was awareness of my own inability to put what I felt into words, and also the fact that it was only right and proper to treat his death in a *Belfast Confidential* house-style. Blunt and to the point. In a black box on the same page I pasted in an appeal: *Do you know who murdered Mouse? REWARD!!!!!! Contact* Belfast Confidential *NOW!!!!!!*

Patrick and Stephen looked down at what I'd done and agreed it was the right way to handle it. Also, I was the boss and paid their wages. I signed off on the pages, and that was it: my first issue of *Belfast Confidential* was away to the printers.

It should have felt good.

It didn't.

Patrick and Stephen and the rest of the staff were going out for a celebratory lunch. Seemed that Mouse had treated them every week when the last pages went to press. But I didn't have the stomach for it, or the head, so instead I found a quiet pub just around the corner and sat on my lonesome, nursing a pint and staring at my mobile, trying to work up the courage to phone Trish. I only managed to work up the courage to order another pint. Fortified, I returned to the office full of resolve, eager to take the bull by the horns. I would send Patricia another text. It would be full of love and remorse and she would melt. She wasn't one for flowers or wine or extravagant gestures. She preferred to shout and curse. I was a man of words. Texting was much more appropriate.

If you talk something up enough, you can convince yourself of anything.

I breezed upstairs before Mary could collar me. My office door was open, and there was a strange man sitting opposite my desk. Strange as in his elaborately coiffured hair and his fake tan and his extravagant silk suit and in the way the smile he gave me could light up half of Belfast. He had a small digital video camera in one hand and as I entered he said 'Hi!' in a slightly camp South Belfast accent and extended his other hand.

I shook it and moved behind my desk. He started to speak, but I held up a hand to shush him and pushed the button on my phone. 'Mary, I have Liam Miller in my office.'

'I know,' she said.

'Did I ask you to send Liam Miller up to my office?'

'No, but he gave me a free book and complimented me on my hair.'

'Okay,' I said. My eyes swept the walls of my office, in case he'd redecorated while he was waiting.

'And your wife's on hold.'

'Ah,' I said.

'As she has been for the past sixty-five minutes.'

I cleared my throat. 'When you put someone on hold, Mary, is there a tune that plays?'

'"The Entertainer". Or "The Sting" depending on your point of view.'

If Patricia wasn't pissed off to start with, she would be by now. 'Could you tell her I'm going to be a while? I'm with someone.'

'Of course.'

I hit the button again. I looked at Liam Miller.

'Liam Miller,' I said.

'The one and only,' he grinned. 'Just give the word, I'm good to go.'

'Excuse me?'

He waved his camera at me. 'We use digital cameras, they won't be intrusive at all; you'll hardly know we're there.'

'What are you talking about?'

He smiled. In fact, it wasn't a new smile, it was a continuation of the old one. I suspected that even after a dig in the nuts and a headbutt he would still come up smiling, which would only encourage another assault. 'What am I talking about?' he repeated, like we were both in on a joke.

My head was still sore and my wife was waiting and Liam's teeth were blinding.

'No, really, what *are* you talking about?'

His eyes sort of narrowed, and he was probably trying to frown, but the Botox wouldn't allow it. 'We have a cross-promotional agreement.'

'A what?'

'I scratch your back, you scratch mine.'

I took a deep breath and said, 'We seem to be getting our wires crossed, Liam. Perhaps if you could just start from the beginning?'

'You're not winding me up? A lot of people try to wind me up.'

I could see that, but I didn't say it. Charm and diplomacy.

'As far as I'm concerned it's all signed and sealed.' He patted his jacket. There didn't appear to be anything in there besides some finely honed pecs. He was alluding to the fact that he had a contract for: 'A reality show. Every week we follow a local celeb through his working day, his homelife, we meet his family, have lunch with him, we get his views on life, all that sort of thing.'

'Ah,' I said.

'Then I pop up and give you some advice on how to sort out any inter-relationship problems you might be having, I redesign your kitchen and create a water feature in your garden.'

'Are you taking the piss?'

'Well, not always a water feature. Decking, perhaps.'

My phone rang. Mary said, 'Your wife says if you don't speak to her now she will take your CD collection and Frisbee each and every one into the Lagan.'

I looked at Liam and said, 'Excuse me a moment,' then swivelled my chair round so that I didn't have to look at him. 'When she said this about the CDs, was it with a trace of humour?'

'No.'

I sighed. 'Okay, put her on.'

There was a click and a little static, and then silence. Of the ominous calm before a storm variety.

'Trish,' I said quietly. 'I'm with someone.'

'I don't give a flying fuck. Where were you?'

'I just got waylaid. It was to do with work – you know how mad it's been.'

'And you couldn't phone.'

'No, my battery died, and then I had something to eat and it must have been off so I ended up throwing up and I fell asleep and then I woke up in a blind panic and I've been trying to get you all morning. Is there something wrong with the phone?'

'No, Dan. You slept where – the office?'

'Yes, of course.'

She was silent. Very silent. I know these silences. She knows I know these silences. I said, in a kind of half-joking, half-deadly serious fashion, 'Unless, of course, you know better.'

'Uhuh.'

'Okay – all right, honest-to-God truth?'

'I'm waiting.'

'It *was* work, I did get sick, but not in the office. I talked to you, I was on my way home, then I realised I hadn't updated May Li on what's been happening at work, so I tried to phone her. The battery was dead, so I asked the taxi driver to stop by her house so I could tell her. I went inside, I told her what was what, I got sick, she let me sleep on the couch.'

Silence.

'I'm sorry, I should have called you. I really was sick. I know how it looks, but you can call her. She'll verify—'

'I already spoke to her.'

'Oh.'

'In fact, she called me.'

'Oh.'

'She wanted to check that you were okay, and to say that she appreciated you coming over so late to update her, and to reassure me that you had behaved like a gentleman, because she knows how we women worry about our men.'

'Oh.'

'But she says you were sick on her bra.'

'She wasn't wearing it at the time!'

'She had no bra on?'

'No! I mean, I was sick upstairs in her toilet, her bra was soaking in . . . wait a minute, how did she know I was sick on her bra?'

'Because apparently you opened the bathroom window and threw it out, and the next-door neighbour was just putting her bin out and it landed on her.'

'It landed on her?'

'Wrapped itself around her face, according to May Li.'

'Oh Holy Fuck.'

Patricia laughed. I wasn't sure if it was a good sign. 'You are such a fucking wanker, Dan.'

'Yes, I appreciate that, but that's why you love me.'

'Sometimes I wonder.'

I lazily pushed myself round in the swivel chair. I'd more or less forgotten that Liam Miller was still with me. He had his camera raised, and he was filming. 'Don't mind me,' he said.

'Put that *fucking* camera down,' I spat.

Liam kept the lens trained on me. 'Full and complete access and no editorial control. That's what we agreed.'

'Not with me you didn't.'

'With the company. You work for the company.'

I sighed.

Trish said, 'What's going on?'

'Liam fucking Miller's filming me for a reality TV show.'

'Liam Miller? You?'

'Yes.'

'You're going to be on TV?'

'Yes. And according to Liam, so are you as well. In fact, he's coming round to film us having lunch and then he'll sort out our interpersonal problems and our fucking decking.'

'We haven't got decking.'

'Not yet we haven't.'

'Liam Miller?'

I had witnessed my lovely wife curse Liam Miller high and low; she had used words to describe him that no lady should ever, ever utter; she despised him and mocked him at every opportunity.

'I'm going to have to get my hair done,' she said.

'What?'

'And the lounge is a fucking bollocks.'

'What are you talking about?'

'He can't come round with the place in this state.'

'He can't come round full stop. Have you taken leave of your senses?'

'It's Liam Miller!'

'Exactly!'

Liam still had his camera raised. 'I'm fucking warning you,' I said, and pointed.

'Sticks and stones,' Liam half-sang.

'Trish – no.'

'Dan – yes. Remind me, my darling, as to who has the moral high ground right now?'

I took a deep breath. 'You do.'

'Remind me, my darling, who went sucking around May Li when he was drunk?'

'I did not . . .'

'Dan . . .'

'I swear to—'

'Your punishment, should you choose to accept it, is to allow Liam Miller into our life.'

'No.'

'Yes.'

'Trish.'

'Dan.'

I drummed my fingers on the desk. Liam's camera moved to focus in on them. I raised them into a two-fingered salute.

'If I do, does that mean I'm forgiven?'

'No, Dan. I neither forgive nor forget. I merely extend the time in which you're allowed to travel in my exalted circle.'

'That's one name for it,' I said.

'Well, at least it'll be mine, rather than that bitch May Li's.'

'Oh – she's a bitch now.'

'Of course she is. She phoned up to see how you were? Bollocks. She phoned up pretending to be concerned, but really to let me know that you'd come to her door with your tongue hanging out. She was letting me know she can have you any time she wants.'

'She can *not*,' I said. Then added after a suitable pause, 'She'll have to make an appointment like everyone else.'

Patricia laughed quietly. 'What are we like,' she said.

'We are what we are, and no one can change us.'

'Well – perhaps Liam can.'

I looked across the table at Liam. 'Yes, perhaps,' I said.

He was a one-man band. He said that with the advances in digital cameras he didn't need a crew or a soundman or a producer or a director or an editor. He was all of these things, and *so much* more. It sounded to me like he was just cheap. He followed me around the office like a dog. He swanned around us as we drank coffee, debated the merits of certain photographs, he criticised the lighting, and mocked the office furniture. He talked summer vacations with the girls in the office, performed some kind of wanky Feng Shui ritual and coughed in a loud and exaggerated fashion every time Mary wandered past with a cigarette hanging out of her mouth.

He asked, on camera, if I was aware of a bad atmosphere in the office, and I said only since he arrived and he laughed long and hard and asked me to repeat the story about throwing up in May Li's bra because he'd only caught one side of it. I refused. He insisted. I stormed off. I couldn't get rid of him.

Eventually I put a hand over his lens and said, 'This is about the Power List, isn't it?'

'Power List?' he asked innocently.

'You're doing this to make sure you're on it. If I tell you you're on it, will you go away and leave me alone?'

He smiled. 'Darling, I'm *way* above the Power List.'

He removed my hand from the lens, and I let him do it. I was really pissed off.

Patricia phoned me half a dozen times to update me on her progress. She was shifting furniture and painting walls and hoovering like there was no tomorrow. More than once she said, 'Liam Miller! Wait till I tell the girls!'

She called again just as I was pulling on my jacket. I had to get out. I had to get away. Naturally Liam Miller slipped into his jacket as well. 'I'm like a limpet!' he exclaimed, 'Except I don't smell of fish.'

Patricia asked what Liam would like for dinner. 'Liam, what would you like for dinner?'

'It's not my show,' he replied. 'It's entirely up to you.'

'It's entirely up to you,' I told Patricia.

'Oh shite,' she said. 'What do you think?'

'Well, sausage, beans and chips works for me.'

'No! Jesus Christ, Dan, this is going out all over the country.'

'Are you ashamed of sausage, beans and chips?'

'Yes, frankly. Ask him if he would like Famagusta chicken with bean sprouts.'

'I'd ask him if I knew what the fuck it was.'

'Just ask him.'

I asked him. He gave me the thumbs-up. 'That seems to be a yes,' I said.

'Brilliant. I can buy it in Marksies then tart it up to look like my own.'

'Is that ethical?' I asked.

Liam raised an eyebrow. 'Is what ethical?'

I smiled for the camera. 'Wouldn't you like to know.'

Trish said, 'No one needs to know. How are you getting on with him?'

'Liam? He's a pain in the hole.'

Liam paused his filming for a moment. 'You can't say that.'

'Say what – hole?'

'Yes.' He gave me a thin smile and patted his pocket, home of the metaphorical contract.

'Well,' Trish said, 'I better go.'

'Hold on a mo.' I handed the phone across to Liam. 'The wife wants a word.'

Liam took the receiver and said, 'Well, *hello* . . .'

I moved swiftly across the room, opened the door, removed the key, then closed it after me and locked it.

On my way out I gave the key to Mary and said, 'Leave him to stew for half an hour, and if he starts whining, blow smoke through the keyhole.'

23

I drove from the office to the former green belt site that was now pegged out as the future headquarters of Ryan Auto. Mary was having trouble fixing up an interview with Jacintha Ryan, and as I was determined not to put myself through the indignity of peeking under everyone's mask at the upcoming Ball in order to secure a few words face to face, and also in part to escape Liam Miller's attentions, I decided to drive out to West Belfast and take a look at the lie of the land there for myself.

What had once been green and pleasant fields (with added trolleys), was now completely ploughed up and apparently ready for building work to begin. There were three connected Portakabins situated behind a high wire fence, with entrance gates policed by two burly security guards. Seeing as how I was not only the new owner of *Belfast Confidential* but was also driving one of only three Ryan Jets in existence I thought they might overlook the fact that I was turning up without an appointment.

The gates opened before me and I gunned the sleek little machine through the rutted entrance. It was about the only gunning I'd managed, as every driver between here and there had slowed down to take a closer look, boxing me in and only allowing me to crawl along. I'd driven with my elbow resting on the window frame, and the wind blowing through my hair.

It was rather nice. All kinds of interesting women smiled at me, which made up for the way their husbands scowled. It felt good to be in Mouse's shoes, as opposed to the clown ones I normally wore.

'One careful driver, returning a borrowed motor,' I said when the first guard approached. 'Who's in charge?'

He nodded and raised a walkie-talkie and spoke quietly into it. Behind me the gates purred shut. I was instructed to enter the closest Portakabin, so I splashed through the mud, then wiped my feet inadequately on a rubber mat by the entrance. I opened the door and stepped inside.

'Oh,' I said.

I'd expected your average workaday builders' cabin, but this was all plush carpets and designer furniture. There were three glass desks, each with its own iMac; the desks were arranged on three sides of a larger glass table upon which sat a scale model of the planned factory. There was a man in a grey suit and red tie sitting behind one of the desks. He was thin-faced and his eyes were a little bit too close together for comfort. The other two desks were unoccupied. On the wall behind him was a framed animation cell from *Bambi*.

He looked slightly annoyed as he stood up. 'You should have called,' he said. His accent was difficult to place, but mid-Atlantic probably covers it.

I said, 'Sorry, only time I could get away.'

'And you are?'

I told him who I was and what I did.

'Ah,' he said. 'It was most unfortunate, what happened to your predecessor.'

'Yes, it was.'

'The car is more than a week overdue, but we felt it inappropriate to demand it back, given the circumstances.'

'I appreciate that.'

'Liam understood as well.'

'Liam?'

'Liam Neeson. He was next on the list.'

I nodded, then I tossed him the keys, which took him a little by surprise. He fumbled and dropped them, and they landed silently on the carpet. Thick shag. He didn't make any attempt to pick them up, as if the effort might crease his nice suit beyond repair.

'So,' I said, nodding at the table-top model, 'this is what it's going to look like. Very impressive.'

'We like to think so.' Then he added, 'I'm sorry – I'm Matthew Rye, Project Manager.'

He came forward and we shook hands over the top of the model. There were little buildings and little people and a car park full of little Jets and the fake grass that landscaped the grounds was made out of that powdered stuff model railway enthusiasts swear by. I nodded down at the little people. 'Which one's you?' I asked.

'I'm inside,' he said, without a trace of humour, 'working the phones.'

'Okay,' I said.

'We brought the basic design with us from America, and then Liam Miller added a few touches, more of an Irish feel. The windows will be angled in such a way to maximise the light. There's not a lot of light in Ireland.'

The model was encased in a glass box, presumably to stop the locals from stealing the cars. I gazed wistfully down.

I said, 'I used to play all around here when I was a kid. There was a nice pond and some ducks. We used to frolic amongst the yellow diamond daisies.'

Matthew Rye stiffened slightly. 'Well, all things must change.

Thank you for returning the vehicle. Is there anything else I can help you with?'

'I'm keen to get an interview with Jacintha Ryan.'

'You and everyone else.'

'You're aware of how influential *Belfast Confidential* is?'

'In Belfast, yes. But elsewhere? This is an international operation, Mr Starkey, and with respect, *Belfast Confidential* hardly touches the market we're aiming for.'

'Well, I just thought she'd be anxious to make a good impression.'

'Once again with respect, Mr Starkey, I believe investing hundreds of millions of dollars and creating thousands of jobs does make a good impression.'

'Fair point,' I conceded.

I looked at the model some more. He looked at me. And then at his watch.

'I enjoyed the drive,' I said.

'It's a fine vehicle.'

'Although I know bugger-all about cars.'

'Well, let me assure you, you won't find a better one.'

'Apparently there was a problem with the brakes.'

'I would find that difficult to believe.'

I shrugged.

'The brakes are state of the art,' he said. 'There is no problem with them.'

'Well, there was with these. Seems a pity to spoil such a positive article with negative comments.'

He clasped his hands before him and gave me a look. 'Are you trying to blackmail Ryan Auto?'

'Not at all. Just I have an invite to the Masked Ball thingy but it's not really my cup of tea and everyone'll be trying to catch Miss Ryan's ear and to tell you the truth, we have a

Power List special issue coming out and she's in with a fair chance of being number one, except the Ball's a bit close to our print deadline, so I thought a few words in advance . . .'

He cleared his throat. 'Perhaps if you put your request in writing.'

'Is that press office speak for "Bugger off and die"?'

'That's not for me to say. You would have to contact New York. As I said, I'm only the Project Manager. Press is a separate division.'

'Tell you what.' I took out a business card and handed it to him. The ink was barely dry. It said *Dan Starkey, Editor & Publisher*, Belfast Confidential. I was quite proud of it. 'Maybe you could pass this on to the press office on my behalf. We've tried from our end without any luck.'

Matthew Rye gave a slight nod, then slipped the card into his jacket pocket without looking at it. And that appeared to be that. I took a final look down over the sea of toy cars, then glanced back up at Matthew Rye.

'Don't know about you,' I said, 'but I kind of preferred it when there were yellow diamond daisies.'

Rye just looked at me. Then as I stepped out from behind the table, his attention switched to my feet.

'You've tramped mud into our carpet,' he pointed out.

'Yes, I have,' I said.

24

Belfast Confidential, dealing as it does with all kinds of potentially libellous situations, has a team of solicitors on call virtually around the clock. It's a good thing too, for I was at the
end of my tether. It was a little after midnight, and the phone
was answered on the second ring. I explained who I was, and
what I wanted.

'Okay,' the solicitor began.

'But first,' I said, 'are you sitting in an office, working late,
or are you tucked up in bed, cursing the existence of mobile
phones?'

'The latter,' he said.

'Excellent,' I replied. 'A level playing-field. Now—'

'Before you go on, Mr Starkey, we have received a directive
from Mrs May Li McBride to transfer a forty-nine per cent
ownership of *Belfast Confidential* to your name, and also to draw
up a contract to employ you as Editor on a salary equal to that
of your predecessor.'

'Forty-nine?' I asked.

'Forty-nine,' he said.

'Not fifty.'

'Not fifty,' he clarified.

'All right,' I said.

'However, as far as that ownership is concerned, Mrs McBride has first to supply us with paperwork showing that she is herself in a position to transfer it i.e. proof that she is the actual owner of the magazine. I understand that this will take a while to prepare, given the circumstances of her husband's death and the necessary complications associated with an individual who dies intestate. We have greater leeway on the salary question, as the company must continue to function, and I don't see a problem with putting a temporary contract through immediately.'

'Good,' I said.

'As for the other thing – well, the contract between *Belfast Confidential* and Liam Miller's Vanity Productions is, as far as I can determine, legally binding. It was signed by Mr Mouse and countersigned by – well, by us. Me, to be exact.'

'Shite.'

'Liam Miller insisted on inserting a number of clauses which may or may not be relevant to you, but which Mr Mouse signed off on. Clause 3C, for example, specifies that the subject refrain from using swearwords while being filmed.'

'Fuck.'

'Clause . . . 5F specifies that the subject may not consume alcohol while being filmed, other than as approved by the director.'

'Oh bollocks.'

'And there's a . . . 6A, I think, which specifies that for the course of filming the production company has access to your office and place of residence for twenty-four hours a day, with no parts of the above to be deemed off-limits, save for those mentioned in appendix . . . let me see . . . upstairs bathroom, loft . . .'

'Yes, yes, that's where I am now.'

'In the loft?'

'Yeah, and it's fucking freezing.'

'It's not—'

'Converted? God, no. Just me, some thirty-year-old *Beanos* and the water tank.'

'If you don't mind me asking . . .'

'Because the fucker's downstairs now, going through my cupboards.'

'But it's gone midnight.'

'I know! But it's television, darling, we never sleep! The fucker. Jesus Christ, man, there must be something I can do.'

He was quiet for a few moments. 'Well,' he said, then stopped again and seemed to think some more about it. 'Yes. I suppose. But please bear in mind that technically speaking I'm giving legal advice against my own contract here.'

'I'll bear it in mind.'

'Have you ever heard of Tourette's Syndrome?'

'Yes, I have.'

'It has many and varied symptoms, but amongst the best known are excessive swearing and pronounced facial tics and jerks.'

'Okay.'

'Do you see where I'm going?'

'Not yet, but keep talking.'

'Your contract prohibits you from swearing on film, and imposes severe financial penalties on you personally and the magazine itself for breaching those clauses. So, if you were to swear frequently and cause filming to be halted, you would probably be adjudged to be in breach of contract and therefore liable to those selfsame financial penalties. However, if you were medically certified as suffering from Tourette's Syndrome, then you would be deemed incapable of acting in any other way and therefore not in breach of contract.'

'Only problem is, I don't suffer from Tourette's Syndrome.'

'How do you know?'

'Well, I don't know. Can you catch it?'

'I have no idea. But who's to say you can't? Or that you can't develop it? Or that you've always had it and it's lain dormant until the stress of running *Belfast Confidential* – or indeed dealing with Liam Miller – has brought it to the surface. We can certainly hire enough expert medical opinion to ensure a long and costly trial, and I doubt his people will have the stomach for that. You may have to continue with the bad language for several years afterwards just to keep up the charade.'

'So that's your advice. To curse my way out of it.'

'No, that's an option for you to consider, and bear in mind that if you leave your employment at any time in the near future, and Liam Miller decides to pursue a case against *Belfast Confidential*, our primary clients, then *Belfast Confidential* can countersue you for breach of contract, irrespective of whatever advice we gave you.'

'It's not advice, it's an option.'

'That's what I said, or if I didn't, I should have; it's late and I'm tired. I mean, can't you just go along with it? How bad can it be?'

'You've seen him on TV, and you're asking how bad it can be? That's one hour you see, with commercial breaks. I'm talking twenty-four hours with *no relief*.'

'Okay,' he said. 'Fair point. My wife wants to bear his children.'

'She's aware he's as bent as a threepenny bit?'

'I think that's the attraction.'

When I cut the line, I poked my head down out of the hatch, to find Patricia looking up.

'Who were you talking to?' she asked.

'Mind your own beeswax,' I said.

'Liam's ready for you now.'

'What do you mean, he's ready for me?'

'He's just setting up in the kitchen. He wants to talk about our relationship. I've done my bit.'

'You've done your bit?'

'Yes. Dan, come on, put the ladders down.'

I had drawn them up into the roofspace as a safety precaution. But I didn't move. I said again, 'You've done your bit. What exactly did you do?'

'Dan, for god sake, it's nothing to be afraid of. I said you were a big kid and a pain in the neck, but that I love you.'

'You told him that and he's going to show it all over the country.'

'Yes. And he says the lawn's been planted all wrong – he's going to come back and dig it up. And he's going to help me design a memorial garden for Little Stevie.'

'You talked to him about Stevie?'

'Yes, I did.'

'And you think a memorial garden will sort things out?'

'It would be nice to have somewhere to go and sit in the sun and remember him.'

'I can't believe I'm hearing this.'

'Well, believe it. It's interesting, Dan. And it's important. To me, at any rate. Please do it, Dan – do it for me, eh?'

'Jesus Christ,' I said.

But I lowered the ladders, because she was my wife, and I cared about how she felt, and also because she ruled me with a rod of iron, because I needed it. She steadied the ladders as I climbed down. She gave me a hug and told me it would be fine.

* * *

Liam had placed his camera on a tripod and brought in an extra set of lights. He'd positioned them so that I was properly illuminated, but the background was dark. It made it look like I was being interviewed in a police cell, or on the set of *Mastermind*.

He said, 'This is, if you like, the serious part of the show.'

'As opposed to running my garden down.'

'Well, it's all over the place, Dan. It's supposed to be smooth, but there's lumps all over it.'

'Those will be the bodies.'

He looked at me. 'Shall we get started?'

'Shoot,' I said.

The first questions were about how I'd met Trish, and how did I think she'd changed over the years we'd been together. I answered as truthfully as I could.

On the third question, I began to blink.

He said, 'I think we'll try that one again.'

He asked the question again and I replied in a satisfactory fashion, at least until my head jerked suddenly to one side and I said, 'Fuckin' fuck.'

He held his hand up and said, 'Once more.'

'Sorry,' I said.

He asked the question again. It was about how I was coping with my newfound celebrity.

'Well,' I began, and my head jerked to one side, 'I think it's important to keep your feet . . .' and my head jerked to the opposite side, 'firmly on the ground.' My head moved slowly back to the middle. 'This is quite a small city, it's not like it's—' my head jerked left, then right, then left again, 'London or New York or . . . FUCKING CUNT HEAD!'

Liam jumped in his seat. He stopped the camera.

'Sorry!' I barked. 'I don't know what happened just then.'

He took a deep breath. 'That's okay. I just . . . The contract – there's no swearing allowed.'

'I understand that.'

'So if we could just . . . take our time. Deep breath, that's it. Now another . . . Okay, Dan, tell me, how are you coping with your newfound celebrity?'

'I think it's . . . fuck titwank . . . important to . . . bastard fuckshit . . . to keep your feet firmly on the . . . CUNTING ground.' My head jerked backward, then forwards. 'It's not like it's FUCKING LONDON!'

Liam angrily paused the camera again. He glared across at me. 'What are you playing at?'

'Nothing – swear to FUCKING God! Sorry, I just – FUCK OFF! I'm not trying to do . . . YOU FUCKING FRUIT . . . Sorry, I'm . . . maybe it's just too FUCKING late. I'm sorry, I need a drink.'

I pushed the chair back, and went to the fridge. I took out a can of beer, snapped it open, took a long drink, then held the cold can to my forehead. I turned, standing like that, towards him. 'Look, I know you're only trying to do your job, but perhaps we could try A-FUCKING-GAIN tomorrow. Sorry.'

He gave me a long, cool look. 'You know,' he said, 'swearing isn't big, and it isn't funny.'

'I FUCKING agree. CUNT. Sorry.'

He stood up. He took a deep breath. 'I know you don't want to do this, but I should remind you that you are contractually obliged to complete this programme in a satisfactory manner. Now, I appreciate that it's late, and we're all tired, but I want you to think about this . . . I want you to sleep on it, and then perhaps you'll realise that this isn't the best way to deal with what you perceive to be a negative situation. I'm going to leave this equipment here, and we'll finish off in the morning before you go to work. Shall we say 7.30 a.m.?'

I nodded.

'Very well.' He moved towards the kitchen door. As he opened it, he stopped and turned and said, 'If you are sleeping on it, I find that if you sleep on your side, with your legs drawn up, one hand on your hip and the other under the pillow, that's the best position for optimum rest. And also a cotton pyjama is nice and cool; silk's lovely to the touch but it's not good for sleeping in.'

I nodded again, mutely.

'Nighty-night, then,' he said.

'Nighty-FUCKING-night,' I responded. 'Sorry, I—'

As he moved along the hall, the front door bell rang.

'I'll get it!' Liam called back, remarkably cheerfully given the way the evening had ended up. It was now after 1 a.m., and my first thought was that it must be someone who had come to pick him up, but he hadn't called anyone and we were still supposed to be working, so it had to be for me or for Trish. Then I thought that nobody ever came calling so late, unless they were the bearer of bad tidings. Or, given the anarchy that has been a fixture of our lives, the bearer of something worse.

I stepped out into the hall after him. 'Liam, hold on a—'

He already had the door half-open, but before he could get it any further there was a sudden, deafening crack, the glass in the door shattered and Liam tumbled backwards, his arms flailing up, his legs completely out of control. I threw myself back into the kitchen just as a second bullet whacked into the doorframe beside me.

Upstairs Patricia screamed *'Dannnnnn!'*

But I was fine.

It was Liam Miller who was dead.

25

The world is but a stage, and we are merely players on it. Or upon it. Or something. Sometimes old Shakey really hits the nail on the head. Another Shakey had once written about it being better to burn out than to fade away, and I suppose this was apt for Liam Miller. No declining audience figures for him. No piles of mouldering books in car boot sales. No fading hipster he, but a martyred icon, a James Dean of the throwover rug, a Kurt Cobain of the designer sofa. Live fast, die young, and leave a good-looking apartment, with just a hint of pastel. In the process, be the star attraction at *the* social event of the year, your own funeral.

On this particular stage, a West Belfast cemetery, Liam Miller was transported to the grave in a surprisingly plain coffin. It was the only area of life – death – to which he had given no consideration, possibly because he thought he would live for ever, and so it fell to his mum to pick out his coffin and choose the hymns for the service. The church was small and musty and not at all used to the crush of celebrity, the flash of the bulb or the screaming of three hundred teenagers as the singer Kieren Kitt arrived to pay his respects to the man who had given him a radical make-over after his departure from the boy band, West Bell. The kids darted and sprinted and crouched between and behind the gravestones, trying to catch a glimpse of their idol as the funeral party inched along while playing serious tag with a security team employed to handle crowd control.

Kieren was a diminutive figure in a long black coat and a wide-brimmed hat, and even when the solemn words around the open grave were drowned out by his screaming fans he kept his head down. Others didn't look so happy. Van Morrison stood with his hands thrust into his pockets, perhaps devastated because not one single teenage girl had ever screamed for him; Liam Neeson read a poem by Yeats, but it was drowned out first by the screaming, and then by the clatter of a press helicopter far above. The chopper was a ridiculous and insensitive intrusion. And I'd hired it. The ex-Formula One driver Eddie Irvine had pleaded to drive the hearse, but had been rebuffed, and now stood chatting to Matthew Rye, possibly on the off-chance that he had the clout to get him back into Formula One. Somehow I doubted it. He had more chance of getting a hard hat and a day's work on a muck-shifter.

May Li was there. Black suited her, like every other colour in the world. Wendy turned up, but was kept out of the VIP enclosure by the bouncers and stood forlornly amongst the civilian onlookers, alternately straining to hear what was being said and snapping at Kieren Kitt's teen fans to be quiet. Terry Breene stood on a slight rise, flanked by the two accountants I'd seen with him in *Past Masters*. He took several sneaky sips from a hip flask. Patrick O'Brien, owner of *Past Masters*, came up and shook his hand, then continued on, working the crowd. Most of them were members of his club already, and many had also appeared on the Power List. Those that weren't, or hadn't, but fancied one or the other or both tried to catch his eye, and he was there, eager to throw it. If he could have given out membership forms, I think he would have.

I stood drinking it all in on an incline on the opposite side, within spitting distance of the Republican Plot, although I resisted the temptation. Immediately in front of me, with his back to me and scanning the mourners with his eagle eyes, was Alec Large. I wasn't sure if Large was his real name or a name he'd adopted to help him strike fear into, well, everyone, but I was glad of his presence nevertheless. He was, according to May Li, the best personal security specialist money could buy. He had worked in Iraq, he had guarded the Beckhams, and he swore blind he was supposed to be driving Princess Diana on the night she died but had suddenly had his shift changed, which he thought pointed to evidence of a conspiracy. I didn't care about his conspiracy theories. I cared about my own, and the fact that remnants of Liam Miller's brain were still splattered over my hall, playing untold havoc with both the Feng Shui of the house and my wife's mental health. Someone had tried to kill me, that was abundantly clear. I thought so, my wife thought so, May Li thought so. The cops who took me to Castlereagh station and questioned me thought so. Even good cop-bad cop came in and gave me the I-told-you-so treatment and advised me to shut the magazine down and flee the country.

And I thought about it.

Seriously.

I don't like being shot at. I don't handle pain well. There's nothing like blood spurting out of a dying man to bring a little focus to your life.

If there is a dark corner to hide in, or a lie to get me out of trouble, then that is my perennial choice, but this was different. This was my home. I didn't want to run, I didn't want to hide. Besides, I'd been abroad, and people had tried to kill me there as well. The difference with this was the very nothingness of what I was trying to do – make a little money, compile a vacuous Power List for a fluffy celeb mag – and this insane over-reaction to it perplexed me no end. I hadn't killed anyone by accident or delivered some personal slight to some notorious gangster. Since Mouse's murder I had chatted to the owner of a private club, a car manufacturer's local rep and an ex-professional footballer. My worst crime was getting drunk and falling over. As far as I was aware, I'd offended nobody but my wife, the Belle of Belfast City and the bra of an astonishingly good-looking Thai widow. But now Liam Miller had taken a bullet intended for me, and the only response I'd yet come up with was to bring in a team of freelance photographers to capture every moment of his funeral for the next issue of *Belfast Confidential*. My first issue, featuring Mouse's death, was already on the streets, and was virtually sold out. For the next issue, featuring Liam's funeral, we would probably double the print run. I just hoped I'd be around to benefit from it.

May Li had offered us a safe house, but we'd turned it down.

I urged Patricia to take it, just to keep her out of harm's way. But she said, 'No, we don't run.'

'*I* do,' I protested.

'No, you don't Dan. Not for the important things.'

'And *this* is that important?'

'Yes, it is. It's Mouse. And it's our new house. We've moved all over the place, Dan, this is the first time I've really, really felt like it's our home for ever. They're not chasing us out.'

I think the neighbours might have preferred it. George and Georgina, not to forget Topper, glared at us over the fence; they glared at the cops and the ambulance and the Scenes of Crime tape and the forensics experts in their white overalls. They never offered us a cup of tea or a word of support. To make it worse, Topper never waved his paw at us, not even once.

So we got Alec Large instead. He was tall, but not as broad as you might expect. His black suit was Armani, and looked like one of Concrete Corcoran's better efforts. His eyes were dark and his eyebrows arched and he watched everyone like a hawk. I saw him stiffen as an overweight man in a rumpled trenchcoat came towards me; I recognised him, but not his million-dollar smile. I said, 'That's okay,' to Alec, but he still insisted on frisking him.

'So, Toothless,' I said. 'What're you looking so happy about?'

'To see you alive, of course.'

I would have smiled, but I felt ashamed of my dentalwork. 'So what do you hear, what do you say?'

'Is it okay to talk?' He cast a wary eye across Alec Large's back.

'Sure,' I said.

Toothless nodded warily, then dropped his voice. 'I hear you're as lucky as fuck. I hear the bullet's untraceable and nobody saw nothing. I hear shares in DIY companies took a tumble and garden centres have run up the black flag.'

'Aye,' I said. 'Did you get a look at that CCTV footage yet?'

'No, working on it.'

'The hookers come up with anything yet?'

'Nah.'

'A definite suspect?'

'Nah.'

'Anyone brought in for questioning?'

'No one important.'

'I'm sure there's a reason I pay you a retainer.'

'Show a little faith, Dan. You know, it's like buses.'

'You mean they never show up on time and they're always vandalised.'

'No, you wait ages for one, and then . . .'

'I take your point.'

He stood beside me and gazed out across the gathered mourners. He smiled again and said, 'Give the public what they want.'

I nodded, but there was something about the smile that was bothering me – or in fact, not the smile, the eyes, and the way he grimaced slightly when he spoke.

'You okay?' I asked.

He nodded. But then after a moment he said, 'Fucking teeth are killing me. I don't know, I think they're too fucking big or I've an infection or something. It's all that fucker's fault.' He nodded down towards Liam's coffin, which was now being gently eased into its resting place. 'Wife saw his fucking show about cosmetic surgery, he said "Life's too short to go around with crazy teeth, get 'em fixed". So I did, and they're fucking killing me. They're already calling me Smiler round work. I liked being Toothless, you know what I mean? You spend a long time building a character, and it's all basically fucked overnight. The fucker.'

'Well, maybe *you* killed him then.'

He smiled, without really meaning to. 'Nah,' he said. 'Shooting him would have been too fucking quick. Roast him on a fucking spit, and baste him with aromatic spices. Fuckin' eat him then, with a bag of chips.'

I nodded.

There was a wake afterwards in *Past Masters*. Bouncers on the door, a guest list. A buffet was laid on and most of the faces turned up. And for the extra-special ones, there was a roped-off VIP enclosure. Patrick O'Brien waved me through, but wouldn't allow Alec Large to follow.

'We let him in, we gotta let them all – there wouldn't be room to move. You're perfectly safe.'

Alec didn't look happy about it, but that didn't matter. It had already been three days, and I was beginning to feel as claustrophobic with him as I had with Liam. The difference was that Alec wasn't camp, and he was prepared to take a bullet for me. Liam hadn't been given any option at all about his head exploding.

Once inside I swapped small talk with Power Listers and would have felt warm about their urging me not to give up on the magazine or the list if I hadn't suspected that one of them was behind both Mouse's murder and Liam's accidental execution. I noticed that nobody cared to chat with me for too long, in case sudden and bloody death was catching.

I sipped a beer and found myself standing by three sullen-looking lads who seemed vaguely familiar. They were blond and muscular and wore tight T-shirts to prove it, although they were black out of deference to the deceased. They kept muttering amongst themselves and casting evil looks across the room at Kieren Kitt, so it wasn't hard to figure out that they formed the remnants of West Bell.

'So,' I said, 'do you see much of old Kieren then?'

'Not if we can help it,' one snapped. I wasn't sure of his name, or of any of the others'. The girls screaming outside the club might once have known their names but they'd chosen to stick with Kieren and condemned these good-looking boys to the eternal hell of boy-band obscurity. Still, they were in the VIP enclosure at a funeral, so life wasn't a total barrel of shit for them.

I explained who I was and one said, 'The Power List thing. Yeah, right. We were number seventeen two years ago.'

I said it was before my time.

'We'll be back,' said the third. 'We're working on new material right now. Then he'll be fucking laughing on the other side of his face.'

From where I was standing, Kieren wasn't laughing at all. He sat at a small table, with a cute-looking girl in a black mini-skirt. He still had his hat on, and now that he was indoors he'd added a set of sunglasses. They were probably designer, though for the life of me I'd never been able to figure out exactly what designing needed to go into sunglasses. Or glasses. Or hats. Perhaps it was just a reaction to Liam's death. Through no fault of my own I'd robbed the world of his designing, psychiatric, gardening and self-empowering talents, so there was bound to be a little backlash.

I chatted to the boys for another five minutes, then wandered around the rest of the enclosure, introducing myself and accepting free drinks. They were going on Liam's mother's tab. But what the hell, she could afford it. She'd lost a guru, but gained a fortune. I nodded at Matthew Rye, but he seemed disinclined to talk; he nodded curtly and returned his attention to Eddie Irvine. Terry Breene said hello, and then rested his head on the bar. One of the blonde waitresses asked him if he wanted to lie down, then led him away upstairs, and neither of them returned. A lot of people were talking about the upcoming Masked Ball, as if Liam Miller's funeral was merely another occasion on their packed social calendar, and the Ball was the next. I was asked half a dozen times what I'd be wearing and who I was taking, and was it proper protocol to ask guests to remove their masks to have their photos taken for the maga-zine, because surely no one would buy the next issue just to see a lot of archaic masks and fancy ballgowns. There was much speculation about Jacintha Ryan, about whether she'd had plastic surgery, or who she was in love with, where she'd next be spreading her money around and what sort of an entrance she planned to make. And everyone had their name down for a Jet, except for those who thought it was crass and vulgar.

When I'd had enough of smiling through clenched teeth I tapped Alec over the VIP rope and he spun on his heel, ready to cleave my head off. I said, 'Relax. I was thinking it's time to go back to the office.'

He said, 'We should wait until the crowd outside disperses. They're mostly teenage girls, but there's enough civilians out there to make it dangerous. I don't want anyone taking a pot shot at you.'

I said, 'I have to get back to work.'

'I wouldn't advise leaving the building.'

'Nevertheless.'

He took a deep breath. 'All right. You wait here – I'll go and get the car. I'll park by the front door, but don't leave the building until I come and get you, okay?'

'Okay,' I said.

'No, really – *okay*?'

'*Okay*. Christ All Mighty.'

Alec hurried away. I did some more chatting, then found myself standing by Kieren Kitt's table. I gave it a playful knock with my knuckles and told him who I was and that my office had been in touch about setting up a meeting but he didn't even bother to look up. 'This is a fucking funeral, man, let it go.'

I said, 'I hear you worked closely with Liam.'

'I said let it go.'

'I'm not interviewing you, I'm just making small talk.'

He looked up. He removed his sunglasses. His eyes were small and bold. 'I'm Kieren Kitt,' he snarled. 'I don't do fucking small talk.'

'Can I get you a sausage roll?' I asked.

He began to look about him. His personal bodyguard was on the other side of the rope like all the others, but he was too busy chatting up a canapé waitress to notice.

'Did you ever meet Mouse – you know, he ran *Belfast Confidential* before me?'

Kieren glared at me. The girl in the mini-skirt patted his hand. He looked down at her, and his face softened a little. 'No, I didn't, now—'

'He was murdered a couple of weeks ago.'

'Yes, I heard.'

'He was going to put you into the Power List – you have any problem with that?'

Kieren laughed disdainfully. 'Listen mate, I'm a star in Germany, France, Spain, Denmark, Sweden, Holland, Switzerland. You name it, I'm a fucking star there, so why would I give a shit about your poky little Power List?'

'America,' I said.

'What?'

'You're not a star in America.'

'Oh fuck off.'

He meant it, but I stayed where I was, with a bottle of Bud held close to my lips for fresh breath confidence. He sat fuming, his fists balled tight. He was Monkey-Davy small, and I wasn't overly concerned. If he made a move I could run and hide in the toilets.

'The boys say hello.' I nodded across the floor of the VIP enclosure. They were still staring across.

Kieren slipped his sunglasses back on. 'They put you up to this?'

'No.'

'I know what they're saying. And if you print a word about the gay thing, I'll sue you for every fucking penny you have now or ever will have, do you hear me?'

'Actually, they were just saying how much they missed you.'

He hesitated then. 'Seriously?'

'Yeah. They were hoping you'd write some songs for them, seeing as how you're multi-talented in that department.'

His eyes narrowed. 'You're taking the fucking piss, aren't you?'

'Yes,' I said.

His eyes returned to the security rope, and this time he made eye-contact with his bodyguard. Kieren pointed at me and made a cutting action across his throat.

The bodyguard stepped over the rope.

'Wise up,' I said. The bodyguard kept coming. I took several steps in the opposite direction. 'Seriously,' I said.

'You fucking wanker,' Kieren growled. Usually it was water off a duck's back, but there was a huge skinhead who'd just been blown off by a canapé waitress coming for me so I slipped sharply to my right and ducked down behind Liam Miller's mother. I heard Kieren shout, 'Find him and fucking deck him!' Discretion being the better part of valour, I stayed in my crouched position and hurried back towards the security rope like a hunchback on a promise. As I stepped over it, I straightened and noted that my evasive manoeuvres had worked perfectly, apart from the fact that his bodyguard was coming straight for me.

I crouched down again. I made it safely across the club floor by ducking and diving through the still happily drinking mourners, then darted down the stairs, taking them three at a time. As I reached the bottom, the bodyguard arrived at the top.

I stepped out into the early evening gloom. The waiting teenagers didn't even pay me the courtesy of mistaking me for their gorgeous hero by letting out a few hopeful screams. I struggled manfully on. Alec flashed his lights and a moment later pulled up beside me. I dived into the back and we eased away from the kerb just as Kieren Kitt's massive bodyguard appeared in the doorway. He glared after me. I gave him the fingers, and was just smiling contentedly as I turned to settle myself in my seat, when I realised it wasn't my seat, nor indeed my car. A man in the front passenger seat was already turned back towards me. He extended his hand.

'Christopher Corcoran,' he said, 'but you can call me Concrete.'

26

I said, 'I'm sorry, I appear to—'

'You were wanting to interview me.'

'Was I?'

'Your office called.'

'Did they?'

I had in fact instructed Mary, and advised Stephen and Patrick, that I wanted to follow in Mouse's footsteps by interviewing all of the potential candidates for the new Power List, but I had also taken it as read that this wasn't to include a notorious gangster like Concrete Corcoran. I was more than happy to compile his entry from gossip and innuendo. I mean, I might have been a fearless journalist, but I wasn't *stupid*.

I said, 'Well, this is hardly the best time. Perhaps I could find a window . . .'

'This suits me fine.'

'Okay,' I said.

I hardly recognised him, despite the fact that I'd flicked through half a dozen photos of him just a few days before. They'd all been snatched, grainy efforts, because he wasn't the type to stand and pose, but the best of the bunch, which I was going to use to illustrate his entry on the Power List, showed a somewhat rotund, balding farmer-type in overalls who looked about as threatening as any rotund, balding farmer-type can.

The man in front of me was neither rotund nor balding. He had on a smart suit, and even though he was sitting down it didn't look like there was an ounce of excess fat on him. Of course the photos we had might have been taken a long time ago. And you can sort your weight. And your clothes. Which left the hair. He had lots of it. You don't recover from baldness. It doesn't grow back.

'I thought we'd go down to the farm, and have a chat.'

I reached for my mobile and said, 'I should let the office know. I've people waiting to hear from me.'

He looked at my phone. 'Is that one of the new ones?'

'I'm not sure, I got it for Christmas.'

'Let me see.' He clicked his fingers, motioning for me to give it to him. So I did. He turned it over and examined it. He gave a little shrug, then opened his window and threw it out. I couldn't hear it clattering away, but my eyes followed it, receding into the distance, like hope. He smiled back at me. 'Do you know if you murder someone, the cops can trace you right to the murder scene even if you're not using the fucking thing? I'll get you a new one. State of the art. That was a piece of crap.'

'Okay,' I said.

We were already on the motorway, heading out of the city. The driver was wearing a dark blue denim jacket and when he glanced at me in the mirror his eyes were full of – what was it? Glee?

'So you're the new boss of *Belfast Confidential.*'

'I wouldn't say boss.'

'Well, you edit it and you own half of it.'

'I don't own any of it yet.'

'Not what I heard.'

I cleared my throat and fixed my eyes on the passing countryside. There was no chance at all of throwing myself from the vehicle. We were travelling far too fast, for a start. There was also the fact that Concrete Corcoran could merely stop the vehicle, and then reverse over my already mangled body. And there were child locks.

'I understand I'm being considered for your Power List,' he went on.

'Well. There's a lot of people being considered.'

'But I'm on some kind of a short list.'

I nodded. There was no point in denying it, my loyal staff having already clearly given the game away.

'I'd be interested in what you have to say. It's important to get your facts right. Would you be running a photograph?'

'I haven't decided. Would you – prefer not?'

'Not at all. There are a lot of photographs out there, one more won't make any difference. But I don't look like most of them any more. Do you know what I mean?'

'I do,' I said. 'Perhaps we could take a new one.'

'God Bless Him,' said Concrete.

It sat in the air for a while, until eventually curiosity got the better of me. 'Who?'

'The blessed soul we just buried.'

I cleared my throat and said, 'You were there?'

'Of course I was. And isn't it a powerful testament to his abilities that not a critter recognised me?'

'Yes,' I said.

'He transformed my life. Put me on a diet. Sorted out my wardrobe. And guess what else?'

According to my info he was in his mid-fifties, but he looked perhaps fifteen years younger. His skin was smooth, and there were no obvious sags or bags, or crows' feet.

'Your hair.'

'Implants. And Botox for my face. If I ever catch up with the cunt that killed him, I'll fucking kill *him*.'

I'd been working on the theory that Concrete Corcoran, being the only outlaw on my list, was the natural suspect. But if, as it appeared, he wasn't averse to appearing on the Power List, and was already well used to bad publicity, then what reason could he have had for killing Mouse? And if he'd been behind the attempt to kill me, then he would already know who'd killed Liam and wouldn't need to issue threats against him. This actually made me feel a bit better, but only for as long as it took me to think about people who protested their innocence too much, and about his record, which was second to none.

'Maybe we could stop at Newry or somewhere, for dinner?' I suggested.

'There's plenty to eat at the farm. Besides, there's something I want to show you.'

'Okay. No problemo.'

Concrete took his own mobile out and began to talk to someone. I could hear what he was saying, but it was so inane that I had to presume that he was talking in some kind of code. He used words like wine, and cheese, that set my mind racing.

Wine . . . red wine . . . blood . . . cheese . . . grater . . . what a way to go.

When he finished I leaned forward and said quietly, 'I have appointments this evening in Belfast.'

'Cancel them,' said Concrete.

'Okay,' I said. I sat back. Then I sat forward again and said, 'I have no phone.'

He glanced back at me, then rolled his eyes and passed me his. 'Make it quick,' he said. 'I'm not made of money.'

Actually, he probably was.

I called Mary and asked her to cancel my appointments.

'You don't have any,' she said. 'I'm just on my way home.'

'I know it's inconvenient, but just cancel them.'

'What are you talking about?'

'They weren't set in *stone*, anyway.'

'What?'

'Sorry . . . I'm losing the signal. I said, they weren't definite, they weren't *concrete*.'

'I'm sorry, but I haven't a clue what you're talking about. Are you drunk?'

'Mary . . .'

'Please hold, there's another call.' She clicked off.

'I'll only be a moment,' I said to the back of Concrete's head. 'She's put me on hold.'

I took advantage of this to cut the line and scroll through his phone book. He was certainly well-connected. I found Terry Breene's name, then Liam Miller's, then Mouse's. I took a deep breath, and kept rolling.

Jacintha Ryan's. In New York.

I exited from the phone book, then tutted. 'Lost the bloody line. Still, she got the message. Here.'

I handed Concrete his phone. He slipped it wordlessly into his jacket pocket. We were off the motorway by now, moving along narrow, unlit country roads. In the old days many of them, leading across the border, would have been blasted closed by the Army, but they were all open now, and almost impossible to police. The skinhead driver roared around sharp corners with all the confidence of a boy racer on e.

We finally skidded to a halt in front of a set of high metal gates; security cameras blinked down at us, and then the gates began to open inwards. We drove up a winding driveway until Concrete Corcoran's impressively large and floodlit house came into view. Along with the warehouses and tennis court and vast barn and covered swimming pool was a circle of concrete which could just have been a patio, but looked more like a helicopter landing pad.

I said, 'Nice farm.'

The driver snorted.

I was led into a long, wide lounge with plush carpets and a projector bolted into the ceiling which was beaming pristine pictures of *EastEnders* onto a twelve-foot screen. A middle-aged woman with a blonde bob and an ash tray on her lap hardly even looked up from a black leather couch as we entered.

'Nice lounge,' I said.

Behind me, the driver snorted. Concrete leaned over the back of the couch and kissed the blonde on the top of her head. She gave a half-smile, but didn't take her eyes off the screen. 'I'm taping it for you,' she said.

'Are you sure you're taping the right channel?'

'Of course I am.'

'Just checking.'

He signalled for me to follow him. So I did. I smiled at the woman, whom I took to be his wife, but she didn't notice. It could have been any lounge, in any house, in any country. The only difference lay in what Concrete was now or had once been. He was a smuggler. A counterfeit artist. A bandit. He was IRA. He killed and he bombed. Not always with his own hands, but he directed it. It had always surprised and confused me when I discovered the crushing ordinariness of terrorists' daily lives. They held down normal jobs, they came home at night and watched soap operas and wrote cheques for electricity bills. Except that instead of saying to their wives, 'I'm just popping down to the shops,' they said, 'I'm just popping down to blow up the shops.' But their wives would still keep nodding, and keep watching *EastEnders*.

We walked down a long hall and into a large kitchen. At the back of the kitchen there was a padlocked door. He opened this and reached inside to turn on the lights. Then as they flickered into fluorescent life he led me down a flight of steps into a huge underground cellar which was filled from one side to the other with stacked rows of large cardboard boxes. As we passed through them I noted that many bore Japanese or Chinese or some kind of Oriental inscriptions.

I said, 'So how's business?'

'Fair to middlin',' he responded.

'Are we in Northern Ireland now, or the Republic?'

Concrete stopped and examined his surroundings. Then he took another three steps forward, and waved me over. '*Now* we're in the Republic. Famous for little green men and not taking an active part in any world wars. Their police officers are not armed.'

Behind me the driver snorted.

At the far end of the cellar, there was another door which required a security code to gain access. Concrete punched it in, while the driver stood at my shoulder, rubbing his hands together. 'Christ,' he said, 'have we run out of oil?'

And then they both burst into laughter.

I managed a grin. It was, after all, part of what they did for a living, smuggling oil. I didn't give them a whole grin because I was too busy worrying about what was behind the door, or what they would do to me once they had me in there. They say that in space, no one can hear you scream, but I was willing to bet that they couldn't hear you underneath Concrete Corcoran's house either.

My only hope was that Mary had had a sudden brainstorm

and somehow understood what I'd been trying to tip her off to.

It wasn't much of a hope.

Concrete opened the door, reached inside, and flicked the lights on. *'Voila!'* he exclaimed, then waved me forward.

I stepped hesitantly through the opening, expecting at any moment to be cracked across the back of the head, or hurled forward into a stinking underground cell. But instead there were clean white tiles and brightly painted walls and clear, precise lighting, all of which provided perfect conditions for the dozen or so oil paintings on display in what was quite clearly Concrete Corcoran's private art gallery.

Concrete took me gently by the arm and guided me forward. 'Well, what do you think?'

'I'm . . . not sure. This is most . . . ahm . . . unexpected.'

He was smiling widely. The driver nodded appreciatively as he trailed along behind us.

'It's temperature controlled. I had the best in the business in to sort that out. The walls are three feet thick – there's not a drop of moisture will get through them. They'll last for ever.'

'I'd . . . no idea you were a collector.'

'Collector? Pish! They're mine – *I* painted them.'

'You?'

'Yes.'

'All of them?'

'Every single one – and this is only the half of them. Oh, you've no idea!' He squeezed my arm hard, but not in a threatening way. He was buzzing with excitement. 'It's like the floodgates just opened! Once Liam gave me a few lessons it was just like I'd been doing it for ever. He thought they were fantastic! He wasn't only my friend and mentor, Dan, he was my agent as well. They've been selling like hot cakes!'

Almost all of them were landscapes, and as we made a circuit of the room I realised that I'd seen their like before, decorating the walls of *Past Masters*.

'Well,' I said, 'I'm very impressed.'

'Are you really? Honestly?'

I nodded. I was, kind of. I had no idea if the paintings were any good. The trees looked like trees and the bushes looked like bushes. I recognised Scrabo Tower and the Carrick-A-Rede ropebridge and Wrathlin Island. And there was no reason why a thug, a bandit and a killer couldn't have another string to his crossbow. I said, 'I know nothing about art, but I know what I like.'

'Brilliant,' Concrete enthused, giving my arm another squeeze. 'I'm really chuffed. It's not going to be a problem then, is it?'

'Is what?'

'Dan – what I brought you here for. I knew I could convince you, once you saw them. You see, I'm a different man now, I've seen the light. Half of us, when we get out of all the shootin' and killin', we go and get born again, but I've never been into God. I'm into Art, Dan, I'm a born again painter!'

I nodded.

'And that's what I need from you, Dan – your support, your commitment.'

'Well . . .' I said.

'That means the Power List, Dan. It'll do me the world of good.'

'I'm not sure if I—'

'They say the past is another country, don't they, Dan? We have to move on, to forget it, don't we? Well, this is what I want you to do. My entry in the Power List, it has to be about my art, about how important it is, about the critical acclaim it's getting. Nothing to do with the old stuff, okay? Nothing at all. Not one reference to it, you understand? I want a complete break. Christopher Corcoran, Landscape Artist. That's it. Straight into your Top Ten. Is that all right?'

'That's all right,' I said.

27

Concrete buzzed his wife on the intercom. Then he buzzed her again. She answered just as he was trying it for the third time. 'Delores,' he said, 'you can bring the wine and cheese now.'

There was a pause, and then: 'I'm watching *Holby City*.'

'It's on the same channel as *EastEnders*, it's still taping.'

'But I'm halfway through it now.'

'Will you just bring the *fucking* wine and the *fucking* cheese?'

There was no response. He drummed his fingers on the wall. 'Delores?' He glanced back at me, looked at his watch, and drummed his fingers again. '*Delores?*'

'All right! I'm coming!'

Satisfied, he turned away from the speaker. 'Now then,' he said, 'where were we?'

'I was trying to explain that I can't just *ignore* your past. If I put you in the Power List and don't even mention that you're . . . who you are, then it would look very strange. The List would lose all credibility.'

'Do I give a fuck about that?'

'A true artist would. Your background is surely part of who you are as . . . an artist.'

He thought about that for a moment. 'Right. I see your point.'

I was feeling a little braver now, which was probably a mistake, given my surroundings, but I have always been one to open my mouth before my brain's in gear and I was suddenly and inexplicably feeling quite protective of *Belfast Confidential* and its reputation. 'You see,' I pointed out, 'if it reads like advertising, it probably *is* advertising, and people won't take it seriously. But if it's written objectively, with complete artistic freedom, in the same way that you create your landscapes, then the results will be a much more accurate ahm barometer of your place in . . . society.'

'But what if it's a hatchet job?'

'Well, that's a risk you take in a democratic society.'

'You'll be writing it, though.'

'I probably will. Yes.'

'So you'll make it fair.'

'It will be accurate.'

He thought about that some more. Then he nodded. 'And sure I already have the advert to back it up.'

'You have an advert? In *Belfast Confidential*?'

'Double page centrefold spread, next week's issue. Signed sealed and delivered. We're having a big exhibition at the Orchard Gallery – we'll shift some paintings that night. Then the crowning glory will be our place on the Power List. We will truly have arrived.'

'When you say *we*, you mean *you*?'

'No, I mean we. The whole school.'

'School?'

'I'm not the only one, my friend. There's a whole new generation coming through, and I'm right at the heart of it. It's so exciting. We have our own workshop in Belfast an' all.'

'I hadn't heard.'

'Oh aye, though we've changed our name. Used to be called *Paint Brush*, but that led to too many misunderstandings, of which I was the winner, but eventually I decided to rename it

Easel. Sounds good, doesn't it? Painting fans get it, at any rate.' I nodded. He turned back to the buzzer and pressed. 'Where is that fucking witch?' There was no response.

'She'll be in the kitchen, Boss,' said the driver, 'and the speaker's bust in there.'

'This house is too fucking big,' Concrete snapped. 'Go and give her a hand.'

The driver nodded, and hurried out of the gallery. I took advantage of the distraction to examine the closest landscape to me in a little more detail. There was a white card taped to the wall beside it. *'Fields, Trees and Bushes Outside Lisburn'* by *Christopher Corcoran. £10,000.*

I glanced back at him. 'You get ten grand for these?'

Concrete came up on my shoulder. 'At least. Depends how the bidding goes. I have slides I gave to your advertising guys, but you can use them in your article as well, if you like.'

'Okay,' I said. I nodded around the walls. 'I'm surprised you have the time. What with all your . . . commitments.'

'Ah, sure the business runs itself these days.'

'It must be very lucrative – imports and exports.'

'Oh, aye. It's the paperwork gets you down.'

'You *do* paperwork?'

Concrete nodded. 'Of course I do. Will I let you into a little secret, Dan? You're not stupid, you know who I am, what I've done, but the fact of the matter is that sometimes in business it's good to have that reputation: it helps with the old negoti- atin', you know what I mean? But the truth is, the business is now almost entirely legit.'

'Almost,' I said.

'Absolutely. I'd say, seventy-three per cent legit. And growing every day. It's like *The Godfather*, Dan, the way they were always going legit.'

'Didn't every *Godfather* movie end with a massacre?'

'Ah, Dan, for fuck sake, don't be so cynical, that's the movies.'

'Of course,' I said.

I looked a little closer at *Fields, Trees and Bushes Outside Lisburn*. There was a zebra in the bottom left-hand corner. I pointed this out to him. He smiled and said, 'Let me tell you a story, Dan. When I first started off with this lark, with Liam's guidance, I entered one of my landscapes in a little art competition in Belfast – didn't say who I was, you know, kept it all anonymous.' He smiled. 'Sure haven't I been doin' things anonymously for years? Anyway, I entered it and this guy from the *Irish News* writes this review which comments favourably on my picture in particular but says there's not enough happening in it, and suggests the addition of animals to, and I quote "help add perspective". So I'm really made up with this, my first review, it's a real cracker, but I want to know more about what he means, about not enough happening in the picture, so I go and see him at his house. It's three o'clock in the morning, because that's when I do my thinking, and I'm wearing the old balaclava, 'cos I don't want him to know who I am, in case it colours his judgment, you know what I mean?'

I nodded.

'So I'm sitting on the end of his bed, discussing art with him in his pyjamas, three o'clock in the fucking morning, and it was fucking fascinating. Surreal, but fascinating. Not that I've any time for that shit. The Surrealists. Won't have it in my school. Pile of shite, I say. Anyway, I says to him would it help if I put some animals in my landscapes, and he thought it was a good idea. I asked him for a list of animals which might find favour with the art critics, and he said it wasn't a good idea to try and please critics in this way. But I thought, like, that you have to have the courage of your convictions, so he agreed to discuss the possible animals I might include. He favoured the more traditional approach – you know, pigs or cows or sheep or a goat or something. But to tell you the truth, even as he was talking, I was thinking, It's too tame, fucking goats. What about something exotic, like a giraffe or a water buffalo, you know?'

I nodded.

'You see, if people look at one of my paintings and they see a zebra, they're going to say, "Hey, what's that zebra doing in a field outside Lisburn? Did it escape from a zoo?" There's no doubt about it – great art makes you think.'

I was starting to get a crick in my neck from all the nodding.

'But I mean, the thing is, Dan, most artists, you know they're shy and retiring and all that, but to get anywhere these days you have to go out there and sell yourself. Take this very same painting: after I'd gone home and stuck the zebra in it, the fucking *Newsletter* of all papers prints a review and the critic says, basically, "Forget about the zebra, the rest of the painting is . . ." and it cut me to the fucking bone . . . "*drab*". Drab! Does this look drab to you?'

'No,' I said.

'So, I goes to his house one night and climb in through his kid's bedroom window and get him up against the wall and say, "Drab, who're you calling fucking drab, in your crap wee house?" Sometimes you gotta take the bull by the horns, you know? So I sat him down and explained to him that although on the surface I was only painting hills and trees and bushes and it might look a bit quiet, like, even with the zebra – I mean, it's fucking tiny, you'd hardly notice it – if he was to look *beyond* the hills, out of sight, he'd see the Long Kesh prison camp where I served seven years for attempted murder. He agreed that this completely altered his views on the painting. You see,

Dan, the meaning was in the subtext. Do you get it?'

'I get it.'

'Good. Now where's that fucking wine and cheese?!' He stormed back across to the buzzer again and kept his finger jammed on it for three minutes, without response.

I said, 'You explained all this about your art to Mouse, didn't you?'

'Oh aye. I'm always spreading the word.'

'And what did he say?'

'He seemed to take it all on board.'

'And did he agree to put you in the Power List?'

'I think it went without saying.'

'Without referring to your back story?'

'He said he'd see what he could do, but he didn't bother explaining it to me the way you did, Dan. I appreciate that. You know, I'm a fair man, I can see both sides. So, the best I can say is, like, leave it to your conscience. Penalise me for my past sins, or celebrate my new life. You decide.'

'All right,' I said.

'C'mon – for fuck sake, we'll go and get our own fucking wine and cheese.'

'I'm really not that—'

'C'mon!'

He jerked his head towards the door, and started walking. I followed. He was a big man with a notoriously mean temper, and if I didn't do what he said, he might kill me – or lock me in for the night with his landscapes. He was clearly as mad as a bag of spiders.

As he realigned the temperature control and then punched in the security code, I took a last look at his gallery. 'Ten grand, eh?' I said out loud, without really meaning to.

* * *

Concrete was leading me back through the cellar when he stopped suddenly and yanked open one of the cardboard boxes. As he reached inside he said, 'Have you seen the new Spielberg?'

I shook my head.

He produced a DVD. 'I know you haven't – neither has anyone else!' He pushed it into my hands. 'Plenty more where that came from. Howse about a suit?'

'Don't wear them,' I said.

'Ah, an artist, just like me.'

'Just like you,' I agreed.

He offered me half a dozen other counterfeit items as we crossed the cellar floor. I rejected them all, because I can't be bought, but held onto the Spielberg as it was supposed to be a real return to form. He began to shout as we moved up the stairs. 'Delores! For fuck sake!' He put one hand on the door to pull it open. 'How many fucking hours does it take to—' and then he stopped so quickly that my head banged into his rear end just above me on the stairs.

From the kitchen someone snapped: 'Put your hands on your fucking head!'

Concrete slowly raised them. I couldn't see around him, couldn't identify the source.

'Slowly – come out fucking slowly!'

Concrete took a step forward. 'Now boys,' he said calmly, 'sure you could have just knocked the door and I would have let youse in and made youse a cup of tea.'

'Shut your fucking mouth, Concrete – now where is he?!'

'Who?'

'You know! Where the fuck is he?'

''Fraid you've lost me, boys.'

'Where's Starkey? What have you done with him?'

Concrete, his hands still raised, glanced back at me. 'Dan, mate – someone's looking for you.' He moved a little to the side, so that I could see: a cop with a gun.

The cop shouted: 'Whoever you are, come out with your hands up!'

I moved forward into the light, with my hands raised. There were four cops in body armour and flak jackets, each with their guns drawn and pointed at Concrete, and now covering me as well. Two more cops were on the other side of the kitchen, with their weapons trained on Delores and the driver, who lay on the floor with their hands clasped behind their heads.

'What's going on?' I asked.

'We ask the fucking questions!' They were nervous. Nervous and angry. 'Who the fuck are you?'

'I'm Starkey.'

'Dan Starkey?'

'Last time I checked.'

'ID, show me some fucking ID!'

I made a move for my back pocket and my wallet but one of the other cops rushed forward, screaming, 'Leave it!' I left it. He fished the wallet out of my pocket and flipped it open. My press card was there. It wasn't a great picture, but it was me. He nodded back at his comrades. 'It's him.'

'Are you all right?'

'Yes.'

'You're being held against your will?'

'No.'

'You were kidnapped earlier this evening in Belfast?'

'No.'

'You're being forced to say that.'

'No . . . really.'

'Then what are you doing here with Concrete Corcoran?'

'He was showing me his etchings.'

'What's going on!'

'I'm telling you the truth.'

'Do you wish to press charges?'

'No.'

'You're not being held against your will?'

'*No.*'

'Nor any of your family?'

'No!'

The cops exchanged glances. Then they slowly lowered their weapons. 'Fuck,' said one.

'Are you happy now, boys?' Concrete asked.

'Watch your mouth, Concrete.'

I lowered my arms. Concrete kept his up, although in an ironic fashion. *Artists.*

'We had a report you'd been kidnapped and were being held against your will.'

I shook my head. 'No. No, I wasn't.'

Concrete winked at me. 'I don't suppose you boys have a search warrant?'

'Fuck off, Concrete.'

They turned for the door. One stopped and said, 'Do you want to come with us, Mr Starkey?'

'Okay,' I said.

Delores and the driver were just getting back up. A cop offered her a hand, but she brushed it off. 'Missed the end of fucking *Holby* now,' she snapped.

'Don't worry, boys,' said Concrete, 'she's got it taped.'

They filed out of the kitchen, along the hall and towards the front door, which had been smashed off its hinges. Glass was scattered everywhere.

'Send us the bill, Concrete,' a cop said with the kind of fatigue that suggested he'd said it a hundred times before.

Concrete followed us through the broken door. There were half a dozen cop cars and several unmarked vehicles fanned out in a semi-circle facing the house. Several cops, with their weapons drawn, had taken up covering positions behind their vehicles, only to be given the word that everything was okay.

As I set foot in the garden, one of the unmarked cars flashed its lights, and a moment later Alec Large pushed the driver's door open and stood, looking rather sheepishly towards me. 'Sorry,' he said, 'this is all my fault. I thought you were in trouble.'

I gave him a resigned shrug and crossed to the car. I opened the passenger side door, but before climbing in I looked back up at Concrete, standing with his driver on a small first-floor balcony, watching as the cops bent back into their own vehicles. 'Thanks for the show,' I called, then thumbed behind me down the drive. 'I thought you had a state-of-the-art security system.'

His driver snorted beside him.

'Aye, you'd think that,' said Concrete, 'but it's fucking counterfeit, like everything else around here.'

28

I was tucked up toasty in bed, but I couldn't sleep. Rain was beating against the window, and somewhere beyond it, Topper mewed. For shelter. For his brother. For revenge. Maybe he'd spotted the ghost of Liam Miller wafting across our lawn, tutting. Perhaps I could make it up to Topper by getting him to pose for one of Concrete Corcoran's paintings. It would be a kind of immortality, another life to add to his nine. But no, Topper wasn't exotic enough. If he'd been a walrus or an alligator, he might have been in with a chance.

I asked Trish about the redemptive powers of art.

She said, 'Shut up, I'm trying to sleep.'

'No, seriously,' I said, 'do you think he's genuine?'

'Dan, please, it's late, I've to go to work.'

'I know that. I'm sorry. I understand. But he's a hood of the highest calibre, or lowest, depending on your point of view. And he thinks he's transformed himself, but he's already leaning on art critics. He has no idea at all about how to conduct himself in a civilised society. The question is, have we done this to him, brutalised him, or is he just a sick fuck?'

'*You're* the sick fuck, now shut up.'

'He's invited us both to the launch of his exhibition. What with that and Liam's funeral, our social life is certainly taking off.'

Patricia sighed. 'If you'll recall,' she said wearily, 'I didn't go to Liam's funeral, and there's no way I'm going to an art show organised by Concrete Corcoran. I know I don't get out much, but I know who he is and what he's capable of, and if you think I'm going along there to be nicety-nice and be strong-armed into buying a painting, then you've another thing coming. So count me out.'

We lay quietly in the dark. Then we turned this way and that.

'Do you hear that cat?' Trish asked after a while.

'I do.'

'He sounds like he's pining for something.'

'He's probably just locked out, wanting in.'

'No, they've a cat flap.'

'Well, then he's just being a cat.'

'Well, it's bloody annoying.'

'I know.'

'Maybe you should go out and throw something at it.'

I sighed. 'That would be cruel and heartless.'

'That's life,' she said.

Another five minutes passed, and I was finally beginning to slip into a bit of a doze when Patricia said, 'I'm worried about the garden.'

'The garden?' I asked groggily.

'The grass doesn't seem to be taking.'

'It was starting to sprout.'

'I know, I thought that too, but it's only here and there. We planted the last few weeks of September – maybe it was too late. I was thinking we should get someone round to look at it.'

'Whatever,' I said.

'Show some enthusiasm,' she said.

'It's three o'clock in the morning.'

'You woke *me* up.'

'Not to talk about fucking gardening.'

'No. What was it? The redemptive powers of art? Fascinating.'

'Well, sor-*ry*.'

We lay silently for another couple of minutes. Then she said, 'Liam thought we'd misread the chart in his book.'

'Back to fucking Liam.'

'He said that laying a lawn was a marriage of soil and seed.'

'Just like us.'

'Not just a case of throwing down the first thing that came to hand.'

'Uhuh. That's right. Have another dig.'

'It's not a dig, Dan. It's common sense.' She sighed. 'He was so sweet.'

'Uhuh.'

'He was. You never gave him a chance.'

'I gave him every chance.'

'You did *not*. You know something? I only knew him for a few hours – and I miss him already.'

'Well, part of him's still on the wall downstairs.'

'Dan!' She sat up straight. 'You just never know when to shut your mouth, do you!'

'I was only saying.'

'Sometimes you just make me really sick, do you know that?'

'I was only raking, Trish, for god sake.'

'He was killed in our *house*, Dan. He was *murdered*.'

'I'm aware of that.'

'And the best you can do is some sick fucking joke.'

'Okay! I'm sorry! But it wasn't that sick.'

'Oh fuck you.' She turned in the bed and gave me a hard shove.

'What was that for?'

'You! And this one!' She shoved me again.

'Trish – fuck off! I'm trying to sleep.'

She shoved me again. 'No – you fuck off.'

'Trish . . .'

'I'm serious. Go and sleep in the other room.'

'Trish . . .'

'Go!'

'Trish . . .'

'GO!'

'Ah, fuck you.' I rolled out of bed. It was back to discretion being the better part of valour. We'd be at it all night otherwise. I tramped across the carpet in the dark. I opened the door and said, 'Trish . . .'

'I'm serious. Just go, Dan.'

But I didn't leave. Not yet. I hesitated by the door and said, 'Can you hear that?'

She was silent for a moment; there was the rain still, but Topper had quit his mewing. 'Hear what?' she snapped.

'Listen. There's music.'

She listened. '*What* music?'

'Can't you hear it? It's from a musical.'

'Dan, what are you—'

'Listen . . . *listen*,' I said with enough urgency for her to try again. But still she couldn't hear anything.

So I began to sing it. '*I'm gonna wash that man right offa my wall . . .*'

Trish screamed, and threw an alarm clock, but I was long gone.

The spare room was filled with all kinds of boxes we hadn't yet had time to open. Or might never open. They do say that if you don't need something within six weeks of first moving house, then you don't need it at all. But for every box of shoes and handbags belonging to Trish there was one of football programmes and *Land of the Giants* bubblegum cards belonging to me. She would never wear her shoes again, but once every few years I still took my stuff out and went through it, reminiscing. I would think about the child I had been, and the child I once had, and wonder whether there might be another, one day. I would think about the disparity between how much the programmes and cards were supposedly worth, and the chances of finding someone fool enough to pay that much for them. I'd heard about eBay, but it scared me.

I sat on the bed. The curtains were open and I could see the blue Mercedes sitting in complete darkness across the road. I couldn't make out the outline of the man within, but I knew he was there.

Alec Large.

Someone to watch over me.

29

When I came down in the morning Alec was sitting at the kitchen table, eating a fry. Trish was in her dressing-gown, cleaning the George Foreman Grill.

I said, 'Oh,' and he said, 'Oh.'

I looked at Trish and said, 'What the fuck are you doing?'

She shrugged.

I said, 'The last time you made me a fry it was the nineteen-eighties and you were into Haircut One Pound.'

She shrugged again and asked Alec if he would like another cup of tea. He looked at me, then said no.

I headed for the front door. He dropped his knife and fork and hurried after me, pulling on his jacket. Trish stepped into the kitchen doorway and called down the hall. 'Oh Alec?'

He stopped.

'Nice talking to you. I hope it works out with your girlfriend.'

'Thanks,' he said. 'Oh, and thanks for the breakfast. Lovely.'

On the drive to work he started to say something.

'I don't fucking want to know,' I spat.

I sat down opposite Alan Wells, our Advertising Manager, at a little after ten. I was late for work. Something to do with a broken alarm clock. I said, 'I understand Concrete Corcoran's taken a double-page centrefold advert in the Power List issue.'

Alan didn't look up from his computer. 'Yes, he has.'

'And how much did that cost him?'

Alan kept his eyes on the screen. 'A double-page advert in *Belfast Confidential* costs eleven thousand pounds.'

'He's a first-time advertiser, right?' Alan nodded. 'And it's company policy that all first-time advertisers pay in advance, is that true?'

'Yes, it is.'

'Did Concrete Corcoran pay in advance?'

'Yes, of course he did.' But then his eyes flicked up for the first time as he added, 'Kind of.'

I took a deep breath. 'Explain.'

Alan pushed his chair back. 'This way.' Then he added, 'Please,' when he saw I wasn't moving.

I followed him out of Advertising into the Editorial part of the open-plan office. He stopped, then nodded forwards. I followed his gaze, and then shifted it left and right searching for what he meant. But it was just the office. Everyone was beavering away.

'What?' I asked.

He raised an eyebrow, and nodded forward again.

'Look, for god—' And then the penny dropped. I'd seen it dozens of times, it had just never registered: hanging on the far wall – a landscape painting.

'You didn't!'

'It had a price tag of twelve thousand pounds and rising, so Mouse thought it would be a good investment.'

'*He* okayed it?'

'Yes, he did. Although it didn't actually arrive until after the fire. Weren't we lucky? And we had it valued independently.'

I moved closer. It was a Concrete Corcoran production all right. Trees, bushes, a river, the Antrim Hills, and peeking out from behind an outcropping of rock, the head and trunk of an elephant.

I said, 'Would you pay twelve thousand pounds for this?'

'Of course not.'

'So why did we?'

'Because Mouse wanted it.'

'Did he often swap expensive advertising space for . . . favours?'

'Not that I'm aware of.'

'Right.'

I left him to it. Mouse was starting to piss me off. Of course he was entitled to swap advertising space in his own magazine for a painting, even one with an elephant in it. It just didn't seem like him; so I could add that to the growing list of other things that didn't seem like him. The reason we'd drifted apart wasn't laziness on either side, it was because he had moved to a completely different planet.

My head was still elsewhere as I passed Mary's desk. She smiled up and said, 'You wouldn't guess who called to see you.'

'Mother Teresa?'

'Mother Teresa is dead.'

I gave her a look. 'I know she's dead.'

'Well, that's not funny then.' She pulled out a cigarette and lit it. She already had one burning in her ash tray. When she'd taken a long enough drag on it she picked an envelope out of her in-tray and handed it to me.

'Terry Breene,' she said, as I opened it up.

'He came here?'

'Hand-delivered.'

I took out a Press Pass for the second leg of Linfield's European Championship match against Maccabi Tel Aviv at Windsor Park the following night, with a printed invitation to an 'After Match Reception' in the boardroom.

'What did he say?' I asked.

'I have no idea,' said Mary. 'I was too busy looking into his eyes.'

'Right,' I said. 'Great.'

'Isn't he lovely, still?'

'Yes, Mary, that's right.' I slipped the pass and invitation into my jacket pocket and turned for the stairs. But before I mounted them I turned back and said, 'Mary, do you know how you knew Mother Teresa was a Catholic?'

She looked a little confused. 'No – how?'

'She looked like one.'

I gave her a wink and hurried up to my office.

Half an hour later Pat came up the stairs. He handed over a sheaf of papers and I started to flick through them as he gave me a running commentary.

'The top one's a list from the Arts Council of all the artists who've received lottery grants in the past eighteen months, and I cross-referenced them with our database of convicted terrorists. The last page shows the names of the eight lucky artists who've also done time for being naughty.' I glanced through the names: Concrete's was there, of course, but I also recognised Thomas 'Biro' McFarlane's, Malachi 'Three Strokes' Murphy and Edna O'Boyle. 'All were in the H Blocks, with the exception of Edna O'Boyle who was in Armagh Women's Prison.'

The first two were fairly well-known players in their time; I hadn't heard of the woman, though. 'Know anything about her?' I asked.

'Weapons found in her house, she got six years. She's not a painter, she specialises in textiles. Last year she won an Arts Council Fellowship for crocheting a bulletproof vest.'

'A . . .'

'I believe it was an ironic statement on . . . something.'

'Okay, can you find out if any of this lot are connected to Concrete's school of painting, or to this exhibition that we're so thoughtfully advertising for them?'

'Will do.' Pat took the sheets back.

Around lunchtime I took a stroll across the square. A wrecking ball had been brought in to help dismantle what was left of the old *Belfast Confidential* building. I said to myself, 'Happens to us all,' and it was only when a familiar voice said, 'Aye,' beside me that I realised both that I'd spoken out loud and that Alec Large was with me.

'Where did you pop up from?'

'I'm always here. You won't always notice me. But in future, I'd prefer it if you advised me in advance where you're going – you know, gave me a schedule or something. I can check places out, assess the risk.'

I nodded. 'Well, at eight o'clock in the morning you can usually find me having breakfast with my wife. Unless of course you're there first.'

He cleared his throat. 'That was a bit of a miscalculation,' he said.

'So perhaps in future then we could keep it on a strictly professional basis?'

'Yes, sir.'

'I don't give a flying fuck about your girlfriend.'

'I understand that.'

We walked on.

'I'll need to know your blood type,' he said. 'Just in case anything happens.' I nodded. He said, 'Well?'

'Well what?'

'What is your blood type?'

'I have no idea. But I can find out. I'll stick a Post-it note to your windscreen tomorrow morning.'

'Okay.'

I'd noticed him on more than one occasion touching a finger to his ear and muttering something into his cuff, and now he did it again. He turned suddenly, and I went with him. There was an old lady with a tartan shopping trolley coming towards us. We both gave her a hard look, but she trundled on past without exploding.

I said, 'Who are you talking to?' and I gave a little pull on my own cuff.

He said, 'No one.'

'But you're talking to your sleeve, and you're wearing an earpiece.'

'Yes, I am.'

'So who are you listening to, then?'

'Radio Ulster.'

'You're what?'

He cleared his throat. 'Let's keep moving; best not to provide a stationary target.'

So I started walking again. There was the usual amount of daylight traffic around the square, and none of the pedestrians were noticeably bearing arms. I said, 'No, seriously, who're you listening to?'

'*Talk Back*, Radio Ulster.'

'Is that code for *There's an elite squad of highly trained security agents watching my every move*?'

'No, it really is *Talk Back*. You have to understand, Mr Starkey, that although I'm the best that money can buy, I'm operating on a limited budget. So there's no back-up.' He touched his ear again, and glanced about us as we approached Great Victoria Street. 'But as long as whoever is watching us thinks there's back-up, they'll probably leave us alone.'

'Someone's watching us?'

'I have no idea, but why take the risk?'

I glanced up and around me. At windows. I was thinking about Kennedy and his very complicated public suicide. And Martin Luther King and his penchant for cheap motels.

'Well,' I said, 'if you insist.'

The offices of JJ Howe, the Fine Arts auctioneers who'd given Mouse a £12,000 plus evaluation on the Concrete Corcoran landscape, were a five-minute walk away. I had an appointment, though I'd kept it deliberately vague as to exactly who I was. As far as the guy in charge was aware, I was just a punter looking for a valuation, and as long as he lived down a dark hole and didn't read the newspapers or watch TV he wouldn't suspect a thing.

As we walked, I said to Alec, 'If there's no back-up, who's covering me when you're off duty?'

'I'm never off duty.'

'But you must sleep.'

'Yes, I do. But believe me, when I'm needed, I'll be there.'

'Okay,' I said. 'So if we'd employed you earlier, you would have been able to stop Liam Miller's murder.'

'He wasn't murdered.'

'You what?'

'Liam Miller wasn't murdered. He was assassinated.'

'What are you talking about?'

'The prominence or importance of an individual distinguishes his or her death from an ordinary act of terrorism or murder. Liam Miller was famous, he was known in every home in the land, therefore his death qualifies as an assassination.'

'What, like Gandhi was assassinated?'

Alec nodded.

It was kind of a surreal idea, placing a bent flower arranger up there with the Indian Yoda. But Liam would have been pleased.

'Okay, so if you'd been on duty, you think you'd have been able to stop Liam's . . . *assassination*?'

'You can never be one hundred per cent sure. But ninety-five, yes, I believe so.'

'Well,' I said, 'I can't ask for much more than that. If you stick with me day and night, and I co-operate with schedules and varying the way I travel to work and basically do everything you say, and in exchange you don't get distracted by my wife offering you a cooked breakfast, you can be fairly certain you'll be able to prevent my assassination.'

'You won't be assassinated.'

'Excellent.'

'You're not nearly famous enough or prominent enough. But I will do my best to stop you from being murdered.'

I stopped. Alec stopped. He scanned the pavement around us, and touched a finger to his earpiece. I said, 'Wait just a minute. I'm the Editor and part owner of *Belfast Confidential* – surely that qualifies me for assassination?'

'I would argue that you're new to the job, and most people have never heard of you.'

I glared at him. 'What was Mouse then – murdered or assassinated?'

'Oh, definitely assassinated.'

I snorted. 'Is this how you get your kicks, drawing up infantile lists?'

'Yes.'

'And do these lists exist anywhere outside of your head?'

'No.'

'So there's no global system for checking on whether someone qualifies as murdered or assassinated, no fucking Dow Jones Index of the recently violently departed?'

'No.'

'So why am I even having this conversation with you?'

'I have no idea. But I think we've stayed in this position for far too long. If you wouldn't mind moving along . . .'

I took a deep breath, and started walking again.

'One thing to consider though,' Alec said, moving just a little behind me. 'If you do get murdered, that in itself might make you famous enough to be considered a candidate for assassination next time – that is, if you had the nine lives of a cat.'

'Right,' I said. 'Thanks for that.'

I don't know who was kidding whom. He was bound to be aware just as much as I was that cats didn't have nine lives. They had one, and then they got buried under a badly sown lawn.

30

JJ Howe had been dead for fifty years. The man in charge now was called Peter Marshall, a rotund, bald-of-head chap in a designer-crumpled blue linen suit that was slightly too large. He led me through a showroom full of paintings – mostly modern – to a tidy office at the rear. He said his receptionist and fellow evaluators were off on their lunch, otherwise he would offer me coffee. I didn't see what was preventing him getting up and making it himself. After all, I might have been a billionaire wanting to splash some cash about. Perhaps he suspected I wasn't.

He said, 'Now then, Mr Stark.'

'Starkey,' I corrected.

He nodded. 'Donald.'

'Dan.'

He glanced down at a small notebook on the dark wooden desk before him, then he lifted a pen and made a couple of amendments to whatever was written there.

'Now then, Mr Starkey. Daniel.'

'Dan.'

'Dan. I understand you have an item for evaluation. It must be very small.' He smiled wanly. I nodded. 'May I ask if this is for insurance purposes, or do you wish to sell the item in question?'

'There's a difference?'

'Oh, most certainly. Beauty is in the eye of the beholder, so any valuation for sales purposes is generally quite vague. But if you're merely insuring it, we have to nail down a rather more specific, and usually lower, figure.'

'Well, I haven't decided. Perhaps if you take a look?'

I produced one of the slides Concrete Corcoran had provided for the Advertising Department and slid it across the table. He looked a little pained as he picked it up. 'I cannot base any official evaluation on a slide,' he said bluntly.

'You could give me an opinion, a ballpark figure.'

'I suppose. Although not in writing.'

'I understand,' I said.

He opened a drawer in his desk and produced a small magnifying glass with a slot in one end, into which he slid the slide. 'And the artist?'

'Well – I'd like you to tell me.'

He raised an eyebrow, then began to examine the slide. He tutted almost immediately, then followed it with three more. He lowered the magnifier again and said, 'Are you having me on?'

'No,' I said.

'We specialise in works of high art, Mr Stark, costing anything from tens to hundreds of thousands of pounds. Not this kind of . . . tat.'

'Don't beat around the bush,' I said.

'The problem,' Peter Marshall pointed out as he raised the magnifier again, 'is that I can't tell if it *is* a bush. The brush-strokes are hideous, there's no definition, the scale is all over the place, even the colours are so badly . . .' He trailed off, as he lowered the magnifier. 'If I didn't know Liam Miller had been assassinated I'd think this was one of his reality show set-ups.'

I cleared my throat and said, 'So as far as an evaluation goes . . .'

'I wouldn't give you the skin off my custard for it, Mr Stark.'

'I see. Could you explain to me then how you or a member of your staff recently provided paperwork giving this a valuation of twelve thousand pounds.'

'We – don't be ridiculous!' Marshall angrily removed the slide from the magnifier and began to push it back across the desk towards me. 'This, sir, is not worth *twelve* pounds, let alone twelve thousand.'

'Even if it's painted by Concrete Corcoran?'

'Ah.' He stopped the pushing. In fact, he clawed it back. He raised it up to examine it again, this time without the benefit of the magnifier. 'Concrete Corcoran. That's another matter entirely.'

'I don't understand,' I said. 'If it's tat, it's tat.'

'Well, not necessarily. It's a Corcoran.' He turned the slide a little to throw some extra light on it. 'Ah yes – I see now. It's so refreshing to find an alligator in the River Lagan.' As he lowered it again he said, 'If one of my staff has valued this at twelve thousand pounds, then I don't doubt he thinks it's worth it.'

'But it's still tat, and technically it's all over the place. You said so yourself.'

'Yes, quite, but in this case it doesn't really matter. You see, our valuations are based on a certain number of criteria, Donald, and very few of them actually have anything to do with the technical aspect of the work. I mean, take a look at any of the pieces we have on display out there – who can say whether they are technically efficient? They are what they are. A series of dots on a blank canvas. A square of black paint on a yellow background. We base our estimate on what the piece or similar pieces might have raised at past auctions, and the critical response to that work. So, for example, Corcoran's previous exhibitions have received outstanding reviews. Outstanding. They have also sold extremely well and there is a continuing and expanding demand for them. Naturally we have taken this into account when evaluating the work.'

'But they're crap.'

'You can't say that.'

'*You* did.'

'Before I knew who the artist was. I didn't know about his struggle, I didn't know about his suffering.'

'Most of his suffering was inflicted on others.'

'That may be, but that is part of the attraction. I don't like the term myself, but there's a kind of terrorist chic developing out there, and people will pay to be part of it. It's like Paul McCartney's paintings, or Ron Wood's – you're not actually paying for the painting, you're paying to own a little bit of someone who has excelled in another field. The Beatles, The Rolling Stones, and ahm, in this case, bloody mayhem.'

We talked some more about art and terrorism, and eventually I got around to revealing who I was. He seemed mightily impressed, although not enough to put the kettle on. He said, 'Then you'll be covering Concrete's exhibition.'

'Yes, I expect so.'

'I understand that between him and his colleagues at Easel there'll be over two hundred works on display. His entire *oeuvre*. It's quite, quite mouth-watering.'

'Something like that,' I agreed.

I reclaimed the slide and thanked him for his time. As he walked me back through the gallery, I could appreciate what he meant about beauty being in the eye of the beholder. Concrete Corcoran's paintings might not be technically perfect, or even adequate, but at least they looked like something recognisable. It looked to me like JJ Howes had cornered the market in dots and splodges.

I shook his hand at the door. He held onto it for longer than he needed to. 'It's a queer business, art,' he said.

'I imagine.'

'Concrete Corcoran is a perfect example. If he was to die – say of a heart-attack or stomach cancer – well, it wouldn't affect the value of his work at all. But if he was to die violently, then you'd be talking about a tenfold increase, almost certainly. Funny that, isn't it?'

'Hilarious,' I said.

I stepped out into the crisp autumn air and started walking. A moment later Alec fell into step behind me.

31

Mouse had reinvented himself, and so had Concrete Corcoran.
Who was I to begrudge either of them this priceless luxury?
And I was beginning to realise that it wasn't only those two,
but that possibly the entire country had ducked into Mr Benn's
changing room and emerged fresh and vibrant. The evidence
was all around, like love. Yes, Mouse was dead. Yes, Liam Miller
was gone. And yes, Concrete Corcoran still had his thuggish
side, but he was at least *trying* to move on, just as Belfast, now
increasingly at peace with itself, was as well. Business was
booming instead of going boom. Both communities were
thriving – in fact, in some respects they were beginning to blend
in.

For years Ireland's articulate middle classes had shown the
way forward through their support of an all-island rugby team,
and now it seemed that the rest of us were slowly coming
round to their way of thinking. There was no longer any border
to speak of, the smoking ban was creeping north, the Euro was
almost a universal currency, and according to Patrick, the price
of cocaine on either side of that invisible border had more or
less stabilised. What if I was the only one trying to hold on to
the old ways, the old divisions? I had chastised anyone who
would listen that this newfound beauty was only skin deep,
that we were as bigoted and hateful underneath as we had

always been. But perhaps it was just me, burned by decades of reporting and chastened by harrowing personal experience, who had failed to emerge from a self-imposed political, religious and mental hibernation. How ironic then was it that I was the part-owner and Editor of *Belfast Confidential*, which in its own way was meant to symbolise everything that was new and bold about this country of ours?

I was thinking this, and other deep thoughts, as I arrived back at the office. Alec took up a position just to the left of a small cloakroom where he could leap out and severely frisk anyone who got past Mary without an appointment.

Not that Mary was at her desk when we got back.

Nor indeed was anyone else at their desks.

Their computers were on. There was music coming from a digital radio. But the phones were ringing unanswered.

I called, 'Hello?' despite the evidence before me, and when there was no response I ordered Alec up the stairs to see if they were planning a surprise (and mistaken) birthday party. He took out his gun and moved cautiously towards my office. I followed a couple of steps behind, unwilling to wait in the hold of the *Marie Celeste*, while estimating with quiet confidence that Alec was big enough and stupid enough to take the full brunt of any bullet or bomb that was waiting for me upstairs.

But no, my office was empty as well. Not even a booby trap.

I was just saying, 'What the fuck is going on?' when there was a tap on the front door and a small woman in a grey business suit nodded through the glass and up the stairs at me. She indicated for me to open the door. So I hurried back down and pulled it open, despite Alec's orders for me to wait for him to check her out first.

'I'm looking for Dan Starkey,' the woman said, glancing from me to Alec, who had just clattered down beside me. His gun was held to his side, but she wouldn't have noticed it unless she was looking for it.

'And I'm looking for twenty-seven employees of *Belfast Confidential*. I'll swap you.'

She said, 'This isn't a laughing matter. We need to talk.' She held up a laminated badge bearing what appeared to be a recent photograph. It read *Becky Winstanley, Equality Commission.*

I'd just started into the familiar, 'I'm kind of tied up right now,' routine I use on time-wasting do-gooders when I realised she was also carrying a copy of *Belfast Confidential* under her arm. So I stopped myself and said, 'What's this about?'

'May I come in?'

I gave her a stern look and said, 'If you're holding them hostage you're not going to get much for them. They're pretty useless.'

'Please don't talk about them like that, you're in enough trouble already.'

'Me? What have I done?'

'Perhaps if we could talk *in*-side, Mr Starkey?' She moved forward, only for Alec to block her way.

'Madam,' he said, 'I'll need to look in your handbag.'

'Excuse me?'

'He has to,' I explained, 'in case you're carrying a Luger.'

'That's ridiculous. And no, you may not.'

'Then I'm afraid I can't allow you in.'

She snorted and tried to move past him, but he stood firm. It was good to know he could protect me against small women in business suits.

She wasn't happy with this. Equality Officers wield a particular power around Belfast and have been known to make grown men weep. Mostly over positive discrimination.

'Honestly!' she barked. 'We're not living in the Dark Ages

any longer. You have absolutely no right to look in my handbag.'

'That may be,' said Alec. 'Nevertheless.'

He stood his ground. She stood hers.

'Last time this happened,' I pointed out helpfully, 'we were standing here for three months. Although if you smile nicely at him he'll let you take him home and make him breakfast.'

Becky Winstanley's nose was turned up just enough to hang a coat on, although because she was so short it would probably have to dangle in the dust.

'Well, do you have a badge or something?' she asked eventually.

'No, he doesn't,' I answered on Alec's behalf, 'but he does have the courage of his convictions, and unless you have something to hide, why not give him a quick decko so we can get to the bottom of this?'

Becky Winstanley rolled her eyes, tutted, but finally opened her bag. Alec took a little longer than he needed to going through her stuff, the way security people will when their authority is questioned. When he was done he gave her a polite *thank-you, madam*, then took up his position by the door. I led her upstairs to my office.

We faced each other across my desk. 'So,' I began, 'I pop out for ten minutes and when I get back my entire workforce has vanished. What have they gone and done, staged a coup in Equatorial New Guinea?'

'No, Mr Starkey, *they* haven't done anything.'

'THEN LET MY PEOPLE GO!' I thumped the table for added effect, but she didn't even do me the courtesy of jumping the way Mary had.

'Mr Starkey, you seem to be treating this as some kind of a joke. This is a very serious matter.'

'Okay,' I said. 'All right. Put me out of my misery: what have I done?'

'As Editor, Mr Starkey, you have a very poor grasp of what is going on in this company. You don't even seem to be aware that at this very moment, your staff are in the pub across the road organising a strike.'

'There's a pub across the road?' Her eyes narrowed. 'A strike? What the fuck about?'

'The Equality Commission goes to a great deal of trouble to work hand-in-hand with companies like yours, to ensure that religious discrimination is banished from the workplace.'

'Yes,' I said, 'I'm all for that. Show me religious discrimination and I'll banish it. I'll give it a boot in the hole. Now do you think you could get to the point?'

A haughty smile slid onto her face. 'You really don't know? Well, sir, we have taken great pride in forging a good relationship with *Belfast Confidential* in particular because it is such a success story. You might describe it as the flagship for what we are trying to achieve. It must therefore stand up to even greater scrutiny than other companies of a similar size.'

'Yes, okay, could we just get to the—'

'It's important that the make-up of your employees is not only equally representative of both cultures and communities, but that that workforce is shown to be working in complete harmony. As your magazine reflects the world we live in, it also in some respects acts as a window for that world to look in upon us, and it's vital that that world sees that we are all now getting on well together. This isn't just window dressing, Mr Starkey, it has been shown to have a staggering impact on outside investment in our economy *and* on tourism.'

'Yes,' I said, '*all right.*'

'Good. So why the crack about Mother Teresa?'

'The *what*?'

'Complainant reports that at 11.15 a.m. on this date you made a joke about Mother Teresa being, and I quote, "dog ugly, like most Fenians".'

'Jesus Fucking Christ!'

'That's the complaint, and that's why they're on strike.'

'I said nothing of the sort!'

'You're denying you made a joke about Mother Teresa?'

'Yes – no. For fuck sake, I was only raking around!'

'Well, that *raking around* could mean that we have to close you down.'

'*What?* What do you mean, close us down? You can't close us down! Christ All Mighty, you're the Equality Commission, not the fucking SS!'

She remained cool, and calm, and collected. And of course, superior. I was none of these things.

'I would suggest, Mr Starkey, that you choose your words rather more carefully.'

'You can suggest whatever the fuck you want! Close us down? You gotta be fucking kidding.'

'Do I *look* like I'm *kidding*?'

She did not. It suddenly struck me how serious this was, or could become. I rubbed at my brow. I glanced at my watch. It was a little after two. I'd made the joke about three hours before. It had meant nothing. Everyone understood that, *surely*. I stood up and went to the window. There was a pub across there, somewhere, and I hadn't even sniffed it out, but my loyal staff were in there right now, plotting against me while this half-pint harridan gave me a hard time over my taste in jokes. It was harmless fun! Whatever happened to harmless fun? When did it become harmful fun? Whatever happened to ironic detachment?

'Mr Starkey?'

I turned from the window and said, 'Look, I'm sorry, this is crazy. I don't even understand what you're doing here. I mean, aren't there procedures – paperwork, reports – should you even be here before I have a chance to talk to anyone about this? What about my rights? The company solicitor'll sort you out. I mean, what are you, some kind of rapid reaction force?'

'We like to nip these situations in the bud, Mr Starkey. We confront, we expose, you show remorse, we negotiate and we resolve. Five steps and we have a solution. Isn't it better to get it sorted out right now, instead of dragging it out? Think of the publicity. You bring in the solicitors, that's what's going to happen. It's your choice. Make the call if you want. Or we sort it out now.'

'But for fuck sake, it's like a kangaroo court!' I took my seat again. 'What if I just throw you out of my office, tell you to bugger off?'

'Mr Starkey, the days of you just being able to ignore us are long gone. We take affirmative action. For example, in this case we would contact every single one of your advertisers and explain the working conditions here, and they will most probably withdraw their support. Retailers will refuse to stock you. Very shortly the company will go belly up. In the longer term we will of course pursue you personally through the legal system, and to all intents and purposes make it impossible for you ever to work in this town again. Do I make myself clear?' I nodded. 'This is Northern Ireland, Mr Starkey, image is everything and we intend to protect that image with everything we have.'

She had a tough, uncompromising kind of a face. I could feel the colour in my cheeks and the beginning of heart palpitations. I shook my head and even managed a short, derisive laugh. 'This is so bloody ridiculous. It was only a little joke.'

'Do you call black people niggers?'

'*What?!* No, of course not.'

'I rest my case.'

'Christ. It's not like that.'

'I'm afraid it is, Mr Starkey. You're an anachronism, a throw-back. Your time has gone, sir. You either adapt or you die out.'

'Would it have made any difference if I'd made the joke about Protestants?'

She set her jaw a little harder.

'Okay – all right. You win. Christ. I have a magazine to produce, otherwise I *would* fucking take you on. So what do I have to do to sort this out?'

'You apologise to the complainant, and you make an offer of compensation.'

'How much?'

'Five grand ought to cover it.'

'Five grand for calling Mother Teresa a Fenian?'

'I'm sorry, did I say five? I meant seven.'

I cleared my throat and said, 'Seven.'

'Plus no punitive action to be taken against the claimant.'

'Okay, all right. Whatever.'

'And you undertake to observe your employees' rights and promote harmony?'

'Okay. Done.'

'All right then.' Becky Winstanley nodded. 'We have a deal.' She nodded again. I nodded back. She didn't move.

'What now?' I asked.

'The cheque.'

'You want it *now*?'

'It's standard procedure, Mr Starkey. It's called a short, sharp shock. And it prevents any backtracking.'

'You mean just so as I don't get to think about how I've been bushwhacked. You know we *should* write about this, it's a fucking scandal.'

'Eight thousand.'

'All right! Christ.' I took out the company chequebook. I filled in everything but the name, pausing over it. 'Who to?'

'Leave it blank. We have a stamp.'

I ripped out the cheque and held it out to Becky Winstanley. She took hold of it, but I didn't let go. 'Are you on a commission?' I asked.

She gave me a sarcastic smile, and snapped it out of my grip. She tucked it into her handbag and stood. 'Nice doing business with you,' she said. 'Just watch your big mouth in future.'

As she walked down the stairs I called after her: 'You know, one word from me and Alec could break your neck in five places.'

She didn't look back. Alec, stepping out of the cloakroom at the bottom, looked quizzically up at me. I shook my head and he relaxed. As she pulled the door open I shouted, 'Is there an Equality Officer checking out the Equality Commission?' She stepped out onto the pavement. 'Are all Equality Officers created equal, or are some more equal than others?' The door closed after her. 'Fenian!' I shouted, but only when she had walked away. Alec blinked up at me. 'No offence meant,' I said.

'None taken,' said he.

Twenty minutes later, they all arrived back from the pub. I stood erect, with my shoulders pulled back, just inside the front door, greeting them one by one with nothing more than an icy stare. They needed to know that although I might be bloody, I was unbowed.

They didn't pay me a blind bit of notice.

Even Mary. She kept her head down, though not so far that I couldn't see the small silver cross now hanging around her neck. Or perhaps it had always been there. Stephen and Pat were the last through the door. They were arguing about whether Shane McGowan qualified as Irish, and what was more important, his music or the fact that he'd turned a generation off alcohol.

I couldn't hold back any longer. 'I thought we were a team,' I growled at them.

'We are,' they said together.

'Yeah, right,' I said.

They exchanged looks.

'We're not gay,' said Stephen.

'We're just very close,' added Patrick.

'I mean, the *strike*.'

'What strike?' asked Patrick.

'The one you were plotting over there. In the pub.'

Stephen looked where I was pointing. 'That's not a pub. That's a coffee-house.'

'And what're you on about, a strike? Jesus, man, you're paranoid – it's our monthly staff meeting. We're non-union, but we still need to get together to talk things through away from management's prying eyes. That's you.'

'And if it means anything,' said Stephen, 'we gave you a vote of confidence.'

'Unanimous,' said Patrick.

I looked from one to the other. 'But . . . what about the joke?'

'What joke?' asked Patrick.

'The Mother Teresa joke.' They didn't look any the wiser. 'The one about her, you know, looking like, you know . . . ?'

'There's hundreds of Mother Teresa jokes, Boss,' laughed

Stephen. 'You're going to have to be more specific.'

'I can't. Jesus, I don't want to open a whole other can of worms. But you know the one . . .'

'Is it like the ET one?' Patrick asked. 'You know: How do you know ET's a Catholic? He looks like one.'

'Christ,' I said, 'keep it down. Jesus. How can you tell that, and you're a . . . well, I presume you're a . . . you know.'

'Catholic? Fenian? Left-footer? *Taig*?'

'Yes.'

'Well, of course I can! Jesus, man, it's only a bit of fun.'

'Tell *her* that!' I pointed along the corridor to where Mary was already busy with the backlog of calls.

'Mary? Sure, why would it worry her?'

'Don't you get it!?' I exploded. 'I told *her* the joke! She reported me to the fucking Equality Commission! I just had to pay eight grand because I cracked a fucking joke about fucking Mother Teresa!' Mary was looking up now. So was half the office. I took a deep breath. My chest was going thumpa-thumpa-thumpa; I tried to remember what the doctor had said about panic attacks, but I couldn't, and that got me more stressed. I gulped for air. I staggered a little.

Stephen put a hand on my arm. 'Easy, Boss – easy.'

Patrick pulled a chair out of the cloakroom, then guided me into it. 'Get him some water,' he said, and Stephen darted away. Mary was standing now, peering down the corridor. Patrick held up a placatory hand. 'It's all right,' he said, 'it's okay.' Mary sat down again and lifted the phone to answer another call, but still looked extremely worried. All around the office little eyes appeared over desk dividers, wondering what was wrong with the boss.

Stephen arrived back with the water. I took a sip. Then another. I tried to regulate my breathing. 'Sorry,' I managed to say. 'I just get . . . fucking pissed off with . . . these fucking little Hitlers.' I took another sip. 'And how *she* has the fucking nerve to show her face back in here . . .' I glared down the corridor.

Patrick said, 'Dan, this joke – when did you tell it to Mary?'

'This morning.'

'And the Equality Commission contacted you when?'

'Half an hour ago. They're just away!'

Patrick nodded. 'That's about an hour after we heard it in the coffee-house. She's a fast mover.'

'What are you talking about? Who told it in the coffee-house?'

'Mary did. She thought it was class, although you embarrassed the fuck out of her. But it was a woman who came to see you, wasn't it? Small, very severe-looking, grey suit.'

'Yes! That bitch sent her! No . . . wait a minute, how do you know she was wearing a grey suit?'

'Because she's Mad Hattie.'

'Mad . . . ?'

'Mad Hattie's wired to the moon, Dan. She's always trying to pull moves on us. She hangs out across the road; she probably heard Mary tell it and decided to pounce. What was it with Mouse – the passive smoking? And then she got a cheque out of Alan Wells for crèche facilities.'

'Oh God, aye – remember that?' Stephen laughed. 'Alan was mortified for months after that.'

'You mean she's . . . she's not . . . ?'

'Dan, for fuck sake, when have you ever heard of a Government body moving with that kind of speed? Did you even ask for any ID?'

'Yes, of course I did! She had a – well, a laminated badge. Oh Christ.' I rested my head in my hands. I'd been done. I'd always prided myself on being so street smart, and now I'd been done over by fucking Mad Hattie. 'What am I going to tell May Li about the eight grand?'

Patrick shook his head. 'Relax, Dan. She got twenty out of Mouse, five out of Alan, and she hasn't cashed one of them yet. I don't know if she even can. I don't think it's about the money, anyway, it's about winding us up. And the fact that she's mental. Anyway, you okay now? We should get back to work.'

'I'm fine.' I stood up. I moved the chair back into the cloakroom. I ushered them back to work. I watched them all beavering away for a while and they paid me the compliment of not staring at their sweaty, chastened boss. Alec Large appeared at my elbow and asked me if everything was all right now and I glared at him.

'You were supposed to protect me! She could have been anyone. I thought you were highly trained?'

'I am, sir.'

'Well, how come you can't identify a lunatic when you see one?'

'I searched her bag, sir. I didn't perceive her to be a threat.'

'You didn't *perceive*? She fleeced me out of eight grand.'

'So I understand. And I agree, I shouldn't have allowed her into the building without first checking her bonafides. It was a miscalculation on my part. It won't happen again.'

I sighed. Told him to go guard a door or something. I stood where I was for another little while, willing myself to settle. And after a while I did. Perhaps it was the soothing powers of Concrete Corcoran's landscape with a zebra. After a while I felt up to walking past Mary, but not brave enough to speak. She broke the ice by asking if I was okay.

'Fine,' I said, 'just fine.'

Then I hurried on upstairs to seek comfort from my wife. I picked up the phone and dialled her work number.

She was a civil servant. Naturally, she was out. On a 'wee message', they said, and no, they weren't sure when she'd be back. Sometimes I truly believe that Belfast's crowded streets are made up of civil servants running wee messages. It is the nature of the beast.

32

As a kid I'd walked down the hill towards Windsor Park hundreds of times. If you believed the news, then civil war must have been raging all around us, but all I remember about those Saturday afternoons was the sheer joy and excitement of local football, my dad lifting me over the turnstiles to get me in for nothing, standing on the Spion Kop and screaming for my team, whether it was Linfield or Northern Ireland. The only difference between them was that Linfield always seemed to win, and the national team never did. I saw George Best play, once. He got sent off. Sometimes, if my dad was feeling particularly keen, we travelled on buses to other grounds, and we always outnumbered the home support by ten to one. The songs we sang were exclusively Loyalist, and even though I knew they were about the Battle of the Boyne, and King Billy and No Surrender, they always felt like they were really about football, about the good guys conquering the bad. We even went once to Londonderry, which felt like we were going behind enemy lines. I remember that one because the song we all sang that day seemed so innocuous and yet produced such rage amongst the home supporters.

'Chirpy Chirpy Cheep Cheep.'

It had recently been number one in the charts for Middle of the Road and we laughed as we sang it, pointing all the time at the crowd on the other side of the Brandywell. I asked my dad what it was about and why it made the home fans so angry, but he answered with, 'Never mind, son,' which was a bit of a pisser even then.

A thousand travelling Blue men singing: *'Where's your mama gone? Where's your mama gone?'*

Then: *'Where's your papa gone? Where's your papa gone?'*

And on through an entire family, and all sung with such glee.

It was only thirty years later that I worked out that internment had only just been introduced and that the opposition fans had probably all had innocent family members and relatives lifted by the Army only days before.

It was a different world, and now Windsor Park was a different place. Nice new stands, a perfect pitch, and instead of a mass of supporters standing yelling sectarian abuse on the Spion Kop, it was all seated, and there was a family enclosure. Linfield were two nil up at half-time against their Israeli visitors, Maccabi Tel Aviv. There were only about a hundred travelling fans. A goal from two of Terry Breene's imports: Mark McNulty, late of Arsenal and Southampton, and one Paul Marinelli, last heard of playing in the Italian Second Division, but in his day a mean finisher for Chelsea. When Linfield attacked, everyone jumped to their feet, and when they scored, the entire stadium seemed to rock. The cheering went on for ever, high-pitched because although the days of lifting your son over the turnstiles were long gone, one of Terry Breene's first decisions was to drastically cut the admission price for children.

Half-time entertainment was a penalty shoot-out for charity. First Minister Frank Galvin and representatives of each of the main political parties took part. Galvin scored, and punched the air. There was scattered booing from the Spion Kop end, but that was to be expected. If he'd tried it fifteen years before, the half-time entertainment would have consisted of his being strung up from the goalposts. When Frank Galvin sank his penalty it was the kids who cheered loudest. He was *from the TV*. And most of these kids had been born after the ceasefire. They were lucky. They weren't weighed down by the past, by hatred, by revenge. Not yet, at any rate.

The second half saw Linfield score another, and Maccabi pull one back. The game ended 3–1 to the home side, and by the time I made my way into the newly remodelled corporate lounge (lots of nice pastels and non-smoking), the party was already in full swing. It was Linfield's best result ever in Europe and Terry Breene was on top form. There was a band playing music in the corner, and Terry quickly took the microphone to thank everyone from the players to the programme sellers for their support, not forgetting the sponsors. And then he started singing. Sinatra standards, mostly. Beautiful girls in Linfield jerseys emblazoned with the name of the new sponsors, *Ryan Auto*, and *Like Jets*, passed out food and drinks, but they also looked kind of familiar, and then I saw Patrick O'Brien behind the bar and understood that *Past Masters* was doing the catering.

When I went for a refill O'Brien pumped my hand enthusiastically. 'Good to see you, but where's your minder?'

I glanced behind me. 'Oh shit!' Then I smiled. 'He's at home, looking after the wife.'

'Is that wise?'

'Probably not, but it's a pain in the hole having him trailing around everywhere. Can't even go to the bog without him casing the joint, and that's in my own house. So he's making silhouette shapes in the front window in case anyone's watching, and I nipped out over the back fence.'

'Well, I hope you've done the right thing. Class game, eh?'

'Yup,' I said. 'You're doing the nibbles, then?'

'Please, if you say "nibbles" my chef will have a hissy fit.'

'I thought he was from these parts.'

'He is. But he's on a mission to transform football catering. Did you not see the stalls on your way in? Out with the pie-sellers, in with the mushroom vol-au-vents.'

I had seen them, and resisted the temptation. I did though note a lot of people spitting them out and saying, 'What the fuck is this, where's me pie?' The fact that they were free, the cost apparently underwritten by Ryan Auto, whose logo was on the pastry, was neither here nor there.

So I said, 'Aye, right enough.'

'We moved eight thousand vol-au-vents tonight.'

'Well, I hope someone picks them up in the morning.'

Before he could respond, spontaneous applause broke out behind me, and I turned to see that Frank Galvin had entered. He began to work the room, starting with the Linfield players, getting royally pissed in one corner, and then briefly commiserating with the Maccabi coaching staff and players, and even posing for photographs with them, in another. When he was finished with that he started in on the rest of us, shaking hands and swapping jokes. It was an odd sort of a crowd, not the kind you would normally have associated with Linfield Football Club. There were a certain number of old fellas, mumbling incoherently into their whiskies about how it wasn't like it was in the old days, and a spattering of reformed hoods in suits pleased to be mixing with the in-crowd, but for the most part it was made up of the same faces I'd encountered at Liam Miller's wake, and had stared at every day over the past few weeks as I shuffled their pictures for inclusion in the Power List. Terry Breene, despite being an alcoholic with someone else's liver, had brought a little bit of celebrity magic to the club, and Belfast's social elite were paying him back by including Windsor Park on their social circuit.

Eventually, Galvin began to make his way along the bar, and then he was smiling at me and extending his hand. As he did, an aide whispered into his ear, clearly giving him my name.

'Dan!' he said, pumping my hand. 'Good to see you.'

'Good to see *you*,' I said.

'Great game, eh?'

'Magic,' I said.

'Did you see my penalty?'

'Oh, I was cheering you all the way. Although there was someone behind me shouting, "Miss, you fat fucker".'

The smile looked a little more fixed. 'Well, that's democracy for you.' Then he winked and said, 'If you give me his name, I'll have him picked up.' He let go of my hand and reached behind me to accept a glass of Bush from O'Brien. 'Cheers, Pat,' he said, then returned his attention to me. 'So, you're the new man at *Belfast Confidential*.'

'Aye.'

'Didn't you used to be big in newspapers?'

'I'm still big, it's the newspapers that got small. Tabloid, actually.'

He nodded and dropped the smile. 'Shame about what happened to Mouse. Nice guy.'

'Yeah,' I said.

'Police found anyone yet?'

'Not yet.'

'Well, they will. They will. And you'd a brush with danger yourself.'

'Yes, I did.'

'Dreadful. Dreadful. I thought those days were gone.'

'So did I.'

'And poor Liam. Terrible loss.' He nodded around the lounge. 'He designed this place, you know.'

I nodded with him. 'He was certainly a busy bee.' Across the room I noticed for the first time that one of the walls featured a Concrete Corcoran landscape, but it was too far away to see what exotic animal he'd managed to introduce into the local surroundings.

'Well,' said Galvin, 'I hope you won't let it stop you. You're doing a grand job. I make sure my office gets *Belfast Confidential* every week.'

'Good to know.'

'And I'm especially looking forward to the Power List issue. I was number one last year, do you know that?'

I nodded.

'So what about this year?'

'Too early to say.'

'Oh, come now.'

I smiled. 'What's it worth?'

He smiled back. 'A Housing Executive house in Twinbrook?' He laughed. I laughed. 'No, seriously, what are the chances?'

'Fair to middlin',' I said.

'I reckon my only competition will be Jacintha Ryan, what do you say?'

'You may have a point. You've met her?'

'Oh yes. Lovely woman, lovely – we had dinner in New York. You put her on your cover, you'll shift a few copies. And as for that car!'

'You've driven it?'

'Not yet, but I hear it handles like a dream.'

'Yeah, it does.'

'*You've* driven it?'

'Oh aye. I think Jacintha has her priorities just about right.'

Galvin gave a fake sigh. 'You know something – you're probably right.' He extended his hand again, and I shook it. He moved on. His aide whispered another name into his ear, and the relentless glad-handing began again.

Patrick O'Brien set me up with another drink. 'Grand man,' he said, nodding after Galvin. 'Grand man.'

'Don't tell me,' I said, 'he's a regular down at the club.'

'Well, *of course* he is. Where else would he go?'

I shrugged. I sipped my drink. Terry Breene sang 'My Way'.

Two hours later, and twenty minutes after the shutters had gone up on the bar, Terry called for silence. He was hoarse, both from screaming at his team from the touchline and from completing the Sinatra songbook. Also, coughing as if he lived in the trenches didn't help matters. 'Ladies and gentlemen,' he said into the microphone, 'please, please . . .'

'Please release me!' some wag shouted.

'Thank you, Engelbert. Ladies and gentlemen,' silence was slowly falling, 'I think you have to agree – it's been a fantastic night!'

There were roars and cheers from all around Liam Miller's pastel-flavoured corporate lounge.

'And the good news is – it's not over yet!' Another cheer went up. 'Our kind sponsors at Ryan Auto,' and he nodded at Matthew Rye, standing beside him, 'have decided that the party must continue – and to that end there are three coaches waiting outside to ferry you all back to *Past Masters*, where my friend Pat O'Brien assures me we can all drink and dance through to the early hours. And it's all on Ryan Auto!'

A fresh roar went up. Terry gave Matthew Rye a hug. Rye,

in the same grey suit and red tie as I'd seen him in the other day, looked sober and embarrassed.

'Oh . . .' Terry raised the mike again. 'And if you're driving, don't forget to take the car!'

The partygoers, including me, were soon ushered downstairs and out into the players' car park where three Ulster Bus luxury coaches were waiting. The Linfield and Maccabi Tel Aviv players and staff were led onto the first, the rest of us crammed onto the other two. Most of the people around me had brought their drinks with them. I had a bottle of Bud in either pocket and one in my hand. *Past Masters* was only a mile away, but the lights could easily have been against us.

There weren't enough seats, so I stood in the aisle examining Belfast's social elite as we pulled away from the ground. They hadn't made many concessions to the fact that they'd been at a football match. In fact, I was willing to risk a wild guess that 90 per cent of them hadn't actually bothered watching the game. I decided to test this theory by asking a pretty young lady to explain the offside rule to me, but before she could address this important question the bus lurched to a sudden halt and she spilled her glass of red wine down her dress. 'Oh fucking fuck,' she hissed, wiping at her bosom. Sensing that she probably wouldn't appreciate an offer of help, I ducked down to peer out of the rain-speckled window. We'd only been moving for three or four minutes, and had made it as far as the bottom of the Lisburn Road. We appeared to be stuck at the traffic lights at the junction with Sandy Row. This was fortunate, because instead of having to look at luxury apartments and chic coffee-houses we got to appreciate exciting wall murals celebrating the UVF. Most of the surrounding streets had been gentrified in recent years, but when they came knocking on the Sandy Row doors the gentrifiers had been gently told to fuck off.

The girl beside me was still complaining about her dress. Everyone else was contentedly drinking and jabbering away. After a couple of minutes, and still no sign of any forward progress, I pushed towards the driver. I could see the rear lights of the bus ahead of us, also stopped.

'What's up?' I asked.

'Lights are stuck on red.'

'Well, if they're stuck, can't you just ignore them? It's one o'clock in the morning – you're hardly going to disrupt the traffic.'

'More'n me job's worth, mate,' he responded.

I was about to give him a drunken mouthful when movement to my left, outside, caught my eye, and I ducked down for a closer look. There were figures hurrying out from the shadows of Sandy Row, and I thought at first that they might be Linfield fans rushing to applaud their stalled heroes, but then I saw one streak past the front of the bus carrying a baseball bat.

It was a little bit late for team sports. Despite the din around me I heard breaking glass from up ahead.

I said, 'Open the doors.'

The driver, who appeared to be the only one on the bus who'd heard the glass break as well, said, 'Not on your fucking life.'

'Open it!'

He gave me a wide-eyed look, then pushed a button. The doors hissed open and I jumped down. A moment later they hissed closed again. Ahead, there was a crowd standing round the front of the first bus, the team bus. The door had been smashed in, and at least a dozen boys, either in balaclavas or with Linfield scarves tied around their faces, were pulling people off. As I drew closer I could see from their distinctive green tracksuits now emerging into the rain that it was the Maccabi players who were being forced off. The bus driver was sitting on a kerb, cradling the side of his head. Then Terry Breene was off as well, and he was pushing and prodding the lad who seemed to be in charge, a skinhead with a pierced eyebrow.

'What are youse doing! You can't do this!'

'We'll do what the fuck we like,' the boy snapped. 'Now get out of my fucking face!'

'No! For Christ sake, man, do you know who I am?'

'Yeah, you're the chief Fenian, now fuck off, old man, or you'll get fucking brained too.'

But Terry wasn't for moving. The Maccabi players were now lined up along the side of the bus. Above them I could see the pale faces of the Linfield players, staring aghast out of the rain-speckled glass, although not aghast enough to get out and help. I tried to move up closer, but another kid who apparently couldn't afford a baseball bat stopped me in my tracks with the pointed end of a rusted railing spike, and a growled, 'Where the fuck do you think you're going?'

'Taking a piss, mate,' I said.

I often add the word 'mate' when I'm talking to tough guys. It's like we're brothers. Arguing ones, in this case, as he gave me a quick jab with his makeshift spear and said, 'You fucken piss off over there then,' and he nodded in the opposite direction. I gave him the thumbs-up sign with my bottle and backed away. I went round the back, then hurried down the blind side, along the length of three buses, before crossing the front of the team bus. I stood behind the crowd of hoods, unnoticed.

The Maccabi players were plainly terrified. Maybe coming from Israel made it harder; they knew about casual violence and weren't naïve enough to think that this was just an elaborate way of being asked for autographs.

The lead hood was walking up and down in front of them, swinging a baseball bat. In the few moments it had taken me to move around the back of the buses Terry Breene had been laid out flat. He lay motionless on the cracked tarmac. The Maccabi manager was trying to get off the bus. He was shouting loudly, but he didn't seem to know any English. Even if he had, it wouldn't have made much difference. One of the lads poked him in the groin with his bat and he stumbled backwards. A few moments later he tried to get off again, but this time he was dragged back by several of the Linfield players.

Further up the road, the excited chatter from the other buses had not dulled one iota. If they were aware, they didn't care. Party on.

The lead hood was doing what hoods do best, threatening and slabbering. 'You bring your fucking Jew noses over here, contaminating our air, you're going to fucking pay for it. We beat you to a fucking pulp on the pitch, and now we're gonna do it right here, just to make sure you get the message.'

One of the players tried to reason with him. 'It is *football*,' he began, then struggled to find the correct English. 'Beautiful game . . . we all . . . brothers.'

'Brothers fuck,' snapped the hood, and whacked him across the knees with his bat. The player let out a groan and collapsed to the ground. The hood stood over him and hit him five more times.

Sickening.

As he raised it for a sixth, I stepped forward.

I'm not brave, but I am stupid. There are many who will testify to this.

I said, 'Lads, lads, for fuck sake.' The hood paused; two others came forward and grabbed me. But like Chamberlain, I persevered. 'Lads, you gotta look at the bigger picture.'

'What the fuck are you talking about?' the lead hood snarled.

'The bigger picture, lads. I'm sure youse have your reasons like, but if you do this, then Linfield are gonna be kicked out of the competition – and that means no Bayern Münich or Barcelona, no magical nights at the Bernabau, no Real Madrid galacticos playing at Windsor Park, no European Cup glory . . . Lads, youse'll talk about those nights for ever, youse'll tell your kids, lads! You can't do this!'

'Can't we fuck,' said the hood, and whacked me with his bat.

It didn't knock me out, but it knocked me down. I lay on the damp tarmac with blood oozing down my scalp and into my eyes, and it blinded me, but it didn't deafen me. I could hear the Maccabi players screaming in pain as the hoods bore down on them.

33

I was given the all-clear to leave the City Hospital at nine the next morning. I'd four stitches just above my hairline, but the delay in my release was more to do with the overcrowding in Casualty than the seriousness of my injury. The medical staff were all busy dealing with the Maccabi Tel Aviv players – nine of whom were suffering from broken legs. There were also smashed knees, fractured arms, and vicious, gaping head wounds. They looked suitably miserable, but still only half as forlorn as Terry Breene, who had little more than a mild concussion. He lay on his bed staring at the ceiling, totally lost. I tried talking to him, but he wasn't interested. Just. Stared. At. The. Ceiling.

Patricia had arrived at four, with Alec Large in tow. Her initial concern gradually gave way to her usual pissed-off demeanour over me getting involved in the first place. *Why didn't you just get a taxi home? Why do you have to drink on and on? Why didn't you stay on the bus? What sort of a wanker are you?* I told her to fuck off and leave me alone, and she told me to fuck up. It went back and forward like that for a while until the nurses told us to shut up, and then Alec Large tried to broker a peace deal by explaining how he would have dealt with the situation. For a start he would have provided armed security for each bus, and he certainly wouldn't have allowed anyone to get off. If by some remarkable chance the hoods had managed to board the team bus, Alec would have tackled the ringleader first. 'Cut off the head and the body will die,' he said. It was easy for him to be wise after the fact. He went on and on about it, how he would do this, how he would have done that. Patricia and I gradually forgot our differences and instead formed an alliance against Alec. As he yittered on, I closed my eyes and she rubbed my arm and whispered that she'd have me home soon.

When we left the hospital there were reporters waiting outside. They were anxious to interview anyone who'd been involved. I knew most of them, but I kept my mouth shut and my eyes averted. Alec Large walked ahead of us, clearing the way. I'm not normally so shy, but my head hurt and I wanted to lie down with Patricia. We'd already watched the Power Listers who'd been on the buses with me give their views on a TV in the Casualty waiting room, despite the fact that they'd been too busy drinking to even realise what was going on outside until long after it was over. But they weren't wrong in what they said, almost uniformly, that this would be damaging not only to Linfield Football Club, but to the Province in general. UEFA, European soccer's governing body, had already announced a full enquiry and both the news and sports media were saying that any hopes the local team had of taking further part in European competitions were hanging by a thread. Tourist chiefs were saying that this kind of incident would scare tourists away. Frank Galvin condemned it. The police said it was too early to say who was responsible, but they suspected Loyalist paramilitaries or a far right group or the Arabs who ran the kebab shop down the road and around the corner. Well, not quite, but they didn't seem to have much of a clue. I continued to listen to all of this informed commentary as we drove home, the undamaged part of my head leaning against the window in the back. Patricia drove. Alec watched out for trouble.

'I'll make us all a nice fry when we get home, then you can go to bed and sleep it off,' she said.

Patricia and Alec chatted easily. It was never an effort to talk to Trish, but there and then it was a relief to have Alec as a distraction for her. She'd picked me up from too many hospitals. She'd rescued me too many times. And I'd put her in the way of danger so often that a certain part of her almost expected it. But it didn't mean she liked it, or could ever get used to it. She'd given me a hard time already, although it was laced with love and sympathy, but sooner or later her patience was going to run out. That, or one of us would die. The chances were that it would be me, but my luck was also such that it could just as easily be her.

I couldn't imagine a life without her.

I was nodding gently against the window, nestling into that almost-asleep state from which novelists and painters and sleuths and inventors sometimes grab their best ideas. I was none of these things, but eternally hopeful that the images that were cascading through my brain might somehow assume a pattern or suggest an answer. I'd just left Terry Breene staring at a ceiling in the hospital, his dreams all but shattered by a pack of hooligans. The attack on the footballers' bus hadn't been a random one, that was for sure. They hadn't just *noticed* the bus, they'd stopped it deliberately and come ready for violence. The question was, was it just an unfortunate but isolated attack motived by race or religion, or could it in any way be connected to everything else that was going down? I'd spent every day since joining *Belfast Confidential* looking for those connections. They didn't *have* to be there, and if they were, they wouldn't connect everything to everything else, but I felt certain that they were there, somewhere. They *had* to be.

It helped, actually, trying to concentrate, because my head was thumping from the crack and the hangover, and the traffic was still in rush-hour mode which gave our journey home a stop-start-stop motion which brought me to the edge of throwing up.

Focus.

Focus.

I began to run the timeline through my head

It all started with Mouse's murder. Tied up, burned to death in his own office. Before I could even begin to investigate that, I'd been warned off by the police. Then I'd been too busy trying to organise *Belfast Confidential* to do much beyond chat to some of the potential new entries on the Power List – no penetrating interviews, no revelation of information which *must not* make it into print. At least, none that I was aware of. Then an attempt to murder me which had resulted in Liam Miller's death. My virtual kidnapping from outside Liam's wake by Concrete Corcoran, and a private viewing of his works of art. Now the assault on the Maccabi Tel Aviv team. Of all the things that had happened, this last one seemed the least likely to be connected to the others. For a start it hadn't involved me at all, or wouldn't have if I hadn't stuck my big nose in. If it was an attack on anyone, apart from the victims, it was on Linfield Football Club in general, and Terry Breene in particular. The hoods had talked about Jews, but it seemed just as likely that it was because Terry was a Catholic.

Was there anything to connect it to the other incidents?

Well, there was the fact that last night's match was an attempt to bring some middle-class sophistication to Belfast soccer, which meant the Power List types. Which also meant vol-au-vents and nibbles provided by *Past Masters*, of which Terry Breene, Liam Miller, May Li and Mouse were all members. Liam had redesigned the corporate lounge at Windsor Park; he was involved in the design of the Ryan Auto factory in West Belfast; he had also signed an agreement with Mouse to make a reality TV show. Liam acted as mentor and agent to Concrete Corcoran, whose artwork hung in *Past Masters*, the Linfield corporate lounge and the *Belfast Confidential* office. Concrete Corcoran was a man with a violent past who was making his way in the artworld by leaning on critics. Yet while he might conceivably have had a reason to murder Mouse, he hadn't harmed me when given the chance. He was also keen to get hold of whoever had killed Liam Miller. And the attack on the Maccabi Tel Aviv players was carried out from the ultra-Loyalist Sandy Row, whereas Concrete came very much from the Republican side of things. There was, of course, nothing to say that in these peaceful days the two sides couldn't co-operate, but it seemed unlikely.

Which left, what?

Confusion.

The easiest thing would have been to say – you know what? These are random acts of violence, and *none* of them are connected.

Mouse could have been murdered for a hundred reasons, professional or personal.

The cops had leaned on me because they *genuinely* don't like interference.

Killers came to my house because . . .

It brought me back to Mouse, and what he might have found out; the same thing that whoever had killed him was trying to stop *me* from finding out, or publishing.

But there wasn't anything.

At least nothing major, nothing that stuck out. I knew from my many years as a reporter that it was usually the little things that pissed people off. You could report a gruesome murder trial, and then the accused would phone you up and threaten your life because you referred to him as 'balding'. You could write a glowing review of a play and then lose a theatre's advertising because you misspelled the name of a sponsor. The thing was, you could never second-guess what would annoy people.

We weren't far from home now, but traffic had stalled. Patricia laughed. Alec giggled. I missed the punchline. Maybe there wasn't one. She glanced back at me and smiled; I smiled back and closed my eyes again. She said, 'If you're going to be sick, let me know. I'm not cleaning this car up again.'

I nodded.

Why me?

Why send someone to kill me in particular?

In thirty-odd years of Troubles, I could think of only one reporter who'd been murdered, and barely a handful who'd been injured in any way. *Belfast Confidential* was a money machine; surely whoever had killed Mouse had to know that that wouldn't be the end of it, that the magazine would continue, and that if they killed me as well, then another Editor would be appointed, and then another, and another. And there would always be reporters, and the more people they killed, the more interest those reporters, let alone the police, would take in the reasons why. Eventually they would find out. They always did. And they had to know that. So why Mouse, why me? Why the hurry?

Well, you hurry because of time: you're late, you're early, something to do with timing. What if it was something that was happening soon, something time-specific, something that meant that action had to be taken *now* to prevent it happening, or to prevent revelations coming out that might interfere with it happening?

Back to the Power List Issue.

Or Concrete Corcoran's upcoming art exhibition.

Or Linfield becoming a power in European football.

Or Jacintha Ryan cornering the market in fast cars.

Or Liam Miller pastelising another unfortunate building.

Liam.

What if my justified sense of my own importance was getting in the way? What if the target had actually been Liam, and not me? What did that do to my tangled web of connections – apart from widen the range of suspects to the one million men in the country who despised everything that he represented? What if a rival lifestyle guru had pulled the trigger?

A bloody turf war between make-over specialists.

Tarantino does Feng Shui.

I needed to sleep.

Warm bed. The smell of grilled bacon and the sound of gentle laughter wafting up. My hair was matted with blood. Sleep came. I dreamed of chaos theory and May Li. I had not spoken to her directly since throwing up on her bra; and this was the image that kept coming back to me. I seduced her in a dozen ways, and she was more than keen, but every time I came to the point of entry, I charged up the stairs and threw up on her bra. And then, as I gripped the sink and tried to regain control, there was a shot from downstairs and Liam Miller was shouting, 'Not on the rug! Not on the rug!' and then Patricia was in the doorway waving her finger and saying, 'You have twenty-four hours to move out,' in the softest, gentlest, most hurt voice I could imagine.

And I could imagine a lot of things.

34

Alec drove me to work three hours later. I'd had a sleep, but it was a tossy-turny exhausting one, and even a cold shower hadn't done much to re-energise me. He said, 'I should have gone with you last night.'

'My fault,' I said.

'I should have insisted.'

'Don't worry about it.'

'I miscalculated. It won't happen again.'

I'd called ahead, so that Stephen and Patrick were waiting in my office when I arrived. They complimented me on my stitches and said that not content with occupying the West Bank, Israel now also wanted to invade Northern Ireland. When I'd finished giving them each a fixed grin, we went over the pages for my second issue of *Belfast Confidential*. It was dominated by photographs from Liam Miller's funeral and wake. There were quite a few of Kieren Kitt, including one for the cover of him crying at the graveside. There were also photos of May Li, and Terry Breene, Liam's mother, and even one I'd had blown up of Concrete Corcoran, standing in the background.

'You've done a grand job,' I said. And they had. They gave each other high fives, and began to reach across the desk to include me, but I kept my hands on the desk because I wasn't twelve.

We went over the Power List for an hour. We were getting to the point where we had to make a decision about who was going to be number one.

Stephen was arguing for Frank Galvin.

Patrick was for Jacintha Ryan.

'It has to be Frank,' said Stephen, 'if people are going to take it at all seriously. Jacintha Ryan hasn't *done* anything yet. Next year – that'll be her time, once she's proved herself. Frank was number one last year, and if anything he's more popular now. Give me one good reason why he should be displaced?'

'Sex,' said Patrick. 'Sex always sells.'

'This isn't about selling,' Stephen argued. 'It's about the Power List. Put her on the cover if you want, but don't make her number one.'

'No, we should change it. We've done Galvin to death. We need a breath of fresh air. Okay, so she's done nothing yet, but she's transformed West Belfast already: it's going mental over this factory, everyone who matters is in a frenzy over this Masked Ball, and think of all the sponsorship money she's putting into sport and the arts and community projects. She's really going for it.'

'What money is she putting into the arts?' I asked.

He glanced down at his laptop, then scrolled through some notes. 'She's sponsoring a painting school . . .'

'It wouldn't be called Easel, by any chance?'

'Ahm, let me see . . . yup. That's it. You know it?' I nodded. 'And then she's commissioned dozens of local artists to provide artwork for her corporate offices.'

'You have their names?'

'The artists? No.'

'Well, see if you can find them, and see how many of them match the born again terrorists the Arts Council are funding.'

'Will do.'

'Anything else on Jacintha Ryan herself?'

'Well, we're kind of hampered by her being over there and us being over here. If you would care to provide me with a first-class return ticket to New York, I'm sure I could find out a lot more. Knock on a few doors.'

'That's what the phone's for, Patrick. That's why we have the internet.'

'Well, I had to try.' He smiled. 'Meanwhile, back at the ranch, I've spoken to a number of business reporters in the States, in New York, in Detroit – you know, Motor City – and they all seem to think that (a) she's pretty dynamic (b) that if anyone can make a go of starting a motor company from scratch, she can, and (c) what sort of a lunatic is she, locating that company in Belfast? They argue that you can't build a sustainable company when you're halfway round the world from your main market – the States – even with Government support. They think she's going to struggle.'

'And how do her people respond to that?'

'That America isn't the centre of the auto-business any more, that she'll sell as many cars to China as she does to America, and every place in between. It's not *where* she's based that matters, it's the demand for the product.'

'And how do the boys in Motor City view the product?'

'They haven't seen it.'

'What do you mean? Sure, I was driving around in it the other day.'

'Well, you would think that, wouldn't you? What you were actually driving around in was a mock-up. It has the chassis design of the Jet, and much of the interior is pretty unique, but the most important thing, the engine – well, that was a Ferrari engine you were driving, because they haven't finished tinkering with the Jet engine. And even if they had, they wouldn't let it out of their labs because it'll be another eighteen months before the first Jet rolls off the production line and they don't want to let all their secrets out before that. They're promising that it'll be revolutionary. Whatever that means.'

'Maybe it runs on milk. Or eggshells.' They didn't look convinced. 'So what about her personal life, anything we can use there?'

'Not much. She sits on the boards of half a dozen charities and they basically exist to mount fundraisers, but she tends to stay in the background. Not keen on the press.'

'Any particular reason?'

'Who can say?'

'What about connections back here? I mean, from before she went to America.'

'Well, that was thirty odd years ago.'

'Some of them very odd,' said Stephen.

'There's not even any old neighbours we could talk to. All the old houses were knocked down about fifteen years ago and the people dispersed all over the place.'

'But if we wanted to,' I pointed out, 'we could track them down, see what they could tell us about the family.'

'If we wanted to,' said Patrick, rather glumly.

Downstairs, Mary handed me a small padded envelope and said, 'Guess who left that in?'

'Mother Teresa' was on the tip of my tongue. But I held back. I said, 'I've no idea.'

Inside, there was a mobile phone. It appeared to be state of the art. With it there was a scrawled note: *As promised!* And then a *Christopher Corcoran* signature followed by a smiley face. By my reckoning, given the size of the scrap of paper and the technical excellence of the smiley face, it was probably worth well over a thousand pounds.

'He's really rather attractive,' said Mary, 'for an older man. But then I'm an older w—'

'He was here?'

'Oh yes. About five minutes ago. He dropped it off for you personal, like, while he was picking up the painting.'

My eyes shot across the room – to the blank space where Concrete's landscape had previously hung. 'He took the painting?'

'Oh yes. He said it was for his exhibition. He's taking them all back, he said.'

'And you just let him walk out of here with a twelve-thousand-pound painting over his shoulder?'

'Oh no. It wasn't over his shoulder, he had two fellas to carry it for him. Anyway, what's your problem? He said he was bringing it back.'

I turned at the sound of a flushing toilet, and saw Alec Large emerge from the gents, just down the corridor. He immediately looked concerned. Something to do with the thunderous look I was giving him.

'Is there . . . is there anything wrong?' he stammered.

'Concrete Corcoran just walked out of here with a twelve-grand painting.'

'Really?'

'Yes! Really! You're supposed to be on guard!'

'Well, I have a bit of a gyppy tummy. I think it must have been the fry.'

'Fucking hell,' I said. 'First you let Concrete Corcoran steal a painting, now you're having a go at my wife's cooking.'

Alec pondered that for a brief moment. 'I'm sure it wasn't your wife's cooking. Eggs work funny with me.' I took a deep breath. 'But yes, I shouldn't have left my post without first securing the office. A bit of a miscalculation, that.'

As if to prove that despite this he was still on top of his game, he tensed suddenly as the office door opened, then rushed away down the corridor to confront this latest intrusion. I shouted after him, 'Alec – for god sake relax, would you!' But then I saw who it was coming through the door. She had half a dozen smart men in suits with her. Alec stood before them, briefly examined a piece of paper she thrust into his hands, then turned and gave me a rather forlorn look. She saw where he was looking, then marched past him towards me, with the suits following immediately behind. She stopped in front of me.

'Wendy,' I said, as pleasantly as I could. 'Long time no see.'

'Dan,' she said.

Mouse had only been dead for a few weeks, but his first wife appeared to have lost a stone since his funeral. She was still an elephant short of being svelte, but her cheeks were pink and shiny, her smile was wide, her eyes were bright, and she gave off every indication of being in ruddy good health, with revived spirits to match. All of which made me a little concerned, frankly.

'Wendy,' I said again.

'Dan. Thrilling good news.'

'Oh? I'm happy for you. Do you care to share?'

'Oh yes. You see, that's why I'm here. It turns out, Dan, that Mouse's marriage to that Philippino bitch isn't worth the paper it's written on, because in his rush to screw her, he neglected to sign his divorce papers, which means that we were still married when he died, which means that full and total ownership of *Belfast Confidential* has passed to me.'

'Oh,' I said.

'Which means that you, who showed me no loyalty whatsoever, who froze me out and made your bed with that slant-eyed cow, have five minutes to clear your desk.'

'Oh,' I said.

35

Of course, when Wendy McBride *said* five, she didn't mean it. She actually meant about three. That's how long it took from her making the announcement for me to be escorted by her smart-suited bouncers up the stairs, for me to rescue a photo of Trish, a few odd pieces of paper from my desk, and then, with Concrete Corcoran's free mobile under my arm, to be escorted back down the stairs again and out onto the pavement. Before they closed the door on me I half-heartedly suggested that we consult the *Belfast Confidential* solicitors to work out a compromise, or compensation, or even my first month's pay, which I hadn't received yet, but it turned out the men in suits *were* the *BC* legal team. One of them said, 'Last time I spoke to you, you were hiding in your roofspace. Now bugger off.'

Through all of this my staff, my loyal staff, kept their heads down and kept working. I suppose they were becoming used to working in a state of flux. Nobody said goodbye, not even Mary, or Patrick or Stephen. As I stood rather forlornly on the pavement, with my meagre possessions in my hands, Brian Kerr, the erstwhile Deputy Editor of *Belfast Confidential*, came walking up with his possessions in his. When he saw me, his lip curled up and he spat, 'Told you, you cocksucker.'

'At least I can,' I snapped back. And then I thought, *Christ*

All Mighty, not only have I been sacked, but the power of the witty riposte is also deserting me. And he was through the door before I could say anything else.

My mind was reeling as I crossed to the car. I ought to have felt quite relieved, because putting the magazine out had been quite a grind. Acting responsibly and showing discipline had both gone against the grain, even if I hadn't been entirely successful. And if I was no longer in charge, then surely there was no longer any reason for anyone to take a pot-shot at me. So that was a weight off my shoulders. But part of me had enjoyed the challenge, the responsibility, the investigation and the prospect of untold riches. And I was angry at being dumped out on the street and generally treated like shit. Then I thought about May Li and what sort of a state she must be in. Had she been in court, fighting to have her marriage recognised, and to therefore keep control of Mouse's assets? Had she been left to fight that fight on her own? Alone and confused in a strange country? Or did she even know? What if she was sitting at home now, blissfully unaware that her whole world was about to fall apart? What if *that* was Wendy's next port of call?

Surely not.

May Li was beautiful, and smart, and rich in her own right. Wendy might have convinced some doddery old judge to hand *Belfast Confidential* over to her, but it was surely just the first skirmish in what might become an extended war. Wendy was strictly Belfast, May Li was *international*. She had run multi-million-pound businesses, published magazines, run satellite channels; she wasn't going to let a bitter frump like Wendy win the day. May Li would have something up her sleeve. And I was suddenly determined to look up it.

As I opened the car door, there were footsteps behind me. I glanced back and saw Alec Large hurrying up.

'I just wanted to say . . .' he started to say.

I held up my hand to stop him. 'It's all right,' I said. 'I've been sacked before. It's actually for the best. I didn't particularly—'

But then he stopped *me*. 'No, I just wanted to say what an arsehole you are, the way you treat your wife.'

'What?'

'A little bit of care and consideration would make all the difference.'

'What?'

'You treat her like dirt, you speak to her like she's a pain in the hole, and yet she's a fantastic woman and why she sticks by you I've no idea.'

'I'm sorry?'

'And so you should be. You behave like—'

'No – I mean, I'm *sorry*, but what on earth gives you the right to talk to me like that?'

'I don't need a right, I'm just stating what's plain for all to see. You treat me like shit, but that's what I'm paid for. But you shouldn't treat your wife like that.'

I shook my head. I laughed. 'This is *so* not your business,' I said. I turned back to the car, but before I could climb in he put a strong hand on my shoulder, turned me back and thumped me once across the mouth.

I staggered back, banging into the car, blood already pouring from my split lip. Alec Large reeled away as well, blood erupting from a long thin line across the top of his knuckles. It was a narrow thing as to who'd come off worst. I wouldn't be kissing anyone for a while, and he wouldn't be tossing any left hooks.

My lip was swelling up. I found some tissues in the glove compartment and gingerly dabbed at it. Alec was trying to tie a handkerchief around his hand, but it was a difficult thing to do with one hand. I climbed out of the car again. He sat down on the kerb and renewed his efforts. I stood over him. He didn't seem frightened.

'What the fuck brought that on?' I demanded, nevertheless.

'You've been asking for it. Things just came to a head.'

'You're telling me. Jesus Christ, man, I've just been sacked, I really don't need—'

'So have I!'

'You?'

The hanky fell away from his hand. I picked it up and gave it back.

'They said that technically speaking I was employed by the company, not by May Li. They said there was no longer any reason to protect you.'

'That didn't mean you had to go out and fucking thump me.'

'I know that. It was entirely of my own free will.'

The hanky fell away again.

'For Christ sake, give me that,' I said, and took it from him. I began to tie it over the impressive wound I'd inflicted on him by striking his knuckles with my teeth.

He mumbled, 'Thanks.'

I shook my head. 'You're not married, are you, Alec?'

'No.'

'And no girlfriend.'

'Not at the moment. No.'

'But when you have, you give them a hundred and fifty per cent, don't you?'

'Of course. Why not?'

'Because it's impossible to sustain. It's too much pressure. It drives them away. I find about sixty-five per cent works for me.'

'Sixty-five?'

'Sometimes less, sometimes more. And that's exactly what Trish gives to me. Alec, you can't judge other people by your values. Trish and I are just fine.'

'No, you're not.'

'Alec.'

'I've talked to her. We've talked about—'

'Alec?'

'What?'

'Mind your own fucking business. All right?' I finished his bandage and stood back. He glared at me. I glared back. 'All right?' I asked again.

He gave me a vague kind of a shrug. I shook my head again, and turned back to the car. Alec got to his feet. I started the engine and wound the window down so that I could see to reverse properly. As I passed he said, 'Your tax is out of date.'

'I know,' I said.

36

When I arrived at what had once been Mouse's house, there was a large removal van parked outside and big men in overalls were carrying out the furniture. 'Wendy, you vindictive bitch,' I said under my breath, and hurried up to the open door. There were more men inside. Everything that could be boxed, had been, and was on the move. I called May Li's name, but there was no response; one of the furniture removers barked a gruff, 'She's upstairs.'

I went up. She was in her bedroom. It was empty. She was standing by the window, looking out. She was wearing a short denim skirt and jacket, with a black T-shirt. Her hair was in a pony tail. 'I saw you parking,' she said, without looking round. 'So you've heard.'

'Aye. She's a fucking cow, throwing you out like this. Taking the fucking furniture.'

'She's not taking it, Dan. I'm taking it.'

'What do you mean? Have you come to some kind of agreement?'

She turned to look at me, finally, and her eyes were thick with tears, and her eyeliner looked like it had smudged and dried and smudged and dried. 'No, Dan. No agreement. I'm taking it before she gets the chance to. I have to sell it. It'll pay for my ticket back to Bangkok.'

'Your *what*?' I managed a disbelieving laugh. 'What're you talking about?'

'I'm going home, Dan. Because I can't stay here.'

'Of course you can. You just have to—'

'No, Dan, and it's not up to me. The court said my marriage wasn't legal, which means I'm here illegally. I either go now or they'll throw me out.'

'But you can fight it, put a legal team together. You could be here for years before—'

'Dan – I can't. I have no money.' She took a deep breath. 'There was never any money.'

'But . . . you're a publisher . . . the TV stations . . .'

She shook her head.

'Then phone your dad. He'll support you.'

'I can't phone him.'

'Of course you can!'

'Dan! He has no phone! He lives in a swamp!'

Then she burst into tears and began to crumple down. I ran forward and grabbed her and she cried against my chest.

From downstairs someone shouted, 'We're all done here, love.'

I held her in my arms for five minutes while she cried, and I could have held her for an hour longer, even though I'd a thousand confusing and accusatory thoughts firing through my brain. Even when she gently pushed me away I did not press her to explain more; the van driver was pumping his horn. She insisted on getting out of the house right away. I did not stop her. In fact, I gave her a lift. We pulled away in the wake of the van, and just as it swept around the first corner I noted in my mirror a small fleet of vehicles swinging into the opposite end of the road. They came to a halt outside Mouse's house, and a moment later Wendy and her solicitors climbed out. May Li didn't look back. Then we were around the corner.

There are places you can take vanloads of furniture to and they'll give you about a third of its value, no questions asked. But they're no mugs on Donegal Pass; they wanted to take a couple of hours to evaluate what May Li had sent before trying to rip her off. So we walked the extra few hundred yards into the centre of town. We found a bar and I took her in. Heads turned as she entered in exactly the same way that they didn't when I did. She'd fixed her eyes in the car and now sashayed through the bar as if she hadn't a care in the world; or, in fact, as if she owned that world. And if I hadn't known the truth, I might have believed that she did.

I had a pint of Harp. It was purely medicinal, for the scab on my split lip and the stitches in my head and the confusion in my head. She had a glass of water. It sat on the table, as still as she was. She said quietly, 'I am sorry.'

'What for?'

'For . . . everything. I just wanted to be with Mouse.'

'You could have had him without lying.'

'I didn't lie to him. Well, at first I did, but then he found out, and it didn't matter to him. He loved me.'

I took a sip of my drink, winced a little, then said, 'Start with the swamp.'

She nodded. 'It used to be a swamp, then a rich man came and drained it, and in exchange for that, he took me away. My parents did not want me to go, but they had no choice. The rich man lived in the city and he owned a bar and he made me work there.'

'As a barmaid. A waitress.'

'No.'

'Okay.'

'One night another rich man came in, and he liked me, and he gave me good things. He was a businessman who flew all over the world. He owned magazines and television stations and he wanted me to travel with him. Not just me – many girls. He paid for all of us – to learn English, how to behave in Western society. It was a different world for us and we loved it, and it was worth it, what we had to do. He was good to us. Then he brought me with him to England. To Oxford. A publishing convention. There I met Mouse and for the first time I fell in love, but I had to go home at the end of four days. But Mouse had fallen in love as well, and he could not live without me, so he came to my country and found me and he met the rich man and convinced him to let me leave. We stayed together for two weeks, and at the end of two weeks we were married. Then we came here, and we knew it would be difficult for us if my background became known. So we made a history. I had learned much of publishing in my time with the rich man, so it was not hard to pass myself off. But then my Mouse was murdered, and my life destroyed.'

She had tears in her eyes again.

I took a sip of my beer.

'How did you get into the country if the marriage wasn't legal?'

'I came on a tourist visa. We were to be married again here. We loved each other. But we were so busy . . . and we thought we had all our lives.' She put her hand on mine. She said, 'You do believe me, Dan?'

'Of course,' I said. Then after a moment's reflection I added: 'Although a more cynical person might look at it another way – that you suckered Mouse into getting married, but once he found out you were a penniless hooker he tried to dump you but you had him knocked off first, thinking you'd inherit all his money. Only thing is, it turns out you aren't married at all and you inherit fuck all squared in a box. Which I suppose is fair enough, because if you'd died first, all he would have gotten was some shares in a mud hut.'

She stared at me. 'Is this what you believe?'

I sat back. I took a deep breath. Another drink. Men at the bar were looking at us. No – it was still May Li they were looking at. She was astonishingly beautiful, and she had ended up with Mouse, who even in his reshaped form was no oil painting. And yet, why not? If I had learned anything in the past few days, especially after examining Concrete Corcoran's paintings, it was that beauty was in the eye of the beholder. If she had fallen for Mouse's qualities as a man as I had once as a friend, then why wouldn't she choose to be with him, in love, rather than spend her best years as the paid concubine of a rich man?

I set my drink down. 'May Li – I want to believe you. I *have* to believe you, because it would absolutely kill me to find out that you were somehow involved. Do you know why? Because I know for a fact that Mouse was in love with you, that you totally transformed his life, that I had never seen him so happy. And because of that, I am going to give you the benefit of the doubt.'

I had half-expected her tears of sadness to be transformed into tears of gratitude. All through this her hand had remained on mine, soft, warm, a subtle but impossible-to-ignore pressure, skin against skin. Now the pressure grew a little. Then her nails, exquisitely manicured, razor sharp, sliced into me. She jumped to her feet, swept up her glass and threw the contents in my face. My lip was sore already, and now my hand was bleeding and I was soaked.

'May—' I began.

But she cut it off with a scream of incandescent rage: 'You give *me* the benefit of the doubt? Who do you think *you* are!'

'May—'

'I will tell you! You are *wanker*!'

She cracked the glass down on the table and stormed out of the bar.

I sat where I was for a while. I blew air out of my cheeks. I became aware of the guys at the bar looking at me. I shrugged at them. *'Women,'* I said.

37

I phoned Patricia at work, but they told me she wasn't at her
desk. I tried her mobile. When she answered I said, 'Guess what?'

'What?'

'May Li *was* a hooker.'

'*Really?*'

'Yup. And she's just sold all of Mouse's furniture and made
a run for the airport.'

'*Really?* Why would she do that?'

'Because it turns out her marriage wasn't legal, and Mouse
never got divorced, so Wendy now owns *Belfast Confidential*. In
fact, she called into the office to tell me personally, and then
gave me five minutes to clear my things.'

'Christ, Dan.'

'She lied though. She only really gave me about three. But
it was plenty of time.'

'Oh Dan. I'm sorry.'

'I'm not.'

'Are you sure?'

'Yes. Kind of.'

'Well – everything will be all right.'

'I know.'

'Although it's a pity you burned your bridges at the *Belfast
Telegraph*. I did warn you.'

'I know that. You were right. Once again. So what are we going to do?'

'Well, we have my wage. And we don't have to eat every day, do we?'

A car pumped its horn from her end. I said, 'Where are you?'

'Just – driving around.'

'What do you mean, driving around?'

'What I say, driving around. Just driving.'

'But why?'

'Just – felt like it.'

'Trish? What's wrong?'

'Nothing's wrong. Can't a girl go for a drive if she feels like it?'

'Well, you're a civil servant, so you probably can. But I'd say it's not like you, and that something's troubling you.'

'Well, there's not. I just fancied a drive.'

'Trish.'

'Honestly.'

'Is it me again?'

'No.'

'Or a delayed reaction to Liam Miller?'

'I don't know.'

'Trish – talk to me.'

She took a deep breath. 'Dan – Mouse is dead. He was our friend. And our boy is dead, and I know he wasn't really yours, and I desperately want to have another baby, with you this time, but it doesn't look like it's going to happen. And you got beaten up by the police and then Liam got killed in our hall and sometimes I think that this is going to go on for ever – you know, this cycle of brief periods of being very, very happy and then there's violence and people die and I spend every waking minute worrying about you or checking under my car in case there's a bomb, or I'm scared to go upstairs at night in case there's someone waiting for me. I don't want to keep living like this, Dan, and I know we used to joke that you were like a shit-magnet, but I think you really are and as much as I love you it worries me that there's always going to be this edge to our life. Some people might like living on the edge, Dan, but I'm getting too old for it and I don't know for how much longer I can do it.'

'Trish – I said talk to me, not bore the arse off me.' Before she could respond in a suitable fashion I said, 'Trish, I love you. I know it's been hectic and dangerous, but I'm out of it now.'

'You might be out of *Belfast Confidential*. But you're still going to find out about Mouse.'

'Well yes, of course. You asked me to, remember?'

'I know I did. But I forgot what it was like, and I don't like it.'

'It won't last for ever.'

'I know – but what if *we* don't last for ever? What if one of us dies? And the chances are it will be me, because you always seem to pull through.'

I sighed. 'Trish. It's just the way things are. And they were quiet for a long time. And we were happy, weren't we? Mouse died, it wasn't our fault, but we owe it to him to find out what happened, don't we?'

'Yes, I suppose.'

'Well, then.'

'I know, but – I just don't ever see it ending. Alec doesn't think you'll ever—'

'Alec?'

'He doesn't think you'll ever change.'

'Oh great. Well, it's important what he thinks. When the fuck were you talking to him?'

'About twenty minutes ago.'

'Twenty? But you're . . . you mean he came to your office?'

'Yes. Don't be angry, Dan.'

'Why the fuck did he come to your office?'

'He asked me to move in with him.'

'WHATTT?!'

'He asked me to move in with him. He says he's fallen in love with me.'

'Jesus Christ All Mighty!'

'Yes, I know.'

'I hope you told him to fuck off!'

'Well – not exactly.'

'Trish! For fuck sake. You're not . . . you haven't been . . . Trish?'

She was silent for maybe ten seconds. Then she laughed gently. 'No, Dan. But got you worried, didn't I?'

I breathed out a long sigh of relief. 'Don't do that to me.'

'If you'd heard him go on about all your obvious problems. And he just about nailed every single one.'

'Christ All Mighty.'

'He brought me flowers to work.'

'Christ All Mighty.'

'And we went for coffee.'

'Christ All Mighty.'

'And he listed all your faults . . . and sympathised with my suffering.'

'Jesus H Christ on a stick.'

'And then he said he'd fallen absolutely and totally in love with me and wanted me to come away with him, right then right now.'

'Trish?'

'Oh yes, and he said how happy he would make me, and also that he could protect me, and treasure me, and that he had an exceptionally large penis.'

'He *fucking* what?'

'Yes, I know, it turned a few heads in the café, I can tell you.'

'And you *didn't* tell him to fuck off?'

'No, Dan, I didn't. He was just so . . . you know, keen. I haven't had that in a while. It makes a girl feel good.'

'I don't believe I'm hearing this.'

'Well, you are. He's just a big stupid puppy and I didn't want to hurt his feelings.'

'*His* feelings?'

'Yes, Dan. Feelings. Remember them? He's young, he's *in love*. You have to let people down gently. Didn't you ever do that?'

'It was always the other way around. Except they usually just told me to fuck away off.'

She laughed. 'That I can understand.'

'So what way did you leave it?'

'I said I loved you despite your many and varied faults, that I was touched by his feelings for me and I'd have to think about things.'

'Trish – I don't understand why you didn't just tell him straight. Isn't it worse, just keeping him hanging on? That's cruel.'

'Dan – I *do* need to think about things.'

'About running away with him?'

'No. About everything. About us. Dan, I do love you, but you're very hard work, and if a fit young man with an exceptionally large penis comes along, you can't blame me for being tempted.'

'Of *course* I fucking can.' It struck me then that she was in her car and driving. I said, 'He's with you in the car, isn't he?'

'No, don't be stupid.'

'You *are* running away together.'

'No, Dan.'

'Then where are you?'

'I'm on the M2. I'm going to my sister's. I haven't seen her in ages.'

'And he's not with you?'

'No, Dan.'

I drummed my fingers on the dash. 'Swear to God.'

'Swear to God. I might stay the night. It's a long drive, and I fancy a few drinks.'

'And he's really not with you. Or meeting you there. Or you're really going to a hotel with him.'

'Dan, you're going to have to trust me.'

'Well, you've strayed before.'

'Pot. Kettle. Black.'

'I thought we were past that.'

'We are. I'm going to my sister's.'

'When will you be back?'

'Tomorrow.'

I took a deep breath. 'Swear to God?'

'Yes, Dan.' She cut the line.

I was aware that she hadn't actually said, 'Swear to God.'

My lip was sore. I checked it in the mirror. I must have been picking at it while Patricia threatened to break my heart, for it was bleeding freely again.

Alec Large had caused me damage twice in one day. Once to my lip, and then an assault on my marriage. He had had the temerity to sit in a public café and invite my wife to run away with him, and then casually thrown in as an added incentive the fact that he had an exceptionally large penis.

Large by name, large by nature.

As Oscar Wilde had once never said, 'What a cunt.'

38

Patricia was gone for the night, maybe longer, and her mobile was switched off now. She wanted to be *alone*. With her sister. Or, for all I knew, Alec Large. There was nothing I could do, except call her sister, or drive down the motorway and camp outside the house and spy. But I wouldn't. I knew her too well. It would only make matters ten times worse. She would be back in the morning, and we would laugh about it. Then we would fall into bed and make love, and we would both try to ignore the fact that May Li and Mouse had enjoyed four orgasms a night, and that Alec Large had an exceptionally large penis which was probably capable of delivering the same. We would fail, but that was the nature of life, and fantasy. We would both keep quiet about it, unless she wanted to score points.

I didn't want to go home to an empty house. Besides, although I was no longer working for *Belfast Confidential*, I still had a job. I had set out to discover who had killed Mouse, and I intended to see it through. Of the eight names on my list of suspects – six Power Listers plus May Li and Wendy – Liam Miller was dead and May Li had fled the country; Jacintha Ryan was still in America; Wendy McBride had assumed control of *Belfast Confidential*; Patrick O'Brien was still in charge of *Past Masters* and Terry Breene was nursing a sore head and tarnished dreams. Purely on past form, Concrete Corcoran was the one most capable of painting the town red. With added wildebeest.

I drove to *Past Masters*, parked outside and went upstairs and ordered a drink. The barman said, 'I'm sorry, sir, but you have to be a member to drink here.'

Patrick O'Brien had given me a membership card. I produced it. The barman took it, and ripped it up.

'News travels fast,' I said. He smiled. I said, 'One minute you're in, and hot, and the next minute you're out.'

'Tell me about it.' It wasn't the barman. I turned to find Terry Breene standing beside me, cigar in hand.

'They haven't cancelled you as well?'

'Here? No, of course not. Out there – yes, it's starting.' He coughed suddenly, a long phlegmy effort which sounded like two parts smoking and three parts pleurisy. Then he rubbed at his throat. 'All the fucking things I've done in my life, and it takes something I had nothing to do with to turn me into a fucking pariah.' He glared suddenly at the barman. 'So give the man a fucking drink, he's my guest.'

'Yes, sir,' said the barman, and asked me what I wanted.

'My usual,' I said.

Mine was a pint, his was a tall glass full of vodka with a little ice and even less Coke. We went to the same table as before. He walked slowly, his shoulders slumped. Despite the fresh liver, he now looked his age. Overnight. As he sat down he said, 'Christ, you have to laugh,' but gave no indication of being able to. 'You hear the latest? Ryan *fucking* Auto have withdrawn their sponsorship. Talk about kicking a man when he's down.'

'What did they say?'

'Off the record? They say in the run-up to the launch of their new fucking car they can't afford to be associated with a football club which has such violent, racist supporters.'

'And on?'

'Corporate rethink. It's all the same shite. The fuckers.' He lifted his drink and drained half of it. It would have had me under the table, but he hardly blinked. He set it down hard and said, 'This is the fucking end.'

'You think so?'

He took a deep breath, and it seemed to catch in his throat, and he gave a ragged cough, and then another. When he'd recovered sufficiently he raised his hand and began to count off on his fingers. 'First, they picked up half of Sandy Row this morning, and it didn't take them long to work out that the boys that did it are all members of Linfield Supporters Club. Second, UEFA are holding an enquiry, and once they hear that they're all supporters, they'll kick us out of the tournament; their fucking president has already said as much. If it had been the fucking Germans nobody would have minded, but Israelis! Christ. Third, that means no television money, no sponsorship, nothing to pay the players with or to repay the loans I've taken out to cover the purchase of the club. Fourth, I've put every red cent I have into this – everything I've saved. I've sold every trophy, medal, I've remortgaged the houses. It's all fucking gone because some hoods from Sandy Row showed our visitors a typical Belfast welcome.' He gave another hacking, chesty cough, then drained his glass. He gave me a terribly sad look. 'Dan – I'm fucked.'

'Well, at least you have your health.'

He smiled at that. He even laughed. 'At least I have my health.' He glanced up at the bar, and with it getting closer to the evening, the shift had changed; the barman who'd refused me service had gone, and now there were two of the tight-sweatered blondes chatting and smoking and getting ready for a busy night behind the bar, and three others on the floor, doing much the same. He smiled across at them, then returned his attention to his empty glass. He lifted it, turned it in his hand. The two cubes of ice hadn't had time to melt. 'You know,' he said, 'it was all so long ago, but it still feels like yesterday.'

'You were the greatest footballer I ever saw.'

He said, 'I was the greatest footballer anyone ever saw. But I never played in a World Cup.'

'Neither did George Best.'

'Best? I could've run rings round him.' He nodded to himself. 'Do you think that's what people will remember, the football? Not all the other mess?'

'Always the football. News gets old, but you can watch old football for ever.'

'Well. That's good to know.' He finished his drink. He stood up and put his hand out to me. 'See you around, mate.'

I shook it. He was a legend. The legend walked to the bar, asked for and received a full bottle of vodka; he pointed across at me, then crossed the floor towards one of the waitresses. He whispered in her ear. Then he went upstairs. A few moments later, she followed. Then one of the waitresses came over with a tray of pints. She placed one in front of me, then a second, a third and a fourth. 'From Terry,' she said, and gave me a wink. I wasn't particularly in the mood for drinking, but it would have been churlish to refuse. So I made myself comfortable. I took my new mobile phone out several times, tempted to call Patricia, or at the very least to satisfy myself that she was where she said she was. But I put it away each time.

Trust.

I was on the fourth pint when Patrick O'Brien came in. He looked surprised to see me. He spoke to one of the barmaids, then came over. 'When you finish your drink,' he said, 'you'll have to go. We've been very patient.'

'I thought we were best mates.'

'It's nothing personal, Dan. Purely business.'

'That means you've been busy signing up Wendy McBride.'

'Like I say, purely business.'

'Is she putting you on the Power List?'

'Of course.'

'What number?'

'I'm sworn to secrecy. But it'll definitely be top twenty.'

'I'm pleased for you. I wouldn't have put you that high.'

'There's no need to be bitter, Dan.'

'Not bitter. Just honest.' I stood and pulled on my jacket. I glanced around the interior of the bar, possibly for the last time. 'I see your paintings are gone.'

'Just loaned out for an exhibition.'

'You get kind of used to them, don't you?'

'I suppose.' He said it with the kind of clipped finality that made it clear he wanted me gone *right now*. Never being one to outstay my welcome, I turned to go. He said, 'Maybe when things settle down, you can apply for membership.'

'Yup,' I said, without looking around.

Just as I reached the top of the stairs leading down to the exit, a scream tore through the air.

I spun back. It came again. A girl, somewhere above.

O'Brien stood by the bar, immobile; the waitresses looked at each other. Nobody seemed to want to make the first move. So I did what I always do, rushed towards the source of the trouble without thinking through any of the possibilities. I hit the stairs leading to the upper floors. When I reached the landing on the second floor I hesitated. Swing doors opened below me and O'Brien appeared. 'Wait! Wait!' he called, but then the girl screamed again and I had a better fix on it. I took the next flight of steps three at a time and emerged into a narrow corridor with six closed doors, three on either side. A girl was crying. Second room on the left. I tried the handle. It was locked. I raised my foot just as O'Brien appeared at the end of the corridor, bargirls crowded up behind him. I struck the door with everything I had, and it flew open surprisingly easily. The bargirl Terry Breene had left with was sitting up in the bed, naked under the covers. She was finally done with the screaming. Her mouth worked like a fish out of water as she pointed at the windows. They opened outwards to give a fantastic view across the Belfast skyline. Unfortunately, they also gave a fantastic view of Terry Breene, lying smashed and bloody and very obviously dead on the pavement three floors below.

39

It took a while to calm her down. This was understandable. As she told it, one minute Terry Breene had been screwing her, then he'd climbed off, taken a long swig from his bottle of vodka, then made a dash for the window and thrown himself out. She'd *heard* him strike the ground, three floors below.

Yuk.

While the other girls tried to console her, Patrick O'Brien spent a long time staring at the pavement. I stood with him for a while, then said, 'You'd better call the cops.'

He nodded, but he didn't move. I turned to the girl. She was sniffing up, then blowing down into a tissue. Her mascara was all over the place and the bedclothes had fallen away, revealing that she was indeed naked, but now she didn't care one way or the other.

I said, 'Did he say anything?'

'Aaaaaaaaaaaaaaaaaaaaaah.'

'I mean, before he jumped. To you.'

'No. He never did. He saw. He came. He jumped.' She looked at her friends. 'It wasn't me, was it? Tell me it wasn't me . . .' She broke down into tears again. The other girls patted and stroked her.

Patrick O'Brien was shaking his head, his eyes still glued to the pavement. 'This is going to kill us, it's really going to kill us.'

I could have said a lot of things to that. But I didn't. I walked out of the room and down the stairs. There was a small crowd of customers grouped around the doors at the bottom, wondering what all the commotion was. I pushed through them, ignoring their questions, then ducked in behind the bar. There was no one to stop me. I poured myself a shot of whiskey, and drained it. I took another. Then I headed for the exit. As I reached the top of the stairs, leading down, another man came racing up them.

'Jesus Christ!' he shouted, and everyone turned. 'Someone's just killed themselves out there!'

Immediately the crowd moved towards him, and around me, and down the stairs for a closer look.

'Any idea who it is?' one of them asked excitedly.

The man shook his head, but then followed it with, 'You know, it can't be, but it looks like Terry Breene.'

No, I thought, it doesn't. Not any more.

It was dark, wet, and I was pissed, but I drove home. Sometimes you have to. Terry Breene was dead, and the last non-lustful words he had spoken had been to me. Maybe he had found some consolation in my assurance that he would be remembered for his football, not his tabloidy exploits. But if that very reassurance had spurred him on to commit his very public suicide, it had also cancelled itself out. He would be remembered now as the supremely talented footballer who killed himself by jumping out of a third-floor window.

Dumb.

Dumb.

A fucking waste.

I punched the dash half a dozen times on the way home. He'd been such a star when he was young, but he'd left the

game early and been written off in the press as a drunken
wastrel. Terry had always maintained that he was having a ball
– making money, and sleeping with gorgeous women. His forays
back into football via management had always started with a
flourish and then quickly petered out, but he'd always bounced
back before.

Linfield was different. His previous fuck-ups had been with
other people's money, and this one was with his own. Just
when he thought he might finally have cracked it, a few thugs
with baseball bats had pulled the rug out from under him. It
didn't matter whether it was an attack on Israel, or an attack
on Terry himself because he was a Catholic messing with a
Protestant team, the result was the same. He'd lost everything
and couldn't bear to start again.

Bastards.

I pulled into the driveway. The house was in darkness. Not
only was Patricia failing to keep the home fires burning, she
hadn't even left a lamp on. I didn't feel like going in. My wife
was gone for the night, I'd lost my job, fallen out with May
Li, been punched in the mouth and my footballing hero had
plunged to his bloody death.

I was knackered. Not just with the alcohol. Fatigue. It was an
effort just to get out of the car. I could just as easily have nodded
off where I was, listening to tapes of The Clash. But I needed a
pee. Topper was sitting on the front windowsill. He hissed at me.
I gave him the fingers. I let myself in. Went up to the bathroom.
When I came out I hesitated at the top of the stairs, torn between
going for a lie-down and liberating a can from the fridge. I had
a DVD of Terry Breene's finest moments, and I half-thought of
watching that, but I wasn't sure if it was a good idea. Too close.
Too raw. But still, it was football, and I was pretty drunk.

I heard a click, off to my right, from our bedroom. The door was slightly open, enough for me to see that the bedside light was now switched on.

Patricia.

You sneaked home to surprise me. To seduce me.

You little hussy.

I smiled happily and turned for the door.

As I pushed it open, we said together, 'I knew you would come.'

Except she was a he, and husky with it.

We stared at each other. Stunned.

Me, in the doorway, Alec Large, naked on top of the bed.

He said, 'Oh.'

I was beyond even an 'Oh.'

He had an erection. At least I think it was an erection. A passing tree surgeon might have grafted on a mighty oak. He didn't even have the good grace to cover it up. Possibly because his hands weren't big enough.

'Holy fucking Christ,' I said, eventually.

'I was expecting someone else,' he said, sitting up.

'So I see.'

He cleared his throat. 'You're never home this early.'

'No,' I said.

'I was expecting Patricia.'

'Uhuh.'

'Bit of a miscalculation.'

'Uhuh.'

I was drunk, and have in the past been known to erupt into violence at the slightest provocation (before, admittedly, receiving a good beating) but there was something about Alec Large, lying naked on my bed, with his big hopeful eyes, and big hopeful other bits, which failed to spark that anger. He was stranded in the hopeless wilderness that lies between being pathetic and a total clown. It was a place I knew well.

Attacking him would have been like attacking myself.

And other psycho-babble.

I just felt kind of sorry for him. Terry Breene had killed himself because an eruption of violence had destroyed his dreams and left him a ruined man. Alec Large was naked in my bed with a hard-on. It was hardly the same thing.

I said, 'How long have you been here?'

He'd left his watch on the bedside table. He glanced at it and said, 'Four hours. I must have fallen asleep.'

'And *that* . . . You woke up with *that*?'

He shook his head. 'Viagra.'

'Well, can't you *do* something about it?'

He looked down at it – well, not down exactly, because the tip of it was almost at eye-level. 'I, well, I didn't want to disappoint, so I took three. I'll still be hard next Tuesday.'

I looked him in the eye. 'How do you know?' I asked. He shrugged. 'Have you done this before?' He shrugged again. 'With just as much success?' No shrug, but avoiding eye-contact. 'Right. Brilliant. Okay. Put some clothes on, Alec. Come downstairs. We need to have a talk.'

We sat at the kitchen table. I made him a coffee. I drank Diet Coke. Too much drink. Alec was in his smart black suit again. He looked at the table a lot. I was glad it was there, between us, keeping his trousers and what they contained out of sight.

'You must hate me,' he said.

'Yes.'

'I can't help falling in love.'

'Uhuh.'

'She is lovely.'

'I'm aware of that.'

'I couldn't help myself. I told her. She said she'd think about it.'

'I know.'

'You know?'

'She tells me everything.'

'What did she say about me?'

'Alec, there is no future in this. You were employed to do a job. Patricia did not pick you out. But she is a friendly soul who made you welcome. That does not mean she wants to come home at night and find you in her bed.'

'I'm beginning to realise that now.'

'I mean, Christ, it's like the separation between Church and State: you have to learn that one thing is one thing, and the other thing is the other.'

'I know. I . . . have an addictive personality. If someone shows me affection, I take more from it than I should.'

'You said yourself it's happened before.' He nodded. 'When you were guarding someone else?'

He shook his head. 'I haven't guarded anyone else before.'

'You what?'

'This is my first time.'

'Your first time working for yourself. It was a company you worked for before. The Beckhams, Princess Diana.'

He bit on his bottom lip. 'No, I never did. I worked as a door steward at *Past Masters*. May Li hired me. It wasn't great money, but it was more than I was earning there.'

'But she paid for some kind of training, right?'

Again, he shook his head. 'There wasn't time. I even had to provide my own suit. I had always wanted to do this kind of work though. I just wasn't allowed.'

I look a deep breath. 'Why weren't you allowed, Alec?'

'Well, I applied. But my eyesight's not great, and I can't wear contacts. And they seemed to think I had a mild case of attention deficit disorder.'

I drummed my fingers on the table. The coffee vibrated. 'May Li hired a blind man with attention deficit disorder to guard me?'

'That would appear to be the case.'

'And all that stuff about assassinations and blood types?'

'Well, I read a lot. I wear glasses at home, but I don't like to wear them in public. Self-conscious.'

'Right,' I said.

'Do you mind if I use your toilet?'

'No, Alec.'

'I also have irritable bowel syndrome.'

He went to the bathroom.

While he was gone I switched on the television news, and read the Ceefax report of Terry Breene's demise. There were three pages in all: one covered the circumstances of his death, one his playing career, and the third was taken up with tributes from other football stars. I had a lump in my throat reading them. The toilet flushed upstairs. As I returned to the kitchen I noticed the message light flashing on our answerphone. I pressed it: Toothless, on his mobile. *'Dan, for fuck sake, will you stay in one place? Been trying to find you all day. I've something for you. Gimme a buzz.'*

Alec began to come down the stairs. He got halfway down, then I heard him retrace his steps, and a moment later came the sound of the bathroom lock being secured again.

I picked up the phone and called Toothless. He answered on the third ring. 'You have something for me,' I said.

'And about bloody time. Yes, I have. Only thing is, I'm

worried about your ability to pay. I heard you got the chop.'

'I'll sort something out. What is it?'

'Oh, wouldn't you like to know. Listen, I'll bring it round.'

'Hold on a minute.' I set the receiver down and walked to the bottom of the stairs. 'Are you all right?' I shouted up.

'*Yus.*'

'I'm expecting a visitor.'

'*Okay.*'

'Which means you have to go.'

'*Christ.*'

He sounded like he was in considerable pain.

'Are you sure you're okay?'

'*Yus.*'

'Well, are you going to be long?'

'*Christ.* Sorry. Have you any idea . . . *how* . . . *hard it is* . . . *to do a plop* . . . when you have an erection?'

'No,' I said. I returned to the phone. 'Toothless, it's not convenient right now.'

'Well, it has to be. I can't hold onto this.'

'Okay. All right.' I thought quickly. I was new to the neighbourhood, and hadn't really had a chance to work it out yet, but I had noticed a children's playground with a small car park beside it, just around the corner. I asked Toothless to meet me there in twenty minutes.

He said, 'I love cloak and dagger stuff, don't you?'

'No,' I replied. 'Familiarity breeds contempt.'

40

Alec Large was still in the toilet twenty-five minutes later.

'Any joy?' I shouted up.

'Not . . . *yet*. I'm really . . . *sorry* . . . about this.'

I sighed. 'Don't worry about it. But I have to pop out for ten minutes. If everything works out for you in the meantime, just pull the door closed after you and never darken it again. All right?'

'All . . . *right*.'

I pulled my hood up against the rain, and hurried down the drive. I was late for my rendezvous with Toothless Malone, mostly due to the fact that I wasn't keen on leaving Alec alone in the house again. But I had no choice.

I slipped down one avenue, then another, and out onto the main road. The playground was a hundred metres up on my left, and I could already see two cars sitting there. One, the closest, had its engine running, and there was a small plume of exhaust fumes coming from the rear. There was a vague outline of someone sitting behind the wheel. The other car was about ten metres further on, and appeared to be empty. There was a small copse beyond the car park, and a high wire fence surrounding a disused tennis court beside the playground. I walked along the far side of the road until I was roughly parallel with the first car, then waited for a gap in the traffic and splashed across. As I drew nearer I could hear the beat of heavy rock coming from within. Loud. I'd no idea what Toothless's car looked like, and didn't want to embarrass myself in front of some courting couple, so I stood by the window for a moment, hoping my presence might register and it would either be him, relaxing with Deep Purple, or some randy teenager telling me to fuck off. But he or they didn't notice, so I knocked lightly on the window, and then a little bit harder. Still nothing. I pressed my face to the glass and shielded my eyes against the glare from the streetlight above. It was Toothless okay, but he was turned slightly to one side, lost in the music. I could under- stand that, although not his choice.

I drummed on the window, then tried the door handle. As I opened it, I said, 'Turn it down, would you?' in a chummy voice – only for Toothless to fall sideways. I stepped back instinc- tively as he sprawled half out of the car. I thought at first that maybe he was drunk, but he didn't move at all. I crouched beside him. 'Toothless, hey, Toothless – are you all right, mate?' I turned his head slightly, then recoiled in horror. His expen- sive teeth were all smashed and jagged and his jaw hung brokenly to one side. His nose seemed to have exploded outwards. His eyes were wide and vacant. 'Smoke on the Water' was booming out, and Toothless was lying dead.

My chest felt suddenly constricted. My brain popped and fizzed. He could only have been there for ten or fifteen minutes, maximum. And it definitely wasn't suicide. I stared towards the other car. Then into the trees. Across the tennis court. The swings were swaying gently. Deep Purple sang on. My heart thundered. I stared again at Toothless – what had he brought me? Was it still there? No, of course it wasn't! Whoever had killed him had taken it. Or what if it was just a random murder, wrong place, wrong time? Deep Purple sang on. No, of course not, of *course* not. Then, just for confirmation, the other car door opened. I was still crouching down. I stayed in that position, but took a step back. A man climbed out. With the rain and the glare of the light I couldn't quite see his face. I took another step back.

'Police – stay where you are!'

I raised myself a fraction, just enough to see over the edge of the bonnet.

Brian Mooney. Detective Inspector. The good cop who'd warned me off. I took another step backwards. He must have followed Toothless. And if he'd followed, he must also have killed him. There was no other explanation. There wasn't time for anyone else to be involved. He hadn't just stumbled on a murder by accident. It had to be him.

'Don't move!'

Good cop.

Bad cop.

Where was the other one?

Smoke on the Water.

Movement, off to my right, coming from behind a twisting slide. A fuller figure, hurrying forward. It was Mayne, his partner. Had to be. I pivoted to my right.

'Stop! Police!'

There was traffic coming – but what the hell.

I darted out. There was a screech of tyres and a Subaru planed sideways on the soaking road; it missed me by centimetres. Another car screamed to a halt behind it, just avoiding a collision. Mooney yelled something. I reached the other side and then jumped a set of gates and charged up the driveway of a detached house. Just as I reached the cover of the garage, a bullet cracked off the wall beside me.

Fucking hell.

I ducked down and raced up the side of the garage into a back garden. There was a low hedge at the rear. I dived over it into the adjoining garden. I rolled once, and was back on my feet and running again. It's amazing what you can do when someone puts the fear of God up you. I leaped a second hedge, then ran through to that house's front garden and crouched down behind a low wall. I peered out into one of the avenues I'd quite happily sauntered down just a few minutes earlier.

All quiet.

In the distance – angry motorists pounding their horns.

Mayne and Mooney. They'd shot at me. No warning, just shot. And beside them, the dead body of their colleague, Bobby 'Toothless' Malone.

Killers. In it together. No time for the whys or wherefores. The question was, had they recognised me? Or merely followed Toothless to see who he was meeting, killed him and left him as bait? I'd had my hood up the whole time, one of those big ones which seemed to swallow your whole head, so it was conceivable that they hadn't seen my face. What if they had? Then it wouldn't be hard for them to find out where I lived, and they could easily be on their way there now, thinking that I might just have run home They'd find Alec Large, and probably kill him too.

Somewhere close at hand, barking erupted. I crouched down further. A door opened and a woman called her dog in. I scanned the road again. Still empty.

If they *had* recognised me, would they take the chance of calling at my house, with Toothless dead and hanging out of his car so close by? Maybe not. So perhaps I had time to get back there, pick up my car, get Alec offside. If they *hadn't* recognised me, they would surely soon work it out anyway. They were cops, after all. And Toothless had called me just a short while ago. Getting access to his phone records wouldn't be hard for them.

I decided to risk it. I had no particular fondness for Alec Large, but having one person shot in your house was unfortunate; two would hit the resale value. I hurried along the avenue, ready to dive over a wall at the slightest hint of someone following me or if a car turned in. I stopped at the end of the street and spent several minutes observing the house from the shelter of a pine tree in the corner garden. The lights were on, but was anybody in?

No way to tell.

There was a mucky lane running along the back of the house. I decided that was the safest way in. No reason for it to be, really. One could cover the front, one the back. But I had to take some sort of precaution. That or I could just charge up to the front door, unlock it, slip inside and hope that a cheap deadbolt and some double glazing would keep out a couple of gun-wielding rogue cops.

But it was something.

I stepped over our garden fence and hurried down the garden path. I'd left the back door unlocked, so didn't need to bother with a noisy lock. I let myself in. Everything seemed to be as I had left it. I crossed the kitchen, opened a drawer and removed a breadknife. Into the hall.

Then a low groan.

From upstairs.

Then another.

I gripped the knife hard. 'Alec?' I called softly.

'For *god sake* – I'm going as fast as I can!'

I breathed a sigh of relief, then turned the light off in the front room and crossed to the window and peered out. Everything quiet. I returned to the kitchen; Alec's jacket was draped across one of the chairs. I checked the pockets. I found his gun in his inside left. I know little about guns, but have handled enough to know when the safety is on. I slipped it into my own pocket. It wasn't particularly heavy. He probably wouldn't notice the difference, what with the weight he was already carrying in his pants.

The phone rang suddenly behind me, and I nearly jumped out of my skin. It seemed louder than I could ever remember it.

A criminal mastermind on the other end, telling me the house was surrounded.

I picked it up.

'Hi, hon.'

'Trish.'

'How you doin'?' Like Joey from *Friends*.

'Fine.'

'You're angry with me.'

'No.'

'You sure?'

'Yes.'

'You sound angry.'

'No. Just stressed.'

'That's my fault. I just needed a break. I'll be home tomorrow.'

'No. I mean, may as well take a couple of days. Absence makes the heart grow fonder.'

'Aw. That's sweet.' Upstairs, the toilet flushed. A hundred miles away, Trish heard it. 'Who's with you?' Immediately suspicious.

'Alec Large.'

'*Alec?*'

'Yup. He came to whisk you away to paradise. Unfortunately, he got me.'

'Oh God, I'm sorry.'

'You will be. Relax. I put him straight. He's fine.'

'Really?'

'Yes.'

'Did you let him down gently?'

'Yes. Of course I did. I'm not entirely insensitive.' He was moving down the stairs now. I didn't want to turn it into a three-way conversation. Or have him grab the phone and beg my wife to run away with him. 'He's coming, I have to go.'

'Okay. Listen, it's lovely up here. I will stay an extra night, if that's all right with you?'

'Yes, of course. As long as . . .'

'Yes, I love you, and I'm coming home.'

'All right.' I put the phone down. Alec Large stood rather sheepishly in the kitchen doorway; his cheeks were flushed, and his weapon of mass destruction continued to poke a menacing shape in his trousers. Worryingly, I was getting kind of used to it.

'You took your time,' I said.

'Well,' he replied, 'you gotta load them up before you shoot them out.'

41

We moved to the lounge. He went to put the light on and I said, 'No, leave it.' I stood at the corner of the window, looking out again. He sat on the sofa, a whiskey in his hand.

He said, 'You're clearly very upset by all of this. I'm sorry. I've acted like an eejit.'

I kept my eyes on the road.

'I had a lot of time to think about things up there. I misread the signals. I do that all the time.'

A car turned into the road. It passed the house. I caught a glimpse of a young woman, singing along to something.

'I should go. I've done enough damage.' He went to get up, then winced, and clutched his stomach. 'Christ.' He sat down again, massaging himself. 'I'm sorry, I'm in no state to go anywhere right now. It flares up when I'm stressed.'

A woman came walking past with her dog. She examined our front garden while it peed against our gatepost. They moved on. I glanced back at Alec, with his bulged-out trousers and his spastic colon. 'Relax,' I said. 'Drink your whiskey. Watch the TV, have a doze. I know what it's like to be in love.'

'But you married her.'

'Yes, I did. Although she put up a fight.'

I stood there for an hour and a half; Alec talked about himself and I did the nodding and shrugging. I was a Samaritan with a revolver in my pocket. Eventually I couldn't take it any more. Stress. Fatigue. Boredom. I left him in there and went upstairs to our bedroom. Again I kept the light off. I packed a small bag in the dark. I'd no idea where I was going or what I was doing, but the house wasn't safe. I stood by the window. I could see further along the road in both directions. Between the houses I could even see glimpses of the road where Toothless had been murdered, and traffic appeared to be flowing freely. Suburban Belfast, as far as I could see, was at peace.

I needed a plan. But how do you plan for the unknown?

Our bed was high enough to give me a view of the road immediately outside our house, so I lay down on it and kept watch while I tried to gather my thoughts. About Mayne and Mooney. And Toothless. Once I had known a lot of cops, but not any longer. I'd gotten myself in so much trouble over the years that only Toothless was prepared to work with me. If Mayne and Mooney were on the take, who was to say that they were the only ones? And even if I was to call an ordinary plod on the desk, what would I say? Mayne had already shown me how easy it was to entrap someone. I was quite certain that if I let slip anything to do with the playground murder, I would be the one arrested for it, not the men I knew to be responsible.

Who you gonna call?

No one.

Because in this day and age, who else would I get into trouble by calling them up? I could hardly wire a plug, but other people could, and if they were determined enough, would surely trace every last person I spoke to. Not that there was a huge list anyway. I'd been reasonably nice to Stephen and Patrick from work; if I needed a little help there was no real reason why they shouldn't come through. Yes, that made sense. I'd go and see them in the morning, before they left for work. Brainstorm it out. There had to be something we'd missed. Mayne and Mooney had to be working for someone. There would be a connection somewhere. Toothless had found it, and then they had found him.

I'm not sure at what point I fell asleep. You never are. I was vaguely aware of the *Newsnight* music coming from the TV downstairs, and then I jolted suddenly awake and it was daylight. My neck was stiff from sleeping in an awkward position. I sat up and peered out into a misty morning.

Mooney and Mayne's car was parked about thirty metres up on the left.

I ducked down quickly, crawled across to the window and raised my eyes half an inch above the sill. Yes, it was definitely their car. And they were both inside.

Christ.

How long had they been there? And what were they waiting for?

Then the answer presented itself – the postman, wheeling his bike along, then resting it against our gatepost. He came up the drive. Somewhere close by, Topper hissed. I crossed the bedroom on my hands and knees, then stood as I went through the door. I looked down the stairs. Two envelopes were pushed through the letter box and dropped on the floor; then a thicker, padded envelope appeared, but he had difficulty getting this one through. He pushed at it for several moments, then decided to leave it, half in, half out. He walked away.

I hurried downstairs and picked up the two envelopes – one with the *Nationwide* logo, the other with bright red letters saying *Competition Winner – Important! Do Not Destroy!* My eyes went to the thicker item jammed in the letter box. I crouched down beside it. There was enough through the door to see that it was addressed to me. It was also franked with an official stamp – the Police Service of Northern Ireland.

Toothless.

He must have been aware that he was being watched and had sent a back-up copy of whatever he'd found in case anything happened to him. And they knew. Perhaps they had beaten this information out of him, or been unable to stop him putting it into the internal mail system at work.

Whatever – there it was. Right before me. And I had to grab it. I had to know. But if I did, they would realise I was in the house. If I left it, they would surely come and retrieve it, and I could take the chance that that would satisfy them. I'd be hiding and they'd be walking away with my one chance to see the evidence Toothless had uncovered. Or they could take it, then break into the house and kill me.

Was I a man or a mouse?

A mouse, always.

I stared at the envelope.

There was a slight buzz of conversation coming from the TV in the lounge, but it was otherwise empty. Alec was gone.

I stared some more.

And it suddenly came to me, simplicity itself. Tear the bloody thing at one end, slip out whatever was inside, then hightail it out the back.

I took hold of the end of it and started to tear, but almost immediately a shadow fell over the glass and two hands grabbed the other end of the envelope and pulled.

I pulled back, hard.

It must have come as a surprise. It slipped from Mayne or Mooney's grasp and I fell backwards, pulling the envelope right through the box, ripping it on both sides. I jumped to my feet and tore down the hall and into the kitchen. Behind me, the front door exploded off its hinges. I yanked the back door open – and saw Mooney hurrying up the garden. I slammed the door again and darted to my left. There were two entrances to the kitchen, one through the lounge and another along the hall. As Mayne pursued me through the lounge, I doubled back along the hall, heading for space where the front door used to be.

Or at least, I thought he was pursuing me.

Instead he had doubled back himself, and we virtually collided at the end of the hall. He was big and strong and trained in unarmed combat, and I ate a lot of crisps. There was only ever going to be one winner. He slammed me hard against the wall, thumped me once in the stomach, then grabbed my T-shirt and threw me into the lounge. I virtually bounced off our expensive, deeply shagged carpet. As was I. Mayne stood over me, and was joined very quickly by Mooney.

'You stupid fucker, Starkey,' Mayne growled.

I was gasping for air.

Mooney crouched beside me and lifted the envelope where it had fallen. He removed a half-inch of a videotape, nodded at Mayne, then slipped it back in.

'You were told to keep your nose out,' said Mayne, 'and now we've got no alternative.'

'There's always . . . an alternative,' I wheezed. 'Have . . . thirty years of Troubles . . . taught you . . . *nothing*?'

I was playing for time, but badly out of tune.

Mooney kicked me hard.

'You were . . . were supposed to be the *good* one . . .' I stammered.

'Yeah, *right*,' he growled, and kicked me again.

'You know,' said Mayne, 'killing a colleague is a real mind-fucker. But killing you is going to be such fun.'

He pulled his foot back for another kick – then stopped. He'd noticed that his colleague was slowly raising his hands. Mayne turned, rather bizarrely balancing on one foot, which he then slowly lowered, just as he raised his own hands.

I blinked through the pain at the figure standing in the doorway.

Alec Large.

His coat on, ready to leave, his hands in his pockets – and his extraordinarily large and drugged-up penis pressing against the front of his coat and forcing it out, like he had a gun concealed in there. He looked as surprised as they did. But they only had eyes for the pistol in his pocket. Which was actually in my pocket, upstairs.

'What on earth is—?' Alec began.

I kicked out hard against the back of Mayne's legs, wincing at the pain of the effort. But he was taken by surprise and collapsed down. Mooney took a step backwards. 'Don't shoot,' he said.

'What?' said Alec, blissfully unaware. But then he made the mistake of taking his hands out of his pockets.

I didn't give Mooney time to think. I forced myself up and charged into him, knocking him backwards. As he fell, Mayne tried to get up, so I gave him another hard shove. He rolled over and I jumped on him, both feet. He groaned. I groaned. He tried to get up. I pinned him back down; I pushed my hand into his jacket pocket and drew out his gun.

Alec's mouth was hanging open. 'What the fuck is happening?'

Mooney pushed himself up. I held his partner's gun on him, then spread it a little to cover them both.

I didn't look at Alec, but I said, 'I thought you went home.'

'Nah, I've been stuck in the bog for hours. You're out of toilet roll.'

'Noted.'

'Do you want to tell me what . . . ?'

'Later,' I said. I knelt and picked up the envelope. I gave it a little shake. 'Anything good?' I asked.

'We're going to fucking get you, Starkey,' said Mayne. 'This isn't over.'

'I know,' I said, 'it's just the commercial break. See ya later, alligator.'

I backed out of the lounge, taking Alec with me.

I didn't much like leaving them in the house, but I wasn't about to shoot them. I wasn't that desperate. Not yet. I tossed Alec the car keys, then held the gun on the front door while he got it started. Then I jumped in, and Alec reversed at speed down the drive.

As we hit the road, Alec pulled the wheel hard left, then slammed on the brakes and threw the car into first. Mooney and Mayne appeared through the open door as Alec gunned the engine again and we heaved forward.

There was a sudden thump and squeal and he slammed on the brakes again. A moment later Topper, having been hurled into the air, splatted down onto the windscreen. Blood and guts and fur obscured the view.

'Just fucking go!' I yelled, and Alec hit the pedal again. I caught a glimpse of Mooney and Mayne in the mirror, racing for their own car. As we approached the corner, Alec fumbled for the windscreen wipers in this unfamiliar car. I stretched across and flicked them on. Topper went back and forth, and back and forth, then as we rounded the corner on two wheels, he fell off.

42

Alec thought it was all very exciting. I'd left his gun in the house, upstairs in my jacket. He said that was okay, it didn't work anyway. It was a replica. May Li had recruited an idiot. He wanted to know who was who, and what was what, and I told him patience was a virtue. I turned the car into a BP garage and instructed him to purchase coffee and sausage rolls. He climbed out, then put his hands in his pockets as he approached the shop, doing his best to cover up the evidence of his Viagra overdose. He seemed to appreciate being given precise orders to follow, although probably to a lesser extent when he emerged to find that I'd driven off. He was a nice enough fella, when you got talking to him, but he was also thick as a plank and embarrassing to be seen with, given the state of his pants. He was fairly harmless, but I didn't want him to end up dead.

I called Stephen's mobile. 'Are you away to work yet?' I asked.

'I'm just going out the door now.'

'Well, don't. Stay there. Give me your address.'

'Dan – I'm sorry, but I don't work for you any more.'

'You don't want in on the biggest story of your life, then?'

He hesitated. 'What story?'

'Give me the address.'

He gave it. It was in North Belfast, up past Carlisle Circus. It had been a dangerous place to live in the old days; now you could hardly afford to live there. A second-floor apartment. I parked outside and he buzzed me up. The door was open. There was modern art on the walls and the smell of fresh flowers. It was all open-plan. Stephen was wearing black jeans and a jersey and standing a little awkwardly by a breakfast bar. He glanced towards the bedroom. Patrick, wearing a blue towelling bathrobe, was in there, fixing his hair in a mirror.

'Okay,' said Stephen, 'the secret's out.'

'Believe me,' I said, 'it was never in.'

Stephen got coffee. I said, 'So how's the new boss?' and he rolled his eyes.

Patrick emerged within a minute, pushing his T-shirt into blue jeans, then smoothing down his damp hair. 'So, what's all this about?' he asked.

I reached inside my jacket and produced the torn envelope. I removed the videotape and held it out. 'This,' I said. 'Someone got murdered trying to deliver it to me last night.'

They exchanged glances.

'That cop?' I nodded. 'Yeah – heard it on the news this morning,' said Patrick. 'They haven't released his name yet. Beaten to death. Shit.'

'So?' I shook it at them again. Stephen took it. He crossed to the video recorder and ejected a tape. He made a point of not letting me see what they'd been watching together. He placed it face down above the machine and slipped my one in. He handed the controls to Patrick and sat back down on a sofa. A moment later the picture came onscreen: passers-by outside the old *Belfast Confidential* office, taken from a high angle, probably from the insurance company HQ next door. I was used to CCTV footage being black and white and poor quality; this was crystal clear and in full colour. There was a time-code running on the bottom left-hand corner. It showed it to be 9.45 on the night of Mouse's murder. I had called Mouse's mobile at 7.25 and spoken to a stranger. Then I'd left several messages. At ten I'd decided to drive down to gee him up, arriving ten minutes later when the fire was already raging. So, hopefully between the start of the tape, and the start of the fire, *something* would show up. The temptation, of course, was to scroll forward, but I insisted on it being played out in real time.

We sat, glued.

Hookers drifted in and out. Cars stopped, started. Kids drove past, yelling insults; the girls screamed back, harsher, wittier.

Nothing.

Nothing.

Nothing.

Then.

We were seventeen minutes into it when a man emerged from the *Belfast Confidential* office. He was wearing a grey suit, appeared tall and quite thin, but he walked with his head down – until just a moment before he moved out of frame, a car honked its horn and the man instinctively looked up.

'Freeze it!' I yelled.

We missed it. Patrick rewound, then let it play again. This time he nailed it. The man. The face.

Matthew Rye, Project Manager for Ryan Auto.

43

We kept his face like that, frozen on the screen, while we walked back and forth and around, debating the possibilities.

'So he pays an after-hours visit, when Mouse is alone, and he kills him. Cops on the take try to stop the tape getting out.' Stephen nodded to himself. 'We take this as read?'

'It would seem that way,' I said.

'You're not convinced?'

'Well, if I've learned anything, it's that life is twisty-turny. Until he signs his confession I won't be completely convinced. Say ninety per cent right now. But if for the moment we say yeah, then, *why*? Why kill Mouse?'

'Well,' said Stephen, 'perhaps Mouse was gay, but hid it better than we do. They were having a fling, they were into bondage, it got out of hand, Mouse died, Matthew Rye decides to torch the place, he calls in Belfast's Gay Police Mafia to protect him.'

Patrick cleared his throat. 'You're projecting your fantasies again, Stephen.'

'And Mouse didn't have a gay bone in his body,' I added.

'That's what *I* said,' said Stephen, 'and look at me now. And even if it is a fantasy, is it any less likely that it's a lovers' tiff rather than some kind of superconspiracy?'

'Who mentioned a superconspiracy?' asked Patrick.

'We're getting there,' said Stephen. Then he glanced at me. 'Aren't we?'

I nodded. We were, and we could have spent the next forty days and nights batting around the different scenarios, but we were hampered by a lack of useful information. 'We need to find out more about Matthew Rye,' I said. 'Who he is, where he's from, what exactly he does, where he eats, drinks, does his shopping, who he screws, if he screws. Everything. All right?'

I looked from one to the other.

'We're due in work . . . five minutes ago,' said Patrick.

'This is more important,' I said.

'I know it's more important,' said Stephen, 'but it's our *job*.'

'We could phone in sick,' said Patrick.

'Both of us?'

'Well, when I get the flu, *you* certainly get it. Besides, Brian Kerr is such a wanker, he's destroying that place. I could do with a day off.' He glanced at me. 'Not that it would be a day off. You know he's postponed the Power List?'

'I didn't, but I presumed he would. Okay, then, make your calls, and let's get to work.'

Patrick gave me the thumbs-up. 'Yes indeedy,' he said. 'Woodward and Bernstein, watch out!'

Stephen smiled beside him. 'Absolutely,' he beamed. 'Forget yer Watergate, this is . . . Ryegate!'

I cleared my throat. 'Isn't that a small town in—'

'Fuck that!' exclaimed Patrick. 'It's fucking Ryegate from here on in!'

They were young and enthusiastic, and not yet beaten down by the horrors of life. It was still early in the day, though.

I used the phone in their bedroom. Patrick sat with his mobile in the lounge and Stephen sat at the kitchen table, using his laptop to track Matthew Rye on the internet. Once in a while we emerged to compare notes. Gradually a picture emerged. He was a member of *Past Masters*, but according to the guest book not a regular visitor. He wasn't married. He was born in Chicago, raised in New York. A profile of Ryan Auto staff included with the initial press pack showed that he attended and graduated from Harvard Business School.

'That's what it says,' Patrick said from the bedroom doorway, 'except Harvard has no record of him.' He raised an eyebrow and went back to work.

About noon Stephen let out a delighted 'Bingo! I love you, Google!' and we rushed out to find him drumming on the table. He finished with a flourish, and went: 'Ta-da!' before pointing at the screen and saying, 'Am I great or am I not?'

Onscreen was a newspaper article culled from the archives of the *Miami Herald*. It was a five-year-old report of a court case in which three Miami residents were acquitted on charges of racketeering and money laundering. One of the three was named as a Matt Rye, an ex-Green Beret. The case against them had collapsed due to the non-appearance of a crucial witness who had, according to the local DA, 'disappeared without trace'.

'Interesting,' I said, 'but who's to say it's the same—'

Stephen pressed another button. *'Voilà!'*

A second, earlier report appeared, filed at the time of the original arrest, but this time also showing photographs of the three men. One of them was undeniably Matthew Rye. Younger, of course, slightly more ragged-looking, but definitely him.

Stephen rubbed his hands together excitedly. 'Have you any idea how many web pages for Matthew Ryes there are out there? Thousands! Luckily most of them are about a musician with the BBC Symphony Orchestra. So this one stuck out a mile.'

Patrick put a hand on Stephen's shoulder and squeezed.

'Well done,' I said, 'but what does it tell us? He was arrested, not convicted. He's innocent.'

'Bollocks!' Stephen exploded. 'It more or less says the chief witness was disappeared. He's a gangster. And he was in the Army, a Green Beret, so he knows how to kill people. And we already know he never went to Harvard Business School. He's up to his neck in it, Dan.'

'In what?'

'This!'

'This what?'

'*This* this.'

I was playing Devil's Advocate. 'Go on.'

Stephen glanced at Patrick, who gave him a nod of encouragement. 'Well, isn't it clear? Matthew Rye cons his way into Ryan Auto, with his fake degree from Harvard and who knows what else kind of shit, with the intention of fleecing money out of the company. He gets sent here to oversee the project, he has a huge budget, he's thousands of miles from Jacintha Ryan, so he thinks he's free to milk the company, maybe use his previous experience to launder the money. Except Mouse somehow finds out about it, and gets killed for his trouble. Matthew Rye's worried that the information might have been passed on to you, so he tries to take you out as well, but gets Liam Miller instead. Plus he's got enough company money to throw around to buy himself some protection from the police as well.' He gave a little bow. 'I rest my case, Your Honour.'

We had the tape, we had Matthew Rye's dodgy background, and we had a lot of presumptions about what might have happened. The tape was enough to put him with Mouse close to the time of the fire; it certainly wasn't evidence of his having been involved in the murder, but this was Belfast: people had been convicted of a lot worse on a lot less. And clearly he had lied to get the job with Ryan Auto. Even though he had not been convicted of anything in the States, even to be accused of such serious offences would cause any company with an eye on its corporate image to run a mile.

The question was, what to do with this information?

Mooney and Mayne had withheld the tape, and murdered Toothless. But who was to say they were the only cops who'd been bought off? But we still needed to get it out there, it was just a matter of deciding on the best method. There was the local TV news, or the radio, perhaps my old newspaper, the *Belfast Telegraph* – or all of them at the same time. We needed to set up a press conference. No chance of anyone burying it then. I suggested this.

Patrick and Stephen, sitting on a black leather sofa, both shook their heads.

'Dan, we work for *Belfast Confidential*. That's where we're taking it.'

'Oh no.'

'You brought the story to us – as soon as you walked through that door it became a *Belfast Confidential* story.'

'Bollocks. It's my story. I only asked for your help.'

'Yes, as *Belfast Confidential* reporters.'

'No I didn't, I asked you as friends.'

They smiled. 'We're not your friends, Dan. We're your colleagues.'

'Ex-colleagues, at that,' added Patrick.

'It's an important difference,' said Stephen. 'Don't get me wrong, Dan, we like you, but that's not why you're here or why we let you in. You *gave* us the story. If you were thinking anything else, you should have said right from the off. I'm sorry, but that's the way it is.'

I shook my head. 'It's my tape.'

'Dan, let's not be childish over this. It's *not* your tape. It's a stolen tape.'

'Yeah, right,' I said. I stood up and made to cross to the video recorder. And would have made it, if Stephen and Patrick hadn't beaten me to it. They blocked my way. I laughed and said, 'Wise up.'

I tried to push past them.

They pushed me back.

'Come off it, will ya?'

I went for it again.

Patrick chopped me across the throat.

Stephen punched me in the stomach.

As I crumpled down, Patrick chopped me across the back of my neck.

'Just because we're fruits,' said Stephen, standing over me, 'it doesn't mean we can't protect ourselves, or our gear.'

'Black belts in karate, each of us,' said Patrick.

'It's a jungle out there,' said Stephen.

When I eventually got my breath back, and they'd given me a cool drink and a bit of a massage, they led me to the front door. They were very apologetic. As I stood on their doormat, Patrick squeezed my arm. 'We want to thank you for this, Dan, and we'll acknowledge your contribution.'

'Absolutely,' said Stephen.

'We couldn't just allow you to take it like that. You came to us.'

'Be careful out there, Dan,' said Stephen.

Then they closed the door.

I sat down on the stairs, trying to get my bearings. The back of my neck still ached, and there was a dull throb in my head. My already bruised ribs were in shock. Something had gone badly wrong, and I was too giddy to quite work out what it was. I had arrived full of hope and now I was sitting on a dusty step. I'd thought there was some light at the end of the tunnel, but instead I'd manoeuvred myself into a position where I could get beaten up by two gay reporters with ambition.

I pushed myself up. Perhaps I was thinking too negatively. Getting beaten up had always gone with the territory, and what difference did it really make if they had the tape? Matthew Rye would be exposed, and once it was in the public eye the police would have no choice but to arrest him for Mouse's murder.

That was why I'd started this thing.

For my friend Mouse.

And now he could rest in peace, and I could just rest.

Perfect.

It was all over bar the shouting.

Really.

44

I wasn't quite sure what to do with myself.

I wanted to go and tell Mouse that the end was in sight, but May Li had had him cremated, and I had no idea where she'd scattered the ashes. I couldn't go home in case my cop friends were waiting for me. Nor was there any prospect of being able to until *Belfast Confidential* published its exclusive. I just needed to keep out of everyone's way until then.

Although, of course, it wasn't in my nature to do so. And there were other things I could have been doing. The boys might have my tape, which was the hard evidence tying Matthew Rye to Mouse's murder, but all the other stuff about him – the fake qualifications and the racketeering charges – that was all still out there. I could gather it in again fairly quickly, but what was the point in taking it elsewhere? If it got out, it might only encourage him to go on the run, and I couldn't have that. No, best to wait until all the evidence was presented together in *Belfast Confidential*. I'd been outmanoeuvred and beaten up again, but curiously I didn't feel too bad about it. Patrick and Stephen kind of reminded me of how I was when I was young. Not gay. But wildly ambitious and absolutely certain that I was in the right. Let them be the focus of attention now. I'd had my time in the spotlight, and didn't like it. Move on, hand over that poisoned chalice to the next generation. I also had to admit that despite my ignoble sacking from *Belfast Confidential*, I did retain some fondness for it. It was onto its third Editor in as many weeks; if it was to prosper it needed to show that it was still made of the same stuff, and this was just the kind of story to prove that. So Brian Kerr was a bit of an arse. He was still enough of a reporter to recognise the power of the story he would shortly have in his hands. He might not exploit it with all the flair and imagination I would have shown, but he didn't need to. It was a big enough story to make it on its own.

So I drove for a while. I bought Diet Pepsi and sausage rolls and a bag of Jelly Beans. I sat in a lay-by and scoffed them. I phoned Trish, but she was out. It was kind of a relief, because I didn't want to explain to her how I was up to my neck in bad guys again, and why, by association, she was too. I left a message on her phone telling her to stay where she was for the next few days, and then everything would be fine. Then I switched mine off so she couldn't respond.

I couldn't go home, so I checked into a small guest-house in South Belfast. The landlady, Mrs Watson, three chins and eyes like Puffawheats, smiled when she saw me coming and said, 'Thrown you out again, has she?' I nodded, and she showed me to my usual room. 'How long this time?' I shrugged. She said she'd had to put the price up since last time, but on the plus side, she now had over one hundred digital channels on the TV.

She did too.

And a TV in every room.

The only problem was that, whenever she switched channels downstairs, every TV in the house did as well. I was trying to take my mind off things, trying to relax, but every time I got engrossed in some movie, away the channel went: she liked shopping on QVC.

I did my own shopping in late-night, out-of-the-way super-markets. I bought fresh clothes and paperback books and beer and built a little nest for myself. My resolve not to contact Trish again failed completely, very quickly. I missed her. She ranted and raved, but understood. Eventually. She wanted me to come to her, but I resisted the temptation. I was a shit-magnet. We both knew it. If I went, somehow *they* would find me. So I stayed put. I read. I slept. I did a push-up. I suffered hangovers. I watched the local news, but there wasn't much happening. Police were still looking into the murder of Toothless Malone, and had staged a reconstruction. I caught a glimpse of both Mayne and Mooney overseeing it. It looked pretty accurate. But then they had the inside track. Nobody had come forward with any new informa-tion. It was probably out there, but old habits die hard in Belfast.

Another night I saw a feature on how Belfast City Hall was being transformed for the Masked Ball which would serve as the official launch of the Ryan Jet project; an interview followed with First Minister Frank Galvin outside a Social Security office in West Belfast which had been deluged with applications for employment at the new auto factory. He hoped that as many people as possible would attend the official ground-breaking ceremony at the factory site the day after the Ball, and help make it into a memorable, nay historic, event. 'People talk about the peace dividend,' he said, 'but this is more than that – it's the peace jackpot. Not only will Ryan Auto transform this part of Belfast, it will lure other companies to our city, it will attract investment and jobs and help to raise both our standard of living and quality of life.'

And then there were shots of Galvin being shown the site – by Project Manager Matthew Rye.

Rye looked confident, plausible, very much at home in the public eye.

I wondered if he had any idea at all that he was so close to being exposed.

Probably not.

If they kept to the usual schedule, Brian Kerr and his team would now be putting the finishing touches to the next issue of *Belfast Confidential*. Then it would be two days at the printers, and straight onto the streets.

I kind of hoped that the big story didn't leak out before publication day. There was something wonderful about a good old-fashioned scoop. You really wanted Matthew Rye to wander into his local newsagent's and pick a copy up himself.

I know it doesn't work like that, but it would have been nice.

Time dragged.

I almost bought a pearl necklace on QVC.

I doubled my push-up regime.

On the evening news UTV ran an interview with Concrete Corcoran about his art school's exhibition at the Orchard Gallery, which was opening that night. They hardly mentioned that he was a terrorist. They referred obliquely to his 'past life' and heaped praise on his landscapes. Concrete explained about the wild animals. When the interviewer said she'd heard that the paintings on show had been valued at over £3 million Concrete smiled enigmatically and said they were just paintings to him.

I was bored senseless in my glum little room, but thankful that my circumstances prevented me from attending. I knew from the boys' research that Ryan Auto had sponsored the exhibition and the chances were that their Irish representative would be there as well.

Keep your head down.

Relax.

It will soon be over.

I drank some more and watched seventy-five minutes of a Liverpool v Porto European Champions League game. My team were one down but had been awarded a penalty. Just as they were about to take it, the channel switched to QVC.

I cursed Mrs Watson loudly, and opened another can.

I called Trish and we had a kind of married phone sex, which involved me begging her to come to the guest-house and her ordering me to drive out to the country. But we were both drunk, and neither of us were prepared to make the effort. So we kind of lost interest. I drank some more and fell asleep, and when I woke in the morning, my first thought wasn't about my wife, or the fact that it was one day closer to *Belfast Confidential* hitting the stands, but whether or not Liverpool had won.

I poked the television news on. The first thing that came onscreen was another view of Concrete Corcoran's exhibition, with guests milling about, drinking wine and admiring the paintings, and I was just wondering how short of news they could actually be, giving him this sort of saturation coverage, when it cut back to daytime, and a reporter standing outside the remains of a burning building.

'. . . all the police will confirm,' the reporter was saying, 'is that at around ten p.m., just as the party was winding down, five armed and masked men entered the gallery and ordered the guests to lie on the floor. They then made a heap of Concrete Corcoran's paintings, doused them in petrol and set fire to them. According to the police, Concrete Corcoran made a desperate attempt to save his paintings, but when ordered to retreat refused to do so, and was then shot in the head by one of the gunmen. He died later in hospital.'

'And Frank – do the police have any idea who might be responsible for this?'

'Well, Karen, the phrase I have most heard over the past few hours from other reporters is the one which says, "your sins will come back to haunt you". But as far as the police are concerned, they aren't saying anything just yet. Whether it was indeed someone from Concrete's past, or perhaps a business rival, only time will tell.'

The camera cut back to the studio.

'That was Frank Waddell, from the ruins of the Orchard Gallery. Christopher Concrete Corcoran was a . . .'

They launched into a potted biography, a brief history of one man's war against the State, and then his reinvention as an artist of international repute but disputed talent.

I sat on the bed, too stunned to move. Concrete Corcoran's life had indeed been played out on a broad canvas, a landscape into which he had inserted himself. He was the wild animal, hiding in the trees, ready to pounce. He had never quite grasped the concept of the pen, or the brush, being mightier than the sword, but had instead fallen to another, equally famous cliché: that those who lived by the sword also died by it.

From downstairs Mrs Watson yelled, 'Danny – your break-fast's ready!'

She was the only person I knew who called me Danny. She made me a fry every morning. It usually cured my hangover, but this morning I just sat over it. Mrs Watson said, 'What's wrong with you, Danny?'

I said, 'Nothing. Could you call me Dan?'

'Dan?'

'Yes. Not Danny. I don't like Danny.'

She raised her eyebrows and said, 'Please yourself.'

She lifted her plate and went into the kitchen. I felt kind of numb. Concrete was dead. Mouse was dead. Liam was dead. Terry Breene was dead. It was like God had come up with a fifth, killing season. And they were all, in one way or another, connected to both *Belfast Confidential* and Ryan Auto. And to me. Connected, yet not connected. They had all died in such a short period of time. But it was such a small city that there were bound to be lots of connections which, ultimately, didn't mean anything.

So don't even think about it.

Ignore it.

None of your business any more.

As soon as *BC* hit the shops, everything would become clear. Matthew Rye would be unmasked, and then arrested. If there was a connection to the other deaths, it would be revealed; if there wasn't, then they were just unfortunate in their timing.

So forget it. Get on with your life.

Liverpool lost.

45

I went to the movies at noon. I watched three in a row, drifting
between screens, sneaking in like a big kid. By early evening
I was all movied out. I returned to my room and ate a Chinese
while watching QVC. I was beginning to find it quite hypnotic.
I was missing my wife. All the little things. Even the bickering
and fighting. She was my love, my passion and I wanted to lie
in bed with her in our new house, or watch TV and hold hands
and order diamanté bracelets. I wanted to wave good morning
to the neighbours and go to a steady job. There were too many
musty boarding-houses like this in my past. I phoned Trish and
told her some of this and she told me to catch a grip.

I slept fitfully, then got up shortly after eight. As I packed
my trunk I thought about Matthew Rye and wondered where
he was: racing for the airport, or languishing in a cell. I didn't
even bother with the TV news. I wanted to see *Belfast
Confidential*. I wanted that feeling, firsthand, that we'd got him.
I wanted to hold it in my hands, then punch the air and shout
like a lunatic.

'I had to charge you for the breakfast you didn't eat,' said
Mrs Watson, when I went down to settle the bill.

'That's okay,' I said.

As I walked out the door with my plastic bags of laundry
and beers I hadn't yet had time to drink she folded her arms

and gave me a knowing smile. 'See you soon,' she called after me. I was too excited to shout anything back at her.

I drove about a hundred yards to the local newsagent's, and waited impatiently while the young girl behind the counter unpacked the morning magazine delivery. As soon as I saw the *BC* banner, I snatched a copy up, threw the money down and hurried outside. There was a photo of Terry Breene on the cover. And lots more of his funeral inside. But there was nothing about Matthew Rye and his shady past and present. Not a word.

I couldn't believe it.

Couldn't *fucking* believe it.

There was only one plausible explanation. Brian Kerr had bottled out of it again. I'd spent the best part of a week holed up in a crummy guest-house for no reason at all.

I threw the magazine to the ground, then pulled out my phone. It was now a little after nine. I called *Belfast Confidential* and Mary answered.

'It's Dan – will you put me through to Brian.'

'Dan who?'

'Dan Dan the baker's man – who do you think, Mary?'

'Oh. Right. *That* Dan. He's in a meeting. How are you?'

'I'm fine. Can you get him out of the meeting?'

'No, I can't.'

'Give me his voicemail.'

'He doesn't believe in it. I can take a message.'

I took a deep breath. 'Right. Do you have a pen?'

'Yes, I do.'

'Good. Write this: *Dear Brian.*'

'Dear Brian,' she repeated.

'*You are a chickenshit cocksucking cuntbag.*'

She didn't repeat this.

'*Yours sincerely, Dan Starkey.*'

She was quiet for a moment. Then, 'Is there a hyphen in chickenshit?'

'No. I don't know.'

'What about cocksucking?'

'I'm not sure.'

'Cuntbag I've never heard before, but I'm willing to bet there's a hyphen in that.'

'Mary, it doesn't really matter.'

'Oh, but I think it does. He's a stickler for good punctuation. You wouldn't want to get on the wrong side of him.'

I sighed. 'Right. Whatever you think, Mary. Are those other two little shits there?'

'Which particular shits?'

'Stephen and Patrick. Who else?'

'Oh, I see. Stephen and Patrick. It's your funny half-hour. No, they're not, as a matter of fact. I expect they're still feeling poorly. Haven't been in all week. It's that bug. The shite just strolls out of you. They called in sick on Tuesday, haven't seen hide nor perfectly parted hair of them since.'

'They didn't come in Tuesday, later on?'

'No, I told you. Patrick called and said—'

'That was the morning – later, I mean. The afternoon.'

'Nope. Not through me anyway.'

I thanked her and cut the line. I leaned against the car. What were they up to? If they hadn't even made it into work, then Brian Kerr wouldn't have seen the video.

Or they might have called him on his mobile. Perhaps it was so sensitive they'd decided to view it outside of the office. Yeah, that could be it.

Or what if, between the three of them, they'd devised some alternative strategy for exploiting the information about Matthew Rye. Since none of them had stock in *Belfast*

Confidential, maybe they'd decided to sell it to the highest bidder. To television. Or one of the big English tabloids.

Or what if they were even tempted to sell it to Matthew Rye himself?

Or Ryan Auto? It had to be worth millions to keep it out of the public eye.

I drove across town. I parked well away from the boys' apartment, not wishing to tip them off, then stood at the corner of their street and watched it for a while. No signs of life. I buzzed them, but there was no response. I tried their phone, even aimed a few stones at their windows . . . but still nothing. It wasn't beyond the bounds of possibility that they'd already started throwing their money around. Maybe they were off to Ibiza. Or San Francisco. Or Portrush. Or what if they were still out negotiating? Would they take the tape with them? What would be the first thing they would do with the tape? If it was me, I'd copy it, in case anything happened to the original. Would they be naïve enough to leave that copy just lying around the house? Or would they have stashed it in a bank vault? How many of us *ever* stash anything in a bank vault? *Can* you even stash things in a bank vault any more? Can you take your Clash collector's items into the Ulster Bank and say, 'Look after this lot for me'? No. You hide your valuables where you don't think anyone will look for them. In that underpant drawer. Behind your CD collection. You mix it in with other tapes of recorded TV programmes you will never, ever watch.

If the boys had copied the tape, then there was a reasonable chance that that copy was still in there.

I buzzed the ground-floor apartment and said I was trying to get up to the second floor.

An elderly man growled, 'Do you live there?'

'No, I—'

'Then I can't let you in.'

'But I—'

'Bugger off.'

I buzzed the first floor. A youngish-sounding woman said, 'I sympathise, but you could be anyone, like a mad rapist with a machete.'

'I'm not,' I said.

'Well, you would say that. I'm sorry.'

I tried the third floor, but there was no one in. I hung around for twenty minutes waiting for someone to come out, and eventually a woman in a green windcheater with the hood pulled up emerged. I had to presume that she was the one I'd spoken to, so there was no point in rushing up. She made a point of quickly closing the door behind her and then waited for it to click before walking away with her head down.

I moved to the back of the apartment block. There was a window half-open on the first floor. It was most probably the young woman's apartment. By shinning up a drainpipe I could conceivably stretch across and haul myself in through the window. I hadn't shinned anywhere in a long time, but I'd convinced myself that the tape was in there. I had to have it. So I shinned. With my sore ribs and my stitched head and my cut lip. It wasn't a lot of fun, but there was a weird kind of adrenaline rush that went with it, and once I got started, it wasn't too hard. After about ten minutes of puffing and blowing, I pulled myself in through the window, tumbled noisily forward, then crouched on the linoleum floor, waiting to find out how many people I'd disturbed.

None, as it turned out.

Satisfied, I wandered into her kitchen and stole a Penguin. Then I went to her bathroom and had a pee, taking care to leave the seat down. I opened her front door, checked the hallway, then slipped upstairs to the boys' apartment. I knocked, but there was no response. I tried the door, and it wasn't locked.

It should have been, of course.

If they'd gone out, they would have locked it.

If they were in, they'd have answered the door, or the phone.

I did not have a good feeling about this. My life to date was the reason why.

I stared at the door. It was open just a fraction.

I ate my Penguin.

Then I pushed the door fully open with my foot, and the stench hit me at exactly the same moment as I saw their bodies.

46

Of course, the first instinct was to run. To pull the door closed and hurry downstairs and let myself out and pretend I'd never been there at all. I'd always scoffed at movies where the hero or heroine entered a dark house or cave when they should have known *fine well* that death or horror awaited them. And I'd been around long enough and been through enough shit in my time to know that the last thing I should have done was enter that apartment, even though it wasn't dark at all, but nice and bright.

But of course I did. I always dive in, head first.

It is the nature of the beast.

Their heads were half-blasted off. Their bodies bloated and stinking. Four days they'd been lying there. For sure.

My eyes fell on the video recorder. I hurried across and slipped my hands through the flap, but there was no tape. In fact, there were no tapes of any description, anywhere. Every drawer and cupboard in the apartment had been emptied; shelves and worktops had been swept clear. As I returned to the lounge I happened to look out of the window and saw that an old man with a rake had appeared in the front garden, and was busy tidying up the fallen leaves. I had a sudden flash of envy. How marvellous it would be, to just have to deal with autumn.

I began a second tour, this time checking for a laptop or notebooks, anything where the boys might have stored any additional information about who they might have talked to about the tape. In the bedroom, their mattress had been ripped open and its contents strewn across the floor. Several porno-graphic magazines lay on the floor. Back in the kitchen the tape had been removed from the answerphone; and then the machine had been smashed. But I noticed that it wasn't actu-ally connected to the phone anyway. I lifted the receiver and listened, and heard the interrupted dial tone which showed there was a message waiting on their callminder service. Same as we had at home. I called 1571 and listened. The Joanna Lumley voice said the message had been recorded at 4.45 p.m. on Tuesday afternoon, shortly after the boys had chopped my throat and thrown me out. Then I heard a familiar voice. *'Pat – it's Brian, got your message, very mysterious, we keep missing each other, give us a buzz back.'*

They'd never checked their messages, and never would.

From outside, despite the double glazing, I heard the old man shout: 'I don't care who you are! Keep off the bloody grass!'

I darted to the window – and saw two uniformed cops. And across the road, just climbing from their car, two more. Another vehicle, this one unmarked, was just pulling in behind them. Mooney and Mayne climbed out.

Shite.

Rumbled.

They'd been watching the apartment. Because they'd killed the boys and taken their tape back and guessed I'd come looking for it. And now they could frame me for a double murder. I had to get out. Now.

Fingerprints.

I'd been careless, once again. But I could only afford a cursory wipe around the telephone, video and kitchen counter. There were more raised voices from below. I peeked down and saw that the old man was doing his valiant best to stop the police from gaining entry. But they weren't for stopping. As the old man gave up the security code and they surged forward, I bolted out of the apartment and down the stairs to the first-floor landing. Luckily the young woman's apartment was along a short corridor which was out of sight until you were halfway up the first flight of stairs, so I just had time to dart along it and slip inside. I'd taken the precaution of leaving it on the latch, which was most unlike me. Maybe I was getting better at this life. Maybe in a thousand years I'd be almost good at it.

I closed the door gently, then leaned against it until the footsteps had passed by; then I crossed to the window I'd gained entry by earlier and peered out. They hadn't posted anyone at the rear, because they hadn't yet found the bodies, and Mayne and Mooney had to play dumb. For a few more seconds at least. I ducked under the frame and reached out for the drainpipe. I pulled myself across, then shinned back down. I jumped the last few feet onto the grass, then turned to find the old man with the rake looking curiously at me.

I said, 'Hi.'

'They're looking for you?'

'Seems like it.'

'What have you done?'

'I stole a Penguin.'

'We're not allowed pets,' he said, somewhat ruefully. 'Had to get rid of my Benji.'

'It's a cruel world,' I said, and hurried on.

Brian Kerr ate his lunch at *Past Masters*. I followed him there, then waited across the road. When he came out, an hour later,

I waited until he had his car door open then hurried up and gave him a shove. He tumbled inside, letting out a surprised yell. When he tried to push himself up I punched him in the ribs and banged his head down on the gearstick. Then I did it again. I wasn't much use in a fight, but given the element of surprise, and the fact that I was younger and bigger and had employed underhand tactics against a scrawny bald guy, I wasn't doing too badly.

He was going, 'What . . . what . . . what . . .' as I hit him.

I hadn't intended to give anything away at all, but I found myself shouting, 'You bastard, you fucker, you bastard, you fucker,' in time to the beating.

Luckily, although the car park was full, there was no one close at hand to witness my attack or hear either my curses or his shouts. Eventually I stopped, and he slumped down, crying into his trenchcoat sleeve.

Honestly.

A trenchcoat.

I know *nothing* about style, but twice as much as him.

After a while I pulled him round, and his hands rushed to protect his face. When he wasn't struck again he lowered them a fraction and stared wide-eyed at his attacker, and it took a few moments for recognition to dawn. He mumbled a hesitant, 'St . . . Starkey?'

I nodded.

'I don't under . . . I don't . . . What have I done?'

'You tell me, you fuckin' fucker.'

'Dan, please! I don't understand.'

'Why did you do it?!'

'Do *what*? Please, I didn't—'

'You sold them out! Sold them down the river!'

'What are you talking about?'

I grabbed him once more and he flinched as if he'd been hit, but I didn't, I held back. But I shook him and said, 'You *know*.' Then I let go of him. He wiped the blood from his face. I'd struck his head twice against the gearstick, and now there was a vague imprint on his forehead, showing the layout of the gears. The numbers 1–4 and an R for Reverse at top right.

'Patrick and Stephen,' I said.

'What about them?'

'Tell me a-fucking-bout them!'

He gave a hopeless shrug. 'What's to tell? So they're gay – there's nothing *I* can do about it.'

I jabbed a finger into his chest. 'Not that, you stupid fucker. Just fucking stop messing and tell me, or I swear to God . . . Brian, I *know* they called you on Tuesday. I know they told you about the video. So don't fuck me around.'

I had him. He knew it.

'What's it got to do with me?' he spat. 'Ask *them*!'

'They're fucking dead!'

This appeared to hit him harder than my punches. His eyes shrank to pinpoints, then expanded again. Tears which had already sprung once, welled again as disbelief rolled across his face. 'J-Jesus Christ. Jesus Christ,' he whispered before turning tortured eyes back to me. 'You're not serious. You're not . . . they're *dead*?'

'Shot dead. Their heads blown off.'

'But that's not poss—'

'Oh yes, it is. And the last thing they did was call you.'

'No! No!'

'They did. You returned their fucking call – you left a message for them!'

He shook his head, as if he was trying to convince himself that he was innocent. 'I just returned *their* call – and they called me back . . .'

'About the tape.'

'Yes – all right! They mentioned a videotape!'

'They told you what was on it.'

'No, they didn't say. They didn't spell it out. They just . . . you know . . . *hinted.*'

'But you guessed – you must have guessed.'

He gave a pained little shrug. 'Look, they said they had this tape, they wanted me to come and see it at their place, but they wouldn't say exactly what it was, just that you'd brought it in so I guessed it had something to do with – you know, Mouse, or something – but I was trying to get the bloody magazine out and they'd phoned in sick already, so we were short-staffed and everyone was shouting at me to do this and do that and do this and do that, and I couldn't just go traipsing out to their place, so I told them to bring it in. And that was it, that's all I said to them. They're really dead?'

'Yes, Brian.'

'But who—'

'Well, he's on the fucking tape, isn't he, Bri?'

He stared at me. '*Who* is?'

Fuck it. He didn't know. He really didn't. I was sure of it. I shook my head.

'Dan – who is it, man?'

'Wouldn't you fucking like to know.' I pushed the door open again and climbed out. I walked away.

He shouted after me, 'The cops are looking for you!' I ignored him. 'They'll fucking get you too!' I kept walking. 'For all I know, *you* killed them! You're fucking mental, you are!'

I stopped then, and looked back. He quickly ducked into the car and started the engine.

I scare few people.

But one is better than none.

47

Patricia emerged from the costume shop looking quite pleased with herself, and lugging two large bags over her shoulders. As she approached the car she said, 'Don't bother giving me a hand, these only weigh a ton.'

'I'm in hiding,' I said. 'It's not worth the risk.'

'Swell,' she said.

'Swell?' I queried. 'Have you been watching too many old movies? Have you missed me that much?'

'Yes, and no.'

When she'd stowed the bags in the boot and climbed back into the car I asked her how it had gone.

'I played the role of a harassed PA to an unnamed but obviously very important mover and shaker who simply doesn't have the time to pick up his own costume. They said I was very late, that most of their best stuff had gone already. Phenomenal demand, they said. They even had to bring in extra stock from their branch in Dublin.'

'And it looks like?'

'There were some fantastic outfits for women. I would love to be going.'

'And it looks like?'

'But you could only rustle up one measly ticket.'

'And a stolen one at that. To get back to the point: it looks like what?'

'You'll love it,' she said, and started the car.

Patricia was there because I'd nowhere else to turn. I didn't think it was safe any longer to use the mobile that the late Concrete Corcoran had given to me, nor to phone Patricia at her sister's. If they were capable of bugging the *Belfast Confidential* office, and I was convinced they had, then they were also more than capable of either tracking my mobile phone calls or monitoring the calls received by members of my immediate family. Call it paranoia, but there were enough dead bodies littering the landscape to justify it.

The look of shock in Brian's eyes when I told him about the murders of Patrick and Stephen was enough to convince me that he hadn't betrayed them. So I'd phoned Trisha's sister's work from a call box; gotten her to drive home, pick up her sister, and take her to another call box, and then she'd phoned me. In a state of panic.

I'd said, 'So how're you doing?'

And she'd screamed at me for putting her to such trouble, flying to the phone like a banshee because she thought I was lying mortally wounded somewhere.

'I'm not,' I reassured her, 'though my pride is a bit dented. Do you know I haven't got a single friend in the world to phone and help me out? What does that say about my life?'

She cleared her throat. 'That you're happily married, and I'm your best friend.'

'Ah,' I said. 'So you're the one going to get me out of this hole?'

'Yes,' she said.

And she did.

Now, we were on our way to a hotel she'd had her sister's niece book by phone, by credit card. She picked up the key, and I went up the fire escape. Once inside we began to get amorous.

Patricia said, 'Put on your mask.'

'My . . . ?'

She nodded at the plastic bags. I'd been so intent on getting her clothes off that I hadn't even peeked at my costume for the Masked Ball.

'Sex first, mask later,' I said.

'No, mask first, sex better.'

'You like me better with a mask on?'

'No, I like you different, with a mask on.'

'But I could be anyone.'

'You would think that. But no, Dan, there's only one you. You're unmistakable.'

'Then why the mask?'

'Would you humour me, before I go off the whole idea?'

I sighed. I rolled off the bed, opened the bag and took out a formal black suit. So far so good. Then the mask. I said, 'What the fuck's this?'

'It's a silver and blue full face Moon eye-mask.'

'Uhuh,' I said. One half was silver, one half was blue, with little stars. I tried it on. I looked at myself in the mirror. 'I look like a robot,' I said.

Patricia nodded beside me. 'It's *weird*, it's creepy.'

'This was the best they had?'

'Well, they had some Marquis de Sade masks left, but I guessed the bad guys would be wearing those.'

'The Marquis de Sade was a bad guy?'

She thought about this. 'Depends on your point of view, I suppose. Relax – you look good.'

'You said I looked weird and creepy.'

'Mmmm. But in a good way.' She smiled. 'Come on, weird and creepy guy, take me to bed.'

'With the mask on?'

'With the mask on.'

'If you ask me, you're the weird and creepy one. If you ask me, you should be wearing a mask as well, but seeing as how we only have one, maybe I should put a pillow over your head, or an oven glove.'

She smiled patiently. 'Do you want sex or do you not?'

'Yes, please,' I said.

We lay in bed. The mask was off. It was impractical for what we'd gotten up to. She said, 'I missed that.'

'So did I.'

'And if you're not careful, you'll be late for the Ball.'

'Did you ever think, in all your wildest dreams, you'd get to say that? "You'll be late for the Ball".'

She smiled, and snuggled against me. 'You don't have to go,' she said.

'No, I don't,' I agreed.

'You're just putting yourself in harm's way again.'

'Yes, I am.'

'And for no good reason. What can it achieve?'

'I don't know, Trish. I honestly don't. I just know that this guy Rye killed Mouse, and that he might have been responsible for Liam Miller's death, and he must have been involved in Stephen and Patrick's murders. And I can't go to the police because he appears to be in cahoots with them. So the only thing I can think of is to go to this Ball and do my usual thing.'

'Act like a shit-magnet.'

'Exactly.'

'In the hope that Rye and whoever else is involved will somehow betray themselves.'

'Yes. You know me too well.'

She stroked my chest. 'Will it work?'

'I have no idea.'

'And if it doesn't?'

'Well, I'm up shit creek without a paddle already, so it can hardly get any worse.'

'Yes, it can, Dan.'

'I know. But I'll be wearing a mask. Nobody will recognise me.'

'I am not reassured.'

'Look – it's the best I can manage.'

'And you just expect me to lie here, tearing my hair out, wondering?'

I nodded.

'And if for some reason, you don't come back to me?'

'Then you go to Paul McDowell or someone else at the *Telegraph* and tell them everything you know.'

'And what's to stop us doing that right now?'

I pointed at the television screen. It had been on throughout our lovemaking, and every once in a while, to slow things down, I'd taken a peek at the Ceefax page we'd called up as soon as we'd gotten into the room. The headline said *Journalist Sought In Gay Murder Horror*.

We read it again, just to see if it had been updated, or if I'd been arrested and nobody had let me know. Patricia hugged me a little closer as she read. Nothing had changed.

'On the bright side,' she said eventually, 'it must feel good to be wanted.'

48

I travelled by taxi, mask already in place, and thanked God that He hadn't decided to have another laugh by granting me the Belle of Belfast City as my driver. I got a fat fella in a baseball cap who glanced at me a dozen times in the mirror, but hardly said a word. When he did, it was about the weather, not the fact that there was a moonman in his back seat.

In five minutes we were approaching Belfast City Hall. I had always found it to be a hugely impressive building, despite all the crap talked in it. Its four towers surrounded a huge central dome, which dominated the city centre. Massive beams of light swept across it, as if it was hosting a Hollywood première, or being defended against an air raid. Fleets of executive taxis and stretch limos vied for dropping-off space close to the gates, and barriers held back crowds of onlookers as Belfast's finest arrived for the social occasion of the season. I had attended hundreds of events here over the years, but I'd never seen it look quite like this, or felt such a buzz of anticipation in the air.

Getting inside was surprisingly easy. Everyone was wearing masks, including the bouncers. They weren't going to ask everyone to provide ID or reveal themselves. That would have spoiled the whole atmosphere. Perish the thought. If you had an invite, you were in. And I had one. One of the few things I'd rescued from my desk at *Belfast Confidential*. I watched as a

group of a dozen or so guests, already half-drunk, spilled out
of a white stretch, then slipped in amongst them. I made small
talk with them as we approached the bouncers, then laughed
at some imaginary joke as I handed over my invite. The
bouncers didn't even look at it. We were all waved through.

We moved into a vast entrance hall, its walls lined with
Italian marble, the floor equally impressive in black and white
marble. Ahead of us there was a noble staircase, richly carved
and lighted by seven stained-glass windows portraying various
scenes from Belfast's colourful history, although I noted there
wasn't one showing The Clash's arrival in 1978. The building
has four halls, of which the Great Hall is the largest. I had
presumed that this was where the Ball would be held – and it
was, but Ryan Auto had also taken over the other three halls,
decking them all out in vast swathes of dark cloth and netting
laced with autumn leaves and providing subtle lights which
completely altered the character and atmosphere of the
building. In one word – gothic. And I suppose in its own way
it was quite classy, in that as hard as I looked, I couldn't find
one single reference to Ryan Auto, the Jet itself, or to our host
for the evening, Jacintha Ryan herself.

The Ulster Orchestra had been split into four sections, the
largest in the Great Hall, the smaller ones providing the music
in the other three. Each of the halls also boasted a free bar;
these were, understandably, already packed. I wasn't sure
exactly what I was looking for, or hoping to find out, so I sought
out a place by the bar in the Great Hall, ordered a drink, and
waited for something to happen. It was bound to. I was there.

Most of the men were also wearing full face-masks – at least
fifteen of them, I noted, exactly the same as mine. However,
because of the small mouth openings, they'd had to push them
up on top of their heads or take them off entirely in order to

drink their pints without spilling them down their fronts. The ladies, on the other hand, resplendent in shimmering silk ball-gowns, were mostly wearing eye-masks, which allowed them to drink freely without fully revealing their identities.

I saw Brian Kerr, standing with his Advertising Manager, Alan Wells. I saw Paul McDowell, my old Editor from the *Belfast Telegraph*. I saw TV stars. I saw Kieren Kitt, his mask pushed up onto the top of his head, but still wearing sunglasses. He was deep in conversation with his three former band members; they were laughing and joking and I crossed my fingers that a reunion was on the cards.

At one end of the bar: Mooney and Mayne.

They were the only ones I'd seen so far who weren't dressed for the occasion. No formal suits, no masks. They had their drinks, two each, but they were scanning the packed room and looking rather frustrated because so many people were still wearing their masks. I perused a long list of cocktails spelled out in gothic lettering on a silkscreen print hanging above the bar, and ordered from a waitress in a cat mask, but whose proportions and smile I recognised from *Past Masters*. It seemed that Patrick O'Brien had his fingers in every pie. Almost literally. Cocktail in hand, I went and stood by Mooney and Mayne.

Keep your friends close, your enemies closer.

Not that I had any friends.

Mayne was saying, 'Once the dancing starts, they'll take them off then, won't they?'

Mooney shook his head doubtfully.

'Christ,' said Mayne, 'it shouldn't be allowed. C'mon, let's circulate.'

As they moved past me I said, 'Sorry, mate, you wouldn't have the time, would you?'

Without thinking, Mayne turned his wrist to check the

time, and spilled the top of his pint over the sleeve of his jacket and down his trousers. 'Fuck!' he said. He shook his head at his own stupidity. 'Ten past *fucking* eight,' he snapped, then moved on, still shaking his head. I was smiling widely, but no one could tell. As I mingled, I heard my name mentioned several times, and at first I froze, thinking that I'd somehow been recognised, but then I realised that I was being talked about and was perfectly free to stop and listen, and even join in. I kind of liked that. The masks were a great equaliser.

A man said, 'Oh yes, they had their heads blown clean off, and I heard they were mutilated as well – you know, down there.' He nodded down at his crotch. 'Oh yes – cut them off and put them in the fridge, that's what I heard.'

'Nonsense,' said a woman in a gold eye-mask with a design like a starfish. 'I heard they weren't shot at all but they were – you know – *fucked* to death.'

'Oh Christ,' said another man.

'I suspected it all along – that Starkey was gay. There was something about him.'

I said, 'You've got it all wrong – he's as straight as they come. I have it on good authority from a woman who should know that he's the best lover in Belfast. A sexual wildebeest, she said. Not a gay cell in his body.'

Another lady said, 'I heard he was straight, but crap in bed. I heard that from his wife's best friend.'

'Who's his wife's best friend?' I asked.

'Well, I couldn't say here, it wouldn't be polite.'

'I heard he was a fruit,' said yet another man, this time with a devil eye-mask with black horns on either side, 'who was living a lie. I guess the pressure got too much for him and he just exploded.'

'Inside those poor boys,' said the starfish lady, and they all started laughing.

'Oh Ruth, you are awful. I just hope they catch him. Gay or straight, he's a menace.'

'But what if he's innocent?' I ventured. 'What if he's been *framed*?'

They exchanged glances, then burst into laughter again. 'Framed?' asked one, incredulously. 'In this day and age? And in our home town? That'll be the day!'

I heard variations of the same conversation half a dozen times. I'm sure the Ryan Auto people were livid. The way things were going I'd sell more copies of my autobiography than they'd sell cars.

Everyone was getting progressively drunker and drunker. By nine they'd run out of ice at the bar, and the beer was running low. Emergency kegs were cheered in. I drifted from hall to hall to hall to hall without hearing anything but gossip or spotting anyone suspicious or having any kind of a brainwave. I kept my eyes peeled for Matthew Rye, but it was impossible to tell. I supposed he would be wherever Jacintha Ryan was, and she had yet to make her grand entrance.

I had another cocktail and wondered whether Liam Miller would have approved of the costumes on show or of how the City Hall had been transformed for the occasion. And then I thought about Terry Breene and how under different circumstances I might have stood at the bar of the Great Hall getting quietly pissed in the company of my hero. Or what sort of an impression Concrete Corcoran might have made, his exhibition a sell-out, a critical triumph, surrounded by his reformed terrorist cronies, the pride of West Belfast, embraced but also kept at arm's length by the city's elite.

And how I would have liked to have had Patricia by my side, looking fantastic in a ballgown. I could have walked her down that staircase, and led her onto the dance floor and she would have stared lovingly into my eyes while we tripped the light fantastic.

Something like that.

I snapped myself out of it as the music suddenly changed: one moment a soothing chamber piece, then suddenly trumpets blasting out. The main lights began to dim and be replaced by swirling spotlights. People started to rush into the Great Hall and I found myself squeezed back towards the bar. Then there came an audible, 'Oooh! Look!' from somewhere behind me, and I saw a woman pointing up at the ceiling. A bright and shiny Jet, which must have hung unnoticed there all evening, was beginning to descend. It was suspended from what appeared to be impossibly thin wires. It was only as it cleared the shadows of the highest part of the ceiling that we could see that there was something perched on the roof of the vehicle. The car itself was a bright green, with what looked like a giant yellow flower stuck on top. All around me people were pointing and whispering and trying to work out exactly what it was . . . and then an elderly woman just in front of me let out a gasp of recognition. 'Why, it's a yellow diamond daisy!' All around her, other partygoers nodded and agreed. As it reached the halfway point between the ceiling and the floor, people began to scatter to make room for its landing. Then the petals of the flower suddenly began to move and spread and open. A voice boomed out:

'Ladies and gentlemen, your host – *Miss* Jacintha Ryan!'

The flower opened fully at last, and there she was, resplendent in an equally yellow dress. Jacintha Ryan beamed down at her adoring public; she waved royally, acknowledging the cheers which resounded around the Great Hall and far beyond.

The Jet finally touched the floor. Giant sparklers exploded out of the ceiling and thousands of little specks of glitter began to rain down harmlessly around us. From the four sides of the car, Armani-suited and silver-masked attendants hurried forward to help Jacintha Ryan down from the roof.

It was way over the top, and could easily have been very, very tacky, but somehow it seemed to work.

It was an entrance to tell your kids about. And she did look absolutely devastating as she almost glided forward. She stopped suddenly and in a very theatrical manner, raised a confused finger to her mouth. Then, acting as if a bulb had suddenly gone off in her head, she turned back to the Jet and opened the driver's door – and out stepped First Minister Frank Galvin, to huge applause. Hand-in-hand they then began to make their way through the crowds, shaking hands and smiling and laughing.

If I'd been Frank Galvin, I'd have shot the PR who'd okayed the stunt. It made him look like he was playing second fiddle, the dumb side-kick to the Queen of the North. A Prince Philip, a Denis Thatcher, ladies and gentlemen, Mr Olga Korbut. But God love him, he probably wasn't even aware of it. He was lapping up the attention and the applause, his familiar smile fixed in place, and a minder following behind, whispering the names of the devoted followers.

The crush was too great for most of the guests to get close. So, to appease them, *Past Masters* waitresses began to pass out little gift boxes wrapped in perfumed yellow paper which, when opened, revealed a Matchbox-sized model of the Ryan Jet. The box said *Limited Edition*, and they went down a treat with all the drunk men, who immediately began making brmmm-brmmmm noises.

Too many people, too much chatter, and all of it insubstantial. I had learned nothing, yet it was possibly the only opportunity I might ever have to mingle unrecognised with the surviving major players in my own divine little comedy. I stood at the bottom of the grand staircase and stared up. I knew the City Hall well enough to know where the VIPs hung out when they weren't required to gladhand the plebs, and had been at enough official functions to know that when the A-list ladies needed to powder their noses they didn't want to have to do it in full glare of the bitching squad. There was a Green Room on the first floor, which came complete with its own toilet suite. That's where I needed to be. Sooner or later the royal couple would retreat there.

I hurried up the steps, expecting at any moment to be stopped by the two security guys at the top, but they hardly blinked as I passed. Just like outside. It came down to confidence and acting like you belonged. Most of the VIPs who were still upstairs weren't actually in the Green Room itself, but standing outside it, watching over the rail as Jacintha Ryan continued her stately progress through the Great Hall. I stood with them for a moment, and saw that Frank Galvin had finally let go of her hand and was now following just a few steps behind. Then I stepped into the Green Room. There were half a dozen other VIPs sitting around drinking and talking; several also stood by a long wooden table weighed down by a massive buffet. I walked up to take a closer look, and found myself standing beside a man with an identical silver moon-mask to mine; he was looking at the dozens of different types of sandwiches, trying to decide. He finally settled on a plain ham one, raised it to his mouth, then laughed as he realised that his mask was still in place and there was no possibility of squeezing it through the narrow gap.

'Bloody nightmare, aren't they?' I said, tapping the side of my own mask. I was starving, actually. I couldn't remember the last time I'd eaten. The man beside me nodded, then pushed his mask back.

Matthew Rye.

My eyes darted to the food.

He took a bite, then nodded. 'Lovely,' he said. 'You should try one.'

I raised my glass. Our eyes met. He didn't blink. I did. Three times. Couldn't help it. 'Think I'll stick to these,' I said, and took a sip through my straw.

He smiled, nodded, then said, 'Nice mask.' He gave me a wink, then pushed the rest of the sandwich into his mouth, pulled his mask back down and turned for the door.

I should have grabbed him by the throat and demanded answers or a confession. The only thing that stopped me was a fear of death.

I had spoken to him once before, in the Portakabin on the West Belfast factory site. But then he'd just been a company man in a decent suit and access to a lot of hard hats. He hadn't been a threat. But knowledge is a powerful thing, and the fact that I knew he was responsible for Mouse's murder and possibly for any number of others changed my reaction to him entirely.

Shiver.

Christ.

I lifted a handful of sandwiches, then pushed through a different door into a small corridor leading to the VIP Ladies and Gents toilets. I knocked on the door of the Ladies, and when there was no response I entered. It was plush and smelled of roses. Aerosol roses, but still roses. There was a sink, and a long mirror, and an armchair and a small pile of towels. There were two cubicles. I opened one of them, slipped in and locked it behind me. I sat on the toilet and pushed up my mask. I ate my sandwiches and waited.

She would come.

I know women.

She *would* come.

49

. . . but not yet. Two cultivated ladies came chattering in and one went into the next cubicle and closed the door, while the other tapped on mine and asked if I was going to be long. Alec Large's line came back to me: *You have to load them up before you shoot them out*, but my voice wasn't high enough to carry it off. She tapped again and said, 'Excuse me?' and I still didn't respond. She tutted.

The toilet beside me flushed. I could see under the gap that she was wearing Prada shoes. I wouldn't ordinarily have known Prada from a clown shoe, but Patricia had recently taken to pointing them out and lamenting wistfully, 'Perhaps for Christmas.' Meanwhile I smiled knowingly, because she was bound for disappointment. Life was too short to spend that much money on shoes. Prada giggled, and clipped across to fix her face while the other woman came in and sat down; this one was apparently less modest, for she left her door fully open. She said, 'Do you think she's had a tuck?'

'Who, Jacintha Ryan?'

'Who else?'

'I think she has. And her eyes. You can always tell with the eyes.'

'You didn't guess with mine.'

'You *never* . . .'

'Yes, I have! New guy on the Malone Road – he's *fantastic*. I'll give you his number, not that you need it.'

They yittered away for another five minutes.

I bided my time.

I had nothing else to do but bide.

Lots of biding. The sandwiches were gone. My mask was back down and breathing into it was kind of weird and steamy. The sounds of music and partying drifted up from the halls of fun and brmmm-brmmmm. I searched for graffiti, and eventually found some in very neat handwriting near the bottom of the door. It said: *If you need some ironing done, phone Belfast* . . . A better class of vandal, indeed.

Three minutes after Prada and her mate went out, Jacintha Ryan came in. I could tell by the hem of the yellow diamond daisy dress, and the yellow high heels that went with it. There was a small gap between the door and the frame, and I was able to watch as she leaned on the sink, let out a small groan, then slipped off her shoes. She gave a sigh of relief, opened her handbag and removed a cigarette and lighter. She lit up and took a long drag, then pressed her face close to the mirror. It had one of those very bright lights that shows *everything*.

She was still looking in the mirror as I unlocked the cubicle door and came out, but was self-confident enough to continue to concentrate on herself, so it wasn't until I approached the cloakroom door, and instead of opening it, bolted it shut that she looked round and realised that I was a man in the Ladies toilets. But there was no panic at all.

She smiled, checked an eyelash in her reflection and said, 'Matthew – you're always one step ahead of me.'

I didn't say a word.

She turned from the mirror and came up close. She smelled of peaches. She said, 'It's such a strain, smiling all the time.

And I can hardly feel my fingers at all. Shaking all those hands, they're numb.' Her hand slipped around behind me and caressed my arse. 'But I can feel *you*.'

Oh.

'You're so strong.'

Her other hand began a circular motion on my other cheek. 'And it's been so long.'

Her left hand began to move round to the front. She started to caress me there.

'Didn't you miss me?'

Her right hand lifted my hand and rubbed it across her breast. And back again.

'Didn't you miss *this*?'

I gave a little grunt.

'Oh, it's the strong, silent type, is it? Are your lips *sealed*, Matthew? Because mine aren't . . .'

She sank slowly to her knees and kissed my crotch. Then she reached for my zip, while continuing to kiss me.

'Do you like this, Matthew? Did you miss this?'

She rubbed her hand across me, then slowly eased down the zip. Then she hesitated. 'What's wrong, Matthew? Aren't you interested?'

Someone tried the door handle. Then they knocked on the door.

'Jacintha – are you all right?'

Matthew Rye's voice.

Jacintha lurched backwards, lost her balance and ended up on her arse on the floor. 'Who the *fuck* are you?' she hissed.

'Jacintha!'

'Tell him you're fine.'

'What?'

'Tell him you're fine. This will only take a minute.'

Jacintha scurried backwards, like a spider with two legs pulled off. 'You wouldn't—'

I charged across the floor after her. Catching a glimpse of myself in the mirror, a weird moonfaced robot man on the attack, I understood the fear that had now enveloped her. She was backed up against the far wall, with nowhere else to go. Nothing else to do but scream. I knelt down beside her, put a finger to my moulded lips. 'Shhhhh,' I said.

Her mouth was half-open, her eyes wide. 'Please,' she begged, 'don't hurt me. Please.'

'There's nothing to be scared of,' I whispered. 'Just tell him you're fine – *now.*'

A brief moment of decision. Gamble on a scream? The door was locked. *What this madman could do before it's forced open.* She nodded. 'Matthew!' she called. 'Matthew! I'm fine. I'll just be a minute.'

There was a pause, and then: 'You're sure?'

'Yes!'

Then silence.

She stared at me. She was shaking. 'Who are you?' she whispered. 'What do you want?'

'A free test-drive of the Ryan Jet.'

'*What?*'

'Nah, that's just to break the ice.' I pivoted forwards, until my knees were on the floor. 'Relax, okay? What is he, Matthew Rye – your boyfriend, lover?'

'He's . . . what does it matter? Please, just—'

'Need I remind you that I'm the scary one in the mask? Just answer the questions.'

'He's just . . . someone I know.'

'You pull the oul' zipper with everyone you know?'

'No, we just . . . sometimes . . .'

'Casual.'

'Yes. Please, if you want money, I—'

'I don't want money. I want to know about Matthew Rye.'

'Like *what*? Please, I'll tell you anything you want to know, just don't hurt me.'

'Like why he's killing people.'

Her eyes widened. *'What?'*

'The Editor of *Belfast Confidential*, Liam Miller, two gay journalists, Toothless Malone . . .'

'I'm sorry – who are these people?'

'You don't know?'

'Why would I? I'm not from here any more.'

'They were important people here, in this town, and your boyfriend killed them.'

'No, look, I'm sorry if these people are dead, or murdered, but Matthew – you don't know him – he works for me. He builds factories, he oversees—'

'He oversees *murder*.'

'No.'

'*Yes*. There is evidence. On videotape.'

'That he killed someone?'

No, actually. It was purely circumstantial. 'He tied a man up, then burned him to death.'

'Oh my God.' Her hand went to her face; her fingers covered her lips. She pulled at the bottom one nervously, exposing perfect white teeth. 'I don't . . . Matthew?' I nodded. 'But *why*?'

'Well, I was hoping you could tell me that.'

'*Me?* What would I know about it? I came here to build cars. Why would— How could Matthew do this?'

'I don't know.'

She sucked up a deep breath, but couldn't stop a tear from

springing. She wiped it away, then hugged herself. 'Tell me,' she whispered. 'Tell me everything you know.'

There was another sudden rattle at the door. 'Jacintha?'

Matthew Rye, getting impatient.

'I'm just having a cigarette, I'll be there in a minute, all right?' Silence again. She clutched my arm. 'Please tell me, I have to know.'

I pushed my mask back. It had done its work. She was clearly distraught. So I gave her the shorthand version, about the *Belfast Confidential* Power List and how people started dying and our big break was getting the surveillance tape showing Matthew Rye, and how we did some checking on him and he turned out to be a sometime gangster from Miami who'd faked his credentials from Harvard. And how he was spending Ryan Auto money to pay off local cops and tap phones and how I was on the run and framed for the murder of my two young gay friends. 'Which is why I'm sitting on the floor of a Ladies toilets in a penguin suit and a moon-mask, frightening the Great White Hope of Irish industry half to death.'

'I'm not frightened,' she said.

'Well, I did my best.' I gave her a reassuring smile.

She shook her head slowly. 'My Matthew?'

I nodded.

She raised her hands to her face and tried to wipe her tears away. Her mascara had run. She looked a bit of a mess. 'I can hardly believe it.'

'I know.'

'Why would he do something like that?'

I shrugged. 'Deep psychological problems, or a bad hair day. You never know.'

'But what am I supposed to do?' Her eyes were pleading. 'I've spent my whole life planning for this moment. This was supposed to be the best night of my life – and it was – and *now . . .'*

I patted her arm gently. 'It's not you, it's *him*. You go to the police and—'

'But you said he was paying them!'

'Good point. Then go higher. Frank Galvin – you trust him, don't you?'

She nodded slowly. 'Yes. Frank. I'll talk to Frank.'

The door was rattled again. 'Are you sick, Jacintha? Please. People are waiting.'

'I'm all right,' she called back. 'I'll be right there.'

I helped her to her feet. She straightened her dress, touched my arm and said, 'Come with me. We'll sort this out together.'

I shook my head. 'That's my way out.' I nodded at a window just above where she'd been sitting. I'd enjoyed numerous escapades in this building, mostly involving copious amounts of alcohol, and/or angry local politicians, and I'd had reason to work out the best escape routes. I knew that beyond this window there was a small drop to a terrace below, and from there I could jump down to a garden of remembrance and make my escape that way. 'You've been gone a long time, Jacintha. Round here they shoot first and ask questions later. You do your stuff, I'll hide.'

I gave her a reassuring wink. She managed a weak smile, nodded, and turned for the door. But then she noticed the state of her face in the mirror, tutted, and quickly dabbed at her eyes with a damp tissue, to no great avail. She pumped up her hair again, then swept across to the door. She hesitated for a moment, took a deep breath, then unlocked it. She opened it just wide enough to slip out, then pulled it firmly closed behind her.

She was vulnerable, but tough. She reminded me of Patricia

in many ways. Scare the pants off you one moment, need a hug the next. An acquired taste, but worth the effort.

I turned to the window. It opened easily enough. Then I saw the security grill.

When the fuck did they install that?

I grabbed it with both hands and gave it a shake, but it wasn't for moving.

Okay.

Okay.

It wasn't the end of the world. I still had my mask. It was just a question of one more walk through Belfast's elite, then lie low until Jacintha Ryan did her work.

Just as I fixed it back in place, the toilet door opened, and I was already launching into a fake drunken spiel about thinking it was the men's toilet, when I saw that it was Matthew Rye, without his mask, and he was flanked by Mayne and Mooney, and beyond them, Jacintha Ryan.

'Oh,' I said.

To cover the mess around her eyes she had donned a devil eye-mask with black horns, like the one I'd seen earlier. It was very effective. So was the way she pointed at me and said: 'Get rid of him. Get rid of him *now.*'

50

They bundled me out of the toilet. I put up a valiant struggle for three seconds, but they were too big and too strong, and they had guns which they hit me with, which probably wasn't in the user's manual but which was nevertheless very effective. On the way past Jacintha I said, 'Nice tears,' and she just smiled, and they hit me again, harder, so that when they dragged me through the VIP room I was hanging like a drunk and shouting accusations which made no sense. Outside in the corridor they turned away from the main staircase and led me towards a fire door, and then the fire escape beyond. I fell several times as they led me down it, then when we reached the ground they pushed me up against a wall at the back of the building where it points towards the Dublin Road, while Mayne hurried away to get a car. Nothing was said. I slumped down on the damp lawn. Music and laughter soaked through the walls. Mayne was back in just a couple of minutes. Mooney hauled me up and then pushed me into the back and got in beside me. Matthew Rye stood and watched while I was driven away.

We were halfway up the Dublin Road before Mooney said anything. 'You stupid fucker, Starkey.' He ripped my mask off. 'You stupid cunt.'

'Well,' I said groggily, 'a cunt's a useful—'

But he smacked me again, and the lights went out.

I was slapped awake. Back of a car, nothing but the light of
the dash, the end of a cigarette, and the fleeting sweep of distant
headlights. No engine. No sound but the soft whisper of trees
moving in the gentle breeze. And then Mooney grabbed my
lapels, pulled me out and threw me down in the damp autumnal
leaves and churned-up mud of a country lane. Mayne came
round from the other side, and between them they hauled me
to my feet and then led me forward.

'A Forest'. Song by The Cure.

Other songs were 'Love Cats' and 'Killing an Arab'.

Long time ago.

My legs were as heavy as lead. My head kept falling forward.

Patricia in bed, waiting for me.

Jacintha Ryan in a devil-mask. In it up to her neck.

Once again I had badly misjudged a good-looking woman's
character. And it didn't matter. I was dead. They weren't taking
me on a nature trek. Mayne had his gun out, and Mooney had
picked a shovel out of the boot.

I'd faced death before. Lots of times. Now here it was, popping
round again, like an old friend. I wondered if it had anything
to do with the cats, and the killing of them. That if Mouse had
rested his chucking arm, neither of us might have ended up
dead. Maybe that's how it worked. You kill one thing, it comes
back to haunt you.

The wind was picking up, or we were in a more exposed
area. We might have been walking for five minutes, or five
hours. Pushed and prodded. I might have swung back suddenly
and struck one or the other, but not both. Sometimes you just
have to give in. Go with the flow. Perhaps the trees would
come to my rescue. Or a small army of Disney creatures would

spread the word and Thumper would . . .

'Here,' said Mayne.

I don't think it was a prearranged spot. I think it was picked quite arbitrarily. Miles from civilisation. Deep in the woods. Pliable soil. Somewhere for me to rot undisturbed until the turning of the world. The playground of Elves and Orcs. I was just wondering why Tolkien had never tackled leprechauns, when I was shoved hard in the back and I toppled forward onto my knees. I steadied myself with my hands. The ground was cold and wet. I didn't turn.

'All right, smart cunt,' Mayne growled. 'This is it.'

'This is it,' I agreed.

'You should have left well enough alone.'

'Hindsight is a wonderful thing,' I observed.

'You can say that again.'

'Hindsight is—'

'Shut the fuck up.'

'Sorry,' I said. 'Wouldn't want to make you angry.'

I heard a click. I let out a sigh. *Oh well, Trish. Fucked up again.*

Mooney said, 'Wait a second.'

'For *what*?'

'Well, you know – any last words.'

'Get away to fuck, just fucking blast him.'

'I know, I know. But just say it, okay? Make me happy.'

'Starkey?' Mayne barked. 'Any *fucking* last words?'

Oh Trish. Waiting there. Throughout our lives we had been continuously cast somewhere between *Romeo and Juliet* and the Krankies. I was tempted to think that this would be just as hard on her as it would be on me, but then I realised what utter crap that was. I was about to die, with damp knees, in a distant wood.

'Any time today, like,' said Mooney.

I turned slightly. I nodded at Mooney. 'I forgive you.'

'Cheers,' he said.

I nodded at Mayne. 'And as for you, your mum gives great head.'

It was too dark to see his reaction properly. But he did spit out, 'My mother's been dead for eight years.'

'I know,' I said, 'but still curiously attractive.'

He lunged forward. Kicked me hard. I fell over.

Good. Go for it. Go for it!

I felt him standing over me. 'Fucker,' he whispered.

I closed my eyes; and then my head seemed to explode with sound and light and I knew I was dead. I thought, *That was surprisingly painless.* And then there was a second shot, but it seemed to come from further away, and I thought, He's making sure, and also, It sounds further away because *I'm* further away. I'm moving down the tunnel, towards the light, always towards the light.

It was quite a relief. I'd seen so many bad things in my time, and caused many of them. I had hurt people, I had killed people, I had betrayed people and been very, very cheeky to them.

Now it was over.

Heaven.

Hell. Reincarnated as a bat. Or a tortoise. Pearly Gates. Who'd be there to welcome me? My son? Mouse? Liam Miller? Or would he be in hell, redesigning it? *Too much red! Turn down the heating, open a window, for god sake . . .*

'Dan!'

Calling me now. Heaven or hell.

'Dan!'

Towards the light, towards the light . . .

'Dan!'

I opened my eyes. The light was *too* bright. I winced. Shivered. Maybe hell wasn't hot at all. Maybe it was cold and damp, like Northern Ireland always was. No place like home.

The voice said, 'Are you all right?'

It was vaguely familiar. And not at all ethereal.

'The light,' I whispered.

'Oh – sorry.' It blinked off again.

'I'm dead . . .'

'No, no – I got them.'

'You . . .'

'I got them, Dan. I got them.'

'I'm not . . .'

'No!'

'I don't understand. Who are you?'

Suddenly his smiling face was illuminated, a torch held under his chin. Not St Peter at all.

'Holy fucking *fuck*,' I whispered.

Alec Large.

51

Alec grinned like a moron. I pushed myself up, my heart beating like thunder. He flicked the torch off, then on again, still under his chin, then off, then on. He laughed wildly. 'I did it!' he shouted. 'I did it!'

He swept the torch around my little death scene. There was Mooney, shot in the back of the head. There was Mayne, mouth open, eyes vacant, with a hole in his neck, and there was me, too confused to show how happy I was.

I stared at him. 'I don't understand, Alec. What the hell are you doing here?'

'I followed you.'

'*Why?* And . . . and *how?*'

'I've been training myself to do this properly. You gave me great advice, Dan. My life really sucked, and I think because it sucked I attached myself to good things, hoping they would rub off on me. Like your wife. Not that she ever, you know, rubbed off on me.' He stifled a laugh. 'But as soon as we had our chat, and I thought about things, it was all so clear – and you know, even my tummy is better. I haven't been to the toilet since. I mean, I'm not constipated. I'm fine. Really fine. It was all, y'know, *psychological.*' He was giddy with joy. And barking mad. 'So I've been watching out for you. You thought you had lost me, but you hadn't really. I staked out *Belfast*

Confidential and followed you following Brian to his club. I watched you beat him up. I've been with you ever since. Couldn't get into the Ball, but I saw them bring you out, and I thought, Being kidnapped once is unfortunate, but twice is murder. So I followed you. Good thing you kept them talking though, or I never would have made it.'

'You got yourself a real gun.'

'Well, they're not hard to come by, and since our chat, I thought there's no point in wanking around.'

I got to my feet. I asked him for his torch, then shone it at Mayne. His gun was lying by his side. I picked it up and slipped it into my coat. Then I turned to Mooney.

'He doesn't have a gun.'

'I know. He had a spade. You can do a lot of damage with a spade.'

'I hate to nitpick, but if you hadn't killed them both, I might have had a chance to get some information out of them. If you'd just made them, like, put their hands up.'

Alec thought about that. 'Mmmm,' he said after a little while. 'Bit of a miscalculation, that. But it was dark. I couldn't be sure. I did save your life, you know.'

'Yes, you did,' I said. 'Yes, you did.'

I went over and gave him a hug. I'm not very demonstrative at the best of times, and this, despite my survival, was one of the worst. But I did it. I think I needed to do it more than he needed to receive it. He didn't hug me back. He stood rather awkwardly. Stiffly, even. Though I was close enough to note that the swelling in his pants had gone down. We were just two guys hugging in the dark and the mud, with two corpses beside them. I stepped back then, and cleared my throat. 'What'll we do with these guys?'

Alec picked up the shovel. 'We bury them.'

I nodded. 'At least until this is all straightened out.'

'What is?'

'This whole thing.'

'*What* whole thing?'

'Alec – everything that's been going on. Haven't you taken any of it in?'

'Well, you play your cards pretty close to your chest. So I'm not really sure.'

'If you're not sure, why the hell did you come and save me?'

He shrugged. Looked at the ground. 'Because you're married to the woman I love.' Then he shook his head and looked at me. 'I'm sorry, did I say that out loud?'

I couldn't help but laugh. 'Right, Alec, let's bury these fuckers. Then I'll tell you exactly what's going on, all right?'

'All right.' He plunged the blade of the shovel into the soil, then smiled up at me. 'I saved your life, you know.'

'I know,' I said.

The sky was lightening. I'd lost track of time, what with the party and the drinking and the being knocked out and kidnapped and nearly shot. Alec drove me back to the city. I was fairly confident of moving freely within it. The days of roadblocks and random searches were long gone.

I asked him to stop at a twenty-four-hour garage to get some breakfast. He looked at me and said, 'Aye, like I'm going to fall for that one again.' I tried to reassure him, but he wasn't having it. So I got out and bought sausage rolls and coffee, and passed them through the window. Then I went to a call box and phoned Patricia.

She said, 'Thank God. I thought—'

'I know. Nearly, but not quite.'

'Christ, Dan.'

'I know.'

I gave her a brief rundown of the night's events. She said, 'Alec saved you?'

I glanced out at him, sitting in the car. He was still grinning. His face had to be sore by now. 'Yes, kind of. Although I would probably have managed by myself.'

'Uhuh. So you're safe. Are you coming home to me? I'm naked in my hotel bed.'

'I can't. Not yet.'

'You have to sort this out.'

'Something like that.'

'It ain't over till it's over.'

'Yup.'

'Is there anything I can do?'

'You can keep safe. You can go back to your sister's.'

'I feel like I should be doing something. You know, in this day and age it's not enough for me just to lie here looking beautiful.'

'It's enough for me.'

'Well, that's always been your problem. Easily pleased. But I'm serious.'

'I know that. And if I need you, I'll call.'

'Or if you can't manage it, get Alec to give me a call and I can thank him properly.'

'Bugger off,' I said.

She laughed. 'If only.'

The pips went, and I didn't bother to insert any more change. It was a nice way to leave it. She has a very dirty laugh, my Trish.

52

We drove to within a hundred yards of the building site that would soon become Ryan Auto and parked on a slightly elevated part of the road. It was 8.30 a.m. The cutting of the first sod ceremony was due to start at 11 a.m. As well as the Portakabins, I could see that a small stage had been erected, behind which a backdrop emblazoned with a rich red image of a Ryan Jet was attached. A large area of the site now boasted a clear plastic covering, with a single corridor of red carpet leading from the entrance gates, which stood open, towards a section which was being laid out with plastic chairs by what appeared to be teenagers in Ryan Auto plastic smocks.

I drummed my fingers on the dash.

Alec said, 'Do you think if you stare at it for long enough, you'll have a brainwave?'

I shrugged. He didn't seem to have anywhere else to go. But I didn't mind that. He had saved my life.

The stretch of land before us had once been the home of the yellow diamond daisy. Its sudden demise had led to its reclassification for industrial development. Jacintha Ryan's entrance at the ball and her dress had been a tribute to the daisy. Was that irony? Or rubbing our noses in it? Or was she trying to tell us something? Perhaps there was something shady about the destruction of the yellow diamond daisy, but was it enough to set off such an orgy of murder? No. There had to be a more substantial reason than that.

Alec said, 'She used to live around here, didn't she?'

'Yeah. Pearse Street, I think.' I waved vaguely towards the houses on our right.

'Must be nice to be able to come back and say, "Look what I made of myself." You know, drive up in a limo or something.'

'I don't think there's anyone left to actually show off to. All the old houses are gone, everyone's dispersed.'

'Pearse Street? They're not all gone.'

'Yes, they are, Alec. Take a look.'

He laughed. 'No, they're not. What about Aggie O'Fee?'

'Aggie who?'

'O'Fee. She's ninety if she's a day. Sure, do you not remember the big to-do about her? She was the last person still living in Pearse Street, and she refused to budge. It was all over the telly, and the Shinners mounted a big campaign to let her stay in the house she was born in, and then when they got into power they mounted a big campaign to get her out. But she wouldn't move, and they didn't want to have to drag her out, so they ended up building around her. Still there, far as I'm aware.'

'I didn't realise you were from around here.'

'Aye well, I don't advertise it.'

Aggie O'Fee.

'All right,' I said. 'Take me to her.'

'To Aggie?'

'Yup. We're getting nowhere fast here – might as well go back to the very beginning, start from scratch.'

'Alrighty,' said Alec.

It was literally around the corner. There were rows and rows of nice neat new houses, each and every one bearing a satellite dish. Then, in one corner, slightly elevated and with what must once have been a fine view across the fields of yellow diamond daisies, there was a single two-up two-down terraced house. Its partners had all been knocked down and now it stood, bent out of shape, broken and lonely, on a narrow band of wasteland overlooking the Ryan Auto factory site.

We parked outside. Alec waited in the car while I knocked the door. When there was no response I tried again, then peered through the age-thin net curtain hanging across the window to my left. As I looked in, Aggie O'Fee looked out. We both jumped a little. She put a hand to her lips and hissed: 'Shhhhhh! He's sleeping upstairs. What do you want?'

I said, 'I'm a journalist, I just wanted a quick chat.'

'Who do you work for?'

'Belfast Telegraph.'

She pulled the net curtain back, and stared out at me properly. She was small and wrinkled and her hair was white and tied back; she had wispy clumps of hair growing out of her chin and huge liver spots on her spindly arms. But it wasn't a beauty competition, and even if it was she would still have finished in front of me.

She said, 'You don't look like a journalist.'

'Thank you.'

'Do you have any identification?'

'No. I'm sorry.'

'Then I can't let you in. I let someone in last week and they stole my spoons.'

'You spoke to another journalist?'

'No, they said they were here to check for rats. They didn't have ID either. Mr Graves was most upset with me.'

'Mr Graves?'

She put a finger to her lips again and lowered her voice.

'Lodger. Peace and quiet, doesn't like strangers in the house.'

'I understand. I don't need to come in. I just need to ask you a few questions about Jacintha Ryan. She's the—'

'I know who she is. I'm ninety years old and I still have all my own teeth.'

'She used to live right here in Pearse Street. Back in the early seventies. You were here then too, weren't you?'

'Aye. But they weren't Ryans.'

'What?'

'I've seen her on TV, she's the dead spit of her mum, but they weren't Ryans.'

'I'm not sure what you mean.'

'They weren't Ryans, they were McAuleys. Must have changed her name. The McAuleys were a great wee family and she's done awful well for herself. It was just a real shame what happened.' She nodded, then seemed to lose herself in some distant memory.

I tapped the window gently. 'Mrs O'Fee? What happened?'

At first I wasn't sure that she'd heard me, and I was about to repeat my question, but then her eyes seemed to clear and she looked directly at me. 'Well, they were chased out because of the soldier.'

'Soldier?'

'Aye. The soldier.' She seemed to be warming to me a little. The lounge window was made up of three panels, and the side ones both opened outwards. She pushed the closest one open, and set herself gently down on the inside sill. 'Them were awful days, weren't they?'

I nodded. I was only a nipper myself then, but I remembered. Everyone does.

'There was so much trouble, but I remember this because they were such a nice family, and we were neighbours, and it was so different in those days. Your neighbours were like your friends, not like today.' She smiled sadly. 'Not that I have any neighbours left. They're all upstairs now.'

'The soldier?' I prompted gently.

'All right,' she snapped suddenly, 'I'm getting there. Did I tell you I'm ninety years old?'

'Yes, Aggie, you did.'

'Aye, well. The soldier. There was always shootin' an' all goin' on. But this day, this young soldier was just passing outside the street here, just where your car is, and he got shot and he was just lying there and, I don't know, he must have been separated from his patrol or something, and he was crying for help and for his mum, but everyone knew better than to go and help him because, you know, in those days you couldn't do that. But Mrs McAuley, she couldn't bear to see him lying there and she went out and comforted him and held him while he died. Terrible. And then when he was taken away, the soldiers came and they searched the houses and they smashed them up, and everyone pointed the finger at the McAuleys, saying they'd squealed an' all, but she'd done nothing of the sort, she'd only held a dying boy's hand. But there was a meeting, and a big gang came up and Mrs McAuley and the girls were dragged out, taken down to the field over there and they were tarred and feathered and beaten up. If the dad had of been there, he might have protected them, or died trying, but he was at work, and there were no mobile phones in those days. Hardly any phones, even. It was really awful. They were taken to hospital, and they never came back to the house after that. 'Twas the last time I saw them – till I saw Jacintha on TV. Knew her straight away, so I did. The dead spit of her ma, so she is. Dead spit.' She nodded to herself for a few moments. 'I wonder if she remembers me? She was only a wee girl, like.'

I made some more small talk with her, then thanked her for her time. I was just turning away when I had a sudden thought. 'I'm sorry, Mrs O'Fee – you said Mrs McAuley and the girls were tarred and feathered. You meant *girl*, didn't you?'

'I'm ninety. Doesn't mean I'm stupid. Girls. The twins. Carmel. That's it, Carmel. Ah, they were like two peas in a pod.'

'And you wouldn't happen to know where the sister is, Carmel?'

She smiled sadly. 'I do, as a matter of fact. It's awful sad.'

'How do you mean?'

'Well, Jacintha making such a success of herself, and Carmel locked away like that.'

'Locked away?'

'Well, I don't know if she's *locked* away, but I think she's still in Purdysburn. You know, the big Home where they put all the daft ones. She . . . well, I don't think she ever recovered. They were all going off to America, and I don't think she was well enough to go. I think she was supposed to follow on later, but she never did. Awful sad. Awful. They were such beautiful girls. Beautiful.'

Then there was the sound of footsteps on wooden floorboards behind her. 'Mrs O'Fee!' an angry voice growled.

'Better go, better go,' whispered the old woman. 'Sorry, Mr Graves,' she began as she closed the window and ducked back under the net curtain.

53

Purdysburn has a new name these days. It's part of a hospital trust. And there are lots of new buildings and different wings. You can tart things up as much as you want, but once something has entered the public psyche, it's very difficult to shift it. For decades Purdysburn had been synonymous with madhouse. Or mental asylum. Or looney bin. It still conjures up images of gothic horror and bedlam. There's hardly a misbehaving child or errant adult in the land who hasn't been warned at one time or another that they'll 'end up in Purdysburn'.

Purdysburn.

Carmel.

Sister of Jacintha Ryan. Terrorised and abused as children. Carmel moves to Purdysburn, Jacintha heads for America.

There was more to find out. There had to be.

We drove around the outer ring, then turned left by the big new shopping centre where Supermac used to be, and headed out towards Saintfield. One always thinks of places like Purdysburn being hidden away, secret, but it was surprisingly well-signposted. The gates were open and unguarded, and once through them there was only a short drive up to the main building, which was a huge Victorian-era redbrick effort, set amongst wide, sweeping lawns. It was actually quite picturesque. I'd half-expected to find screaming women in night-dresses being chased across the grass by white-T-shirted heavies with butterfly nets. But it was all calm and quiet, yet busy. There were half a dozen small car parks, all of them full. Alec left me off by the door to the main reception area, then went looking for a space.

Luckily, it was quite busy inside, so that for a few minutes I was able to stand and take in the area without having to explain myself and my bruises. I noted that relatives visiting patients were free to come at any time, but it was advised that such visits be restricted to outside of mealtimes. When I approached the desk, a pretty receptionist smiled at me.

'Hi. Ivan Carruthers – I'm a solicitor representing the estate of the late Mr Marcus McAuley. His daughter Carmel is a patient here.'

'Yes?'

'She was left a small amount of money by her father, but it's been sitting in an account gaining interest for twenty-five years.'

'Well for some,' said the receptionist.

'Once a year the office has to send someone out to check that Carmel does not wish to access those funds.'

'Uhuh.'

'So I'll need to see her.'

The nurse nodded, then checked her computer. She did some tapping. 'Yes, she's in Sinclair House, Ward Three.'

'Thank you.' I started to turn away.

'Sir, I'll need to see some kind of ID.'

'The office did call ahead.'

'Nevertheless.'

I began to pat my pockets. 'I don't seem to have . . .'

'Unfortunately we have strict guidelines.'

'I don't even need to talk to her, just satisfy myself that she's still a patient here.'

'I understand that, sir. But unless—'

'Ah, there you are!'

I turned, and saw Alec hurrying towards me. He was wearing a white button-up doctor's jacket, designer glasses and carrying a clipboard. 'Thought I'd lost you for a moment. If you'll just come this way.' He pointed ahead, down a corridor leading into the hospital proper. Then he waved and smiled over at the receptionist. 'It's quite all right. He's with me.'

She nodded. We walked on. A dozen yards along I said, 'Where'd you get the coat?'

'Liberated it outside.'

'Does that mean stole?'

'You're here, aren't you?'

'You're starting to get good at this, Alec.'

'Dr Large to you,' he said.

There were various different houses within the hospital, some of them secure and to which it would have been a great deal more difficult to gain access. Fortunately for us, Sinclair House was dedicated to longterm voluntary patients. There was a nurse behind a desk. Before I could say anything, Alec launched in.

'Hi, Doctors Large and Stark, here to see a patient, Carmel Ryan.'

'Carmel McAuley,' I said quickly.

'And I'll need to see her records.'

The nurse looked us over briefly, before directing us down a hall. Evidently, once you were in, you were in. 'You'll have to ask for her records down there,' she called after us.

There was a television switched on in the corner of her room, which seemed comfortable. A different nurse said, 'We don't normally allow them TVs in their rooms, but she won't sit with the others.' Carmel was facing the TV but she was staring out of the window, across the hospital lawn. Before we crossed to her, the nurse handed Dr Large the patient's file. He began to peruse it.

I said, 'How has she been?'

'Well, actually, she's been quite agitated these past few days.'

'Any particular reason?'

The nurse smiled indulgently. 'They don't really need one, do they?'

'And is she talking much?'

'Well, yes – she has lucid periods.'

'What about visitors?'

'I'm really not sure, Doctor. You would need to check with the desk.'

Alec nodded down at his notes. 'Thirty years as a voluntary patient. It's a very long time.'

The nurse nodded in agreement. 'It's sad. No family here any more.'

'But no attempts have been made to assimilate her back into the community?'

'I think, if you check further back, there was some effort made in the early days. But it didn't work out.'

'Very well.' Alec smiled down at her. 'You run along then. And if you don't mind me saying, I like your hair.'

'My hair?'

'You've changed it recently, haven't you?'

She blushed.

'Makes you look younger.'

'Thank you, Doctor.'

She skipped happily away. I shook my head at Alec and his 'into bed' manner, then I crossed the room and stood in front of the window, so that I was blocking Carmel's line of sight to the gardens outside. She stared straight through me at first, and then slowly her head moved to one side, so that she could see the grass again.

I pulled up a chair beside her and said, 'Carmel?'

Her eyes drifted lazily towards me. She was, without doubt, Jacintha Ryan's twin sister – but she was also quite different. She was a Ryan or a McAuley in her natural state. No hairdye. No plastic surgery. No make-up. No care and attention. She had bags under her eyes, and her brow was deeply furrowed. She had never been Botoxed. She probably didn't know what it was. In itself, no bad thing.

I touched her arm. 'Carmel. Hi, I'm Dan. This is Alec.'

'Dan,' she said.

'Dan. I need to ask you some questions.'

'Dan. Have you come to get me? She said she was coming.'

'Who said that, Carmel?'

Her eyes softened a little. 'My sister.'

'Jacintha.'

'Jacintha's coming for me. She's taking me away. To her house, in the fields.'

'When is she coming?'

'Soon. Did she send you?'

I glanced up at Alec, who was busy going through Carmel's drawers. 'Alec,' I said, 'leave it.' He left it. I smiled at Carmel. 'That's right, Carmel, Jacintha sent me. She's coming to get you soon.'

She was wearing a black top and corduroy trousers. I noticed that she had one hand nestled inside her top, moving it round and round, round and round. 'Home,' she said.

'Home,' I agreed. 'But before you go, you have to pass a little test, like at school – is that all right?'

Her brow furrowed slightly. I could see that her eyes were slightly unfocused. 'I just want to go home,' she said. 'Mummy has my Communion dress.'

I looked up at Alec. He was back going through her possessions again. 'Will you leave it?' I snapped. He closed another drawer. 'The notes. Does it say what she's on?'

Alec opened her file again and quickly scanned it. 'There's a whole list of stuff,' he said, then gave a little shrug. He showed me the list. It was long, but the names meant nothing to me, though I was willing to bet they weren't all vitamins. Keep them drugged, keep them docile. For thirty years.

I said, 'Carmel – when did you last see Jacintha?'

'Yesterday.'

'And before that? When was the last time before that?'

'My birthday.'

I glanced up at Alec. He checked the file again. 'This time last year, give or take a couple of days.'

'My birthday present,' said Carmel. 'I'm going home.'

'Does she come every birthday?'

Carmel nodded. Her hand seemed to be moving faster under her top.

'Carmel – how long have you been here, in this hospital.'

'Long time.'

'And have you never left?'

'I'm not well. I'm sick. Not safe.'

'But now you are, you're going home?'

'Yes.'

'You feel better now?'

'I have to go to Communion.'

'But you feel better?'

'Yes. Jacintha says I'm great, I'm a good girl, and as soon as there's no bad boys left, then it's time to go home.'

'What do you mean, bad boys?'

'The bad boys.'

'Which bad boys, Carmel?'

'Bad boys who cut my hair.'

'Why did they cut your hair?'

'I don't know. Carmel was bad . . .' She was starting to get agitated.

I patted her arm. 'It's all right.'

'Carmel was bad, Mummy was bad.'

'It's okay.'

'Carmel was bad, Carmel was bad!' I glanced nervously back at the door. It was a madhouse. Nobody was paying any attention. As I turned back, Carmel's hand suddenly shot out from beneath her top. It was covered in blood. She began to wipe it across her face. 'Carmel was bad! Carmel was bad!'

The movement also pushed the top up to reveal that her stomach was criss-crossed with wide gaping sores and scars which were bleeding and weeping freely.

'Christ All Mighty,' said Alec.

'Bad,' said Carmel. 'Bad, bad, bad, bad!'

There were no nurses nearby. I grabbed her hand. 'It's okay,' I said.

'Bad, bad, bad.'

'No, Carmel, *no*.' I began to force it down.

She suddenly looked very frightened. 'Sorry . . . sorry. Didn't mean . . . didn't mean . . . Please don't. Please . . .'

'Shhhhh, it's all right. It's okay.' I let go of her hand. She pulled her top down.

'Won't happen again,' she whispered. 'Won't happen again.' Tears sprang. 'I just want my dress. I just want my dress.'

I patted her arm again. 'It's coming,' I said. 'It's coming. Isn't Jacintha bringing it?'

This seemed to calm her. I stroked the top of her hand, then set it gently down on her lap. My own hand was covered in her blood. I wiped it across my trousers. 'There's nothing to worry about, love, nothing. The bad men are gone, the bad men are all gone.'

She nodded slowly. Then, as I stood up, her bloody hand slipped back under her top, and began that same rotation again.

'She'll be here soon, Carmel. You keep watching. You keep watching.'

We crept out of the room.

As we hurried down the corridor, the nurse with the nice hair came beaming across. 'Well? How is she?'

Alec handed her the file. 'Still barking,' he said crisply, then led us out of the hospital.

54

The pieces were starting to fall into place, but it was as if we'd bought a jigsaw in a charity shop: you could be certain that several pieces were missing – stuck down the back of a settee or swallowed by a toddler. Carmel was a child in a middle-aged woman's body, living on the promise of a new life with her sister. Once Jacintha had finished dealing with the bad men who'd tarred and feathered them. But who were the bad men, and what did they have to do with the trail of death which had been left across the city?

As I sat behind the wheel, still in the Purdysburn car park, running through the possibilities, I noticed that Alec was smiling again, and snapped an angry, *'What?'* at him.

He reached inside his jacket – he had thrown the doctor's coat into the back seat by now – and removed a small photograph album. I realised that I'd caught a glimpse of its cover when I shouted at him to keep his nose out of Carmel's drawers.

'You didn't,' I said.

'I did.'

He opened it on his lap and flicked through the pages of childhood snaps, mostly small prints in the kind of washed-out colours that we put up with in the 1970s. Carmel and Jacintha playing in a sandpit, on holiday in what looked like Portrush, their parents dancing with them, toys being opened at

Christmas. Innocent. A good-looking family.

So what?

Like most photo albums, there were a number of empty pages towards the back – and wedged sideways into one of these was a larger, and slightly creased black and white photograph. Alec pulled it out and turned it round. 'This'll be what you're after.'

It showed a group of kids, ranging I guessed from nine or ten up to maybe twenty. The fashions were very much of the 1970s – tank tops, perms, flares, sideburns. There were two rows of them standing, and a third sitting on a bench. There was a banner held just above the head of the kids in the front row, reaching to the chests of those in the second. It said *St Patrick's Youth Club*. The twins weren't difficult to pick out – blonde, beautiful, the only difference between them being that one, and I couldn't tell which, was missing her front teeth. She looked cute and happy. A thousand grannies must have said to her, 'Who kissed those out?'

'Very nice,' I said.

'Look again,' said Alec.

I scanned the faces. 'What exactly am I looking for?'

'A familiar face.'

I tried again, one by one, top row down to bottom, my finger hesitating over each of them. And then I stopped over one little lad who had a real cheeky look about him; his eyes were half-closed as if he'd been laughing, and the tip of his tongue was just sticking out. He was familiar, but only in a vague kind of way – but what gave it away were the white shorts stained with mud, the dirty knees, and the black and white baseball boot he had resting on a football. And as soon as I added that to the face, I had him.

'Terry Breene,' I said.

'Oh,' said Alec. 'Right enough. Didn't mean him.'

He nodded at the photograph again. I ran my finger along the top row, then the second, and at the very end on the right, there was another boy who caught my attention. He was definitely one of the youngest, and he was undeniably the best turned out. He had on a flowered shirt and a waistcoat and well-pressed trousers, and whilst the rest of them looked like they'd just been charging about the park for half an hour, this boy didn't have a hair out of place. He looked like he'd just been for a job interview with a gospel showband. I kept staring at him. Something about the eyes. They weren't looking to the camera, but rather condescendingly across at his youth-club mates. A girl directly behind him had raised her fingers above his head to give him rabbit ears. The message seemed obvious – he thought he was better than them, and they thought he was a wanker.

'It's Liam Miller,' I said.

Alec's eyes snapped down to the photo again. 'Christ – it is. But it wasn't him I was thinking of.'

'Alec, for fuck sake, we haven't got all day, just fucking—'

He jabbed a finger towards the middle of the back row – at the two oldest boys in the photo. One was clearly the hard man of the group. While the others luxuriated in their big hair, his was cut back into a skinhead; he was wearing a cut-off denim jacket, skinners and Doc Marten boots.

'Our old chum,' said Alec.

Christ. *Portrait of the Artist as a Young Man*. It was Concrete Corcoran, back in the days before he'd fully set.

Alec nodded, but he wasn't finished. He pointed at the next boy along. Altogether a more respectable-looking character – round-faced, horn-rimmed glasses, healthy big perm like he was the drummer from Slade, an attempt at a bandito moustache, but just too young to pull it off. It looked like he was the focus of the group, their natural leader. Although there were three almost even rows, they looked as if they had all formed up around this one boy. But I didn't recognise him.

'Without the hair,' said Alec. 'Recede it right back, lose the bumfluff and glasses.'

I tried it. 'I still don't see it.'

'Add thirty years – he's still in charge.'

'I'm still not getting it.'

'Ladies and gentlemen, please be upstanding for the First Minister.'

The penny dropped. And as it dropped, a shiver ran directly up my spine.

Frank Galvin. Frank fucking Galvin.

'Jesus Christ,' I said.

'Exactly,' said Alec. He gave a slight shake of his head. 'You know something? It's not a youth-club photo at all.'

'I know,' I said. 'It's a hit list.'

55

What do you do? Do you sit there with your mobile phone and call people? Do you say, 'Guess what we found out? Yep, yer man Liam Miller and Concrete Corcoran and Terry Breene and Frank Galvin were all members of the same youth club. What a year that was, eh? And you know what else? So was Jacintha Ryan, and if you put two and two together, and divide by three corpses, you get one left over and that's Frank Galvin. Except not for long because Jacintha Ryan's been paying Matthew Rye to knock off all her old chums, and there's only one of them left now and he's about to get on a stage in the middle of a field and jump through hoops for her and he has absolutely no idea what's coming.'

The people at the other end of the line say, 'Well, why would she do something like that?' And you say, 'Revenge.

'She went away and reinvented herself, but she never forgot what her friends, her pals, did to her and her sister, and all because her mum gave some comfort to a dying soldier. Maybe it was what drove her to such success in the States, this burning need for revenge, and maybe it took thirty years for her to get into a position where she could do something about it. And now that class of 1972 or 1973 or 1974 is paying the price.'

But then whoever you call says, 'And who is this I'm speaking to?' and you say, 'Dan Starkey.'

They say, 'Not the gay journalist-killer Dan Starkey? The one that's plastered all over the papers and the TV? *That* Dan Starkey?'

And you cut the line because you know nobody is going to believe you, not yet – that whatever has to be done you have to do it yourself, or perhaps with the help of one other, the grinning idiot sitting beside you.

Except he's not such an idiot, having stolen the last piece of the jigsaw, having completed the picture.

11 a.m. The cutting of the sod was due at eleven, but when did things ever get under way on time?

First Minister: busy schedule, everything timed to the second.

Jacintha Ryan: efficiently building an auto-empire.

Of course it would be on time.

We roared out of the Purdysburn car park, careered across lanes, cut corners, the vehicle soaring over humps and speed-traps. Alec was a Belfast version of Steve McQueen in *Bullitt*. In about eight minutes we were able to turn onto the Falls, but then we had to stop dead because the traffic was tailed right back. Everyone was turning out for the ceremony. The footpaths teemed with young mothers and their children, hurrying towards the factory site. Every once in a while they pointed up at the Goodyear Blimp. She'd gone and hired that out as well. Money was no object. Hot air balloons, Matthew Rye, the local cops, probably, it now seemed, even the hoods who'd attacked Maccabi Tel Aviv and hastened Terry Breene to his suicide. It was all part of her revenge. Mouse had obviously suspected, and paid the penalty.

Alec pumped the horn, he yelled out of the window, but we weren't going anywhere. A cop started to take interest. I ducked down. Alec gave him a pacifying wave. The cop's attention was diverted to a thirteen-year-old girl who'd dropped her flagon of cider.

We jumped out of the car and started running. People are always running in West Belfast, so nobody paid any attention. It was at least half a mile and five minutes before we puffed to the top of the slight rise which looked down over the factory site. The great and the good were already in position, and there were hundreds of locals standing behind crash barriers watching, just as Jacintha Ryan and First Minister Frank Galvin began to mount the steps onto the stage. As they did, 'Johnny Comes Marching Home' roared out of huge speakers and vast sparklers erupted around them. The people cheered. The shadow of the Goodyear Blimp drifted across the former home of the yellow diamond daisy.

We stood watching for a moment, not quite sure what to do. There were too many people, too much noise. Cars stuck in the traffic were blasting their horns; other drivers, with more patience, had climbed out, abandoning their vehicles, and were hurrying forward. Everyone loved Frank Galvin, local boy made good, and they were starting to fall for Jacintha Ryan, local girl made big, and now bringing it all back home. Could we be wrong? They seemed like such a great team. Was Matthew Rye really out there somewhere, preparing to kill Frank Galvin in front of all these people, all those cameras? Why not just leave it for some dark night when the First Minister was going home to his wife and kids?

Because that's not the way she wants it.

She wants to do it *now*. When he's basking in his popularity, when he's revelling in the fact that he's brought the good times back to the troubled streets he grew up on. It's how she does it.

Terry Breene, on the cusp of football triumph.

Concrete Corcoran, at the launch of his exhibition.

Liam Miller? The Lifestyle King. A fixture in every house. And an expert on fixtures.

Maybe it hadn't all gone according to plan, since there were complications like Mouse and me and Stephen and Patrick, but I had no doubt at all that Frank Galvin was the big fish she was after, and that if she was going to have him killed at all, it would be here, a very public murder.

No, an assassination.

'What now?' Alec gasped.

'I don't know.'

'We can't just stand here!' Alec shouted.

'I know! I know!'

An assassination. The difference between my death and Galvin's. He was important. He was a household name. For every assassination, an assassin. Kennedy. King. *A sniper.*

Christ, that was it. But where?

I spun, scanning the skyline.

And there was no deduction to it at all, really, because there was only one point nearby that gave an unrestricted view of the factory site and its little stage, but also the privacy and elevation required to line up a perfect shot.

Little old lady.

Aggie O'Fee.

And her lodger.

Upstairs.

I stared at the house, about two hundred metres away. The upstairs window was open. A glint of sunlight on metal.

Christ All Mighty!

I took off running again, and Alec charged after me. I pushed and shouted my way through the crowds still arriving to watch the ceremony.

'Where? What?!' Alec was shouting.

'The house, the fucking house!'

I had the gun out now, and even as I ran I was able to check that it was ready to fire. I was becoming *used* to being in these situations. But familiarity does breed contempt. I hated that after all these years I was still chasing someone with a gun. I felt sick, and my legs were as heavy as lead, and my heart was ready to pop.

But these things you do.

Right.

And wrong.

I was at the door. I raised my foot and kicked it in. Or tried to. It stayed firm.

I kicked it again. It wouldn't budge.

Alec arrived beside me, but without stopping he raced on and put his shoulder to the wood and it came straight off its hinges. He tumbled in with it and lay there long enough for me to jump in over him. Mrs O'Fee was just emerging from the lounge with a tray in her hands and a pot of tea and a plate of biscuits on it.

She said, 'Oh.'

I took the stairs three at a time. Two bedrooms. Left and right. I chose left, pushed the door open with the gun held out in front of me and screamed, 'Put it fucking down!' – except there was no one in there, just a window open and a curtain flapping.

Crack.

From the next room.

And a second later, distant screams.

I pivoted back out of the room and rammed the second door open. 'Put it fucking down!' I yelled as I charged in.

There was a rifle in the window, mounted on a stand. But no gunman.

At least not until he put a pistol to the side of my head and said, 'You first.'

Matthew Rye stepped out from behind the door. There was sweat on his brow and stains under the armpits of his white shirt. He had loosened his tie. Hot work, killing someone.

The screams grew louder.

Police sirens.

'You fucking did it,' I said.

'I fucking did. Drop the gun.'

I dropped it. I was thinking: Right, Alec, do it now. You've sneaked up the stairs, you have your gun out, *do it now!*

But there was nothing, no creak of a floorboard, no hint of support. He had to be there; he was just taking it very, *very* slowly.

Talk, talk, you have to keep talking.

'We know what you're about,' I said. 'You've got them all now, haven't you?'

'Really?'

'St Patrick's – anyone who did well, anyone who stuck their head above the parapet, she put them on the list and you killed them.'

'Very good,' he said.

'You're a hired killer.'

'That's me. This gun for hire. A million dollars. Easy work if you can get it. And only fools like you to annoy me.'

'Well, I was bored. And here we are.'

'Here we are.' He changed the angle slightly on the gun. He took a step back. He didn't want to get covered in blood.

'You think it's over, don't you? You think it won't come out?'

'I know it won't.'

'You assassinate the First Minister, you think they won't track you down?'

'Well, the thing is, Dan Starkey – I didn't assassinate him.'

'What?'

'It's a business, Dan. I kill for money, but I'm not fucking stupid. Of course you don't kill First Ministers or Prime Ministers or Presidents and get away with it.'

'I . . . I don't understand. You shot . . .'

He smiled. 'I shot Jacintha Ryan.'

'Ja . . . she's . . . ?' I looked to the window, but the angle wasn't right, standing up, where we were. I couldn't see anything but sky and distant houses and the tail of the Goodyear Blimp.

'Of course she's dead. I don't miss.'

'But why *her*? Why Jacintha?'

'Anyone ever tell you you talk too much?'

'Well, conversation's a dying art.'

'Yes, it is. Yes, it is. Fair point. Well, let me explain, then you can write this up and file it in hell. Jacintha made the fatal mistake of paying my final instalment before I pulled the trigger. It went through at exactly eleven a.m. – electronic transfer, you see. Once I knew that, there was really no necessity to kill Mr Galvin. I don't need that kind of a shit storm. And, seeing as how Jacintha was the only one who knew our little secret, then it seemed clear that all I needed to do was remove her, and I was home free. I just skip out in the confusion.'

'Except . . .' I pointed out.

'Except she wasn't the only one who knew our little secret. There's you.'

'The fool.'

'Still the interfering fool. So.' He smiled 'Time to go. Any last words?'

'Nah,' I said. I'd been there once too often. And the words were never right. The only thing I could think of was that Alec had let me down, that there wasn't enough Viagra left in him to make him rise to the occasion. Or that he was waiting for Matthew Rye to try and leave, and then he could grab all the glory for himself.

And my wife.

'You're sure?'

'I'm sure. Fucking just do it.' I closed my eyes.

He pulled the trigger.

Everything exploded in light and smoke, but even as I reeled sideways I knew that I was still alive. There was pain and incredible noise and my ears were fucked, but I opened my eyes and saw Rye slump to his knees. He was cradling his left hand. Blood was spurting. He was missing a finger. No, two. The gun lay in two pieces on the floor beside him, smoking.

I charged across and kicked him. Hard. He fell over.

I jumped on him. I grabbed his hair and cracked his head off the floorboards. Everything was *fugged*, the sound like it was underwater. But I kept cracking his head.

I knew exactly what had happened. He'd pulled the trigger and the gun had exploded in his hand, for the simple reason that he'd bought the weapon either directly or from an associate of Concrete Corcoran, and like everything that came out of Concrete, it was crap or counterfeit and worked half the time, or some of the time, or none of the time.

I was so busy thinking this, and banging his head, that I didn't even notice Rye's good hand snake out and grasp hold of my own gun, lying on the floor beside us. Wasn't aware until it was too late and he had it against my leg, and he groggily pulled the trigger and there was a second explosion, and this time I felt the pain.

I toppled off him, clutching my leg and yelling.

He tried to scramble to his feet, to shoot me again, but I

retained enough wit to kick out hard with my good leg, and his feet went from under him before he could get fully erect. He hit the floor hard and the gun was knocked from his grasp. It landed between us.

We both dived on it. We wrestled and poked and cried and screamed and gouged and bit because we were both bleeding and desperate; we both had a hand on it at the same time, then banged it back and forth on the ground, trying to dislodge each other's grip while still biting and tearing and yelling and grunting. It banged down once more, but this time a bullet shot out of it, and it was shock enough for us both to let go of it.

I was the first to recover.

My years of training.

Or his loss of blood.

I grabbed it. It felt unusually hot. It was probably another of Concrete's dodgy weapons, capable of firing one bullet before self-destructing. I couldn't take the chance of it blowing up again, so I managed to turn and throw it out of the open window. There was a brief moment when Matthew Rye looked at me in disbelief, then he jumped to his feet and charged out of the door and down the stairs.

And then, silence.

Blood was oozing out of my leg. I was in agony. My eardrums were screaming. Any moment now, he would come back up those stairs to finish me off.

But still, nothing.

Slowly, slowly, I dragged myself across to the window. I pulled myself up. Heard:

'Put your hands in the air! Armed police officers! Put your hands in the air!'

But it sounded like it was coming from a million miles away.

There were a dozen of them. Matthew Rye was on the ground, handcuffed. Alec Large was standing there with Aggie O'Fee. He was smiling up. She was staring at her battered front door, looking distraught.

'Put your hands in the air! Armed police officers!'

Maybe two million miles.

Alec shouted, 'It'll be all right! I told them who you were! They're just playing safe!'

I almost laughed. *Playing safe.* Sure. Double murderer holed up. And they'll hold fire on the word of Alec Large?

I slumped down, away from the window.

They'd work it out, that I was one of the good guys.

They just needed time.

To speak to someone sensible.

Trish.

Or Mouse. He always had his head screwed on. He could tell them.

I settled myself as comfortably as I could on the floor. There was a lot of blood, some of it mine, and splinters, and there was a picture of the Virgin Mary on the wall. I thought she was smiling at me, but I might have been mistaken. Even if she was, I didn't return it. What was the point? It would only end in tears.

56

These things get sorted out. They always do. Since when has there ever been a travesty of justice in Northern Ireland?

They just needed a little time. I lay in hospital, with various tubes attached, and prayed that I wouldn't contract some kind of Superbug just as one final kick in the hole from yer man upstairs. My leg was pretty messed up. It was looking unlikely that I would ever play for Liverpool now. Me and Terry Breene. My hearing was returning to normal. People sent flowers.

I lay there, in a private ward, nobody really saying who was paying for it, but I think Frank Galvin was involved somewhere. He came round and shook my hand and smiled for the cameras and absolutely denied that he had ever been involved in the tarring and feathering of the McAuley girls, although I knew it was a lie, and he knew that I knew it was a lie. There were others out there who knew it as well, the ordinary boys and girls who hadn't made anything of their lives apart from becoming decent people struggling to survive in a harsh part of a tough city, the very people Frank Galvin championed. I had thought of Galvin as one of those closet IRA men who could never change his spots, but maybe I'd just picked on the wrong species. He was more like a snake, a snake charmer, perhaps, and he had changed his skin. How long this new, attractive skin lasted . . . well, who could tell?

Galvin said, 'Dan, she fooled us all.'

'Uhuh.'

'She never had the money to build the Jet. She only ever produced a couple of dummy cars and several thousand Matchbox toys. But who could ever have guessed?'

I shrugged. 'She *was* a high flier in the auto industry. She *was* tipped to be Head of General Motors. But then she had some kind of a breakdown, and she was quietly eased out. She negotiated a two million dollar pay-off, and a confidentiality agreement. Didn't want anyone else in the industry to know she had, you know, mental problems, told them it would harm her chances of working again. Then she set about spending the money on this . . . con.'

'And a gunman.'

'An assassin. So there was never any car, never any jobs. It was just a very complicated way of getting her revenge.'

'It seems that way, yes. You would think, if she was determined to kill people, she would just have done it quietly, then enjoy her money.'

I shook my head. 'I think she knew exactly what she was doing. She wanted to have a ball, literally, and then go out in style.'

'You think she knew he would shoot her as well, in the end?'

'Possibly. But I think she thought he would kill you first.'

'Then, sorry to disappoint her.' He smiled kindly down at me. 'Well,' he said, 'country to run. What're you going to do?'

'Limp,' I said.

Alec came to see me every day. He said he was thinking about retraining as a psychologist. Or a psychiatrist. He wasn't entirely sure of the difference, and neither was I. Patricia tried to time her visits to avoid him, but it seemed inevitable that they would meet eventually. So one Wednesday when she came in, she opened her arms for a hug and Alec, sitting beside me, enjoyed a very brief moment of hope, and opened his arms to receive it. Then closed them sadly as she enveloped me.

She was very good with him though, and I didn't say anything. He had saved my life, and he had a heart of gold.

Later, when he'd gone home, we were kind of canoodling. Patricia lay on the bed beside me, doing her best not to jar my leg. But before we could get anywhere, there was a knock on the door. I said, 'Leave it,' but Patricia, like Liam Miller, could never resist a knocked door. She rolled off and opened it.

Wendy was standing there, with a bottle of wine. She said, 'Is this a bad time?'

'Yes,' I said, 'but leave the wine.'

'Wendy,' said Trish. 'Haven't seen you in ages.' There wasn't a lot of warmth in it.

'I came to apologise,' said Wendy. 'To both of you. I've been awful.'

'No, you haven't,' said Patricia, again with little to no conviction.

'No, I have.'

'Okay,' I said.

'I was just bitter – at Mouse. You know. And then . . .'

'Crazy with power,' I said.

'Yes. That.'

'Well,' said Patricia, 'no harm done.' Not a lot of conviction in that either.

'You've been through hell,' said Wendy, 'both of you. And I'd like to make it up.'

'How?' Patricia and I said together.

She came fully into the room. She sat on the end of the bed, and shook her head at my shot leg. Then tears began to roll down her cheeks. 'I do so miss him,' she said.

We left her for a respectful twenty seconds. Then I said, 'How?'

She wiped at her eyes. She managed a smile. 'Well, Brian Kerr is a total wanker. He doesn't know his arse from his elbow and nobody wants to work for him.'

'Ah,' I said.

'So I want you to come back and edit *Belfast Confidential*.'

'*Really?*' said Trish, a woman who knew the benefits of a regular wage.

I shook my head. 'No chance,' I said.

'Dan,' said Wendy, 'it needs you. The issues you did were the best. Don't throw the baby out with the bathwater. You know you're good at it, and the money's great.'

I shrugged. 'When May Li owned it, she gave me forty-nine per cent.'

'May Li never owned it. Forty-nine per cent of nothing is nothing.'

'Well,' I said, 'beauty is in the eye of the beholder. I *thought* I owned it. Now anything else would just feel like a rip-off.'

She thought to herself for a moment, then nodded. 'Okay. I can offer you three per cent.'

'Forty-five.'

'Four.'

'Forty.'

'Five.'

'Thirty-five.'

'Six.'

'I see a pattern emerging. Settle at twenty and I'm yours.'

'Ten.'

'Fifteen.'

'Twelve.'

I looked at Trish. She shrugged. I said, 'Okay, deal.'

Wendy put out her hand. I shook it.

'Let me open the wine,' I said.

'Should you?' Wendy asked.

'Of course,' I said.

'I mean, you have to get to work. They're waiting.'

I pointed at my leg. 'I'm seriously ill.'

Trish looked at me. Wendy looked at me. I had just pulled the cork out with my bare hands.

'Start on Monday, then,' said Wendy.

'Alrighty.'

'With one proviso.' I tutted. 'We do the Power List right away.'

'Okay.'

'And you put yourself in it.'

'Me?'

'Yes, you. You're the Editor and part-owner of *Belfast Confidential*. And your part-time job seems to be changing the fate of nations. I think you deserve it.'

Trish leaned across and kissed me on the cheek. 'Yes, you do,' she said.

I smiled at both of them. 'Will it help me get girls?' I asked.

I got out of hospital on a Friday, and I was due in work on a Monday. I was kind of looking forward to it, but also feeling a bit down. I was still on crutches, living on painkillers.

On the Sunday, Trish took me out for a drive for some fresh air. I hobbled along a beach; Patricia collected shiny stones. We ate lunch in a pub. Someone recognised me from the TV coverage and forced me to sign an autograph. On the way home we found ourselves on the motorway, within sight of the graveyard in West Belfast where Terry Breene, Concrete Corcoran, Liam Miller and now Jacintha Ryan had been laid to rest. We turned off and drove up past Aggie O'Fee's house. She was outside it now, giving a television interview, standing proudly by her new front door. She was probably telling them about how old she was and how she still had her own teeth.

We drove on until we came to the factory site. The security gates were lying open, so we drove in and parked. Patricia helped me out of the car, and we stood together in the mud, surveying the scene. The Portakabins had already had their windows smashed and were covered in graffiti. The stage was broken in two, the Ryan Auto banner was flapping, half-burned, in the breeze. The plastic chairs were gone, and the plastic ground cover had been ripped apart by joyriders.

'Well,' Patricia said, 'it was fun, wasn't it?'

'That's one word for it.'

'I thought I'd lost you. But then I think that a lot, and you always come bouncing back.'

'Luck's going to run out sooner or later,' I said. I was thinking about the youth club, and the seemingly innocent kids in that photo, and what they were capable of. Was it a sign of the times, or were kids always capable of that kind of violence? It was *Lord of the Flies*, really.

I wondered about Carmel, and whether she was still waiting for her sister to arrive.

Then Patricia gave an excited little whoop. 'Oh look, Dan, isn't it pretty?'

Before I could say anything, she'd bent down and plucked a yellow diamond daisy out of the soil. She held it up.

'You shouldn't really,' I said.

'Why not?' she asked. Then she nodded across the churned-up field. 'Look – there's dozens of them.'

And there were.

They were survivors. Just like us.

Trish blew on the little petals. Several of them floated away. 'Is it a weed or a flower?' she asked.

'It's a flower,' I said.

'How can you tell?'

'Easy,' I said, taking it from her hand and blowing the rest of the petals off. 'It looks like one.'